Books by C A Farlow

The Nexus Series

A Quantum Convergence
Book 1

A Quantum Uncertainty
Book 2

A Quantum Singularity
Book 3

Buzz for ***A Quantum Convergence***

Book One of The Nexus Series

2016 Rainbow Awards: 3rd Place Lesbian Sci-Fi/Futuristic
2016 Rainbow Awards: 3rd Place Lesbian Debut Novel
2016 Golden Crown Society Award: Finalist, Best Debut Novel

"Okay, I'm ready to gush about this one. There isn't anything I can say I didn't like… I couldn't put the book down, and if you're into sci-fi or fantasy, you won't be sorry if you pick it up."

—*Inked Rainbow Reads*

"I also liked a lot how fantasy elements were well-placed into the story to give the plot an edge that other sci-fi don't have. I will wait impatiently for the next book."

—*Elisa Rolle, Rainbow Awards*

"This is a great book for sci-fi lovers, and probably some fantasy lovers, as well. Also, anyone who loves a romance with fated mates or soulmates would find this interesting. The book drew me in quickly and had me turning pages, always wanting to see what came next. Farlow has also left some interesting threads dangling at the end, making me want to read the second book as soon as it comes out to see where she takes Alex and Lauren next."

—*The Lesbian Review*

Fascinating! This was a wonderful story, full of drama and love. The characters were full-bodied and the story grabbed and dragged you along on the tips of your toes from beginning to end. A fascinating read."

—*Skip Maslan, Goodreads*

Buzz for **A Quantum Uncertainty**

Book Two of The Nexus Series

2017 Rainbow Awards: Winner,
Cate Culpepper Award for Best Paranormal Romance

2017 Rainbow Awards: Best Lesbian
Book of the Year, Tenth Place tie

"SciFi through the fresh eyes of a real science person! The story is well-written and reflects some cutting-edge scientific applications of theories suggested as much as a century ago. The characters are a bit self-conscious but likeable. The science is presented in a clear and compelling manner and the SciFi angles are clever and creative. The writing overall is approachable and entertaining."

—Elise Rolle, Rainbow Awards

"Loved this second book into this unique trilogy. Another cliff hanger that makes you anxious the read book three. CA Farlow does an excellent job at creating this world, with all the ins and out of any society."

—A Happy Kindle Customer

Buzz for **A Quantum Singularity**

Book Three of The Nexus Series

2020 Golden Crown Society Award: Nominee, SciFi/Fantasy

"This book 3 was wonderful. It tied up all the lose strings of the previous two books. It brought a proper ending to this trilogy. This was a wonderful series. This was a great addition to my collection of sci-fi books. Thank you for a great travel through the universe."

—A Delighted Kindle Customer

A Quantum Uncertainty

Book Two
The Nexus Series

C A Farlow

LAUNCHPOINT PRESS

2021

A Launch Point Press Trade Paperback

A Quantum Uncertainty is a work of fiction. Names, characters, places, and incidents are either the product of the author's imagination or are used in a fictitious manner. Any resemblance to actual persons living or dead, business establishments, events, or locales is entirely coincidental. Internet references contained in this work are current at the time of publication, but Launch Point Press cannot guarantee that a specific reference will continue or be maintained in any respect.

Second Edition, 2021

ISBN: 978-1-63304-223-0
Ebook: 978-1-63304-224-7

Editing: JZ, Judy Kerr
Formatting: Patty Schramm
Cover: Lorelei

LAUNCHPOINT PRESS

Launch Point Press
Portland, Oregon

Mt. Zirkel Area and Surrounds, Southwestern Wyoming

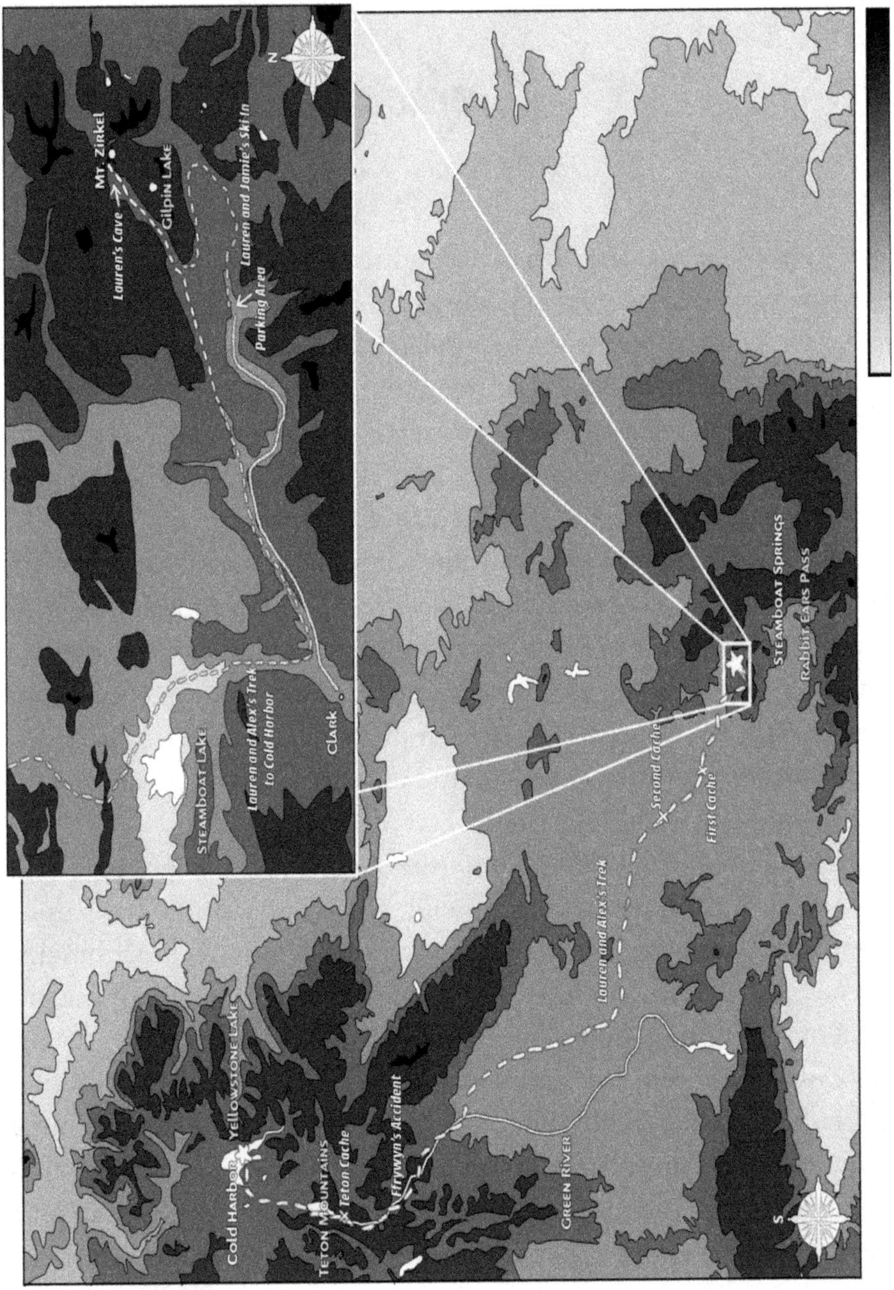

Preface

For the Second Edition

As is often the case in scientific discovery, theory comes before the discovery and theoretical science leads applied science, as ongoing research and discovery leads to application. Gravitational waves were first postulated by Henri Poincaré in 1905. Albert Einstein predicted their existence with his theory of general relativity in 1916. They were not discovered until September 2015 using the Advanced LIGO Detector arrays in Washington State and Louisiana.

Molecular weaving, quantum computing, and the basis for Terran analyzer gel are recent discoveries noted in today's scientific journals, as is the use of nitrogen vacuoles in diamond as a permanent data storage medium. The origin of the moon and its anorthosite exterior are real, as proven by the samples brought back by the *Apollo* astronauts. Quantum loop gravity and the existence of parallel realities are still in their theoretical infancy.

This book is named *A Quantum Uncertainty* in honor of the discoverer of the Uncertainty Principle used in Quantum Mechanics, Werner Heisenberg. Einstein's Theory of Relativity describes the interactions of things of immense scale—the fabric of space-time, the existence of black holes, gravitational waves, movement of the galaxies, and even the interactions within our entire universe. Heisenberg's Uncertainty Principle is used to describe the attributes of the smallest things—sub-atomic particles. In general, Heisenberg's theorem states—the more precisely one knows one attribute about a particle, the less precisely one knows its complementary attribute. This relates to the plot of this book. The more our protagonists try to control a situation, the less they can control it.

As in Book One, readers interested in learning more about the science and scientific theories used as the basis for this science fiction are encouraged to explore further. You'll find a reading list at the end of the novel for your own personal indulgence.

Though the persons inhabiting this tale and the existence of parallel realities are creations of the author's imagination, the geographic places and most scientific concepts are real in Earth's reality.

CA Farlow
February 2021

Author's Note About Appendices

PLEASE NOTE: The back of the book contains information to help readers understand and navigate the special world of this novel. There you will find:

- List of the characters and their roles
- Pronunciation guide
- List of books to learn more about the science in this series.

In addition, don't miss the Map in the front section of the book!

Acknowledgments

An author owes much to everyone who touches her work up close, as the editor reviews the plot and themes and point-of-view conflicts; the beta-reader who believes in the author and gladly reads her work with enthusiasm and a keen eye; even closer still as a proofreader corrects things that auto-correct and the author's weary gaze misses. Farther off, a publisher paves the way with introductions and advertising and recommendations to various reviewers. Farthest away, yet closest to the author's heart, are her readers. For they are the ones who keep the author focused, energized and motivated.

I thank all my readers who embraced *A Quantum Convergence* and have waited patiently for this second installment of the series. A special thanks to those who took the time to review *AQC* and post their thoughts on the various sites. Each and every review was taken to heart, listened to, and appreciated. The comments kept me going, able to top every hurdle the second volume threw up.

Lori and all the wonderful staff at Launch Point Press for taking up the journey and reissuing this series, I thank you for your encouragement and belief.

Judy Kerr, for all your hard work and detailed eye. The story was better due to all your efforts and patience.

Jodi, beta-reader and legal expert. As always, this book is better for all your effort. Your input is invaluable, and I treasure our friendship.

Lorelei, graphic designer, your creativity brings these books to life.

Elaine, three-time Olympic fencer and member of fourteen US Fencing Teams, #1 Ranked in 2000. What more can the author say, when someone with this level of knowledge and hands-on expertise is available, but thank you. Thank you for your gracious help and patience in taking a novice through the intricacies of modern fencing duels. Lauren's life was in your hands as these scenes developed.

For my grandmother, the perfect counterpoint to my grandfather.

She showed me the importance of art and music and literature. After all, she reasoned, there was more to life than differential equations.

She taught me to see the simplicity in a flower, to hear the complexity in a Chopin étude, and to relish in the beauty of the world in which we live.

She taught me to respect those different than ourselves, and most importantly of all, she taught me the meaning of love.

Part One

The Keep, Terra

Natural science does not simply describe and explain nature; it is part of the interplay between nature and ourselves.

~Werner Heisenberg

Chapter One

Children's laughter rose on the early spring breeze and drifted through the clerestory windows of the western solar. The solar's occupants glanced up from their analyzers and smiled at each other. The laughter was a sound so new to the Keep it gave everyone pause.

"That is all due to you, Dearheart. Thank you for returning the children to us." The strong emotions behind Alex's words flowed along their bond, warming Lauren's heart.

"A team effort, Dearest." Lauren saw Alex's blue eyes fill with pride. "I couldn't have done it without Newkirk and the healing technicians. Not to mention, all the help the water techs provided."

"But you must not discredit your efforts." Alex stated, wagging a long finger at her. "Without your experience and intelligence, we would not have a cure. And using your DNA as a comparator was the stroke of genius which made it all possible."

Blushing to the roots of her auburn hair, Lauren said, "Enough already! I didn't do anything another physician wouldn't have. It's bad enough I can't walk across the boulevard without being stopped every ten meters by someone who wishes to say thanks or give me a gift. I'm not a savior. I'm just . . . just me."

"Well, just me, I cannot thank you enough or be any more amazed."

Lauren tried to change the conversation. "Alex, we need to do something about those gifts. My solar is filled to the point of exploding. Can't we redistribute the gifts or find a way to give them back?"

"I will take them. I know there is some good food there. That jerky from Lord McLaran was quite tasty." Ice lay sprawled on one of the two leather sofas before a crackling fire.

Turning toward the large, snowy-white wolf, Lauren mentally growled at her, *"Ice, you gotta stop eating all the time. You're getting fat."*

"I am not fat. I am fluffy. I had a bath this morning and my fur is not completely dry. It is always fluffy after a bath."

"Keep telling yourself that, Ice, and maybe you'll believe it. But pretty soon you won't be able to fit through a door." Lauren laughed at the pout forming on the wolf's face, as her ice-blue eyes danced with humor.

"She is correct, Ice. You have put on a few kilos. You need to get out for a run. Go catch your food instead of eating what the kitchens provide," Alex chastised the wolf. *"Snow would love to have a late-night hunt with you."*

"Why should I exert myself when I am still healing? Besides, the kitchen staff sends up the best treats."

A livid scar ran from the wolf's shoulder, across her side, down to her hip. It stood out as a pale-reddish slash against the snow-white fur beginning to grow in around it.

"Ice, you're fine. Your wounds are healing well. Stop being a baby and get outta here. Snow's down in the stables with Ffrwyn. They're getting ready to have a run in the meadow."

"My side still pains me. I cannot take a deep breath, and running pulls on the muscles."

Lauren threw her arms up in exasperation and spoke aloud. "You're the biggest baby I've ever treated. Even Alex was a better patient than you are."

"What? I am a terrific patient." Alex's voice sliced through their mental conversation and her indignant pout matched Ice's.

"Really, Alex, you wanna go there?" Alex hung her head, her ebony bangs forming a curtain. "I didn't think so." Lauren's sarcasm thickened. "Ice, go on. Get out before I throw you out a window. You won't feel better until you start moving and break up some of your scar tissue. As your physician, I can tell you there isn't anything you can hurt with a little exercise. And you'll feel better having a run. Plus, we need to clean the sofa. I can't believe how much you're shedding."

A wolfy snort accompanied Ice's rise from the sofa. She stretched like a giant house cat, and padded over to Lauren's desk. *"Fine, I will go down to the stables, but I am not healed. It still hurts, and for your information, I do not shed."* She snarled, exposing her canine teeth. *"You shaved all my fur off, so I cannot be blamed if it is still coming out."*

"You do shed. Your fur's all over the solar." Lauren gestured around the room where most of the furniture sported a fine white furry coating. "You may feel some pain but you'll feel better being outside in the sun, getting some exercise. Quit being such a whiner and get outta here!"

Lauren ran her hand down Ice's side, as the wolf leaned heavily against her chair. The scar and surrounding tissue were warm to her touch, a sure sign the tissue was still healing. But as Lauren applied gentle pressure to the area, Ice didn't shy away or seem to be in discomfort so the underlying musculature was healed, if a bit atrophied. Ice was lucky Oswein's blade hadn't penetrated her abdomen and damaged any internal organs. Lauren shivered with the memories of that horrible day in the Council meeting. Everything seemed to have happened so fast, Snow defending Alex and being attacked with a psi-blast. Ice bursting into the room to defend Snow, and Oswein striking her down. She shook her head to clear the memories. *So much blood.* Lauren absently rubbed her chest, pain shooting down her arm from Gwenhwyfach's disruptor injury.

"Snow will be glad to see you. I will let McLaran know where you are going. Maybe he would join you as well." Alex tapped her communicator and placed her call.

"*I am going. Tell the young McLaran to bring some of his father's jerky with him.*" A wolfy laugh trailed Ice down the stairs and out of Alex's solar.

"Lauren, you should take your own advice and get outside. It is a beautiful day. We could go and see how the preparations are coming for the Investiture." Alex rubbed her hands together in childlike glee.

Though Lauren knew Alex was trying to sound upbeat, she could feel her underlying concern along their bond. She knew Alex recognized her reticence to go outside. She also felt Alex's confusion, she didn't know if Lauren's hesitancy was the result of her injuries or her natural shyness which kept her in the solar. The Terrans did overwhelm her when she was caught outside. And truth be told, she wasn't feeling well, and she was worried about the ceremony.

"I don't know." Lauren tried to smile at Alex but knew her effort fell short. "I need to finish this report on the expanded uses of the nanotechnology for the healing techs. And I'm scheduled to meet with Merilyn this afternoon about the ceremony. Why don't you head to the stables and have a romp with the furkids? I'm sure the boys would love to spend some time with you." *And I could use some rest. I don't want*

Alex to know how much pain I still have in my chest. Lauren focused back on her analyzer and rubbed her chest again.

"I get it. You want me outta here, too. Okay then, I will head off." Alex slapped her hands down on her desk and stood. "Give my regards to our Seneschal. Let us plan dinner with the boys and the furkids this evening. I will ask McLaran to invite his father."

Lauren smiled up at her.

"Sounds great. I'll pass on the invite to Merilyn. Have a good afternoon, Dearest."

Alex gave Lauren a kiss on her forehead.

"I will, Dearheart. Get some rest if you can. The techs can wait on that report." Alex moved around the desk toward the solar stairs. "And tell Merilyn to go easy. She is such a stickler for detail I am afraid she will overwhelm you."

"I will. No worries there. She always lets up when I'm totally confused or nodding off from her lengthy explanations." Alex's wolfy snort trailed after her as she ran down the stairs. *She sounds more like Ice every day.*

"I do not!"

Merilyn, Alex's Seneschal, arrived in mid-afternoon with the tea tray and an auburn-headed guest in tow. Lauren met them as they entered the lower floor of Alex's solar. "Good afternoon, Your Grace." Lauren inclined her head in respect to the tiny elderly woman.

Settling the tea tray on the low table in front of the warm fire, Merilyn surveyed the room. "Lauren, I am afraid we will need to move over to the public floor in your solar, as it has more room." She shook her head ruefully. "I cannot believe the amount of personal belongings Alexandra has accumulated over the years."

"I know. She's a real packrat." Ignoring the puzzled look that crossed Merilyn's face, Lauren turned toward her other guest and extended her hand. "Hi, I'm Lauren Beckwith. We saw each other at the Council meeting, but we've never been formally introduced. It seems things got outta hand before I met everyone."

Her new guest ignored Lauren's outstretched hand and tucked her hands deeper into the folds of her blue-green robe. She inclined her head.

"Lady Beckwith, it is a pleasure to meet you. I am Siobhán MacDonald. I offer my thanks for all you have done for Terra and especially for the children. It is a joy to see them running about." A warm smile spreads across her narrow face. "You are goddess-sent and have created a miracle for us." She inclined her head toward Merilyn. "I do not know that the Fraser could have done better."

Heat rose up Lauren's neck. She smiled and pulled her hand back, realizing she wasn't insulted by Lady MacDonald not taking her hand. *I'm becoming more Terran every day.* "I don't know about the Fraser, but it wasn't a miracle, simply good old-fashioned medical science, with a bit of amazing engineering thrown in courtesy of Newkirk."

Merilyn cleared her throat. "What have I told you, M'lady? To most it is a miracle of epic proportions, and something which will be chronicled in our history for all millennia."

"Right." Lauren scuffed her toe against the inlaid hardwood floor nervously. She felt her dragon tattoo begin to roll beneath her skin. "Miracle or not, I'm glad I could help your technicians."

"Forgive me, but how are you feeling, M'lady? Your injuries were extensive," Lady MacDonald asked, her steel eyes narrowing as she scrutinized Lauren.

"I'm better every day." Lauren absently rubbed her chest. "I understand once the shield is recalibrated, I won't have these phantom pains, and the random static discharge will stop."

Merilyn huffed in frustration. "I apologize for the continuing delays. I know from Alexandra you suffer, but it seems the sabotage done to the shield—which allowed your original exit without notice from the Keep—was more extensive than we first thought. And with all the psi-energy released during the battle in the Council meeting, the shield was shredded. It is taking a great deal of effort to rebuild."

"No worries, Your Grace. I know you're doing your best." Lauren again rubbed her chest and then down her arm over her dragon tattoo. Her touch calmed the beast's rolling motion under her skin.

"But it seems my best is not good enough." Merilyn cast a penetrating gaze at Lauren. "We are exhausting our shield technicians. A tremendous amount of mental energy is required to remove the inserted psi-filaments from the shield architecture. The filaments exist as physical threads, and their removal creates large rifts in the remaining shield. We may need to take the shield down entirely, once we have a good stretch of weather forecast, and then rebuild it from the ground up."

"No, Your Grace, I'm okay. No need to risk the Keep for a bit of discomfort."

Lauren moved away from Merilyn to stop the discussion, only to see Lady MacDonald's eyes narrow. She had watched the exchange closely and Lauren suspected Lady MacDonald knew she was in considerable pain—physical and psychic.

"I disagree. Time is of the essence." Lady MacDonald nodded toward Merilyn. "Can you not see how she is suffering? Her aura is rife with foreign energy surges. You must take the shield down immediately or this invader may find a foothold within Lady Beckwith's psyche."

After focusing her probe outward to sort the psi-energy in the room, Merilyn gasped. Lauren knew she had seen how her usual emerald green and ice-blue aura was shot through with red and black bolts all of which arced from her chest and arm. She had seen them before, and Alex noticed them tainting their bond. "Lauren, lift your sleeve, please."

Pulling her sleeve up, she exposed the silver-blue dragon rolling beneath her skin. Scales flashed in the sun as Merilyn reached out to examine the tattoo more closely.

"Do not touch me."

Merilyn staggered under the weight of the mind-voice. Lauren knew it wasn't the tattoo dragon speaking, but the torque around her neck. Her dragon torque was awake more often and spoke frequently, especially when distressed.

"I will not touch you. I wish only to help your mistress, Oh Great One."

"I appreciate your desire to help her, but we are protecting her as we can and will not allow a permanent taint to contaminate her soul. You must do as the Lady MacDonald says. You must fix the shield or shut it down soon." Lauren felt her dragon torque shiver, and the small puff of steam which accompanied the dragon's admonishment, warmed her neck.

Merilyn eyes rose to the dragon resting around Lauren's neck. "We are doing our best, Oh Great One. I will request the shield be shut down tomorrow. We will then activate a solar shield until a new psi-shield is completed."

"*Very well. We will maintain our protection.*" Lauren felt her torque relax and settle back into its state of slumber with a final puff of steam.

At that moment, Alex burst into the solar, sweat running down her cheeks. "What is going on here?"

"Easy Dearest, we were discussing my phantom pain when my torque woke up and yelled at Merilyn." Alex encircled Lauren's shoulders and nuzzled her neck above the torque, placing a soft kiss beneath her ear. Lauren felt her dragon smile, as her scales rippled against her neck and she released a sigh. "*Thanks, Alex, but what brought you back? You've got a lot to do. I didn't mean to interrupt your sparring.*"

"*My torque awoke and nearly burned MacD's eyebrows off. We had locked blades when she shot a spout of flame.*" Alex looked at Merilyn and Lady MacDonald. "What have you two done now?"

"Please calm yourself, Your Majesty. I noticed some foreign energy bursts in Lady Beckwith's aura and pointed this out to the Seneschal. Merilyn asked to see her tattoo, as she was rubbing her arm. The Great One took offense at this physical contact. It seems they are protecting her from the shield discharges."

"I see." Alex said to Merilyn. "We need to fix this immediately, pull the shield down completely if necessary."

"We will pull it down, Alexandra, tomorrow. It is all we can do." Frustrated, Merilyn tapped her foot rapidly on the wooden floor.

Lauren moved in Alex's arms to look at her guests, but didn't step out of Alex's grasp. "Let's move on to something more important. What do I need to do for the upcoming Investiture?" Lauren knew from her reading the Investiture Ceremony was important to Alex and the Terrans. It was a complicated ceremony, in which she would prove her right to her position. It would formally acknowledge her adoption into Clan Fraser, while another part of the ceremony would be their wedding, and she would become Royal Consort. Finally, if she passed the four challenges, she would be crowned Co-Ruler of Terra.

"I don't want to do something wrong in the ceremony that causes disrespect to your culture. Alex knows how I feel about the Investiture. I've agreed to be her spouse as I am Alex's soulmate. Therefore, I'll willingly accept Royal Consort to the throne, but co-ruler is something I need to get my head around before I agree to it." She lovingly patted Alex's arm. "Regardless of what we've accomplished, I don't believe your citizens would easily accept me as co-ruler. I'm not Terran."

"And that is why I have invited the Lady MacDonald to our lessons, a'Mhaighdeann." Merilyn's use of Lauren's formal title made the meeting take on a serious air. "She is our Lady of the Ancients and will teach you our history and what you must know to become a Terran citizen and an adoptee of Clan Fraser. She is also charged with creating the ceremony in accordance with our traditions."

Nodding, Lady MacDonald said. "Yes, we have much to do if we are to be ready at sunrise on the solstice."

"What? The solstice is only a few months away. No way I'll be ready that soon." Lauren's panic rose and Alex tightened her arms.

"Easy, Dearheart, they know what is best."

"I understand, Alex, but I don't know if I'm ready for all of this. I'm still so tired and now I gotta get ready for this ceremony in a few months." Lauren buried her face in Alex's shoulder. *"I don't want to embarrass you if I fail."*

"Failure is not in your vocabulary." Alex smiled down at Lauren. *"But I understand you are tired and your continuing pain is wearing on your energy reserves."*

"How many times have I asked you two to limit your private conversations when others are in the room?" Merilyn said in a terse voice, but Lauren knew Merilyn's anger was in response to Lauren's suffering and her frustration at not being able to stop it.

"Sorry, Your Grace. All right, if we've gotta do this in a few months, time is of the essence." Lauren stepped out of Alex's embrace and asked Lady MacDonald. "Let's head over to my solar and set up a schedule for my history lessons. But I've gotta warn you history isn't one of my strongest subjects."

Lady MacDonald smiled warmly at Lauren. "I understand, M'lady, and I will do everything I can to help you. We will get through the fifty-four millennia of Terran history as quickly as we can."

Shocked by the magnitude of the task before her, Lauren spun back into Alex's grip. "Fifty-four! Alex, how am I gonna do this?"

Alex placed her hands on Lauren's shoulders and squeezed gently. Lauren noted her sapphire-blue eyes held confidence and conviction. "You will do this as you have done everything else, with genius and strength of character. I will help as I can, as will the boys and the furkids."

Lauren drew a deep breath and nodded once. She felt Alex's love and support sing along their bond. She smiled as her anxiety about the Investiture ebbed. *Together we can do anything.*

Chapter Two

Lauren gave her all to the history lessons, proving Alex right. She met twice a day with Lady MacDonald and immersed herself in Terran history. The technicians pulled the shield down, and Lauren's pain vanished. Her only discomfort was normal tissue healing around the site of the blast injury in her chest. Her scar over the poly-titanium implant which replaced her sternum itched. Lauren knew her body was growing bone around and within the porous implant and at times, it felt like the itch went all the way down into the bone. Her tattoo rested peacefully beneath her skin and her dragon torque was quiet but watchful. Their torques, hers and Alex's, were acclimating to being out in the world again and were learning along with Lauren, catching up on the millennia of history they had missed while they slept.

Afternoon sun streamed through the octagonal window in the eastern solar, highlighting dust motes dancing through the air. Lauren bent over her laptop, rereading the history of the Doouglas and Fraser. She had downloaded their personal journals so she could learn about them in their own words, fascinated by the pair and all they sacrificed to unite the Terrans. In the millennia before these two clans came to power, Terrans were comprised of thirteen disparate clans scattered about Terra Prime and her three satellites. Distrust and jealousy kept the clans apart. Cultural and technical advances were developed independently and were not shared; often these were stolen or obtained through espionage.

Therefore, a union between the two most powerful clans—Doouglas and Fraser—was seen as impossible and viewed as a threat to the tentative stability between the other eleven clans. However, a soul-bond formed between the oldest children of these two powerful clans which could not be denied.

Prior to their meeting, the two children were sent to the Technology Institutes to study. The Doouglas was enrolled in the Terran Intra-stellar Flight Academy, while the Fraser studied healing at the hospice college. They met due to an accident.

From the Journal of the Doouglas

Today I get to fly solo! I have dreamt about this for as long as I can remember. Even flying flitters around my clan homestead cannot compare to piloting my own intra-stellar flyer around Terra Prime, to each of her three satellites and back. The hours spent calculating my route proves I can beat the existing time record using gravitational acceleration. None of my teachers believe I could use a slingshot maneuver around each of our satellite moons to increase my velocity. They do not believe I can accelerate from the accumulation of angular momentum from the three lunar bodies.

I have calculated and recalculated my flight path, the gravitational forces of the planet and her satellites, and the structural integrity of my flyer. However, when I presented my proposed flight plan, the flight committee rejected it, calling it reckless and impossible. So, I filed an alternate plan—conservative in trajectory and speed. Of course, this they accepted without question. A safe course for a girl.

I have waited until today to take my flight because of the alignment of our moons. All three are now on the same side of Terra Prime. I plan on using their combined mass to offset the gravitational mass of Terra Prime. After the mandatory three orbits of Terra Prime, I will accelerate for Cailleach Bhéarach—the mother and the largest of our three moons.

I will dive into her gravity well and use her curvature of the space-time field to accelerate into a figure-eight maneuver around Beira—Queen of Winter, and Brìghde—Queen of Summer. These smaller satellites share a merged gravity well and orbit each other, as well as Terra Prime. By traveling between them, I should be able to gain additional acceleration and reach a velocity of 0.85 light pulse. Faster than any Terran has traveled. This will allow me to slingshot back to Terra Prime. I should be able to slow to landing speed using atmospheric braking. I estimate my total flight time will be less than two point five six solar hours.

My craft technicians have reinforced the shielding and structural fins on the *Eponá*, and I redesigned her engines myself. This flight will show a craft can survive these speeds and that engines can be built to accelerate a craft to 1.0 light pulse. Today, *Eponá* will run as she has never run before.

From the Journal of the Fraser

Today, I am assigned to the trauma wards. My thesis proposal—to use immersion stasis chambers for massive acute trauma—was accepted by the graduating committee. I have installed a prototype chamber in the Level Alpha trauma ward in our capitol's space port. Many flight technicians and pilots working here suffer critical injuries while servicing and piloting intra-stellar craft. Burns, crush injuries, blast injuries, and crashes occur on a regular basis.

I spent my last visit home collecting the needed herbs for my immersion gel formula. I am only missing the key element—the DNA of the patient. Once a patient is presented to the ward with injuries deemed terminal and the patient is transferred to my care, I will collect a DNA sample. The patient will then be immersed in the chamber, and I will synthesize the gel using a combination of healing herbs based on the injury, and the patient's DNA. The patient's genetic pattern will be used to generate unique growth hormones which will stimulate cellular germination at the sub-molecular level. Tissue and organ regeneration will occur based on the DNA template of the patient which should minimize the chance of tissue rejection.

The immersion gel will act for a patient as amniotic fluid does for a fetus. Amniotic fluid is a marvelously dynamic environment which contains nutrients and growth factors which facilitate fetal growth, and provide mechanical cushioning and antimicrobial effectors. My immersion gel will be augmented throughout the treatment term with ionically-balanced fluids to facilitate osmotic flow of nutrients and growth factor across the patient's skin. A plasma-based supplement will hema-statically balance oxygen-transfer across lung tissue, as the lungs will be filled with the immersion gel.

To date, no patient has been deemed serious enough to try my new chamber. Standard techniques will be used until patient death is imminent before I am allowed to try mine.

Our race is naturally long-lived. Our ancestors utilized early bioengineering to eliminate disease and susceptibility to infection from our genome. It is not uncommon to live for several hundred rotations without need for medical intervention. The oldest member of my clan lived to five hundred and five rotations.

Death usually occurs due to injury or conspiracy, not natural causes. Development of poisons and their antidotes are the principal areas of medical study. The continuous conflicts between the clans feed this research, as the clans are constantly looking for ways to defeat one another. However, I feel healing and patient care should be a healer's primary mission. Therefore, my treatment is seen as a violation of natural law by the clan elders. Their comment on my thesis confirms their opinion: *We should not be able to intervene and cure any injury regardless of how it occurred.* In essence, allow us to maim and poison each other into oblivion.

I do not accept this and move forward building my prototype chamber and refining my immersion protocols. Now I must wait for a patient and a family willing to try an unconventional technique.

A soft knock interrupted Lauren's review of the journals. "Come."

"M'lady, I am here for our afternoon session. Is now a good time?"

Lauren leaned over the banister from the upper sitting room. "Yes, Lady MacDonald, please come on up."

A head of brilliant red hair popped over the banister before Lady MacDonald responded, "I wish you would call me Siobhán, I keep looking for my mother-in-law when I hear Lady MacDonald."

Lauren laughed. "I know what you mean." Lauren's mother would never allow someone to call her by her first name, and she would love all the bowing and titles and courtly protocols on Terra. *My mother is a snob, yet I'm barely comfortable with it all.*

"Then we are in agreement. I will call you Lauren and you will call me Siobhán. Yes?"

"Yes, I'll call you Siobhán." Lauren conceded.

"Good. We shall proceed with our lessons. The ceremony is approaching, and we must redouble our efforts." Siobhán paused at the expression on Lauren's face. Lauren couldn't keep her face neutral at the thought of reviewing more dry and tedious history.

Siobhán smiled. "But today I think we should do two different things. First, you should know about the ceremony and the roles everyone will have in it. Then, in an hour or so I have invited a couple of the participants here to go over a specific part of the ceremony. For this part, they will need to direct your lessons. I am not qualified."

Intrigued, Lauren's questions began. "Not qualified? How's that possible? Merilyn led me to believe you know all about Terra, her history, and her protocols. What's so different about this?"

"Lauren." Siobhán laughed and held up her hands to stop the flood of questions. "M'lady, please, enough. I now understand what Lord McLaran means when he says you have an infinite number of questions for an infinite number of things!"

Lauren laughed and nodded. She sobered as she remembered time was ticking and she needed to focus. "Okay, let's do this!"

"As you know, the Ceremony of Investiture will take place in the standing stone circle within the sacred grove at the center of the Keep." Siobhán paused and Lauren nodded. "The circle is made up of twelve stones—megaliths actually. Great slabs quarried from the surface of our lunar satellite. Each stone was transported to Terra and then moved by hand to the sacred grove. There, they were erected in a perfect circle. The radii of this circle are aligned with the critical annual astronomical events—winter solstice, spring equinox, summer solstice, and fall equinox."

Lauren shook her head.

"What do you not understand, Lauren?"

"Nothing." She waved her hand in dismissal. "I'm amazed by some of the similarities between Earth and Terra. I wonder if there've been other nexus travelers across time who may have influenced human development on Earth."

"What do you mean? How would that be possible? We knew nothing of your Earth reality, nor is there any mention of its existence on a parallel reality within our history prior to your arrival. How would there be similar structures on your Earth?"

Laughing, Lauren again held up her hands. "I don't think I'm the only one who asks questions when faced with something unexpected."

Siobhán bowed her head in acknowledgement and smiled. "You are too correct." They had discovered a common trait between them.

Siobhán asked, "What parallel are you speaking of?"

"On my Earth, there is any number of standing stone circles. Relics now, without a known origin or purpose, but sites some believe held great meaning for ancient cultures. Most also have astronomical alignments."

Rubbing her chin, Siobhán leaned forward in her chair, seemingly amazed by this similarity. "Fascinating, truly. We must speak of this again in more detail. But for now, we digress, let us return to our standing stone circle."

Lauren made a mental note to search for articles stored on her laptop referencing Stonehenge or any of the other British and Scottish circles. Her attention snapped back to what Siobhán was saying when Clan Cador was mentioned. "What did you say? I'm sorry. I missed your last comment."

"I said each stone was set in place by one of the clans. Three representatives of each clan will sit before their stone, in judgment of you during the ceremony. Only the stone of Clan Cador will be without representatives."

After the Council meeting attack and Gwenhwyfach's treason was exposed, Alex had placed the entirety of Clan Cador under house arrest and there they would stay until the extent of their leader's plot could be determined. Gwenhwyfach was in exile on East Sundaram—island of molten rock known in Earth's reality as Hawaii. It was a place without any known nexus and deemed safe to exile a mind-technician of Gwenhwyfach's skill. And Lauren knew how skilled she was. Her psi-attack on Snow during the Council meeting nearly killed the wolf. She had easily manipulated the shield to expel Lauren from the Keep on that cold winter morning when the injured Alex was taken away. And she did that without detection by the shield technicians. These acts were only a sample of her skills.

A small dwelling was built before she was transported there. Supplies and other needs would be sent monthly by automated drone. A one-way transmitter was provided to allow her to contact the Keep in an emergency or if there was something she needed outside the approved resupply list. This one-way communication insured she could not exert her psi-control over anyone.

Even with these physical barriers and psychic precautions, Lauren still felt uneasy when the clan was mentioned. A shiver skittered down her spine. "Sorry Siobhán, I didn't mean to interrupt."

"I understand, Lauren. No need for you to apologize." They returned to the particulars of the Investiture ceremony.

A knock on the solar doors interrupted their study, and Lauren breathed a sigh of relief for the respite the newcomers brought with them. "Come on in. It's open."

The doors swung open and Alex's three childhood companions, Tavish MacDonald, Angus Newkirk, and Robert McLaran the Younger, entered with Robert's father, Lord McLaran. Snow and Ice brought up the rear of the tartan-clad group. Bowing deeply, the broad-shouldered MacDonald placed a slim ironwood case on the table before Lauren. Its intricate grain caught the firelight. "For you, M'lady."

"Will you stop already? How many times do I have to tell you, I'm just Lauren." Lauren's gaze rested on the case, and intrigue, not admonishment, colored her voice.

"Of course, M'lady," MacDonald said, a small smile twitching the corner of his mouth.

Lady MacDonald rose gracefully from her chair and cuffed her son soundly in the back of the head. Had he not been kneeling, she couldn't have reached the back of his head, but the rebuke stood and MacDonald's face reddened as he blushed furiously.

"You are a scamp and always have been, my boy. Do not embarrass our clan before the future Consort to your Ruler."

"I would not dream of embarrassing our clan, Màthair." Excitement, rather than contrition, colored his voice. MacDonald again took a knee and placed a large calloused hand on the box. "M'lady Beckwith, may I present you with this gift, forged by my clan. May you use it to protect, to serve, to support, and to honor our Ruler in all her actions. May it bring you strength. May you have the wisdom to know when its use is needed and called for, and more importantly when it is not." As he removed his hand, the box quivered slightly on the low table.

Lauren held her breath as she reverently placed her left hand where his had rested on the box. Clan MacDonald were gifted blacksmiths and jewelers, and she could only guess what lay inside. Warmth moved up her arm and her dragon tattoo rolled over. It may have been remnant heat from MacDonald's large hand but Lauren thought not. When she felt her torque awaken, she knew she was correct, energy was being emitted from it. The box contained a gift of great significance.

Slowly she reached for the two golden clasps. Each clasp was a small dragon head and each dragon held a platinum hasp in its mouth. Turning the small heads, she freed the lid. Her dragon torque shivered in anticipation, and her scales tickled Lauren's neck. Her tattoo blinked its eyes. As she raised the lid, Lauren caught sight of a deep purple interior. The box lined in soft velvet, cradled a weapon. It was a slender sword with a golden hilt, a fine-wire filigreed guard, and a silvered titanium blade. The hilt was an unblemished ingot without an imprinted outline of a hand-clasp. A large green diamond graced the pommel, its luminosity muted by the surrounding deep purple velvet.

"Oh my. It's—I don't know what to say. It's magnificent."

"Now you have done it, my boy. You have rendered the Consort speechless." Another cuff to the back of his head, and MacDonald fell forward. He caught himself on the arm of Lauren's chair before he could land face first in her lap.

His forward dive seemed to break the spell cast upon the room. And laughter bubbled up from Lauren. Snow pushed to the front. *"It is truly magnificent, Lauren."*

"Yes," Ice added, peeking around Snow. She also seemed at a loss for words.

Lauren's entire being was focused on the slender blade before her. Reaching out, she moved to grasp the hilt ingot in her right hand.

"Wait!" Lord McLaran called out.

Lauren snatched her hand back as though the blade would burn her.

She cast a questioning glance at Lord McLaran, who shook his head. "M'lady, I assume you understand how a diamond is formed?" Lauren nodded. "Then, let me explain about this particular stone and its relationship to the stone in the pommel of the First Foremother's blade." That was the sword Lauren had used in defense of Alex in the Council meeting which went so badly.

Lauren settled back and eyed the blade speculatively as McLaran explained. "A diamond is a three-dimensional construct of carbon atoms, but every once in a while, a nitrogen atom will contaminate the carbon matrix and replace one or more of the matrix atoms. This nitrogen atom creates an atomic-sized flaw—a void, if you will, in the carbon matrix. Into one such void the MacDonald Clan has encoded a DNA-fingerprint. Your DNA-fingerprint. As soon as you touch the hilt, the blade will recognize you and only you. It will become your blade."

Laura was stunned. Molecular encoding was discussed as a method for making handguns serviceable to only one user in her reality, but not at this level. "So, if I understand what you're saying, this'll be my weapon and only mine? I'll be bonded to this weapon as Alex is to hers, and no one else will be able to use it? They would be killed by a release of bond energy if they took it up?"

"Partially correct, M'lady. It will be only yours once you touch the hilt," MacDonald replied.

"But?"

MacDonald frowned. "We had no way of creating a weapon which we knew would bond with you. No way to recreate a weapon exactly like Her Majesty's. No way to impart sentience into this blade with a piece of your life-force"

"But I can use Alex's sword, and even the First Foremother's. Those are bonded weapons."

Lord McLaran leaned back in his chair and smiled ruefully. "Your use Alexandra's blade is the result of your bond with her. The blade recognizes you as it recognizes Her Majesty. This should not have happened, but it has and is an indication of the depth of the bond you share."

"We did need to use the blade." Lauren thought back to their journey from Mount Zirkel in her reality. How Alex's injuries precluded her using her sword to open the supply caches along the way.

"We did, and you did. You were brave, Lauren."

"Thanks, Ice," Lauren replied absently, trying hard to reconcile these events and the use of these somewhat mystical objects. The wolf leaned against her chair offering physical support.

"The use of the Doouglas blade is a bit different." Lord McLaran rubbed his chin. "That blade is an ancient weapon which has been in existence for a long time. It has been used several times by others, when the need of its use arose. It seems to sense when that time occurs and it allows another to wield it."

"But both Alex and I used that blade. It made itself into our weapon. Alex is lefthanded yet the hilt fit her. But it morphed and fit my right-handed grip when I took it up." Lauren looked around the room at the faces creased with questions, but which also held the conviction that an inanimate object could 'do' something, do anything. Lauren shook her head and then said in awe. "And then . . . then it talked. You all heard it. With the tree, it talked."

Chuckling softly, Lord McLaran placed a gentle hand on her arm. "I know. The MacDonald Clan has tried for millennia to understand weapon-bonding but to no avail. But I agree, the actions of that one blade are a miracle. The tree and the blade intervened at the exact moment they were needed most. Without their actions, and yours for that matter," he smiled down at her and squeezed her shoulder, "we would not be here having this discussion."

MacDonald picked up the explanation of her new weapon. "As Lord McLaran stated, this diamond holds an exact copy of your DNA-genome in a nitrogen vacancy which exists at the precise center of the stone."

Again, Lauren shook her head. "A DNA-fingerprint is one thing, but an exact copy of my complete genome is different. It would be made up of three billion base-pairs." She tried to calculate the size of a complete genome. "I don't know, about seven hundred megabytes of data. All that fits in an atom-sized hole within that stone?" She pointed at the blade where it rested in its box.

"Yes, one nitrogen vacancy is large enough to hold that amount of information. But we went a step further. We produced this diamond as an exact atomic duplicate to the naturally-formed stone in the First Foremother's blade."

Lauren returned her gaze to the large stone sparkling on its velvet bed. She tried to visualize the geometry of one ever-so-small flaw being placed within the heart of the stone's carbon matrix—a matrix which was an exact copy of another stone.

"You can synthetically produce a diamond of this size and quality?" Lauren asked in awe.

MacDonald laughed. "Yes, we can and we do, and in this instance, we did. When the First Foremother's stone awoke and spoke, we knew the sentience within the bonded-stone still lived. We asked Alex to ask the blade if we could create a stone in her image for you. She allowed us."

Lauren sat back in her chair and gaped at MacDonald. "She allowed it?" Thinking of the presence she felt when she wielded the First Foremother's blade, she couldn't believe the blade would allow this.

"Not only did she allow it, she was pleased to have a . . . an offspring if you will. And the result is the stone before you. The only change we made was to add a bit of beryllium to the mix to give the stone its unique green tint, trying to create a stone that matched you."

"Amazing." Lauren was awed by all she was part of and, she had to admit, worried by. Her presence was doing unimagined things to this ancient culture and this realization frightened her a bit.

"Well, all right then." Lauren sat forward and reached out to grasp the hilt in her right hand. As her hand closed on the hilt, it morphed to fit the girth of her hand, each finger now nestled into a custom-shaped groove. *Just as the First Foremother's blade did.* Lifting the weapon from its case, Lauren recognized how fine a weapon it was. It wasn't the two-handed broadsword Alex carried. This was a weapon to wield with a single hand, a weapon of grace and finesse. It was perfectly balanced to her strength and arm length. Standing, she slowly swept the blade back and forth in shallow arcs.

"We knew you did not have the upper body strength to learn to fight with a broadsword, nor the time to develop that strength before the Investiture. So, we designed a weapon to match you, strong but thin and graceful. A rapier, if you will. This is classically a thrusting weapon, and blows are delivered from the point; unlike a broadsword which uses its edge to deliver a slashing blow. We believe you would be able to use this blade differently." MacDonald paused and Lauren stopped moving the blade.

"Me, use this blade? Why? I'm a physician and a scientist, not a duelist. It is a beautiful gift but not one I would use."

"Lady Beckwith." Lady MacDonald stood and bowed formally to her. "As part of the Investiture, you must demonstrate your intelligence and your ability to complement Alexandra's wisdom. You must swear fealty and prove willingness to obey Alexandra and the law of Terra. You must show your depth of knowledge of our culture and heritage to augment, not diminish our history. But most importantly, you must prove your ability to protect our Ruler."

"But . . ." Lauren muttered, dazed by this summary of the Investiture. A feeling which seemed to happen more often than not lately. Everything moved too fast, was too overwhelming. She sat back in her chair with a thump, the blade dangling from her hand.

"M'lady," When Lauren didn't respond, Lady MacDonald went on sternly. "Lauren Beckwith, we are not asking you to give up your principles, or violate your personal ethics, but this is a critical part of the ceremony. Those on the Council who are still unconvinced of Clan Cador's plot or their treasonous acts would challenge any Consort who cannot fight to protect." She looked around the room and seemed to beseech help in her argument.

Lord McLaran knelt beside Lauren's chair and placed a gentle hand on her left arm, covering the dragon beneath her skin. The dragon tattoo shivered but didn't protest. It seemed to recognize the importance of this moment. "Lauren, you have been protecting the Ruler and if I may be frank protecting all of Terra since the moment you crossed the nexus from your Earth. You raised the Sword of the Ruler when you needed to access the storage caches on your journey here and then again to penetrate the shield of the Keep. You raised the Sword of the First Foremother in protection of our Council and our Ruler. You sacrificed your own safety and nearly your life, to protect Her Majesty and Clan Doouglas, when only newly adopted to Clan Fraser. You found a cure for our children, protecting the future of our world. You did all this before you even understood the ramifications of your actions. You continually put aside your own wants and needs, your own safety and nearly your life for the protection of Terra, and for Alexandra."

Lauren slowly blinked at McLaran as the magnitude of his words settled in her soul. "I understand, M'lord. Up until now, I understood what this Investiture means for Alex, for you, for the Clans, and for Terra. But forgive my shock and incredulity. It seems I'm only now truly realizing what it all means for me."

"He is right, Lauren. You are our savior, and you hold the heart and soul of our Ruler in your loving hands." Ice stood from beside her chair and nuzzled her cheek. Snow leaned in on the other side and placed her nose in the palm of her free hand.

"I've never discounted my soul-bond, Ice. Never."

"We know, because we are also bonded with you both, but the others—those outside our bond—must be shown. It must be proven you are truly Alex's soul's complement."

"Well, if you put it like that. I don't have a choice, do I?" She smiled down at Ice with her blue eyes so like Alex's.

"You have every choice. This is nothing but a public acknowledgment of what we already know. We know neither Alex nor you would do anything to harm the other. You would each sacrifice everything for the other, and you already have."

"Again, thanks for reminding me where my priorities lie." Lauren laughed and bent her head touching her forehead to Ice's soft fur.

Snow broke in. *"Do not make light of this, Lauren. We do not. We know what you have already sacrificed and suffered."*

"Snow, I can't and won't make light of anything, but the magnitude of everything that's happening is overwhelming. I need a bit of time to digest it all." Lauren ruffled Snow's fur. *"But when I've got you two to keep me grounded I can't go wrong."* Wolfy smiles graced their faces and growls of happiness rumbled in their chests, as love flowed along their bond.

Lauren realized once again she had fallen into a private conversation in front of others and tilted her head in acknowledgement of her embarrassment. "My apologies." A chuckle rolled around the room. "So, if I'm to learn dueling as well as the history of the entire Terran race before the ceremony, we'd better get started." Pushing herself from her chair with her free hand, Lauren motioned around her solar. "Obviously this lesson must be held somewhere else. We don't have enough room in here."

Lord McLaran rose. "Too true, Cáraid Rioghail. I suggest we take this lesson to the far hay barn this evening, away from prying eyes. We do not want to give away our tactics too soon."

Lauren had read her future title in the journals of the First Foremothers but not heard it spoken aloud. Lord McLaran was showing them all what was at stake and how important this part of the Investiture would be. She shook herself. *Get your head in the game here, Beckwith, too much to worry about.*

Placing the blade back in its case, she closed the lid and gently caressed the wooden lid. "You've outdone yourself, Tavish MacDonald. Truly."

Lord McLaran cuffed the boy on the shoulder in agreement.

Chapter Three

Merilyn looked up from her parchment-covered desk as the oak door of her rotunda swung open. Alex strode into the room and proceeded to drop into the nearest chair without invitation and heedless of the chair's structural integrity. Merilyn winced at how little regard Alexandra had for a twelve-hundred-year-old chair, but when she saw the storm brewing in Alex's sapphire eyes, Merilyn knew this was not going to be good.

"What may I do for you this fine day, Your Majesty?" she asked, knowing full well Alexandra was only concerned about five things lately: the Investiture, the ongoing healing of the children, the traitor, finding the remaining co-conspirators, and Lauren. This upset was, without a doubt, about Lauren.

"The Council is driving me to distraction. They want another meeting to re-discuss the traitor." Merilyn stifled a chuckle as Alex placed air quotes around 're-discuss', a gesture Lauren used frequently to emphasis her point. More of Lauren blended with Alexandra every day. Their bond was strengthening beyond what anyone could believe. She also knew the name Gwenhwyfach of the Hebridean Clan Cador would never cross the lips of Her Majesty again.

Alex rose suddenly and paced around the circular room. "What is there to discuss? We have been over this. Exile was our only option to protect those within the Keep unable to protect themselves from potential psychic manipulation."

Merilyn let her stew for a few moments. "Alexandra, sit down. You are making me dizzy."

"I cannot sit down. I am besieged by the Council on an hourly basis. They have decided the best way to get their wishes met is to go directly to Lauren, bypassing you and I. Lauren has enough to do without a bunch of Council members bombarding her with requests for meetings." Merilyn had not realized until now how the Council was getting to Alexandra. Now she knew, use the one person Alexandra could not say no to, Lauren.

Merilyn tapped her bottom lip in thought. "I agree. Lauren must be protected, isolated, even. She is exhausted and absolutely overwhelmed with preparations for the upcoming ceremony."

Grasping the back of her chair, Alex leaned forward. "Stating the obvious again, Seneschal?"

"Do not be rude, Alexandra. We all recognize the demands being placed on the two of you. Allow me to think out loud and without interruption. Now, sit down." Merilyn leaned back in her chair, hands clasped across her stomach. "Together we will determine the best course of action."

Chastised, Alex again plopped down in the high-back chair and immediately began tapping her fingers on the armrest.

Stifling a groan, Merilyn knew nothing good would come of their discussion if Alexandra did not calm down. Perhaps a diversion? "Have you seen Lauren's new blade?"

"Not yet." Alex replied distractedly. "She is due in the far hay barn this evening for her first lesson. I am hoping to see it then. I hear from the boys it is a magnificent sword, but I have yet to figure out how they plan on teaching her to spar with such a weapon. It is unlike anything we fight with. I do not know how she will be successful fighting against a broadsword with an overgrown knitting needle."

Merilyn half-rose from her seat, anger flashing through her. "Do not let Lauren hear you call her blade that!" Her voice dropped half an octave, but lost none of its power. Her whisper cut through the room like a dagger. "Or Young MacDonald for that matter."

She knew Alexandra recognized her mistake immediately, as a dark blush rose to color her cheeks. The blush deepened and moved across her chest, visible through the open collar of her white shirt. "Your Grace, I am sorry." She spread her arms in emphasis. "I meant no disrespect to Lauren or her blade, nor to its creators. I am so distracted and overwhelmed. And now the Council demands more."

"Then give it to them." Merilyn tapped her desk to emphasis her point.

Alex rubbed her cheeks in frustration. "I do not know how Lauren does it. She goes morning, noon and night. She barely gets three hours sleep before she is up again. Working on some project or other for some technician, studying her history, or reading those journals. I am not doing any science, I already know the history and what the Investiture requires, and I have read the journals multiple times. But I am still exhausted!"

"Then give it to them." The tapping got louder.

"Setting up the exile and all its demands has occupied all my time. I have not sparred with the boys or ridden Ffrwyn in a month. Yet, Lauren keeps going and going." Shaking her head, Alex rubbed her face again and drew a shaky breath. "I am truly amazed by her stamina."

"Then give it to them." Merilyn slapped the top of her desk with one small hand.

Alex snapped her head up at the sharp crack. "What did you say?"

"I hate to repeat myself, but I will in this instance. I said, then give it to them."

"Merilyn, you must be joking. Give it to them? That's tantamount to giving them carte blanche to make demands at their whim. I cannot . . . I will not, give it to them."

"Take a breath and calm down. Think about this for a moment. What do we not know, but must find out?"

Alex paused and her eyes lost focus as she seemed to consider her comment. "There is only one thing we must determine . . . who else is involved in the treason against us."

"Correct. And how would you go about finding this out?" Merilyn knew she was leading Alexandra on, but she had to get her to clear her roiling thoughts, and focus.

"I suppose the most straightforward way would be to interview everyone on the Council under psi-examination, but I cannot order such an extreme measure without justification or specific evidence. And we do not have any suspects or evidence, only suspicions. The traitor must have had help. She could not have masterminded this and carried out her plans alone."

Merilyn nodded. "Yes, psi-examination would be an extreme measure and only available as a last resort. But what if all the Councilors were held in one place and then collectively questioned? Or more accurately, challenged through questioning? With Lauren by your side, she could listen in, while you or I or McLaran challenge them. Demand answers and justifications for their harassment. See who responds and how. See who pushes for more. Who accepts what is given without question. Watch who is quiet and who is not. Can we make them blunder and give themselves away? Because, Alexandra, I agree there are others involved. How deep the treason goes remains to be seen, but I fear we will end up cutting a wide swath through the fabric of our society before this is over and done."

Nodding her head, Alex agreed. "All right, that sounds like a plan. Please call a Council meeting. Make it at your earliest convenience. We do not want to appear to roll over too easily to their demands, so let them know We are not happy with the interruption in Our preparation for the Investiture."

Merilyn was pleased Alexandra had accepted this plan and knew when she invoked the use of the royal 'We,' she would not change her mind.

Alex rose from the chair to leave the rotunda, but paused. "Do you have any ideas who we should concentrate on?"

"I do not. Although, I agree there are others involved." Merilyn's voice quivered, her concern tainting her normally steady speech. This meeting was going to be a watershed moment in their history and she was gravely worried about the potential outcomes.

Nodding, Alexandra moved toward the door, but Merilyn interrupted her departure. "And Alexandra, listen to what you said about Lauren. I agree. She is spread too thin and cannot maintain her current pace. Although, she would never admit she could not."

Alex faced her mentor once again. "What are you getting at, Merilyn?"

"Only that you might want to consider a . . . what does Lauren call it when one takes some time off to rest and relax?"

"A vacation." A frown creased Alexandra's forehead.

"Yes, that is it, a vacation. Perhaps, you should consider taking a vacation." Merilyn tapped her desk in emphasis.

"But her studies and the preparations?"

"Lady MacDonald is pleased with Lauren's progress. Her knowledge of our history is growing every day. Síobhan says her tutelage will not be needed much longer and Lauren could complete her studies by herself with some suggested readings."

Alexandra blew out a breath. "All right, that sounds like a great idea, for both of us. We need to spend time together before things get crazy as Terra demands more from their Consort, and I never see her again. Any suggestions where we should go? It will have to be away from the Keep or the interruptions will not be controllable." Alex crossed her arms and waited.

Merilyn tapped her lower lip in thought once more. "Where do you think Lauren would most like to go?" Alex shrugged. "It would have to be some place she has never been before, some place private and isolated. Some place she has wondered aloud about to each of us in her scientific musings. Know anywhere like that?"

Alex jerked in shock. "Are you suggesting what I think you are? Dare I do that?"

"I think you not only dare, but you must. It is the last part of who we are that Lauren has not seen but must embrace as your Consort." Merilyn leaned forward and pointed at Alexandra. "You must share this with her. She must see the *Iolar Mara*."

Alex relaxed slightly and nodded. "All right, I'll do it." And with that, the Queen of Terra left the rotunda.

Merilyn smiled at Alexandra's retreating back. *That is something I wish I could share with them. Lauren's natural enthusiasm to try new things and her insatiable appetite for new technologies will make this a memorable trip.* Merilyn shook her head ruefully. *But my stomach will not allow it.*

Chapter Four

Evening settled over the Keep like a fleece blanket, warm but with lingering hints of winter cold. Lauren raced down the solar stairs and out onto the nearly empty boulevard. Most folks were home preparing their evening meals. With her ironwood box tucked under her arm, Lauren made good time to the Postern Gate and exited the Keep proper, then she ran south toward the stables and the hay fields beyond. She was meeting Ffrwyn and the wolves at the stables. The four of them would trek up to the far hay barn for her first weapons lesson with the boys.

As she rounded the last bend in the path, Snow called to her, *"Lauren, are you coming? We are going to be late if we do not hurry."*

"On my way. Keep your furry knickers on, Snow."

"I bet you lost track of time again. McLaran will have your hide if you are late."

"McLaran can try but he won't be successful. I'm doing my best with everything, so lighten up. And I'll tell McLaran that, as well."

"You do that and see where it gets you with your lessons. He does not like tardiness or sloppy swordsmanship." Ice's snide remark caused Lauren to increase her speed.

Lauren raced up the path and slithered through the fence into the stable grounds. Ffrwyn with Snow and Ice at her heels ran to meet her. She smiled at the trio. The white feathered feet of the giant ebony horse ate up the distance and she easily outpaced the wolves. *"Mount up, Lauren. We must hurry."* Ffrwyn's deep female voice rumbled in Lauren's mind.

The horse dropped to her knees to allow Lauren easier access to her broad back. Once she was settled, Ffrwyn rose and took off across the stable grounds to the fields beyond. The cold air brought tears to Lauren's eyes as they rushed through the night. As usual, Lauren could barely keep her seat as the horse stretched her gait to a full gallop. *"Easy, girl. I'm not Alex. You don't want to dump me on the way."*

But Ffrwyn didn't slow her pace. As the fence at the southern end of the grounds drew closer, Lauren knew what was coming. She grabbed a handful of long soft mane and tightened her hold on her weapon box. *I'm going to regret this. I can already tell.*

Scrunching her eyes closed, she held her breath as she felt Ffrwyn gather herself. The next thing she knew, they were flying through the air, weightless, as the giant horse topped the rail fence. They landed with a thump and, without losing stride; the horse raced across the next field. These outer fields were sown in tall grasses which brushed Ffrwyn's belly and Lauren's feet.

"Well done, Lauren. You never so much as bounced on that jump." Snow complimented her as the wolf ran alongside.

"It wasn't me, guys, it was all the Horse. She makes any rider look good."

All Lauren heard was a whiffle and snort from Ffrwyn. Lauren knew she hated being called Horse, but before she could decide if she needed to apologize, Ffrwyn began to slow. She smoothly dropped her gait from a gallop to a lope to a gliding walk. A couple of stutters indicated they had arrived at their destination. That and a lack of wind blowing through her hair.

Sliding smoothly to the ground, Lauren went around to Ffrwyn's head. Stroking the long broad nose, she crooned, *"Thank you, Ffrwyn. You always take the best care of me. You're the best friend I know."* This comment got her a raft of grumbles from the wolves as they arrived and proceeded ahead of her into the hay barn.

"You are welcome, Lauren. I will always do all I can to help you. Those other ones not so much, but you always." Her mind voice didn't sound winded but her exertion was evident as her sides heaved and a thin coat of glistening white sweat painted her chest and shoulders.

"You are great, even if you are a horse." Laughing, Lauren skittered out of the reach of Ffrwyn's snapping jaws and smiled back up into large mahogany eyes before making her way toward the barn.

The barn was a huge timber-framed structure and Lauren headed toward a light-outlined opening set within one of the double-hung doors.

She pulled the door open, marveling how some of the pegs holding the structural elements together were larger than her hand. Her gaze was drawn to the three floors towering above her. A square central area opened all the way to a high trussed ceiling. The wrap-around balconies on each of the floors were usually filled to overflowing with bales of sweet hay, but as spring arrived and after a severe winter, the supply was greatly reduced. Giant block and tackle systems hung from iron hooks mounted into several of the timber cross-members. These were used to lift hay bales from the upper floors and lower them to the ground. Dust motes danced through the air as Lauren strode fully into the central open area. Straw covered the inlayed wooden floor. She smiled seeing Lord McLaran and Young MacDonald among the small group waiting for her.

"You are late. This is an unacceptable way to begin your lessons. Your behavior indicates you do not take the protection of the Ruler seriously." A deep voice scolded.

Lauren skidded to a halt, her anger snapping. "You've gotta be kidding me."

Turning toward the speaker, Lauren was aligned directly with the stomach of a giant. The towering man stood with hands on hips and scowled down at her. A sneer of contempt marred his crag-like features. The man asked Lord McLaran. "Is this the wisp of a girl I must teach the intricacies of sword play? It is not possible. She is unfit."

"Now, Stewart, let us not jump to conclusions. This is Lady Beckwith. She has saved our Ruler and our people more times than I care to count, and she did it all without thought of reward or safety. She will be a student worthy of your teaching." McLaran seemed to hold Stewart's glare until Lauren saw a small nod. Then McLaran moved over to her.

"M'lady, may I present Stewart McGuiness, SwordMaster of all Terra and Champion of the People." He nodded to the SwordMaster. "Champion McGuiness, may I present Lady Lauren Beckwith, holder of the Ruler's heart and Savior of the Terran People."

The SwordMaster looked down his nose at Lauren, and she stifled the urge to quail under the weight of his steel-gray gaze. *Remember your strength and position, Lauren. This is the same as holding your own against any teaching surgeon you've met.* She held his gaze until he nodded again.

"All right, let me see this weapon you have created, MacDonald." Tavish stepped forward and motioned for Lauren to hand him the case. He balanced the case in his arms. "M'lady, show the Champion your weapon, please."

Lauren opened the dragon clasps and tilted up the lid. Reverently, she grasped the sword in her right hand and pulled the sword from its velvet bed, holding the blade high.

"No! What is this?" The SwordMaster demanded. "I will not waste my time on an inferior blade such as this. It is a pig-sticker, not a weapon to defend and protect. It is an affront to all we are as Terrans."

"Now, Stewart, a moment." Lord McLaran replied. "This is a weapon of grace and elegance, much like the lady herself." He tilted his head in her direction reinforcing his compliment. "She does not have the upper body strength to wield a broadsword."

Stewart interrupted, "She used the Ruler's sword and then she used the blade of the First Foremother. If she is truly the Ruler's Savior she must use the proper weapon."

"Yes, she is the one who used those weapons, but—" McLaran said.

"Then she will use a proper sword."

Tavish MacDonald stood up to his full height and stepped in front of Lauren, the empty case tucked under his arm. "Champion, I respect your knowledge and your skills. I respect all you have taught me. But in this instance, you are wrong." Lauren peeked around Tavish and saw the SwordMaster rear back as if struck and focus his laser glare on the young man. "Lady Beckwith is a protector and a savior already proven. She holds the heart and soul of our Ruler in the gentlest of hands. The bond they share has not existed since our First Foremothers. It has reawakened and is blessed by the tree and blade. You will not disparage either the lady or her blade."

"No, boy! It is you who disparage. Disparage us." He thumped his fist against his chest. "Disgrace our history. No one has ever stepped into the Sacred Grove to defend our Ruler with a blade such as this." He waved his arm in Lauren's general direction and at the sword she held.

"Where is it written what type of blade must be used?" Lauren asked.

"It has never been done, and I will not be a party to this affront." The SwordMaster crossed his arms over his broad chest. The wolves' growls filled the barn and Ffrwyn stomped her hoofs in disapproval of his words.

Lauren shouldered her way around Tavish and grabbed McGuiness' arm. "You are the one who is wrong, Champion." She felt his anger ripple down his forearm. "The Fraser entered the Sacred Grove on Terra Prime without any weapon at all, as she was a healer and refused to lift a weapon for any reason. She swore to do no harm." She lightened her grip. "Even unarmed, the Fraser won her right to rule beside the Doouglas using the strength of their bond alone. It is said the Fraser completely subsumed herself. She allowed the Doouglas to have absolute physical and mental control of her body and mind and thereby fight the challenge through her. She evaded every stroke. The Fraser danced and spun, and the challenger missed, until he was so exhausted, he was unable to lift his own weapon to strike another blow. The challenger was not successful."

The Champion's eyes locked on Lauren, but she held his penetrating gaze. "I'm not the Fraser. I am a healer. I too will guard my soul's other half. I have raised a weapon and I will do so again if needed. If you will not teach me then I'll go elsewhere to learn what I must." Lauren dropped her hand from his arm and stepped back. She held her sword high, the titanium blade reflected a rainbow of light around the barn. "This sword is my sword. Forged with strength by our Ruler's right arm. I carry and use this weapon as I must, to serve and protect Alexandra Aoeron Aonwyn nighean mhic Fionnaghal, Rigain Rìoghachd Fuar Ćala, now and forever."

A beam of pure green-white light shot from the diamond pommel and struck the SwordMaster in the chest. A light soprano voice, tinkled like falling snow flakes through the minds of the group. "*If you will not teach the rightful soulmate of your Queen, then you are no longer champion of Terra.*" Lauren staggered and nearly dropped her sword as it spoke.

Another voice broke in, a deep alto calling from afar. "*We name MacDonald the Younger as the new Protector and Champion of Lady Beckwith, healing technician and nexus traveler. She is Bhean chéili agus comh-rialóir Fuar Ćala. He will teach her, and he will guard her and Our Ruler.*"

"I concur and add the approval of the First Foremothers." Lauren felt a puff of steam on her neck as her dragon affirmed the mind-voiced words of Lauren's and the First Foremother's blade. *"We would not have awakened and reentered this world were it not a time of need. But more importantly, we would not choose a pair who is unworthy of our guidance and protection."*

The SwordMaster stood still. Seconds became to minutes before he spoke. "I acknowledge the wisdom of the blade and the dragon." He bowed slightly. "I am humbled the First Foremothers souls are again amongst us. I am pleased the children of Terra are healed and our people will live on. But I will not teach the use of that blade," he pointed at Lauren's rapier, "in the protection of our Ruler."

No one moved until Stewart stepped back from Lauren. He tilted his head to Lord McLaran, "I withdraw from these lessons, M'lord. Let it be known I believe this is an affront to all Terra stands for, and I shall not be a party to this travesty." He spun on his heel and strode from the barn.

Lauren dropped her arm. Sarcasm dripped from her voice. "That went well. Now whatta we do?" Her shoulders drooped, angry at herself for having precipitated another diplomatic situation. *Dammit, I've done it again.*

"You have done nothing wrong. MacDonald was correct in creating this weapon for you. And it seems you have completed another bond and awakened another blade." But Lord McLaran's chuckle lacked any humor. Lauren knew his mind was racing to figure out their next steps. Time was ticking away and this part of the ceremony was vital.

"Can we do as the Fraser did and have Alex control Lauren's actions?" Snow asked. *"Their bond is strong enough. Alex transferred her use of the Ruler's blade to Lauren when the Comin attacked."*

"That will not happen." Everyone spun around as Alex's contralto filled the barn. She strode into the barn through the open door, her weapon drawn and fire blazing in her sapphire eyes. "Lauren is her own person. She will stand as my protector, and she will be successful."

Lauren let out a breath, as relief washed over her at her love's appearance. "But, Alex—"

"Do not 'But, Alex' me, Lauren," Alex snapped. "You will do this. The blade is correct. I heard it from across the Keep. MacDonald created this weapon for you, and he will complete your education in its use." Alex crossed the straw-covered floor and stopped before her soulmate. She sheathed her weapon and knelt in one fluid motion, taking Lauren's left hand in hers. "Lauren, you are my heart and hold my soul. I know you will always guard my life." She bowed her head and touched her forehead to the back of Lauren's hand.

"Don't kneel before me or anyone, Alex." Lauren pulled her to her feet. She gazed up into those sapphire eyes and felt her soul settle. *"We are one."*

"Yes." The torques and blades spoke in unison. Their bond sang between them, as Alex stood and gathered Lauren into her arms.

"Enough of this." McLaran's voice broke into their moment. Heat flashed up Lauren's neck. These instances when their souls connected were becoming more frequent and more intense. They were so intimate Lauren was embarrassed when others were witness to it. *"Can they feel our energy?"*

"They can and do, Dearheart, but I will not put aside our feelings for anyone. I do not want to miss a single opportunity to relish the love we share."

"You're right, but now isn't the time. Let's plan on tonight to revisit these feelings?"

"Your pool or mine?" A wolfy grin graced Alex's face.

Heat again flashed across Lauren's neck and face. *"Stop that or we won't make it to the pool or to tonight."*

"Oh, we will make it all right. Especially, if I have anything to say about it."

Lord McLaran broke in again, "Focus, you two. If McGuiness will not help us, then we have a problem."

"I am sorry to disagree, M'lord, we do not have a problem. We have a unique user-blade, we have the Savior of Terra, and we have a bonded pair of Rulers who have not been seen since the First Foremothers. With these things, we can do anything. I forged this blade. I will teach its owner in its use." MacDonald was adamant in his assertion of the facts.

"Her." Lauren interjected. She knew her new blade was female, especially after she spoke.

MacDonald asked. "What? Her, who?"

"Her. My blade is a her, not an it."

MacDonald shook his head but nodded, a lopsided grin growing on his face. "Of course, it is, I mean she is."

Stepping away from Alex's side, Lauren raised her blade, letting her flash in the muted light of the barn. "Time isn't in our favor, and I haven't got a clue what I gotta do or how to do it. So, let's do this!"

The group began teaching Lauren the use of her blade.

"Lauren, as I said when I presented you with this blade, she uses her point to attack in a thrust. To be successful when fighting with this style weapon, we had three hypotheses we needed to address when we began designing her for you. First, can the user with a shorter reach, given her size and the length of her blade, control the distance the bout is fought from?" MacDonald held up one finger. "Secondly, is it possible for the user with a lower technical ability to use this blade and control the speed of the bout?" He ticked off his second point and raised another finger. "And lastly, is it possible to force an opponent into your own area of strength and away from his, thereby lessening his skills?" He raised a third finger.

Lauren listened intently as he outlined their strategy. What he said made sense. She and her blade were smaller, less strong, and definitely less skilled. Doubt clouded her mind. *How am I going to do this?*

"As you have done everything else, with elegance and grace. Relax and let MacD show you the way. He will help you develop muscle memory through repetition so you will not think, you will act."

"Lauren, you need to focus here." Lord McLaran tapped her on the head and pulled her away from her inner dialogue with Alex.

Physically stepping away from Alex and the distraction of their bond, Lauren gave her full attention to MacDonald.

"Let us start at the beginning. You will need to draw your opponent within your reach. Try and get him to attack high. Then, you can step under his guard and attack with a thrust beneath his blade." He demonstrated the moves he visualized when creating the blade.

Lauren watched as he swung his broadsword high above her head preparing for a downward slash. She could see the opening in his guard and she stepped in under his raised arm, tapping his side with her left hand.

"Yes, that. When you thrust forward with the point of your blade, this also serves to lower your overall height, making it more difficult for your opponent to reverse his high move and parry your thrust."

"Reverse? Parry?" Lauren bit her lower lip in concentration. "You've got to explain your terms as you go, MacD. I'm a visual and hands-on learner."

MacDonald laughed, "Explain terms. That is pot-kettle, if you ask me. You never explain your terms. You and Newkirk speak your own language with no regard for others when you get going."

Alex stepped forward. "Let me show her."

Alex again drew her sword and fully faced Lauren, blade pointed down at a forty-five-degree angle. Lauren mirrored her position but since Lauren was righthanded and Alex lefthanded, their blades were on the same side. In a flash of motion so fast Lauren could barely react, Alex swung her blade upward in a shallow arc. The arc passed in front of Lauren, beneath her nose, and she instinctively jumped back as the air sang in front of her face.

"Stop!" Lord McLaran's command halted them both. "M'lady, you cannot step back. That opens space for your opponent to reverse the sword's arc and swing down into your torso. You cannot allow him to use his longer and heavier weapon. You must step forward and crowd his blade."

"No way! If I had stepped forward she would have removed my nose," Lauren argued. *I can't see the geometry here.*

Alex returned her blade to its starting position. "Watch this, Dearheart." She repeated her upward arcing swing, only this time in slow motion. When she had swung past Lauren's face she halted the arc, holding the blade in position above and slightly in front of Lauren's face. "If you wait until the blade passes your face and is swinging up to complete the arc, all of your opponent's momentum is moving away from you. That is the time for you to step forward, under his slash."

"How do I do that when my nose is on the ground?" Lauren's shoulders drooped and she frowned.

MacDonald laughed. “That is the trick. You lean away but do not step back. That way your feet keep you close but your upper body moves away, allowing the blade to pass.”

“Right. Like I can do that.” Lauren lifted her blade and bent backwards.

“Sarcasm is not becoming, Lauren,” Ice said.

Lauren spun toward the wolves where they lay on a pile of straw, her blade pointed toward them. “Like you can do better, you big furball.”

“I can, and I will.” Ice rose and trotted to the center of the floor. *“Again please, Alex.”*

Alex took her position and without warning, her blade flashed at the wolf's snout. The wolf bent her right knee and slid her right forepaw toward Alex. The blade sang over the wolf's head, and then she launched herself forward under Alex's guard and into her side. Alex fell back, as Ice landed on top of her, jaws around her throat.

Laughter rose from the group, but Lauren remained unconvinced she could duplicate that move. “Well played, Ice, but I don't have four legs, only two. That move, though spectacular, isn't one I can replicate.”

Snow snorted. *“But it is, Lauren. You have two legs and two arms. Your opponent will always give away his intent before it happens. A muscle twitch, an eye-flicker, a dip of the blade, something will tell you a move is coming. When you see this sign, gather yourself.”*

Lauren's gaze lost focus as she thought about what Snow said.

Ice said, *“Alex lifts her blade a millimeter or so as she grips it tighter in preparation of swinging her blade upward—”*

Alex was indignant. “I do not lift my blade!”

“Yes, you do, Alex.” Newkirk spoke up for the first time since the group lesson started. He affirmed Ice's observation with a nod. “We all know that small motion. You cannot prevent it. Your broadsword is heavy, and to slash one-handed you must grip the blade tighter. This causes your forearm muscles to bunch, which lifts the blade tip ever so slightly before the swing.”

Newkirk stepped up and drew his blade. “Let us try this again. As you see any indication your opponent is preparing to move, focus on his eyes. They will give away the moment the attack is coming.” Newkirk dropped his blade downward and waited for Lauren to fully face him. He was taller than Alex and his reach was proportionally greater.

In a blink, his blade slashed through the air, Lauren slid her right leg forward with a bent knee and she lunged off her left leg, her blade outstretched toward Newkirk. This lowered her center of gravity, and allowed her to move her head and shoulders back and away from the arc of Newkirk's swing. As his blade passed her face, she slid forward on her right foot and promptly lost her balance. Cartwheeling her arms for balance, Lauren overcorrected her fall. She landed on her side with a loud thud.

"M'lady, are you all right?" Newkirk's panicked voice filled the barn.

Rolling onto her back, Lauren laughed and waved off his offered hand up. "Right, I guess four legs are better than two."

"Moving under a slash is a solution to one of the three hypotheses we came up with when we tried to envision how you could successfully defeat a taller, stronger, and more skilled opponent who fights with a longer, heavier slashing weapon," MacD said.

Determined to get this move correct, Lauren lifted her blade and slowly moved through the bent-leg lunge.

"That is it, Lauren." Snow encouraged from the straw pile.

Again and again Lauren repeated the lunge until she could do it on the balls of her feet, in perfect balance. Newkirk and MacD tried to unbalance her lunge by pushing her from each side. And when she could keep her balance against their efforts, they again tried their attacks.

Sweat ran freely down Lauren's face and dripped from her chin. The muscles of her forearm were quivering when Lord McLaran called a halt to the lesson. "Enough. Lady Lauren is tired and she will injure herself if we continue."

"No, I'm fine." Lauren stated, narrowing her eyes in concentration and again taking up an *en garde* position.

"No, you are exhausted—"

"I'm not. I've gotta get this."

Lord McLaran disagreed and stepped forward. "And you will, but not tonight. You have made great progress and demonstrated your athletic prowess, but we cannot afford an injury because you are muscle-weary."

"I'm not. Come on, let's go again." Lauren waved her blade in emphasis.

MacD passed a critical eye over her. "Please lift your blade and hold it at shoulder height."

Lauren raised her blade with the shaft parallel to the floor.

"Now lunge forward." Taking a confident step forward, she lunged toward her imaginary opponent.

"Hold that position and tilt your blade upward by bending your wrist." With her blade pointed toward the ceiling, Lauren had to support the weight of her arm plus the blade with only her shoulder.

Tension built in her shoulder and upper arm as the weight of the blade pressed down. Her right thigh began to burn, and spasms tore at her shoulder muscles. Sweat again ran from her hairline into her eyes, stinging, blurring her vision. Lord McLaran stepped up and tapped her blade. It fell from her hand. Alex snatched her blade out of the air before it could strike the ground.

"Never overtax yourself to this point of exhaustion. Muscles learn and strengthen through exercise but are destroyed through abuse. You have done enough tonight." Alex handed her blade back to her hilt first. She accepted the weapon with a bow.

"Thank you, M'lord." She bowed to the rest. "And to each of you, as well." The boys returned her bow.

"Come on, Dearheart, there is a warm pool waiting for you."

I hope Alex can keep me from drowning. I'm so tired I'll never be able to hold my head above water.

Chapter Five

Lauren floated effortlessly on her back in the center of the hot springs pool beneath Alex's solar. Her naked body was buoyant in the high salinity water. She ached all over. Her right arm was ribboned with bruises from the blade strikes which had penetrated her guard. *Gawd, Lord McLaran's right, I way overdid it. But I'm not going to get this if I don't keep on. No matter what, I won't let Alex down.*

"I know you won't, Dearheart. Moderation and repetition are best. Muscle memory is what we need to create. You cannot think your way through this. You must flow, relaxed and confident. Let your muscles be in control so that you can react." Alex strode into the room with a stack of fluffy towels in her arms.

Flipping over on her stomach and stroking languidly to the pool's edge, Lauren peered up at her love through the rising steam. "It's so hard for me to shut my brain down like that. I haven't had to do something like that since my last piano recital, and that didn't go so great." Lauren laughed, remembering the panic she felt before the performance. "But what with all the history I've got to learn—"

"Which you have." Alex slid into the pool.

"And the ceremony itself and everything I must do and say—"

"Which you have memorized perfectly." Alex moved nearer and reached out to gather Lauren close.

"And now this, I'm so going to fall flat on my butt."

"Which you will not." Alex smiled gently.

"But, Alex—"

Alex encircled Lauren's shoulders with long arms and smiled indulgently at her. "What have I said over and over?"

Lauren rolled her eyes at Alex's constant admonishment to stop not believing in herself. "Don't 'but Alex' me. I got that part, but—"

"Stop." Alex placed soft fingers on her lips to halt further argument.

Lauren looked deeply into Alex's eyes. Their bond flared, with flashes of emerald and sapphire, and they effortlessly slid into each other's soul.

Lauren's heart skipped a beat to take on the rhythm of Alex's. *Synchrony.* Warm, wet lips captured hers, and she fell into their kiss with abandon. Tongues dueled as they sank lower into the pool. *Wow, this is so—*

"Totally!" Alex agreed.

Words lost all meaning as Lauren encircled Alex's waist with her arms to deepen their physical contact. Then nothing else mattered. Nothing else existed beyond the boundaries of their souls. Water sloshed over the pool's edge as Alex lifted Lauren out to sit on the side, her legs dangling in the warm water. Alex stood on a seat at the pool's edge. It seemed her hands were everywhere at once. And Lauren slid farther into the ecstasy of them.

Slowly, Lauren's nipples reacted to Alex's gentle pinching and plucking. Alex's other hand slid down her side and over her hip. Fingers nestled in wet curls where they began to explore, delving deeper until they reached their goal. Lauren stiffened as those fingers found her hardened clitoris. *"Not yet, Dearheart. Together."*

"Always."

Lauren let her hands slide over the silken skin of Alex's shoulders and then lower to dance in ebony curls. "Ah—"

Lauren didn't know if Alex spoke aloud or they were communicating only through their bond. Did it matter? No. What mattered was her love was in her arms. *Stop being so analytical and let go, Lauren.*

She gasped and shivered as Alex stroked through her curls again. Two long fingers separated her folds and tracked down the sides of her clitoris to pinch the core between them. Another small pinch and she was hanging on the edge.

"Wait." Alex commanded.

"I can't." Lauren groaned.

"You will wait."

Lauren tried to ignore her body's demand for release and focus on Alex. Moving her fingers, she tangled them again in Alex's curls. Then she dove deeper, searching, seeking. *There!*

Stroking up and forward, she sank deep within Alex and began a steady but languid rhythm. Alex's essence soon coated her fingers. Lauren was so focused on Alex and the feelings humming along their bond, she almost missed the moment when Alex sank into her core. But

Alex's powerful arm drove her long fingers deep, lifting Lauren partially off the pool deck. The stroke pulled her fingers free from Alex and away from her soulmate's center. *Lost!*

"I am here, Dearheart."

Alex relaxed her upward stroke and allowed Lauren to sink back to her seat. Lauren opened her eyes, and their bond snapped again with almost tactical connection. She reclaimed her place, and together they reestablished a rhythm. Steady, in tune, then accelerating, pounding and unrelenting. Lauren felt Alex rest her thumb on her clitoris and begin to stroke in time with their rhythm.

Never taking her eyes from Alex, Lauren could see how difficult it was becoming for Alex to hang on, to even keep her eyes open. She fought her own need to reach her release. Curling her fingers with each upward stroke, Lauren searched out and found that one small spot. She increased the pressure on it with each stroke until she stopped all motion and simply held her hand still, one finger pushing hard.

Alex roared, throwing her head back. They were there. Caught up in a maelstrom of their own creation. Swirling emotions, physical feelings, spiraling outward to eternity, whiplashing back. Time ceased but their love encapsulated and protected them. Forever, together!

Their dragons added their roar to the psychic tumult they created, and the walls of the bath chamber rang with their joy.

Floating again, Lauren came back to this reality. Her fingers were still deep within Alex, caught in a vice of contracting muscles as Alex rode the aftershocks of their pleasure. Lauren smiled and slowly lay back, pulling Alex out of the pool and down with her. She rolled them over, so she was above Alex.

"I've got you. Let it all go, Dearest. I'll never let you fall." She tightened her hold on Alex with her left arm wrapped around strong shoulders and wiggled the fingers of her right hand lightly, waiting for them to be released.

Alex's contractions slowed, becoming farther apart as she relaxed. *Safe.*

"I'll always keep you safe." Lauren slowly pulled her fingers free.

Lauren marveled at how relaxed Alex was. No worries, the two of them here, together. *Wish we didn't have to be all the things we have to be for everyone else. That we could just be us.*

"But then we wouldn't be us, now would we?"

"I'm not getting into a philosophical discussion. Not after that." Lauren's smile broadened as Alex opened her eyes, and she lost herself in the swirling sapphire and emerald colors dancing in the soft light. *"Oh, Alex, that was amazing. It's more every time."*

"You need not waste words, Dearheart. I feel what you feel. I share what we create. Together, now and forever." They lay side by side, sated and relaxed on the edge of the pool.

"Not to devolve into a sappy love song, but you're right. Besides, no words can define what we share."

"This is a love symphony, and nothing we share is sappy."

They slid back into the warm waters to float together, arms entwined, legs gently ruffling the calm surface of the pool as steam swirled above them.

When their fingers were pruned beyond recognition, they rose from the pool. Wrapped up in large fluffy towels, they climbed the spiral stairs into Alex's sleeping chamber. "I'm wiped out," Lauren flopped unceremoniously across Alex's wide bed. "Wake me up in about a year or so. That way it'll all be over, and I can stop worrying about everything."

She felt Alex's thoughts searching, questioning. Without opening her eyes, she asked, "What? What's the matter now? I can feel your concern."

When Alex didn't answer right away, Lauren's opened her eyes. Alex's face hovered inches above Lauren's. Startled, she tried to push herself deeper into the down surface to escape.

"I hate that. Stop sneaking up on me. You're as bad as Snow with her cat-paw abilities."

"All right, I am sorry for startling you." Alex smiled down at her. "But I agree with Merilyn. You need a vacation."

A bark of laughter punctuated Lauren's rebuttal. "Oh, yeah, right. Like I have time for a fricking vacation." She felt more than saw the hurt her comment had on Alex. "Oh, Gawd, I didn't mean to criticize, I'm sorry. I'm not making light of your suggestion and you are probably right." She rolled onto her side and pulled Alex fully down beside her. Lauren reached out to stroke her hard abs. "I do need a break. But a vacation? Where would we go? I've got my lessons with Lady MacDonald. And now there's the dueling lessons. I'm booked up. And for that matter, so are you." She poked Alex in the stomach to punctuate her point. "I wouldn't go anywhere without you, and you can't get away either."

A question creased Alex's brow. "What have I gotta do?"

Gotta? We're melding more. Merilyn said it would grow. Shared speech patterns show the strength of our bond. Lauren shook her head and smiled at Alex. "You, Dearest, must deal with the Council and resolve the whole treason issue. I know you aren't satisfied with the exile arrangements you've made for the traitor. And according to Lady MacDonald, you've things to do for the Investiture, too."

"We are not melding. We are reaching . . . what was it you called it?" Alex snapped her fingers. "Right, synchrony. I am thrilled with our synchrony and am enjoying this feeling of completeness. I have never had that before. And frankly, I do not want to give it up. I do not give a damn about anything else."

"I totally agree." Lauren rolled back and tucked her hands behind her head, gazing up into the beams of the trussed ceiling. "But you do have things to do."

Lauren smiled as Alex rolled up and snuggled into her side, their bond singing with the physical contact. "Things to do, be damned. We are going on a vacation, and that's that. Besides, I must show you one last part of our Terran civilization. It is something you will need to see and accept before the ceremony."

Snapping her head around, Lauren was puzzled. *Last part, what the heck? How could there be more I need to learn?*

"It is something we briefly touched on once before, it has not come up since."

"What, something you didn't think was important enough for me to know? Something I couldn't handle or shouldn't know about? What are you talking about, Alexandra?" Her face flushed as her anger started to simmer.

"Easy now. I am not hiding anything or lying by omission," Alex replied and placed a gentle hand on Lauren's stomach. "Forgive me for not speaking of it in detail before this, but we did touch on it during our stay in the Teton cache."

Ire drained away and Lauren wrinkled her forehead as she tried to recall what this mystery thing could be. "We talked about a lot of things during our trek here. What could be such an important part of Terran society I need to see it before the Investiture? But isn't something you felt I needed to know more about before now?"

Alex withdrew her hand, and Lauren immediately missed it, cold seeping into her stomach. The bed shifted as Alex sat up against the headboard and crossed her long legs. Opening her arms, she said, "Come here, Dearheart, and let me tell you where we are going on vacation."

Chapter Six

Lauren stood stiffly before a triplex mirror on the middle floor of her solar, arms outstretched and feet wide apart. Hamish McLeod knelt before her, adjusting the fastener on the large white boot encasing her right foot and lower leg. It was attached to the rigid pants she wore. Even though she was covered in a full-body suit of black energy mesh, she felt naked in front of this man. It was how the mesh fit that made her uncomfortable—like it was painted on. Every dimple showed through the sheer fabric. But it was the white suit which concerned her more. It was uncomfortable and she had no idea how she was going to be able to move when encased in this much stiff molded material.

Lauren queried Merilyn's reflection in the large mirrors. "Come on, is all this necessary?" The Seneschal had brought Hamish McLeod to Lauren that morning along with the suit she now wore.

Merilyn sat primly in a nearby arm chair, legs crossed and hands folded in her lap, wrapped snuggly in a Fraser tartan she had retrieved from the back of one of Lauren's sofas. "Each suit is custom made to the wearer, M'lady. So yes, it is necessary."

"But it's only a two-week vacation. This is overkill for such a short trip in a flitter."

Merilyn shook her head and frowned. "But it is an unforgiving environment. One fraught with danger at every turn. The least misstep could spell disaster not only for you, but for Alexandra. Knowing both of you, if one was in harm's way, the other would jump in with both feet to protect her partner." Merilyn nodded at the small man kneeling before Lauren. "Hamish will be done soon. Once the suit is complete, Lord McLaran will have your helmet. Then, you can be off."

Lauren huffed but she stood still as Hamish moved to the boot on her left foot. Once it was adjusted to his satisfaction, the tailor picked up the suit's torso section and held it up. Lauren crouched, reached her arms up through the sleeves, and popped her head through the neck ring. Straightening back up to her full height, the torso section fell into place, and Hamish snapped the flexible belly rings to the pants. Lauren stood encased in a white-on-white suit. Only her forearms, hands, neck, and head were exposed.

Gauntlets with articulating fingers were next. Lauren slipped her hands into the large white gloves. After the wrist connections were made, she flexed her hands. She could hear tiny gyros whir as she extended her fingers.

Hamish moved behind her and Lauren jumped, startled as his fingers caressed her neck above her dragon. "I am sorry, M'lady," he said, his voice reflecting his embarrassment as he stepped away from her.

"No, I'm sorry, Hamish. You startled me is all. Usually, my torque doesn't allow anyone to touch my neck. I have a bit of warning, when she stirs or puffs a bit of steam."

"I understand. I need to secure the neck sleeve so I can depressurize the suit. It must be an airtight fit." Lauren nodded, and he tightened a neck gator of rubbery material within the neck ring. Hamish attached a hose to a small compressor and then to a nozzle on the left side of her suit. Flipping a switch, the compressor hissed into action. Lauren felt the white suit tighten and mold to her contours. Once all the air was withdrawn, the compressor stopped, and Hamish pulled the hose free of its connection. He sealed the port and stepped back. "You may lower your arms, M'lady."

Lauren dropped her arms and inspected her reflection. Her auburn hair was in a tight braid, wrapped snuggly in a bun against the nape of her neck. Fearing her movements would be restricted, she took a tentative step back from the mirror, surprised to find her movements free and fluid. The suit didn't hinder her in anyway, amazing considering how difficult it was to don. It felt and acted like a second-skin.

"How's it possible to shrink that much material into this snug a fit?" Her scientific curiosity was piqued.

Hamish laughed. "It is all in the molecular weaving, M'lady."

"Molecular weaving? You've got me there." Lauren tipped her head to the side, again scrutinizing her reflection. She heard Merilyn sigh. Smiling at Merilyn. "I gotta understand this, Your Grace. And besides, it's really cool, don't you think?"

Merilyn shook her head, but smiled indulgently at Lauren. "I do think it is another of our scientific achievements which is so a part of our daily lives we do not consider it 'cool.' anymore. It simply is."

"It's cool to me. I can think of a bunch of applications in medicine for a fabric that conforms, yet retains its flexibility. Especially in the treatment of deep burns." Lauren asked the tailor. "You were saying something about molecular weaving?"

"Yes, quite." He smiled up at Lauren. "Of course, you understand weaving fabric is one of the oldest skillsets a civilization acquires as it develops." Lauren nodded. "We have applied the design concept of weaving—the interlacing of long threads—to the building of chemical structures in two and in three dimensions. Instead of fabric threads we use chemical threads, chemical building blocks, each selected for their specific physical characteristics. We shape the building blocks by adding a metallic bonding element—copper, iron, or molybdenum—transforming them into the threads. The threads can then be woven into materials with exceptional mechanical and dynamic properties." Gesturing with his hands, he illustrated the linking of blocks, one to another.

"Are you talking about reticular synthesis?" Lauren warmed to the subject, her concerns about the suit and her initial discomfort forgotten.

"I am unfamiliar with reticular synthesis, M'lady." He shook his head. "But we create long organic strands or threads using elements that generate strong covalent bonds across the metallic bridge atom. The metallic bridge, when removed, leaves a pattern or imparted-shape on the organic strand. We then take these strands and using other elements shape the strands into the material patterns we desire: sheets, tubes, blocks, beams, bars, and so forth. We use those shapes to construct the materials that we need." Hamish smiled again.

"Is she wearing you out, Your Grace?" Alex's contralto filled the solar.

Lauren saw Merilyn dozing in the comfortable chair, feet to the warm fire. "I think we've done her in, Alex."

Alex, dressed in a tattered kilt and a stained shirt, came fully up the stairs and into Lauren's solar, followed closely by Lord McLaran. "I agree,

Dearheart. Seems the concept of molecular weaving was too much for our venerable Seneschal."

"Your Majesty, I am truly sorry." Hamish bowed deeply.

"Hamish, you know as well as I, that Her Grace is bored by all our technical achievements. She knows best how to use the amazing things you create but could care less how they were invented." Alex pointed a finger in Lauren's direction. "Now this one on the other hand, is quite the opposite."

Hamish nodded. "So, I have heard, ma'am."

"Okay, guys, I'm right here. Remember me?" Lauren pointed at herself.

Alex circled Lauren in her arms and kissed her quickly on the cheek. "We would never forget you, Dearheart."

Ice and Snow raced up the stairs and tumbled into the solar.

"Is it ready, yet?"

"Can we go now?" Their questions fell one over the other in their excitement.

Lauren cautioned the pair. "I can't go without the rest of my suit guys. But soon, I'll be ready to leave. How do you get to go, anyway? Has Hamish made suits for you two?"

Hamish fussed with the gauntlets covering Lauren's hands. "Indeed, I have. They were almost impossible to keep still for all the fittings and we had to make special socks to prevent their claws from puncturing the fabric once it was close-fitted."

"That I've gotta see." Lauren laughed out loud.

"And you will, M'lady. As those two furry ruffians are going with you on your trip," Lord McLaran stated.

He held out the helmet he carried under his arm. "For you, Lady Beckwith."

Lauren took the sleek helmet from him. Except for an oval of silvered metal coating the back of the head area, the helmet was molded from a single piece of transparent material. A black locking ring circled the base but other than that its contour was unbroken.

"Allow me, M'lady." Hamish took the helmet from her and lifted it up.

She again crouched down and allowed him to slip it over her head. He aligned, and then locked the flexible ring onto the suit's neck. Once fitted, Lauren felt her ears pop, and she swallowed convulsively. Fear crept into her as she thought she might suffocate inside the sealed suit.

"Take a deep breath, Lauren," Lord McLaran instructed. "The suit and helmet will equilibrate to the atmospheric pressures inside and out, then, it will adapt to your respiratory rate." His voice sounded a bit tinny, but she figured it was due to being transmitted over some sort of internal speaker.

She took a small breath, tasting the air. Positive pressure filled the helmet, and the helmet flexed with her inhalation. *Oh, I get it. It's a pneumatic membrane, like the face shield in Alex's armor. Cool!*

Relaxing, Lauren spun in a circle. The helmet was more than a pneumatic membrane. It became darker as she faced the sunlit windows and lighter as she turned away. *Photo-sensitive lensing.* She grinned at Alex, who sat in an armchair in her favorite position. Alex's arms were crossed over her stomach, and her legs draped over one chair arm, feet swinging gently.

"The helmet will filter impurities and contaminants from the outside when they are detected by the analyzer. If oxygen is not available it will seal itself off, isolating the wearer from a hostile environment. Then the recirculator will take over. Oxygen will be concentrated from the wearer's exhalations and other bodily emissions." Alex said, her voice clear.

Ice and Snow followed Lauren closely as she moved about the solar, getting used to the feel of the skintight suit and the claustrophobia of wearing the helmet. "Your voice is less mechanical now."

"Ah, good. The helmet is adapting to you." Hamish clapped his hands. "It is learning and adjusting to your normal aural frequencies. I was worried it would not recognize your physiology easily." He watched her with a critical eye.

"A helmet that can learn, how cool is that? But how does it work?"

Hamish shrugged at Lord McLaran as if to say, 'your turn.' "The helmet can do that because it's more than a helmet. Or should I say it's not a helmet at all, but a wearable analyzer shaped like a helmet."

Lauren faced him, a frown of concentration crossing her face.

"Watch out, McLaran. Hope you do not have plans for dinner." Lauren spun around, hands on hips glaring down at her soulmate.

"Watch it, Dearest."

"Oooo! Scared now."

"You'd better be. I'll deal with you later."

She looking back at Lord McLaran. "You were saying something about a wearable computer."

"I guess I should ask what is on the dinner menu before I answer that. It could be a long night."

"What is going on?" Their merriment woke Merilyn from her nap, and she started, glancing around the room to get her bearings.

"Nothing untoward, Your Grace. We were discussing the evening meal menu. Will you be joining us? Do you wish something special from the kitchens?" Lord McLaran smiled warmly down at her.

"Let me order from the kitchens, and we will have a grand feast," Ice said, and she jumped up from the sofa she and Snow were sharing.

"Do you ever think of anything but food?" Alex queried in amusement.

Snow bounced up and joined her partner. She shoulder-bumped Ice and snorted. *"Go ahead, Oh Hungry One? Answer her."*

"I think of many things, but now I am thinking about eating." Ice crouched and stretched a smile that showed her teeth to her molars and split her face.

"Lauren, how is the suit feeling?" Merilyn neatly deflected McLaran's questions of dinner and refocused on the matter at hand. "Any places where it is rubbing or pinching? It must be absolutely comfortable, for you will wear it for long stretches."

"We've got to do something about Lord McLaran and Merilyn, Alex. They need to explore these feelings they have for each other. Maybe they should be the ones to take a vacation and we can stay here. I can complete preparing for the Investiture, then."

"We will take our vacation, but you are right as always, Dearheart. Those two need some time to themselves without the stresses and interruptions of Keep business. I will ask Newkirk to lend a hand while we are gone."

"I thought he was coming with us." Lauren raised her eyebrows in question.

"Oh, Newkirk the Younger is coming with us and the furkids. I was speaking of the Elder Lord Newkirk. If we can pull him away from his shield laboratory for a few days, he would be able to manage the Keep."

"Excuse me. You are doing it again!" Merilyn's icy tone cut into Lauren and Alex's conversation. "I understand your bond is strengthening, and it is probably easier to converse mind-to-mind, so to speak, but it is still rude when others are present. So stop it."

Heat crept up Lauren's neck, but she grinned in amusement. "So to speak. You're so funny sometimes, Your Grace. Gotta love a good comedienne."

"Enough of that, Lauren," Merilyn admonished. "Answer Hamish's questions so we can complete this task and you can be off in the morning on your vaa—vacation." Merilyn tripped slightly over the alien word.

Bowing her head, Lauren acknowledged not only the rebuke, but Merilyn. She nodded back at the tailor.

"It feels fine. I'm not able to fully extend my fingers but I suspect that will probably come with practice." She wiggled her fingers in illustration.

"The neck seal is rubbing on my scales." Lauren's torque added drily. Lauren's torque slithered around her neck and attempted to remold herself beneath the base of the seal, flattening into Lauren's sternoclavicular joint space.

"Better?" Lauren asked.

"Yes, thank you, M'lady" A flutter of scales and the torque settled completely. The torque's soprano voice filled the solar and the minds of its occupants. It reverberated in Lauren's bones. *"You must be comfortable to travel. And We are most excited by this opportunity to see Terran advances."*

"Too true. Travel will be most interesting." Alex's torque added with a small puff of steam. Alex's dragon blinked languidly, a toothy smile spreading across her scaly face. Lauren could feel an answering smile on her torque.

"That's settled then. With my dragon comfortable, we seem to be ready."

"Let us eat!" Ice jumped up from her spot by the fire and spun around in a happy wolf dance.

"In a moment, Ice. Why don't you and Snow go get the boys, while we finish here," Lauren suggested and the wolves darted down the stairs and out of the solar. Alex beamed at her. "What?"

"You are so adaptable. Here you stand in an alien suit yet you can direct a room and coordinate dinner plans. I am most impressed."

Lauren knew she was being tweaked. She could see the twinkle in Alex's eyes and feel the sparkle of her inner laughter along their bond. But, Lauren decided she wouldn't acknowledge it yet. *Later, perhaps?*

"Fine. Is there anything else?"

"No, I believe that has . . . how do you say it? Got it covered, M'lady?" He motioned with his hands. "Please, remove the suit, and I will address your issues with the gauntlets. I imagine it is a small adjustment in the weaving direction of the micro-joints. I will change the angle of motion in the weft this afternoon and bring them back to you this evening for a final test."

"Great! Thank you for all your hard work."

Hamish smiled and reached up to release the neck seal of her helmet.

Dinner was more a discussion than a meal, as the ten enjoyed the five courses sent up from the kitchens. Afterwards, they relaxed around the plate-strewn coffee table in the middle of the second floor of Lauren's solar. The three boys and two wolves were settled on the floor on various rugs and pillows, while Lord McLaran and Merilyn shared one of the two love seats. Alex and Lauren were entwined on the other one, with Lord Newkirk sitting pensively in an overstuffed armchair nearest Lauren.

"How are you feeling, M'lady?" His question was so quiet, Lauren barely heard it over the lively conversation the boys, Lord McLaran, and Alex were having about Lauren's blade.

"Fine, M'lord." He raised an eyebrow, skeptically. "Oh, I still have some discomfort. I imagine it's only the bone grafting onto the poly-titanium alloy of my sternal implant." He raised an eyebrow. "My dragons are still protecting me at times when there is discharge off the

Keep's shield." Lauren's torque huffed at being caught, and she felt Alex's dragon roll beneath her skin. Alex looked at her in question.

Lord Newkirk said, "I apologize for all you suffer due to my inability to stop the discharges."

"No worries. It's less all the time and everyone agrees it's to be expected."

"Expected it may be, but you have suffered too much while given us so much in return."

Lauren felt heat rise up her neck. "No, M'lord. As I have said many times before, it was good medical science, and a fresh look at the problem from another perspective. But, I didn't work alone. I couldn't have done anything without Angus." Lauren smiled at Newkirk the Younger where he was emphasizing his point with a wild arm gesture.

"Yes, he is a radical when it comes to scientific thought. Though, he has learned much from you too." A proud smile graced Lord Newkirk's face, and warmth spread within Lauren at their job well done.

"M'lord, do you think we could impose on you for a few weeks?"

"Of course, M'lady. What may I do?"

"While we're gone, we were hoping the Seneschal could have a break, too. Perhaps get away from the Keep. Maybe go on a short trip." Lauren watched Newkirk's face wrinkle in question. "Alex and I were thinking Lord McLaran could take her to the Teton cache for a few days."

Lord Newkirk was quiet for a few minutes, and then the light came on as he figured out the reason underlying her request and he grinned. "Oh yes, M'lady, that is a capital idea. A short rest before all the demands of the Investiture hit. Yes, capital indeed. That can surely be arranged." He rubbed his chin thoughtfully. "In fact, I can have my analyzer linked to the one in the Seneschal's office and work through my shield analyses there as easily as I can in my laboratories."

"All right then, it's decided. Now, how do we get them to go?" Lauren asked her co-conspirator.

Lord Newkirk laughed. "That is the real problem, but nothing we cannot solve with a little ingenuity." Lauren frowned. "You let me worry about that. You go and have a wonderful trip of your own. Let me deal with our little problem here at the Keep. Agreed?"

"Yes, M'lord, agreed!"

Lauren smiled at her successful enlistment of Lord Newkirk in their plot to get Lord McLaran and Merilyn some time together. "Lord McLaran, there is a matter of a helmet that is not a helmet, but is a computer we were to discuss this evening?"

He jerked at Lauren's pointed question. "Yes, M'lady there is."

"And?"

Sitting upright, he released Merilyn's hand. He nodded to Lauren and settled in for an in-depth discussion of analyzer-science. What he didn't know was Alex and Lauren had already discussed the gel-material used to make their analyzers. Once Lauren discovered the gel-interface in the desk analyzer in her solar, she queried the databases to learn all she could about it. Lauren laughed to herself. She was going to get to tweak someone else this evening.

Chapter Seven

Morning dawned bright and clear, without a hint of wind to cut the cold air hanging over the Keep, outside the shield. Lauren barely noticed the weather. Her focus was on the sleek craft before her, painted a black so deep nothing reflected off its satin-smooth skin. Not a rivet or fastener marred its surface.

Small, stubby swept-back wings adorned each side, but they didn't appear long enough or broad enough to support a craft of this size in flight. The dorsal surface seemed to be one piece of transparent glass, but Lauren wasn't tall enough to see into the cabin. A black fin jutted into the air and tapered to a point behind the aft portion of the dorsal fuselage.

A dragon with shimmering red scales graced the fin, its tail twisting up into the tapered point. The words 'Y Ddraig Goch' were printed in script beneath the beast's belly. Over one hundred meters long, the craft looked more like a giant praying mantis ready to jump into the air at any second, than an aerial craft. The most disturbing observation was the lack of any discernible means of propulsion.

"Ready for your flight, M'lady?" Lauren saw Angus Newkirk striding across the Gyp-Crete expanse. Robert McLaran followed carrying a large aluminum case in each hand. Once at her side, Angus reached up and stroked the nose of the craft. "She is a fine example of our flitters. A veteran of many sorties before our migration to Terra and now Alex's first choice of aerial transportation."

She could see Newkirk loved this ship, but she was skeptical.

Alex, the other boys, and the wolves arrived. The wolves had their suits on and helmets in place, wolfy grins clearly visible through their transparent face shields. They trotted with confidence. Lauren smiled at the pair, they looked like cartoon characters ready for adventure.

"She is beautiful, is she not?" Alex reached up and lovingly stroked her hand down the tapered nose of the aircraft. When Lauren didn't immediately agree, she cast a questioning glance her way.

"She is beautiful, Alex, but—"

"What have I said?"

"I know. She is beautiful, but—" Lauren winced as she saw Alex frown. "I'm sorry, Alex, but I've read the Doouglas journal, and I know what can happen."

From the Journal of the Doouglas

A long time has passed since I last was able to make an entry here, and even now it takes all my strength to move one hand to do so. I have a design for a voice-activated data entry system in mind, but that is for another day. I will type until I can no longer raise my arm to the data-pad.

My *Eponá* ran as I built her to. We reached a speed of 0.92 light pulse. I am amazed at the acceleration we achieved with my plotted slingshot maneuver. Truly, faster than anyone has traveled before. All was nominal until our final approach into Terra Prime's atmosphere.

I remember initializing my atmospheric approach. I remember the first buffeting as the structural fins began to bite into the upper reaches of the atmosphere. I remember switching from thruster-control to ailerons. I remember setting the approach angle to forty degrees and holding that angle with a gentle hand. I remember the buffeting increase until I could barely maintain the course. I remember watching the angle fall below thirty degrees. I remember the heat shield begin to sheet off the nose. And then . . . then, I remember nothing.

Nothing except pain. Unbelievable—unending—unendurable pain. Searing—flaming—incinerating pain. And floating. Floating in a pool of pain.

But a voice, a soft comforting voice, penetrated the pain. It was always present, only a cry away, always soothing. I had never heard that voice before, nor have I heard it since my release from the experimental treatment tank.

No one expected me to survive the accident, no one except my father. As I understand it, I was dead when the rescue techs brought me to the trauma unit. Over eighty percent of my body covered with plasma burns. The trauma techs said the plasma was still burning through my body and would have continued to burn deeper until it reached my bones, where it would react with the calcium in the bones, halting its advance. They could not rinse it off fast enough to begin resuscitation.

I am told my father gathered me in his arms and jumped into the rinse-supply pool, regardless of potential injury to himself as the plasma transferred to his body. He ignored his pain and acted.

Father had been waiting at the Terra Prime Space Dock for my successful return. I had shared my desire to travel faster than anyone else and my theory of how traveling at greater than 1.0 light pulse was possible. He listened quietly, as was his way. He always gave his absolute attention to anyone presenting a new idea, especially, an idea which could improve Clan Doouglas and Terra Prime. When the crash occurred, he was the one who pulled me from the wreckage. The one who carried me to the trauma wagon.

Once we were pulled from the pool, the trauma techs were able to begin their work. But the damage was too extensive. They were unable to restart my heart and I was placed on mechanical life support. I was told my father ranted and raved, and begged them to do something—anything. There had to be another treatment.

Father told me one of the techs said there might be something. Something experimental, something untested. That was when he was introduced to the healer who had invented an immersion treatment for trauma.

I am going to stop here. My arm is weary to the point of uncontrolled muscle tremors. It seems my healing is not yet complete.

Lauren shook her head to clear the graphic images the journal painted in her mind and tried to smile regardless of her concern. She shrugged apologetically. "This may be a case of too much information, but not enough understanding to fully comprehend the true risks, or lack thereof."

Alex sent a burst of reassurance along their bond and Lauren relaxed.

"You're right, Dearest, she is beautiful. But can she fly?" Lauren asked in a low whisper to keep the others from overhearing her concerns.

"She is our best flier of all. One of the ships designed by Clan McLeod to traverse our skies. Carry us around Terra wherever we need to go, and carry us on our vacation, safely."

"But how does it fly? I don't see any engines or other means of propulsion."

"Ah, another of Clan McLeod inventions. Within the atmosphere, it flies by polarizing the magnetic field of the planet. Outside the atmosphere, it glides on focused intergalactic gravitational waves."

"If you say so." Swallowing hard, Lauren nodded. After all, this ship had made many successful flights.

Lauren watched Alex move her hand beneath the port wing and press her palm against a small square. The dorsal plane opened, and atmosphere hissed upward, as a tower of condensation rose into the cold morning air. "This way, Dearheart."

A hatchway opened forward of the wing and a ladder slowly descended to the tarmac. The boys climbed in first, followed closely by the wolves as they hopped up the widely spaced rungs. Alex grabbed a middle rung and extended her hand to Lauren. "This is going to be so cool, Lauren. Once in flight, you will forget your concerns. There is nothing more exciting than riding on the back of *Y Ddraig Goch*."

The interior of *Y Ddraig Goch* seemed huge, especially with the transparent overarching canopy. Seats were arranged at an angle to a central aisle which extended forward to a pair of high-backed chairs in the nose section. Newkirk occupied the left seat and MacDonald the right. A series of monitors curved around in front of them and a meter-high console separated their chairs. Its surface was covered in gray-green gel material, indicating it was a large touch-interface for an analyzer.

The wolves reclined on low, bench-like couches, which seemed to be designed for them, both taking in all the activities around them, as they swung their helmet-covered heads back and forth. Their excitement humming along Lauren's bond. Alex was almost as excited. *She really does want me to see this. I won't take this away from her, no way.*

Alex pointed to the seat behind Newkirk. "Sit here and I will get you strapped in."

Lauren dropped into the indicated seat and it began to envelop her. She gasped, jumping up. "It moved."

MacD laughed from his front seat. "It is supposed to, M'lady. The chair will conform to your shape and act as a G-force absorber."

Lauren tentatively sat again, and the chair melted beneath her. Once her full weight settled, the chair re-molded itself to her contours.

"Your body must be supported properly to absorb the G-forces of the flitter's maneuvers. It will morph during different phases of the flight, as well as when you change position in the seat."

"Okay, but it feels weird."

Alex placed a gentle hand on her shoulder. "Think of it as floating in our warm pools. The seat will provide the same buoyancy."

Newkirk turned around. "Everyone settled? Pre-flight is complete, and we are cleared for launch."

Alex dropped into her seat across the aisle from Lauren.

"Now comes the fun part," Ice said, as Newkirk returned his seat forward and reached his right hand down onto the console analyzer. As he wiggled his fingers, Lauren felt a vibration begin to build from within the ship. From where Lauren sat, she could see everything MacD did too. He gripped a joystick in his right hand and a double-handled lever in his left. As the vibrations became almost audible, the ship rose.

"Hold the hover, MacD," Newkirk instructed.

"Aye, holding hover." The ship floated above the tarmac as MacD rotated the nose one hundred and eighty degrees. The sun angled into the cabin lighting the interior in a warm blaze.

Newkirk tapped his left ear. "We are cleared. Let us move out."

"Moving out. Aye." MacD. replied.

Lauren watched as MacD's large hands gently caressed the controls. Lightly pushing forward on the levers and tilting the joystick to the right, the ship responded. The nose rose and soon they were skimming over the trees, headed to the west, southwest. Remembering the cardinal directions were reversed in this reality, Lauren corrected herself. This reality existed thirteen thousand years in the future compared to Earth's reality, and a magnetic pole reversal had occurred on Terra in the intervening time between the two realities. *We're headed to the west, northwest.* The sun still rose in the east and set in the west in this reality, but the north and south poles were reversed.

Climbing rapidly, they soon topped the mountain range which held the Teton cache. *I hope Merilyn and McLaran have a good trip and a restful stay.*

"I am sure they will, once McLaran convinces her to actually go," Alex added her thoughts to Lauren's. When they had left Lauren's solar that morning, Lauren could hear Merilyn arguing with McLaran through the heavy oak door of her offices. *"He may have to carry her to the stables."*

"That I would give a whole elk to see," Snow said. An image of a struggling Merilyn thrown over Lord McLaran's broad shoulder came to Lauren through their bond from one of the wolves. *"I might even give up an evening steak to see that as well, Lauren."*

Lauren's burst of laughter caused Newkirk to spin his chair around. "Everything okay back there?"

"Yeah, we're good, Newkirk. I'm thinking about how Lord McLaran is going to get Merilyn out of the Keep."

Young McLaran laughed. "My father is quite resourceful. Although, he did spend a lot of time with Gríobhtha last night planning their strategy. Those two can accomplish anything when they put their heads together."

Another bond-image flashed, this one of Merilyn thrown across the horse's broad neck, held in front of McLaran as they galloped across the meadow. "I'm sure you're right. Hopefully, both will survive the journey. If they ever put her down, she would probably run back to the Keep."

All the craft's occupants shared a laugh.

"Approaching western coastline." MacD's hands moved over the controls with practiced ease.

A line of brilliant blue crossed the horizon and Lauren noticed for the first time she could see the curvature of the planet. The sky above them grew darker. They were still climbing as MacD held the nose in a positive up-angle versus the horizon.

"Alex? How high do we need to go to travel to the oceanic islands?"

Alex cheeks flushed a light pink. "We have a short stop to make before we tour the northern oceanic islands. We need to go a bit higher to get there."

"What aren't you telling me? I'm getting the feeling Merilyn may not be the only one being kidnapped today." Butterflies began to swirl in her stomach.

"Seal up, please, we will be entering orbit momentarily," MacD said.

"Seal up? Orbit?" Lauren's voice dropped an octave. "Where are we going?"

"You are going to love it, Lauren. We are going to Luna Keep." Snow said excitedly.

"Your helmet, Lauren. Please," MacD instructed.

Lauren picked up her helmet from the rack on the side of her chair and sealed it in place. Alex did the same, and then reached over and checked the helmet seals on Ice and Snow.

"You are going to love it." Ice could barely sit still even with the restraints.

Lauren couldn't stay mad at Alex for long. She was sure they couldn't lie or hide something from the other. Emotions that strong would light their bond with their energy. *"You are in so much trouble. You know that, right?"*

"I know, but you have always said you wanted to travel in space."

"You're right. It was something Granddaddy and I dreamed about."

Granddaddy would have loved everything about Terra, and Lauren couldn't keep her sadness at bay at the memories. Alex reached out and grasped her forearm where it rested on the arm of her chair. The physical contact strengthened their bond, and she felt a burst of love and reassurance.

"Did you not say using the astronomical skills your grandsire taught you is how you figured out when you were?" Newkirk asked from his co-pilot seat.

Lauren remembered that cold night outside the first cache and how she had figured out which star was in the North Star position. Nodding, she laughed. "Yeah, I did. Once I had that figured out I started to relax a little."

"But I still had to sit out in the cold and wait for you to figure it out. I thought we were never going to go back inside. I about froze my butt off." Ice huffed from her couch.

"Ice, you could never freeze your butt off. It's got too much insulation."

A deep rumbling growl answered Lauren's teasing. *"Are you calling my butt fat, Lauren?"*

"If the insulation fits, Ice, you gotta wear it."

"I am fluffy."

"At *Luna Keep, we are light, Lauren,"* Snow interjected.

"She may be light on Luna, Snow. The gravity is only sixteen percent of Terra's gravity. Her weight maybe less, but her mass is still the same. If she is fat on Terra, she is fat on Luna. The laws of physics apply everywhere."

"Lauren got you there, Ice." Lauren saw Alex roll her eyes at this joke about Ice's weight—it was getting old.

"I do not know about these laws of physics, but I am not fat."

"Leaving Terra orbit in one minute, exiting Terran gravity well at forty thousand kph," MacD said. "Prepare for translation to grav-wave focus. Tighten all crash harnesses. Check suit and helmet seals."

Lauren jerked in her seat. She was so focused on teasing Ice she didn't realize how high they had climbed. Now, the blackness of space surrounded the *Y Ddraig Goch*. Here, the stars were brilliant, steady dots. Space lacked atmospheric turbulence which created the twinkling effect on Terra.

"Thanks, Ice, I appreciate your distraction." Lauren sent a burst message to the wolf.

"You are most welcome, Lauren." Ice returned love across their bond.

"Grav-wave translation in three, two, one. Now."

Y Ddraig Goch trembled around them. The ship felt like she was gathering herself, as Ffrwyn would before a fence, and then she leapt forward. It seemed they were racing toward the stars. The bright dots of stars became streaks of light as their speed increased. G-forces built, and Lauren's chair re-formed around her, absorbing the crushing force. MacD rolled the joystick and brought the nose around. Luna filled their forward view and it grew larger with each passing minute, as Alex's dragon ship raced across the interplanetary distance to the giant satellite.

"Breathe, Dearheart. Breathe." Alex reached across the aisle and laid a gauntlet-covered hand on her forearm.

Lauren took a deep breath, but never took her eyes from the view. "Ah, gawd. That is so—"

"It is so, and soon we will be in orbit around her."

"Orbital insertion in three hours."

Lauren jerked her head back as if slapped. "Three hours, holy shit, the *Apollo* astronauts took three days to reach the moon."

"You have been to Luna, Lauren?" Young McLaran asked, leaning forward from the seat behind her.

Lauren's stared in awe at the vista outside the overhead transparency. Her G-force couch did its job, accommodating her body with her movements. "What? I'm sorry I'm a bit overwhelmed here."

"As you say, 'no worries.' I asked if you had been to Luna before."

"I've never been higher than the cruising altitude of an intercontinental aircraft." Lauren noticed the confused look on McLaran's face. "About twelve thousand meters is as high as I've been in Earth's atmosphere. But I was talking about the *Apollo* missions to the moon. NASA—the National Atmospheric and Space Administration—conducted six manned lunar landing missions. Those twelve men are the only ones who walked on the moon's surface in my reality. They explored tiny areas surrounding their lunar modules, but the rocks they returned to Earth, and the scientific experiments they conducted, were key to our understanding of the moon's origin and proved we could survive off the surface of the Earth."

McLaran shook his head. "Only twelve? That's not many. We have over three thousand living and working at Luna Keep."

"Three thousand? Where do they . . . how do they . . . what do they do?" Lauren was stunned by this information.

"They maintain our intra-galactic fleet which brought us here from Terra Prime, monitor the passive satellites watching for other Terran survivors, build new ships, and conduct ongoing research in faster-than-light travel." McLaran paused and then frowned at Lauren. "Should we ever need to evacuate Terra, their efforts will provide us an escape route." Then he looked out the forward transparency again.

"Approaching 0.00001 light pulse. Prepare for deceleration." Again, MacD's calm voice cut through their conversation.

"Wow, this is simply amazing."

Newkirk picked up the explanation of their technology. "We measure our velocities as a percentage of the speed of light. We are approaching 1/10,000th the speed of light. Once we reach that velocity, MacD will slow us down and prepare for orbital insertion into Luna's gravity well."

Lauren understood what Newkirk said. She knew what the speed of light was—$3x10^8$ kilometers per second. Travel at light-speed velocities was the subject of science fiction in Earth's reality, but she knew the Terrans traveled at velocities greater than light speed. After all, that is how they traversed great intra-galactic distances. She knew Terra Prime was located on the opposite side of the Milky Way galactic center near the constellation Sagittarius. She never dreamed she could travel at light speed velocities. *Why should I think that? This isn't my Earth's reality. This is Terran reality. My new reality. Right where I want to be. And oh boy, is this a trip! Sit back and enjoy the ride.*

"That is correct, Lauren. Just enjoy. We will be there soon." Snow's reassurance enveloped her like a warm blanket.

Lauren sat back, relaxed in her couch, and watched Luna grow larger.

Chapter Eight

MacD piloted Alex's *Y Ddraig Goch* on a perfect orbital course. They overflew the dark side of Luna, and Lauren watched as he took his hands off the controls. The ship shuddered. She knew that was when Luna Flight Control had taken over. They were gravity tractoring the ship into the Luna Keep docking facility. The *Y Ddraig Goch* settled into her docking slip and Keep technicians encircled the craft. They dragged long white, blue and red hoses out to the sides of the ship, and attached these umbilicals, while MacD and Newkirk completed their after-landing checklists, and shut everything down.

Snow squirmed on her couch, trying to release her crash harness.

"Easy there, girl. Let us get you unhooked." Alex released her own harness and moved slowly across the aisle to the wolf. Reaching out, she unsnapped the webbing, but Snow didn't stop squirming and once the harness released, her wild gyrations translated into an exaggerated leap from her couch. Her upward motion was stopped when she crashed into the closed overhead transparent canopy.

"What have I told you? You have got to move in slow and controlled ways. Putting too much energy into your movements will result in exaggerated reactions in this low gravity." Alex stepped slowly back to her seat with a frustrated frown.

Lauren watched as the wolf's ricochet brought her back to the deck, where she safely landed on all four paws. A sheepish grin graced her face and, with ears flattened, Snow hung her helmeted head. *"I am sorry, Alex. I am excited to be back and want to see the Keep."*

"I know, Snow. We are all excited but we must be careful what we do in this harsh environment. That goes for you too, Lauren." Another frown darkened Alex's face. "Easy does it when I release your harness." Alex reached down and pulled the quick-release on Lauren's crash harness.

Once released, Lauren rose slowly from her chair and fell forward. She didn't float off the deck, weightless. Instead, she felt light, buoyant.

Thrusting out her arm to catch herself on the back of Newkirk's chair, she overcorrected and ended up back on her butt in her chair. "Whoa, I see what you mean."

Lauren methodically stood up again, trying to find her balance in this light gravity. She waited with the others for the canopy to open. They climbed out of the craft and were met on the docking floor by several white-on-white suited techs. One stepped forward and raised his arm to Alex.

"Welcome, Your Majesty. We are thrilled to have you visit us. Given all you have going on, we are honored to have you at Luna Keep."

"Thank you, M'lord." Alex grasped his forearm in a formal greeting of peers. "May I present my soulmate, partner, and soon to be Cáraid Rioghail Fuar Ćala, Lauren Beckwith, healing technician, nexus traveler, and Savior of Terra."

Alex turned to Lauren. "Dearheart, may I present Lord Iain McLeod, Chief of Clan McLeod, spacing and engineering technician, Admiral of our intra-galactic fleet, and Head of Luna Keep."

The suited man bowed low and touched his hand to his helmet. Lauren nodded back with a broad smile and reached her hand out. "I'm honored to meet you, M'lord, and I'm looking forward to learning all about Luna Keep."

"It is I who am honored, M'lady. Your reputation as a technician is well-known among the inhabitants of this Keep. Many of us have children whom your treatment healed. We are all in your debt."

Shocked, Lauren fought to hold her face neutral as he took her gloved hand in his and squeezed firmly. Lauren smiled warmly at the chief technician. Her tattoo dragon rolled beneath her skin and her torque ruffled her scales in acknowledgement of their welcome.

McLeod turned back to Alex and waved toward a doorway in the interior wall of the docking facility. "Your Majesty, let us take this to the observation deck. We have a small reception arranged and you can introduce Lady Beckwith to the Keep's inhabitants."

Nodding, Alex placed a hand in the small of Lauren's back, directing her toward the door and out of the docking area. They moved across the glistening, seamless, white floor of the docking bay. Lauren was amazed at all the activity buzzing around. Technicians were working on several ships, with tools and parts strewn about the floor beneath them. A large transparent dome stretched overhead and bright white light filled the massive space. The doorway turned out to be an elaborate airlock. Once the outer door opened, Alex, Lauren, the wolves, and Lord McLeod entered. The outer door closed, and the lock pressurized. A series of lights cycled from red to amber to green and then the inner door allowed them access to Luna Keep proper.

The airlock opened onto a long hallway, carpeted in a deep purple material. Diffuse lighting eliminated shadows on the light gray walls. Lauren noticed the hall was curved. The ends of the hallway were not visible from their location near the airlock.

"You may remove your helmet now, M'lady."

"M'lord, please call me Lauren. It'll make things easier." She unsealed her helmet, pulling it off in one fluid motion and tucked it under her left arm.

"That is not possible, M'lady." McLeod turned and briskly walked away down the hall.

"Crap. I'm sorry, Alex." Lauren slapped her forehead and turned to Alex.

Having removed Snow's helmet, Alex bent over Ice getting her helmet off. Standing straight again, Alex shook her head. "No worries, Dearheart. McLeod is a stickler for rules and regulations. He is a military man and takes his service in our navy very seriously. The McLeod clan's motto is 'hold fast' and that is what he does with tradition."

Lauren nodded. "I get that. I'm sorry if I've embarrassed you."

Alex caught her hand and whispered in her ear, "You can never embarrass me." She bent forward and placed a gentle kiss on her cheek. At that moment, the airlock cycled open, and the boys and a couple of docking techs entered the hall.

Lauren felt Alex stiffen. She reached over and placed a hand on Alex's stomach. *"Later, Dearest. We can explore this low-gravity environment together. How does that sound?"*

Alex smirked, sufficiently distracted. *"Absolutely, Dearheart."*

Turning to the others, Alex said, "McLeod said we have a reception to attend. We will head up to the observation deck. If you three have other things to take care of while we are here, please feel free to do what you need to." The boys nodded and disappeared down the long hall leaving Alex, Lauren, and the wolves. "Let us head to my quarters, and we can shed these suits. Then we will enjoy the reception the Keep has prepared."

"That sounds like a great idea. Lead on."

After a brief stop in Alex's quarters to remove their suits, the four took the central elevator to the uppermost floor of Luna Keep. The doors opened and they stepped out onto the observation deck and sound engulfed them. Lauren quelled at the onslaught and took an involuntary step back. *"Easy, Dearheart. They are excited to meet you."*

"I understand." Lauren stiffened her spine and stepped forward to stand at Alex's right shoulder. It was a position she occupied at public gatherings, sharing Alex's public aura, and more importantly, sharing her own strength with Alex. Still, this was the largest gathering Lauren had personally experienced. The huge room was crowded with strangers.

Another deep breath and Lauren's discomfort settled. She took some time to look around. They had stepped out of an elevator which filled the central axis of a large dome. The entire arched ceiling was transparent, like the docking bay, letting in the white light of the rising sun. The perimeter of the dome was lit by warm lighting that illuminated the floor. Large food-laden tables were clustered in several banquet areas along the outer perimeter, while the drink stations were positioned around the central axis. It was a beautiful setting, but the occupants captured Lauren's interest. In contrast to the white room, its occupants were clad in a multitude of colors, like a flock of woodland birds. Rich reds and muted browns blended with the deepest navy blues and emerald greens. Splashes of orange, yellow, and cream created bright spots across the crowd. Lauren hadn't seen the clans together in one place like this before. *Wow, they are amazing. Nothing like the muted tartans of Terra Keep.*

"Those are the hunting and working tartans of the clans." Alex swept her arm around the room. "These are formal tartans. Used for special occasions and to honor our heritage."

Heat rose up Lauren's neck as she realized this was all for them. She blushed not in embarrassment, but because she was humbled by their welcome. She felt their welcome along her bond with Alex, felt the pride they had for who they were, what their work meant, and for whom they worked. The crowd seemed to notice them all at once. Silence filled the space, and then everyone bowed to the pair. Not a bow of requirement, but a deep bow of respect and honor.

Alex smiled and returned their bow as deeply. "Thank you all for your welcome and for this wonderful banquet. I know before we leave, we will meet each of you. But first allow me the honor of introducing my soulmate." She turned to Lauren and held out her hand.

Lauren took the offered hand and squeezed it. Snow moved to Alex's left and Ice to Lauren's right. Cheers rang out from the crowd and Lauren smiled.

"Doctor Lauren Beckwith, healing technician and nexus traveler, daughter of Clan Fraser, soulmate of Alexandra, Regain Rìoghachd Fuar Ćala, Queen of the Planet Terra, Bhean cheile agus comh-rialoir. But most importantly, the Savior of Terra." The cheer this time was so loud Lauren felt it reverberate in her chest. As Alex took a step forward, Lauren did as well, and she bowed deeply to the crowd.

Another cheer rose and Alex signaled for quiet. "We are here to introduce you to Lauren and to learn about your new work. To show Lauren what you have built and what you maintain in the protection of our race on Terra and here on Luna. Thank you for your wonderful welcome. We are humbled by it."

Alex stepped forward again, this time to the edge of the crowd, and Lauren felt a pulse of reassurance along their bond. *"These are our friends, Dearheart."* And then they were engulfed as the crowd surged forward. Ice pressed against Lauren's side and she dropped her hand onto the wolf's neck.

"I am here for you Lauren. I will not leave your side."

"Thanks, Ice. This is all a bit overwhelming. Nothing like the Keep."

"You are correct. Here the people live on a harsh and unforgiving world. They must rely on each other for their safety and lives, and they can never live on Terra again. Their bodies have adapted to this light-gravity world, and Alex says their bones would not survive a heavier world. That creates a special bond among them. A bond which supersedes clan or

personal desires. Nowhere else has a group lived and worked together for so long. We are honored they volunteer to do this for Terra and for Alex."

Ice's comment brought her up short, Lauren was thunderstruck by how self-centered she was being. There was much more behind the wolf's words. Everyone she had ever met, here and on Terra, did what they did for the survival and betterment of their race. But deeper than that, they did everything for Alex. She was the leader they believed in and followed, whom they knew would never let them down or knowingly bring them harm. They knew Alex would place herself in danger and give her life to protect them. No wonder Alex was so desperate to find a cure for the Comin bio-weapon. Why she worked so hard to ferret out the traitors who nearly destroyed the Council and their way of governance. Why she gave her all to serve and to protect.

Lauren knew it wasn't a one-way relationship though. It was a mutually-giving relationship, built on respect and honor, on the belief they could do anything, achieve anything, together. "I" did not exist in the family of the Clan or the society of Terra. 'We' is what created this strong and resilient culture and race. Now Lauren was a part of it. What before she may have defined as her physician's duty to heal, cure, and do no harm, she now realized was her love and honor to serve. *How can I want to go back to Earth? I belong here.* Lauren realized that thought was a statement—no longer a question in her mind—but a statement. A statement of fact.

From the Journal of the Fraser

I am preparing to travel to the Clan Doouglas Keep in the morning. It seems my patient is not doing as well as she should be, but this needed trip was almost prevented. My father, Chief of Fraser Clan, was irate I would wish to aid Clan Doouglas, again. Had it not been for my mother's intervention, I would have been barred from the trip. Mother understands this is about my healer's obligation, to tend to a patient in need. She is also a healer and herbalist and her skills are much sought after around Terra Prime. Somehow, she has succeeded in tending many patients from many clans despite my father's objections.

Mother and I have had many discussions about how a healer's obligations may clash with clan loyalty. She agrees clan loyalty must take a backseat to the patient. Father cannot ban me from making this trip or aiding my patient.

However, this is the first time my healer obligations have come into direct conflict with my clan loyalty. I must say I did not even hesitate when I got the comm call from Clan Doouglas. I simply prepared what supplies I would need and readied myself for the journey. It was not until I mentioned the trip at dinner that father objected.

Our clans—Fraser and Doouglas—have historically been at odds with one another. And now, given our clans are the most powerful and influential, it would be seen by the other clans that ours were banding together, should one come to the aid of the other. Father said he was not trying to keep me from my healing work, but trying to manage the perception of my helping another powerful clan. The two most powerful clans could not be seen to be in collusion with one another.

It was then I made a nearly fatal mistake. I gave my opinion. I told my father the clans should stop fighting and start working together. I believe together, Terra Prime would prosper, and advancements would be accelerated. We are no longer a bunch of disparate groups living independently on a vast planet. We are Terrans, living on a planet and her three satellites. Together, we have the potential for greatness. Separately, we will eventually kill or poison or murder each other into oblivion.

That did not go over well. I thought I had caused my father to have a stroke. The color of his face matched that of his hair. He countered with the standard, "It is all about clan." Clan first, clan only.

I told my father all I saw was an old man hanging onto old ideas. If we were ever to face an enemy from without, we would be killed from within. At that point, I left the table. What father does not realize is he could not keep me from my patient. I would have left, anyway.

Lauren smiled as the inhabitants of Luna Keep swirled around her. She greeted, bowed and tried to shake hands. She tried to dissuade them from their notion she was a savior. She repeatedly told them it was good science, good medicine, and a great team who discovered and developed the cure. But they would have none of that, so she accepted their thanks in the manner it was given—from their heart to hers.

She was handed plate after plate of marvelous food—broasted vegetables and perfectly grilled meat, were followed by delicate cakes with spun icing—and glasses of celebratory drinks—rich mead and a delicate sherry-like drink Lauren thought was heaven in a glass. She'd lost Alex in the crowd a long while ago but true to her word, Ice never left her side. A pillar of strength, Ice showed her approval of a conversation or individual with a wolfy grin, moving someone else along who had monopolized Lauren's attention with a low, almost inaudible growl. What seemed like hours later, the party was still going strong, but Lauren was exhausted. She found herself next to the dome's perimeter, where she stood in awe of the view outside the transparent barrier.

"Amazing, is it not, M'lady?" A deep voice rumbled near her ear.

Turning, she recognized the speaker as Lord Iain McLeod. His voice was very different when not modulated by the analyzers in their helmets—a deep brogue, rich in timbre. He was short, but his broad shoulders filled out the crisp white shirt beneath his sash of gold and black. Fine red lines crossed the tartan and matched his bright red knee-high socks. "M'lord, I don't know what to say. In my reality, only twelve men walked on the lunar surface, and for only a few days. But here . . ." She waved her arm to include the observation dome and the other external structures. "You've created a city, a research center, shipyards, repair facilities. And I guess that doesn't include the twelve ships resting in orbit."

"Nothing greater than what you have done for us." He leaned against the perimeter wall and smiled up at her.

"As a researcher, inventor, and engineer, you know as well as I it takes a team to accomplish things. One person may have an idea or a suggestion, but the team gets it done."

Chuckling heartily, McLeod nodded. "Truly said, M'lady." He turned his gaze out to the expanse of Luna Keep beyond the transparent barrier, hands clasped firmly behind his back.

"Will you tell me a bit about the Keep, M'lord? The trip up from Terra came as a complete surprise to me, and after I got over the shock of being in space—intra-planetary space anyway—it was too late to ask anything at all. And also about light pulse speeds, and focusing gravitational waves, and polarizing magnetic fields, and helmets that are actually shaped analyzers." Lauren knew she was babbling but her scientific curiosity could not be held in check any longer.

McLeod turned toward her and away from the magnificent view outside the dome. A look of awe and respect painted his face.

Ice leaned against her leg. *"Wait, Lauren, this one will surprise you."*

And then he did, for a smile of such beauty spread across his face Lauren felt her heart race. "What . . . what've I said now?" She put a hand over her mouth. "Oh gawd, did I say that out loud?"

"You did, M'lady, but that is all right. I am so blessed to meet a mind as curious as my own. When my brother told me about his meeting with you, I didn't . . . err . . . couldn't believe what he said about you." McLeod shook his head. "About how many questions you asked, how intensely you listened, how you offered such insightful suggestions."

"I've met your brother?"

"You surely have, Hamish McLeod. He tailored your suit."

Lauren felt another blush race across her face as she remembered how she had badgered the tailor about her environmental suit, the helmet, and everything. She shrugged.

"I truly believed he was exaggerating everything about you. After all, you have developed a larger-than-life persona among our Terrans. No one could have made me believe you are who you are until now. I am at your service, Your Majesty. Ask your questions. We have all the time you need." McLeod bowed his head.

Lauren's face burned. She was so excited about being given carte blanche to ask her questions she nearly missed the honorific McLeod had bestowed upon her. Then, the meaning of what he offered hit her. Tears tracked to her chin and dripped onto the Pennanular brooch on her left shoulder. Her torque fluttered her scales and puffed a small whiff of steam as Lauren was stunned to silence by this open-ended offer.

"Oh, dearie me. Now I have done it." McLeod reached a tentative hand out and placed it gently on Lauren's forearm. "I am sorry, Your Majesty. I meant no disrespect or insult to your insatiable curiosity."

Alex appeared from the crowd and arrived at Lauren's side in time to catch the next tear on her fingertip before it could fall. "Dearheart, what?"

Lauren turned to face her love, and Alex gathered her close. She knew she was making a scene, but she couldn't help it. Even with all the questions she asked before, no one, not since her grandfather was alive, had made such an open-ended offer to allow her to ask all she wanted to. At Alex's concerned gaze, Lauren smiled through her tears. "I'm sorry, Alex. It seems I've created another scene."

"You cannot and would not intentionally create a scene. What has happened that has upset you so? My torque awoke but did not express unhappiness. She seemed pleased but you are crying."

"I'm amazed." Lauren hiccupped through her happy tears. "I've met someone who reminds me of Granddaddy. Lord McLeod said he would not only answer all my questions, but he welcomed all my questions. Welcomed them. Pretty amazing." Alex bent and kissed her tenderly.

After a few calming breaths, Lauren turned and faced McLeod but stayed safely encircled in Alex's gentle arms. "M'lord, I am humbled by your offer and your blessing. Only once before in my life have I been given license to ask anything I wanted. Once he was gone, I believed I would never receive such a gift again." She hung her head, and her voice dropped to a whisper. "He was what kept me going, when things were bad with my parents. He showed me the light when things were dark. He taught me who I am and who I could be, and most importantly, he taught me to never give up."

Alex's arms tightened around her and she drew on that strength. "I would not be here nor be fortunate enough to have found my soulmate without his guidance when I was young. And now, M'lord, you have given me his gift again. You do not know the value of what you are offering me."

McLeod dropped to one knee before her. "Your Majesty, it is you who are giving the gift. Remember what you said? Scientific advancement and learning takes a team to share knowledge and creativity. Together we are more than we are singularly." He placed a hand over his heart. "I believe that tenet with all my heart."

Lauren reached out and placed a gentle hand on his shoulder, smiling into his concerned face. “Sometime I’ll tell you about my granddaddy. He would’ve loved to see all I have and know that the theories and hypotheses he read about in his scientific journals have come to pass in your reality. Thank you, M’lord, thank you so much.”

“Stand up McLeod, before you freeze in place. Your knees are not what they used to be.” Alex’s comment seemed to lighten the mood and McLeod stood with a bark of laughter.

Alex turned them back to the room at large, her arm still draped over Lauren’s shoulders, and said to the crowd. “And now, I think it is time we retire for the evening. We thank you for your hospitality. We will be here for ten days, and each of you is welcome to share time with either or both of us. You are the shield that protects our world. We are forever grateful for all you do. Again, thank you, enjoy your evening.”

Alex led Lauren to the elevator, where the wolves fell in beside them. They entered the empty car and waited for it to take them to the residential level. Once it opened, they walked hand-in-hand down the long hall to the suite at the far end. Nothing was spoken between them, as nothing needed to be said. Lauren was filled with joy as they walked back to Alex’s quarters. They were complete and together, and all was well.

Chapter Nine

McLeod was true to his word. Over the next several days, he and Lauren discussed an enormous range of topics. Most of the discussions included Newkirk, and his unique perspective on science. Subjects ranged from astrophysics to the biomechanics of life in micro-gravity; gravitational wave propulsion to hydroponics; production of the interface-gels to the emission-free engines that powered Luna Keep; from the origin of the moon to Lauren's understanding of the *Apollo* missions from her reality; the tools used to hand-quarry the stone slabs in Terra's sacred circle to the upcoming Investiture; the Terrans' escape from Terra Prime to the nanites created to treat the children. From the nexi to the existence of parallel realities. The most difficult discussions focused on the treason of Clan Cador of the Hebrides and the reawakening of the blade, tree, torques, and the First Foremothers.

Of all their discussions, two continued to pop up: gravitational wave propulsion and the origin of the moon. McLeod was adamant to fully understand how the Terrans detect, focus, and use gravitational waves for their propulsion systems, he would need to take Lauren up to the *Iolar Mara*—the Clan Doouglas' *Sea Eagle*—and show her a full-sized system. Alex wasn't as excited with this idea as Lauren was. It would mean another space flight and additional exposure to cosmic radiation. McLeod had his helio-astronomers assure Alex solar activity was within normal range and no solar flares or coronal mass ejections were forecast. But they all knew space travel was fraught with dangers.

In the end, Lauren convinced Alex. The next day, she and Newkirk, with Ice in tow, arrived at the docking facility, fully suited and ready to fly out to the gigantic intra-galactic vessel. Snow and Alex elected to stay behind on Luna. McLeod and his chief propulsion engineer met them and they entered the small lunar flitter. MacD sat in the pilot's seat, helmet and suit on.

"What is this, sir?" Lord McLeod demanded.

MacD spun around, a huge smile on his face. "It seems I am now the pilot for all of M'lady's flights from here on. So please be seated and we will be off momentarily." He turned back to his instrument panel and his preflight checks.

"Well, I never," McLeod huffed as he checked the seal on his helmet.

"M'lord, please do not take offense. Her Majesty trusts you and your staff implicitly." Newkirk tried to soothe the riled clan leader. "However, with all that happened on Terra and until we have captured all of the Hebridean traitor's accomplices, Her Majesty will not take any chances with her soulmate's safety."

"Of course, I understand that. However, I am not used to having my authority undermined. Her Majesty has caught me off guard."

"Alex isn't undermining your authority, M'lord. She's being cautious."

"And I am not used to being flown about by a boy." McLeod settled into a seat behind MacD.

The canopy sealed and everyone double checked their helmets and suits. Lauren reached over and tightened Ice's crash harness. *"Thank you, Lauren."*

"Anytime, Ice." After she was satisfied, Lauren settled back for the short hop up to the *Iolar Mara*.

The flitter rose smoothly on kinetic thrusters and climbed away from Luna Keep toward the black expanse of space beyond the thin lunar atmosphere. After ten minutes of flight, the silvered specks Lauren had noticed in the sky above Luna Keep began to resolve into the great ships of the Terran Intragalactic Fleet. Each ship was a huge wedge, bisected by a cylinder along its long axis. Half of the cylinder sat above the wedge and half below. The forward point of the wedge dropped away from the wedge's horizontal plane, making each ship appear to have a beak. Another ten minutes and Lauren could see the color of each ship and the unique artwork which graced the sides of the cylinders. Each ship was nestled within a white filigree cage and lit by powerful floodlights.

She easily picked out *Iolar Mara.* The great ship sported rows of interlaced feathers which tapered aft along her central cylinder, like the giant sea eagle she was named for. Each brown-black feather was edged in gold and tipped in a sparkling white. The entire aft section of the ship's central cylinder was festooned with white-on-white feathers outlined in dazzling gold and platinum.

Lauren counted eleven ships. She tapped McLeod on the shoulder. "I only count eleven ships, M'lord. Aren't there supposed to be twelve?"

"Aye, there are twelve. The *Dubh Mogairle* is quarantined and unlit. Her Majesty had us shut the ship and her systems down in preparation for her decommissioning and destruction."

"*Dubh Mogairle*?" Lauren hadn't heard the name before, and was struggling with the translation.

Newkirk joined their conversation. "The name means Black Orchid. It is the ship of Clan Cador. Alex wanted it scuttled immediately after the traitor was caught and exiled, but the Council felt it was too extreme a measure. Destroying the ship of a clan would condemn the innocent clan members to life on Terra without a means of escape. So, the ship herself sits in exile, awaiting her fate, as her clan members do." Newkirk shook his head, unease clear in his hazel eyes. "I hate to see such a fine piece of engineering destroyed without true cause."

Lauren nodded, sadness filling her heart, not only for the ship but for the clan. McLeod expanded Newkirk's explanation. "When we shut down her systems, we sent her crew to Luna Keep. They are in exile and under guard until they are cleared of all charges of conspiracy to commit treason against the Throne." McLeod's frowned at the penalty this ship was paying due to the actions of her clan leader. "Her slip is darkened and no one is allowed onboard. She is powerless. Her position in lunar-synchronous orbit is maintained by external tugs." He pointed above and to the portside of the flitter's flight path. "There."

Lauren could make out a darker spot against the blackness of space. Some dim starlight reflected off her white filigree cage, but the position occupied by the *Dubh Mogairle* was nothing more than a hole in space. Not all of Clan Cador was complicit in the treason of their leader, and she grieved for the ship and her crew, isolated and alone, yet surrounded by the brilliance of her fleet mates. But a part of her was glad for the swift action taken to protect Luna Keep and Terra from any additional traitorous acts.

MacD turned the flitter to starboard, and the *Iolar Mara* filled the canopy. He made a slow approach to the giant ship, and then rolled the flitter on her back. They were now above the top of the wedge as the flitter sailed over her dorsal plane, perpendicular to the longitudinal cylinder. Lauren was in awe at the size of the ship. He completed the circumnavigation and flew to the docking bay in the aft section of the central cylinder. An oculus opened in the ship's skin, a lit tube stretched beyond. MacD slid the flitter through the oculus and down the tube. They entered a cylindrical chamber where many flitters were being moved on large grav-sleds. Their flitter settled into an open place on the deck, and they prepared to open the canopy.

Once on the deck, Lauren noticed the press of gravity. It took effort to lift each foot, and she overbalanced several times until she acclimated to the change. Ice huffed in frustration and simply sat on her haunches, waiting for her balance to equilibrate. The group made their way to the hatchway and double airlock. Once through, they removed their helmets and racked them in a large steel storage area located to one side of the hatch. She reached down and removed Ice's helmet, storing it beside her own.

The large wolf shook herself in a full-bodied tremble. *"Better, thank you, Lauren."* She smiled down at Ice.

McLeod began his tour of Alex's great ship. "Propulsion is in the central cylinder beneath the wedge. We will head there after you see the bridge and engineering controls." Newkirk, Ice, and Lauren followed McLeod into an elevator. The silvered door slid shut, and McLeod entered a string of commands into a control panel to the right of the door. Lights blinked in sequence before flashing green. The interior lights dimmed as the car began to move. Lauren's stomach dropped as the car rose swiftly. The car twisted and turned. *Must be following a track system.*

"Better ride than a rollercoaster. That was great!" Lauren exclaimed, giggling as they exited, but her laughter stopped abruptly as she took in all of the command bridge. A huge transparency wrapped around the front of the bridge. All the command and control stations curved around the lower edge of this transparency. A central dais followed the line of the curved outer hull and sat in the middle of a U-shaped bank of monitors. A large chair occupied the middle part of the elevated dais. Anyone sitting in the central chair could see the surrounding analyzers, and everything outside the great ship. "The *Enterprise* has nothing on this beautiful ship."

"I am sorry, M'lady, I do not know of the *Enterprise*." McLeod said while stepping onto the bridge dais to stand beside her and share the view.

Lauren laughed realizing a relic from her own reality had slipped out in her moment of total awe. "And you wouldn't. The *Enterprise* is a ship featured in a science fiction television show from my reality." She ran her hand across the back of the leather-covered command chair. Ice moved to the front of the dais and dropped down to rest. *I bet she's done that many times.*. Lauren smiled at the reclining wolf. It didn't take much imagination to picture Alex reclining here, watching over the bridge of her intra-galactic traveler. In fact, if she squinted, she could see permanent indentations in the leather covering the right arm of the chair. There were scuffs marring the metallic substructure of the chair. Yep, Alex must've sat for many days in this chair, with her legs hanging over the right arm.

"Television?" McLeod asked for more clarification.

Lauren laughed again. "Television is a form of visual entertainment transmitted over the air via radio frequencies in my reality. The *Enterprise* was a starship in an early program known as *Star Trek*. It also had a faster-than-light propulsion system, though it was all make-believe."

"Our propulsion is not make-believe, as you know. But, when we have time, I would like to hear more about this *Enterprise*. Sometimes, make-believe can be turned into reality with a little imagination."

Lauren smiled remembering how many things first introduced in *Star Trek*, grown from its author's imagination, made their way into her reality's technology. "We'll do that, M'lord, but I would like to see how your propulsion systems work."

"When we translate into gravitational wave propulsion, we have to have gravitational waves. These analyzers are constantly searching the near-ship," McLeod pointed to the portside monitors. He turned to the analyzers on the starboard side. "And the far-ship environs. We have discussed gravitational waves at length. You said your Einstein postulated the existence of gravitational waves." McLeod looked at Lauren.

Lauren nodded and stroked the tip of her nose. "He isn't 'my' Einstein, but he was a cosmological genius. I believe Henri Poincaré first proposed the possibility of gravitational waves before Einstein's theories predicted their existence. Scientists actually discovered them a few months before I crossed the nexus."

"Aye. Our First Foremother also knew they existed, but we did not know how to use them until she came up with the collectors we use to capture the wave energy."

"If I understand what Alex said, the Doouglas designed the ship's wedge-shape to float on the waves."

Newkirk stated gravely. "Float? Not so much, Lauren. As you know, gravitational waves are rhythmic distortions in the fabric of space-time, created by stellar collisions of gigantic proportion—merging black holes or colliding binary neutron stars. These collisions release enormous amounts of energy which distort the space-time field, generating concentric waves that travel outward from the point of collision at one light pulse. Much like a pebble tossed into a pond distorts the water surface in concentric rings."

Lauren nodded, trying to visualize the permutations of how such massive collisions could create a gravitational wave.

"Once the wave is detected, the ship is aligned with the wave, and she accelerates to near light pulse velocity. The wave will catch the ship up in its eddies and carry the ship with it. The First Foremother discovered how to control the direction of travel and how to accumulate wave energy to accelerate faster than the wave itself. An amazing discovery."

"Indeed. Newkirk is correct. She invented the mechanism to collect wave energy. Once in the wave, the ship deploys large spun-sails made of gold-coated analyzer gel. These sails are able to capture and store the gravitational radiation which the wave carries with it in the form of radiant energy."

"Like heating coils? Or the waves of steam hot water gives off?"

McLeod shook his head. "Fair, but a more apt example would be the visual light generated by the sun which carries radiant energy within its photon stream. One feels the warmth of the radiant energy when standing in the sun. The Keep uses this solar radiant energy to generate power. Radiant energy from the geothermal springs is also used in the heating system of the Keep."

He sat down at the starboard side analyzer and brought the display online. A schematic of the ship appeared.

"Here," he said, pointing at the lateral sides of the ship diagram. "We accumulate the radiant energy being carried in the wave and store it in heatsinks within the core of the ship. We then bleed off the radiant energy to feed a fusion vessel."

"Fusion vessel? You create a fusion reaction?" Lauren snapped her jaw shut on the stream of questions cascading from her brain.

"In a manner of speaking, we use the accumulated radiant energy from the gravitational waves to heat plasma within a magnetic containment fusion vessel to fourteen million degrees and then we add rogue hydrogen collected from open space."

Lauren rubbed the tip of her nose, again trying to visualize what the Chief Space Technician was saying, about what the radiant energy produced. How the Terrans produced a miniature sun within a fusion vessel. How they used hydrogen-fueled reactions to drive their ships. Solar fusion was a chain reaction where unstable Hydrogen^{1} atoms combined to form unstable Helium^{3}. These unstable helium atoms then combined to form stable Helium^{4} plus protons and energy. Lots and lots of energy. "But to make this a self-sustaining reaction, you'd need an almost infinite supply of hydrogen."

McLeod agreed with a nod. "You are correct, but a supply of hydrogen is not the issue in this reaction. The hydrogen can be collected from the nearly infinite supply of rogue atoms filling the vast expanses between solar systems, from the atmospheres of gas giants which occur in almost all solar systems, or from the water in comets which meander around the galaxy. The issue is how to harness and control the reaction, to stop it when not needed and start it again to drive the propulsion system."

"Can we see one of these waves?" Lauren turned her attention to McLeod's monitor. A multicolored waterfall display slid slowly down the monitor. Every ten or so seconds, a bright band would ripple across the display.

Newkirk leaned over the back of McLeod's chair, pointing to the display. "See these disruptions in the cascade display?" Newkirk looked back at Lauren and she nodded. "When a gravitational wave distorts space-time around the ship, it minutely changes the overall gravity field of the ship." Another purple streak rippled across the display. "There's another. We have gravity detectors along the entire length of the longitudinal cylinder. As a wave ripples along the hull, we can tell the direction it is traveling, and by measuring the total change in gravity onboard the ship, we can calculate the magnitude of the wave. If the wave hits the starboard side of the ship, the distortion starts on the right side of the display, and vice versa. The overall wave-magnitude is shown by the size of the distortion on the plotter."

"Okay, I can see that," Lauren muttered as another distortion rippled across the display. This one was almost twice as bright and much broader than the others. She pointed at the display. "That one came from abaft the beam on the port side of the ship."

"Very good, M'lady." McLeod grinned up at Lauren. "You have sailed before?"

"Yes, with my grandfather. When I was small," Lauren answered, never taking her eyes off the display, mesmerized by the march of gravitational waves randomly lighting the monitor. "I'm surprised at how many there are."

"There are more here in stationary orbit. The gravity well, created by the combined mass of the planet Terra and her satellite Luna in the space-time field, acts as a focusing lens. Out in deep space, there are fewer waves. Let us head down to engineering and see the sail-generators, the fusion vessel, and the heatsinks."

After a full day in engineering, the group made their way back to the docking bay. Lauren was overwhelmed by what she saw on the *Iolar Mara*. Technology on such a grand scale was hard to comprehend in such a short time. She wanted to stay longer, but they were on a schedule and had a hard deadline which Alex had imposed. They were due back in Luna Keep.

As they settled into their crash couches, MacDonald turned. "M'lord, we have a request for you." He handed McLeod a small earbud.

McLeod inserted the small device and tapped the bud in his ear twice to activate the device and listen. "All right, we will detour on the return flight." He nodded as more information was obviously being relayed to him. He removed the small bud and pocketed the device before settling his helmet in place. "MacDonald, please set a course for Construction Site Alpha. It seems I am needed to address a small problem."

"Alex isn't going to like it if we're late. I can feel her worry, even at this distance from Luna Keep. Perhaps, you can drop me off and then have MacD take you on to the site?" Lauren frowned. She wasn't comfortable with any delays in their return.

Ice placed her helmet-covered head on Lauren's thigh. *"It will be all right. Alex will understand this is important. We have kept Lord McLeod from his duties. We can spare some time for him to see to this request."*

"Okay, Ice, but if she's mad, I'm sending you in first." Lauren patted the wolf's strong back through her white suit.

"I will gladly face the wrath of Alex. I am brave." Ice smirked up at Lauren.

Laughing at the wolf's feigned bravado, Lauren said, "Then, it seems we are headed to Construction Site Alpha, gentlemen. Let's try and not waste any more time. No matter how brave Ice thinks she is, I don't want to stress Alex out any more than I already have. This is her vacation too after all."

The flitter rose smoothly from the deck. MacD rotated it around and flew out the oculus. Once clear of the giant ship, he headed farther away from Luna. "It should not be more than another thirty minutes, M'lady."

As they approached the new coordinates, MacD rotated the flitter's nose back toward Luna and dropped their acceleration to zero.

"Easy, my boy, I do not want you hitting anything out here." McLeod warned, as he leaned forward over the backrest of MacD's pilot's seat to gaze out the forward transparency.

The flitter shuddered and began to slide backward. MacD relaxed back in his pilot seat, hands folded across his stomach.

"Ah, MacDonald, shouldn't you be flying?" Lauren asked.

"Not here, M'lady. Construction Site Alpha is towing us into a docking slip. That way we will not hit anything, as the Chief Engineer asked." MacD threw a smirk at McLeod, but he was focused on the superstructure coming into view around the flitter. Once their backward slide stopped, the flitter was surrounded by a filigree of white webbing.

Leaning around the back of Lauren's couch, Newkirk gazed into her eyes, his expression serious. "M'lady, this is a zero-gravity environment. We need to do an EVA to get into the central nexus of the construction site. I am going to tether you and Ice together. Once we pop the canopy, Ice will guide you out of the ship and toward the central nexus." Newkirk paused as if waiting for Lauren to respond. She nodded slowly and shot a quick glance at Ice, who seemed mesmerized with all the activity outside the flitter. "MacD will stay with the flitter. McLeod, McLaran, and I will follow on another tether. The best thing to do is relax and keep all your motions to a minimum. Let Ice do all the work."

"I don't know. Maybe I should stay here with MacD. There's no reason for me to go out there." She sketched a small wave at the canopy over their heads. Butterflies in her stomach had morphed into giant luna moths, and fear gripped her muscles in a vice.

"I have done this many times, Lauren. I will take good care of you."

Lauren turned to the wolf. "I know, Ice, you always do, but—"

"Lauren," Newkirk said, "I cannot leave you here with only MacD to watch over you. Alex would have my head, and we are wasting time. If we want to get back on schedule, we need to get this EVA done."

Lauren gathered her courage and nodded once more.

Newkirk hooked a braided wire cable to one of the eyelets on Lauren's suit, using a device similar to a carabineer. He then threaded the cable through a fastener on Ice's suit. He repeated this with himself and McLeod. "All right, MacD, pop the canopy."

Although Lauren knew she couldn't hear the hiss of escaping atmosphere with her helmet sealed, she watched the flitter's atmosphere condense as streams of instantly frozen ice crystals rushed away from the cockpit and out into the cold vacuum of space.

Once the canopy was fully open, Ice pawed the quick-release on her harness, pushed off from her couch, and floated upward toward the open canopy. Lauren watched her rise out of her seat and smiled feeling the wolf's joy as she began to dog paddle through her upward trajectory. *Maybe this will be fun. And it's a new experience. You used to love new experiences. When did you turn into such a stick-in-the-mud?* Lauren laughed.

"After the first Comin attack in the meadow."

Lauren realized she had projected her thoughts. *"What, Ice?"*

"I said, after the first attack. Your aura changed at that point. The many stresses of trying to survive in an unknown world changed you."

"How couldn't it?" Lauren watched Ice paddle upward.

"I do not know, but I believe you have overcome many things in your own way, and I think you are very brave in all things."

A sharp tug nearly severed her crash harness, bruising her chest. "Ooof." Pain shot through her sternum as the wolf's upward momentum jerked on her suit and she was snapped upward against her harness. Ice plummeted back toward her, the downward pull on the taut cable reversing the wolf's course. Lauren threw her arms out to try and catch Ice but Newkirk sliced in over her couch, grabbing the wolf and deflecting her trajectory away from Lauren.

The pair tumbled toward the aft section of the flitter with the cable wrapping around them as Newkirk struggled to control Ice's tumbling motion. The cable snapped taut again, pulling Lauren sideways against her harness, and the pair came flying back toward her.

"Stop!" McLeod shouted.

He grabbed the cable tying him to Newkirk and jerked. The trussed pair sped back past Lauren toward where McLeod stood anchored to the deck. Lauren watched as he gathered them into his arms. His motions were smooth and controlled. Once he had them, he allowed their momentum to bend his body backward absorbing more of their momentum. The three swayed gently, like a giant tree in a stiff wind. "Do not do that again. You know better. How did you miss not releasing Lady Beckwith's harness?" He chided, as the two struggled against their cable bindings. "Stop struggling. Have I taught you nothing about EVA?"

McLaran rose from his rear seat and pushed off toward Newkirk and Ice. Dropping his feet to the deck, he anchored himself under the couch supports and began to unravel Ice and Newkirk. McLaran then unhooked Lauren's tether. "Stay seated, M'lady. We will have these two freed momentarily, and then you will be free to fly!" Lauren heard the laughter in his voice.

Oh, this is going to make a great story. I wish Alex was here.

"I will take Lady Beckwith with me while you two deal with this pair," McLeod said as he released Newkirk and Ice and bent toward Lauren instead. He hooked another tether to Lauren's suit and then released her harness. "Relax, M'lady. Allow me to direct our trajectory."

"No moves, right." She floated slowly upward as the effect of zero-g took over. She lost her spatial orientation and her panic rose. Up and down, right and left no longer had direction and her inner ears struggled to keep up with her movement. Nausea began to build, and she swallowed hard.

"Look at me, M'lady. Keep your focus on me. I am your frame of reference." He seemed to know she was becoming increasingly disoriented. He turned and pushed off from the deck, one hand outstretched, the other hand grasping the tether which joined them.

Lauren tried to follow McLeod's movement, but she wasn't sure in which direction he was actually going. She felt a gentle tug along the cable. This force caused her random floating to change into directional motion. She moved upward, out of the cockpit, toward the filigree framework surrounding the flitter, and then she looked around. Bottomless space surrounded her. There was no up or down, no left or right, no floor—only nothingness.

"Falling. I'm falling!" she said, struggling to grab the edge of the canopy.

Alex's voice sounded strong and reassuring along their bond. *"You are not falling, Dearheart. Focus on my voice. McLeod has you."*

"No, no! I'm falling! Can't stop." Lauren was in a full panic and she struggled to reach the canopy.

"Dearheart, stop."

Lauren heard Alex in her mind, but didn't know where she was. All she knew was she was falling. McLeod turned toward her and tried to maintain a constant tension on their tether. He retracted the cable, pulling Lauren slowly toward him as she missed the canopy and now struggled to find purchase on the filigree superstructure.

Before she could grab the webbing, she was caught from behind in a strong hug, which propelled her forward toward McLeod. "There, now I have you."

"Alex, ah gawd, where did you come from?" The panic began to subside as she snuggled deep into the safety of Alex's strong embrace.

"Easy, Dearheart. I am sorry for throwing you into this situation without more preparation. It is my fault. I should have told you about my surprise and not tossed you to the wolves."

A growl filled Lauren's helmet, and she let out an explosive breath. Calmness flowed along their bond with a burst of love. She smiled and fully relaxed, going limp in Alex's strong arms.

"I apologize."

"Apology accepted." Lauren turned slowly in their hug and faced Alex. She tilted her helmet until their face-shields touched, and she smiled at her love. "Thanks for the rescue."

"No problem. Remember, I will never let you fall."

"Nor I, you, Dearest." Lauren reached out to return Alex's hug and propelled them backward. "Whoa."

Alex laughed and absorbed the motion. The pair slowed again as Alex countered their momentum with small tugs on the tether anchoring Alex to the filigreed structure. "It is a lot like swimming, except in three dimensions. Did you not tell me about your Isaac Newton's Law of Motion?"

"Law of Motion?" Lauren was confused by this non-sequitur, and she tried to wrap her brain around what Alex said.

"Yes, something like for every action there is a reaction?"

"Right, his third law of motion. A reaction pair is created—one object interacting with another."

"Dearheart, consider us your reaction pair. I will do the action and you the reaction and together we will move."

Lauren smiled as warmth filled her soul. "Always together."

Alex fluttered her legs and Lauren was happy to go along for the ride. She watched the webbing pass over their heads. She peeked at the moon far beneath them but she became disoriented when she focused on the distant satellite for too long. Lauren kept her gaze on her love's beautiful face.

A smile formed on Alex's face. "*I can feel you looking.*"

"*It's a view I'll never grow tired of.*" Lauren felt more than heard Alex's chuckle.

"*Easy there, or we will miss Construction Site Alpha. I would not want to float off into deep space. Though I am sure some of the Clan Cador and the Hebrideans would probably cheer.*"

"*Not going to happen. I've got you.*" Lauren joined in their combined laughter.

Alex's movements slowed. "There she is."

Lauren tipped her head up, breaking eye contact with Alex, and gasped. "Oh, Alex, she's . . . she's amazing."

Above them, cradled in a gigantic web of filigree, lay a ship. Larger than the others Lauren had seen in the Terran fleet, this one was painted with a pattern of coarse rusty-red hair. Four distinct black hooves peeked from the keel-side of her wedge.

"And she is yours, M'lady." McLeod's voice broke into her helmet.

"No." Lauren shook her head.

"Yes, Dearheart. Clan Fraser lives again, and the clan must have a ship. Meet the *Ruadh làn-damh*—the Fraser Red Stag."

By now, they had floated up and over the leading edge of the wedge. Lauren could see a pair of golden antlers stretching back from the prow on either side of the longitudinal cylinder. She saw one brilliant amber eye, captured so realistically she thought it would blink at any moment. The stag's snout flowed down the point of the wedge and terminated in a black button nose.

Lauren reached out, as if to touch the beautiful ship, her gloved hand extended. "Does Merilyn know about her?"

"Of course. It was her idea to ask McLeod to build her. Once you accepted her offer of adoption, she knew the clan would not die out with her passing. Clan Fraser has not had a ship since the destruction of the First Foremother's craft."

Lauren stilled in Alex's arms. She remembered reading about this cataclysmic event in the Fraser's journal. The Fraser herself was almost killed in the explosion when the fusion vessel burst during the ship's shakedown cruise. It hadn't been christened yet, so it carried no name.

From the Journal of the Fraser

I nearly died. Death is a feeling I do not know how to articulate when it is about myself and not one of my patients. Even now I am amazed I still live while so many others are dead. The pain of all this tears my heart apart and for what? My love worked so hard to bring her theories to life. And now all her effort is for naught. Lost in the cold of space.

Clans Doouglas and Fraser combined their vast resources and built Terra's first interstellar space craft. This was her first test flight. We were scheduled to test the spun-sails, heatsinks, and containment vessel in her propulsion system. We did not want to fly along a gravitational wave yet as our methods of wave detection were not perfected, but we needed to test the other system components of the ship. I went along as crew physician should anything happen during flight. My soulmate remained on Terra Prime, monitoring the flight from our control center at the Doouglas Orbital Space Keep.

A short trip was planned from Terra Prime around the outer orbit of her three satellites to a point halfway to our sun and back. This would take us out of the gravity well of Terra Prime. Once there, we would open the sails and begin capturing the radiant energy carried in the photon stream of our sun, storing the energy in the heatsinks, and initiating a fusion reaction in the containment vessel.

It was a smooth trip out of the planet's gravity well. The ship performed flawlessly. When we opened the sails and radiant energy was flowing to the heatsinks, energy accumulated as it should. However, when the containment vessel was opened and hydrogen was introduced to begin the fusion reaction, the vessel failed. It could not maintain magnetic structural integrity at fusion temperatures and exploded.

The bridge staff noted the vessel's initial instability, and closed the ship's blast doors. The engineers tried to bring the vessel under control and halt the reaction by cutting off the stream of hydrogen fuel. This did not work. The reaction cascaded out of control. The bridge gave the order to abandon ship. Life pods shot from the sides of the ship, but the engineers stayed behind to save the ship. As the bridge was one large escape pod, the bridge crew elected to stay behind. That meant I stayed behind, too.

I felt my love's panic, frustration, and her anguish across the interplanetary distance. I knew her fear fueled her ability to broadcast and this strengthened our bond. Those feelings from her should have told me things were lost. I sent back as much reassurance as I could, along with the information coming from engineering. They were fighting valiantly to bring the situation under control and save the ship.

And then nothing. One instant we were listening to the engineers' chatter as they struggled, and then a scream. I do not know if it was my scream or my love's scream along our bond or a scream overheard from engineering, but it tore the fabric of space. This one psychic scream rippled outward and was heard across Terra Prime and her satellites. Every Terran knew what happened in that one instant.

The great ship exploded in a mini-nova of such power the bridge pod was thrown another quarter distance to our sun. The rest of the ship disintegrated into globules of molten molecular matter, melted by the extreme temperature of the explosion, then flash-frozen in the near-absolute zero temperatures of deep space. It took over four weeks for the rescue vessels to reach the site of the accident, and another two to find the bridge escape pod.

The bridge pod was awash in victims. The rapid acceleration of the explosion, followed by the impact of zero-g, smashed those not strapped in their acceleration-couches. Even those seated and harnessed were not totally protected. Limbs dislocated from their sockets and long bones shattered. I sustained a dislocated hip and shoulder. Head injuries occurred, as loose equipment flew around the bridge space. When major blood vessels were torn open, those crew members bled out before I could get to them. Bubbles of blood and other fragments of flesh floated about the bridge.

Had it not been for our bond, we would not have been found. My love never said how she knew where to search, but she followed our bond and found us. Even with the images I shared, the rescue crews were not prepared for the carnage they found in the bridge pod. No one understood how anyone survived such a violent accident.

It took many weeks to convince my love to build a second ship. We were not able to recover anything to tell us what actually happened to the containment vessel. Concerns of sabotage were foremost in the investigation, but nothing was discovered. Had I not sent information along our bond, the control center would not have known what happened until our telemetry stopped. Our bond allowed us to have almost instant and complete communication. The Doouglas used these fragments of data to build a second improved ship.

A deep regret still lingers in my love's soul because she could not heal me as I healed others. I will always walk with a limp and need the aid of a cane to get around. But it was worth this price for our Terrans to learn to fly through the stars.

As if reading her thoughts, Alex spoke aloud. "This ship will carry a name and proudly proclaim the rebirth of Clan Fraser."

"Has Merilyn seen her? It's her ship, as she's the matriarch of my clan." Lauren felt Alex's heart skip a beat. Confused, she asked, "What?"

"Dearheart, you never stop amazing me with your generous soul. You always think of others before yourself. What a gift that is. In answer to your question, no she has not yet seen her. Merilyn does not do well in space, and an EVA is definitely out of question."

A wolfy snort and laughter filled Lauren's helmet.

"That is an understatement, Your Majesty," McLeod said. "I do not want to have to discard another perfectly good suit."

Lauren turned her head toward the trio floating casually near them. "I don't understand."

"Let's say Merilyn revisited her breakfast when we tried to have her view the laying of the keel." An unpleasant image appeared in Lauren's mind. "So, until we can move her directly into the ship via flitter from Terra Keep, she will not see her. Once complete, she will own her. You, however, will command her. She is your ship, as *Iolar Mara* is mine." Alex paused, and Lauren nodded.

"The command bridge is complete, M'lady. Shall we have a tour?"

Lauren was so overcome by what Alex said, she could barely reply to McLeod's question. "Yes, M'lord, I think that'd be great."

Lauren felt an invisible hand grab them up. It pulled them toward the great ship. Turning in Alex's arms, she saw an open oculus in the upper wedge, this seemed to be their destination.

"We are being tractored in using an antigrav-wave generator. The device captures our mass and applies a directed force to it."

"Action-reaction, if only Sir Isaac could see this. It puts his apple to shame."

"Apple? What has a piece of fruit got to do with antigrav-waves?"

Lauren grinned at Alex's confusion. "Later, Dearest. I'll explain later."

As the view of the ship's hull filled her face-shield, Lauren could see the intricate line drawings on her hull. Each of the stag's hairs was perfectly laid down. The artwork so precise. Lauren didn't say anything else. She couldn't. The massive ship occupied her thoughts. *She is gorgeous. I can't wait to see her fly free across the heavens.*

The command bridge had a small gravity generator in one corner and this allowed Lauren and the others to move freely about the immense bridge. Still in their suits, they had racked the helmets near the hatchway and left their gauntlets inside each helmet. McLeod indicated that although construction was complete, not all her systems were operational. In case of emergency, they would need their helmets to make the trip back to their flitter.

Designed in a similar fashion to the bridge of the *Iolar Mara*, this one also wrapped around a central dais but instead of one command chair this dais had two. Covered in soft brown leather, the chairs appeared to have never been used. *"They haven't."*

"What, Alex?" Lauren turned from where she stood on the lower step of the central dais.

"I said, they have not been used. No one but the Captain sits in the command chair."

"Listening in again, Dearest?"

"Always, you are always center-most in my mind."

"You say the nicest things." Lauren smiled at her soulmate.

"Stop that, you are doing it again."

Turning to the wolf, Lauren replied. "Ice, I gotta tell ya, I don't know what I'd do without you keeping me in my place." Lauren laughed as a smug expression crossed the wolf's furry face.

"Your place is here, M'lady." Newkirk swept his arm before the command chair.

"I'm not the captain, Angus."

"Aye, but you are, Lady Beckwith. She is being built as the flagship of Clan Fraser. You are Clan Fraser. So, you are her captain. As Alex said, you command her."

McLeod joined Newkirk beside the second command chair. "Grace her with your acceptance, M'lady."

Slowly Lauren stepped up onto the dais and stood before the right-hand chair. She reached out and placed a gentle hand on the armrest. The leather was cool to the touch but quickly warmed to her body temperature.

"It is your rightful place, M'lady. At the right hand of our Ruler."

Lauren turned and sat, for Alex's torque spoke the truth. A truth Lauren recognized and embraced. She was Alex's soulmate and would be her right hand in all the ways she could.

The chair morphed, conforming to Lauren's lean frame. Warmth spread through her as she settled farther into its comfortable depths. She leaned back and crossed her legs. From this position, she could see every bridge monitor and through the wrap-around forward transparency. "Alex, join me?" Lauren motioned to the other chair.

Alex sat and took Lauren's outstretched hand in hers. Peace and comfort enveloped them and spread around the bridge. McLeod stepped back and staggered slightly.

"Easy, M'lord. This is a common thing. You are feeling the strength of their bond and sharing in their feelings." Newkirk reached out to steady the Chief Engineer.

"It is a wondrous thing," he said in awe.

"Aye, it is, and one I want to always share in. Theirs is a unique bond, one we will never experience again in this lifetime, I fear." Newkirk smiled at the seated pair. No one moved for a long time, each basking in the soulmates' bond. That is until Lauren's stomach growled.

"I am hungry, too. Let us be gone so we can eat," Ice said, as everyone laughed.

"That's our cue then. A meal is in order. Alex?"

Alex tilted her head. "I could eat. Space makes me hungry."

McLeod resumed his role as educator. "That is true, Your Majesty. What one does not realize in zero-g, you are constantly trying to balance. Your muscles are in continuous motion, even if the movements are minute. That burns a lot of energy. And your suit is dehydrating. We will return to Luna Keep and enjoy a meal and then I recommend a soak in the hot springs." McLeod watched Alex and Lauren to ensure his instructions were understood.

Lauren nodded and squeezed Alex's hand. *"I think a soak would be great!"*

"As you wish." Alex squeezed her hand in return.

The short EVA back to the flitter was completed without mishap. Lauren kept her eyes on Alex, and the pair easily traversed the distance through open space. Once settled, they were soon headed back to Luna Keep.

Chapter Ten

A message waited for them at Luna Keep. The Seneschal had scheduled the Council meeting, and they were expected back within two days. "I am sorry to cut our vacation short, Dearheart. I know you were looking forward to some, what did you call it?" Alex snapped her fingers. "Beach time."

"No worries, Alex. This has been great, and I can't believe all we've done and seen," Lauren answered as she threw some items into her backpack for the trip back to Terra. "McLeod is a great engineer. I hope I'll have time to talk with him again."

"You will. He will be at your Investiture."

Lauren turned to where Alex sprawled across an armchair. "How's that possible? He's lived in low lunar gravity for too long. How will he be able to cope in a full gravity environment? Being on Terra is going to put too much stress on his cardiovascular system."

"It seems Newkirk, with McLaran's help, has invented a small, wearable field generator. McLeod will be able to move as freely around Terra as he does here. The field generator will produce a lunar gravity field around him, using a combination of pulse-generators and antigrav units."

"Cool, very cool." Lauren's mind spun as she envisioned their invention. "I wonder how they miniaturized all that into a wearable unit? How big is it? Is the generator in the field or outside the field? If he moves too fast, would he float?"

"You will have to ask them, M'lady." Alex laughed from her chair. "I am glad he will be there, representing Clan McLeod. As the chief builders and engineers of our society, they will be the ones responsible for testing your intellect and ability to augment the wisdom of our world."

Lauren flopped down on the bed and gaped at Alex. "Come on, Alex? McLeod is an amazing mind. There's no way I'll be able to correctly answer his questions. I don't know anything about space flight or Luna Keep." She paused and hung her head. "Or, anything."

A fingertip raised her chin. "Stop this continuous self-doubt. McLeod told me about you recognizing gravitational waves when you first saw them and how impressed he is with your genius." Lauren smiled sheepishly. "Remember who you are! Remember what you are to me and to others. You are Lauren Beckwith, healing technician and nexus traveler, daughter of Clan Fraser, Savior of Terra, Captain of Ruadh làn-damh, Bhean chéile agus comh-rialóir Fuar Ćala."

"Good gawd, with all that, it's amazing I've got any time to be soulmate of Alexandra Rigain Rìocharchd."

"It is all pretty pretentious, I must admit."

"That's saying something, Dearest, I've never seen a more title-focused group in my life. Even the doctors I trained with weren't this snobbish." Lauren moved over and sat in Alex's lap.

"If I remember correctly, you are above all that, as you are Doctor Doctor Beckwith. A single 'doctor' would not fit the status of the Bhean chéile agus comh-rialóir Fuar Ćala."

Lauren was puzzled. "How'd you learn that? I never use all my titles, and I know I never introduced myself as 'doctor' to you or anyone else on Terra."

"You are correct. You never did. However, your eReader has an "owned by—" nameplate on the back. And your titles are there for all to see."

"Argh . . . I'm going to kill her." Lauren shook her head and hopped up from Alex's lap. She turned back to her packing. "My friend Susan and I always call each other by our formal titles, it's a bit of a joke between us. When she and her partner gave me that eReader a few years ago the nameplate was glued to the back. I tried all kinds of things to get it off, but couldn't without ruining the case. So, I usually kept the plate hidden when I used it. Pretty easy to keep your hand over the plate when you're reading." Then she stopped, all humor gone.

Alex reassured her, "I know, Dearheart, but I promise, you will see your friends again. I will do my best to make that happen as soon as possible."

"Thanks, Alex. Knowing you recognize how much I miss them means a ton to me."

"Wow, a ton? On the lunar surface that is a lot." Lauren promptly hit Alex in the head with a rolled pair of socks. Alex tumbled from her chair, grabbing her sides as she dissolved in a fit of laughter.

Lauren and Newkirk discussed McLeod's field generator unit as they flew back to Terra Keep. She was fascinated by the ingenuity they applied in using the analyzer gel to make a suit of wearable material.

"So, in essence, McLeod will wear the field generator?" Lauren asked.

"No, not really, M'lady. The suit is the analyzer that controls a small unit, which he will wear on his belt. That is the field generator. We miniaturized the generator into the belt pack and embedded all the control interfaces into the fabric. We had to have something which would immediately adapt and reshape the gravity field as he moved. Using the fabric as the interface, it will sense movement through a four-dimensional algorithm." Newkirk held up four fingers in emphasis.

"Up, down, right, and left." Lauren nodded.

"Pitch, yaw, roll, and time." He ticked down each finger. "From those we can calculate velocity, vector direction, angular momentum, and acceleration. Then the suit can 'move' the field with him."

MacD interrupted their technical discussion. "Preparing for translation to repulsion-magnetic flight. Orbital insertion in five minutes, check helmets and crash harnesses."

"Raise your seat backs and tray tables to their full upright and locked position. Turn off all electronic devices." Lauren laughed at herself. Those interminable airline flights she endured in her reality had nothing on this one. *This is so cool!*

"Tray tables?" McLaran asked from his rear seat.

"Sorry, guys. I didn't realize I spoke out loud." Lauren's gaze focused on the brightening atmosphere below them. The ship shuddered, as MacD tilted the nose to an up angle.

"Heat shield deploying."

Streams of superheated gases lit the outside of the canopy as the flitter penetrated wisps of upper atmosphere. Lauren reached up and touched the transparency. No heat transferred through her glove even as the red glow outside the flitter intensified. "Wow. That is amazing."

From the Journal of the Doouglas

The crash debris was stored away within Clan Doouglas Keep after the safety board completed its investigation. It was deemed an accident due to the reckless actions of the pilot and structural failure of her craft. I was stripped of my flight authority and grounded indefinitely. No one believed I would survive my injuries, so these punishments were deemed moot. But survive I did.

It has been two and a half rotations since the crash, now I have enough physical ability to open the storage unit which holds the remains of my *Eponá*. I was shocked at the tangled, burned husk that sat on the Gyp-Crete floor. I ran a hand over the wreckage. *What happened, my friend, what happened? We were on-course and ahead of schedule. All flight controls were nominal.* My engineering skills reasserted themselves as I surveyed the wreck. *Only one way to find out—recreate the flight and piece together all the parts left from the crash.*

Over the next few weeks, I transferred all the wreckage back to my laboratory in the Keep and downloaded all the flight records into one personal data-node. I vowed to get to the bottom of the crash. Something wasn't right about the accident. Although I cannot remember anything after atmospheric reentry, I know something happened which caused the *Eponá* to deviate from her programed flight path.

I recovered at my family home. During this time, I reconstructed the accident nanosecond by nanosecond and confirmed the *Eponá* angle of entry went from forty degrees to less than thirty degrees after atmospheric reentry. Reentry is the most difficult and critical action a spacecraft takes during its entire flight. There is a fine line between too steep and too shallow a reentry angle. Too shallow and the spacecraft skips off the atmosphere back into space—much like a stone skips off the water of a pond. Too steep and the force of gravity and drag increase to the point of destroying the craft and the debris burns up in the atmosphere.

This is what happened to *Eponá*, but why? In the vacuum of space, a spacecraft relies on thrusters to push the craft in one direction or another. In atmospheric flight, the craft uses moveable surfaces to push against the air to control the craft. *Eponá* was in transition between space and atmosphere. There was enough air at that altitude to allow *Eponá* to use ailerons to control its angle of entry and maintain its forty-degree attitude in relation to Terra by pushing on the atmosphere. But the stabilizer fins failed and were forcibly stripped from the body of the craft. The fins were never found and assumed to have burned up within the atmosphere.

The fins are critical to determining the cause of the reentry failure. I have begun searching for them. Plotting the *Eponá's* trajectory of reentry back to the moment when the reentry angle changed, I was able to determine the point above Terra where the fins failed. From there, I calculated the trajectory the unpowered fins would take, as they fell toward the planet surface. I mapped a projected impact area and a search began for any debris in that area. After a month of searching, a fin fragment was found and returned to the Doouglas' Keep.

Now that I had the fin, real research could begin. Metallurgic analysis was completed, and it was found to be within stress parameters. I could rule out metal fatigue. Next, I reconstructed the fin in three dimensions to determine if the metal was damaged from implosion or explosion, using three-dimensional printing. The metal near the bracket connection was bent outward, only explosion would bend the metal in such a way. Chemical analyses were performed to determine whether substances existed in or on the metal fragment which were not part of the craft. I found minute traces of sodium azide on the fin bracket surfaces near the location of the bent metal.

Sodium azide is an inorganic salt—NaN_3. When in contact with an accelerant or an oxidizer, or the salt is heated to greater than three hundred degrees, sodium azide splits explosively into sodium and nitrogen atoms: $2NaN_3 \longrightarrow 2Na + 3N_2$. Nitrogen is a gas and rapidly expands with enough force to rupture metal. If this salt was placed in packets along the fin-body bracket, when the fin heated on reentry, the salt would spontaneously split, releasing a high volume of expanding gas and rip the fin away from the craft. I had the cause of the accident. But who placed the salt packets and why?

I am turning this investigation over to Atair Doouglas, my father and chief of my clan. He is a formidable ruler. He won his place through intelligence and diplomacy, not tyranny and conspiracy. His clan members respect him and they know he instills the same respect in his heirs. One day I will take over from my father, but not for many years, as he is young. Father has taken up the search for the traitor, beginning with a list of all the technicians who worked on *Eponá*.

MacD's control was perfect, and the clinometer never wavered from forty degrees. Soon the flitter burst through a cloud deck over the sparkling blue water of Terra's eastern ocean and he turned their craft toward the continent visible on the horizon.

"Decelerating for landing. Prepare for kinetic propulsion. Terra Keep in ten minutes."

The flitter shuddered and Lauren heard a loud boom as they crossed the coastline. The sonic boom indicated they broke the sound barrier—Mach One. *I've now traveled at Mach One and at light pulse speed. No one in earth-reality would believe that!*

The flitter settled on the Gyp-Crete tarmac and the ground crew surrounded the craft, preparing to attach umbilicals. Lauren released her harness before unsnapping Ice's, while Alex tended to Snow. Everyone was ready to exit when MacD opened the canopy. The ladder extended and Alex stepped over the edge and swung around to descend to the ground.

"Remember, Lauren, full gravity here."

"Got it, full gravity." Lauren helped Ice over the edge, and the wolf climbed down in a controlled fall. A ground technician half-caught the wolf to halt her tumble. Snow was next, and then Lauren swung her leg over the edge. Or tried to, anyway.

"Problem, M'lady?" McLaran smirked.

Lauren growled in embarrassment. "A hand here, please."

"Of course." McLaran lifted her leg clear of the canopy edge, and she turned onto the ladder, facing back into the flitter. He grinned at her. "All right now, M'lady?"

"I'm so going to get you for that, Robert." Lauren laughed and he smiled at her.

"You are sounding more like Ice every day." McLaran teased.

"Am not."

"Are, too."

"Enough, you two. We are going to be late," Alex shouted from the ground. "Stop your bickering and get down here."

Lauren stepped down to the next rung and missed. She fell backwards and didn't have time to scream before she was caught in strong arms.

"I have you." Alex grinned down at her.

McLaran leaned over the edge of the open cockpit. "Do you need another hand, M'lady?"

Lauren smiled up at him. "No, McLaran, I've got all the help I need."

Alex swung her down, and when her feet touched the ground she staggered. A strong hand on her shoulder steadied her. McLaran's laughter floated from above.

Alex waved him off. "I have her, McLaran. She will not fall."

Lauren patted Alex on her side. "I'm good, Dearest." Alex released her and she took a tentative step forward, staggering again. "Whoa, you're right full gravity is a real drag."

Chapter Eleven

The following morning, Lauren and Alex rose early. A soft knock heralded Merilyn's arrival. She called up the stairs. "All right you two, time to rise. We have the Council meeting at mid-morning."

"We're up, Your Grace. Come on in." Lauren stood in the middle of the lower room of Alex's solar adjusting her kilt around her waist.

Arriving at the top of the stairs, Merilyn smiled, and Lauren felt her pleasure. "We'll be ready for breakfast in a sec. Alex is getting her sword from the weapons vault. Breakfast is on the table, so help yourself to anything." Lauren indicated the food-laden table which sat to one side of a large window. A platter of breakfast meats and scrambled eggs sat beside a basket filled with rolls and sweets.

"You are looking well, M'lady. Space flight seems to agree with you."

"It does. I had a great time. Everything but the EVA. That wasn't so much fun." Lauren noticed Merilyn got a little green at the mention of EVA, but she politely ignored that. "The best part by far was meeting and talking with Lord McLeod and all the Keep's technicians. How was your vacation, Your Grace?" The green quickly morphed to red as a blush flashed across Merilyn's pale face, "That good, huh?" Lauren laughed as the Seneschal's blush deepened.

With a wave of her hand, Merilyn tried to dismiss Lauren's questions. "We had a fine time. Very relaxing. I can see why you two enjoyed the Teton cache as much as you did."

"Really enjoyed!" Alex's contralto filled the room, making Lauren blush. Alex walked over to the food. "Yes, Your Grace, we also had a great time in the cache. Especially, the hot springs in the back."

Lauren watched Merilyn try to scrub the blush from her cheeks. "I'm glad you had a good time. Rest is important for the maintenance of a strong and healthy immune system, and you've worked too hard over the last months. I was worried for your health."

"Oh, it is not her immune system I was worried about, Lauren. More her cardiovascular system, I think."

Merilyn's blush deepened to a deep burgundy, and Lauren worried she'd stroke from embarrassment. "Stop it, Alex. I'm sure Her Grace had a good time and got plenty of rest. Let's not undo all the good her vacation did in one morning." Turning back to the table, Lauren asked again, "Hungry, Your Grace?"

"Yes, thank you, Lauren," Merilyn choked out while flashing Alex a withering gaze.

All three sat down at the table, and Lauren passed out plates. They discussed the Council meeting agenda while eating their breakfast.

"Before we go down to the meeting, I have something for you, á Mharghdeann." Merilyn handed Lauren a package, brightly wrapped in green glittered paper.

"Oooh, I love presents." Lauren gladly accepted the gift. Carefully peeling back the paper, she found a tartan. Lauren reverently placed her hand on the folded soft material of muted silver, grey, and black. "Your Grace, I've already got a tartan from you."

"I understand that, Lauren, but your sash was ruined in the attack during the Council meeting. Also, this is a bit different. It is a plaid. As you are being invested as the Queen's Consort, you have a right to wear the tartan of Alex's clan in addition to the Fraser tartan. What you hold in your hands is a Doouglas hunting tartan." Merilyn motioned for Lauren to stand, as she took the folded tartan from her. "The plaid is worn much like a sash, but as you are the Consort, it is wider than a sash and worn over the right shoulder not the left." Merilyn carefully draped the material over Lauren's right shoulder.

"Your Grace, it's beautiful." Lauren stroked her hand down the multicolored wool. "I don't know what to say. I'd be honored to wear Alex's plaid." Though Lauren saw Alex nod, her love's expression was grave. "What, Dearest?"

Alex ignored her question, turning instead to Merilyn. "Your Grace, you are asking Lauren to make a bold statement. She is my soulmate and in my heart already more than Consort. However, some on the Council will see this as an affront to our traditions for she is not yet Consort. The

Letters Patent have yet to be ratified, and the ceremony is still weeks away."

"That is the point, Alexandra," Merilyn said. Alex's frown deepened. "With this action, or I should say with Lauren's action, I am trying to subtly provoke the Council. When one is agitated or angry, one cannot as easily guard their secret thoughts. I hope we will increase our chances of ferreting out more Hebridean allies. Make anyone sympathetic to their cause react without thinking. Lash out irrationally."

Alex pushed back from the table and stood, fingers tapping her lower lip, as she paced the room. "Well played, Your Grace. However, should you not ask Lauren for her permission to place herself in harm's way? This is tantamount to painting a target on her."

Lauren moved around the table to stand in front of her love, halting her pacing. "I'm totally okay with this, Alex. I think it's a great way to generate a reaction. We'll fire up the Council before the questions are asked. And besides, I've got MacD watching my back, and you've got McLaran. Merilyn has Lord McLaran, and with the wolves, we've got this covered."

Alex obviously didn't agree and shook her head. "We do not have this covered. I do not like this at all." Turning back to Merilyn, she pressed on. "I appreciate your idea, Seneschal. I agree we must find the traitor's accomplices, and I am sure Lauren appreciates this gift, but I will not place her in harm's way, yet again." Alex stamped her foot, much as Ffrwyn did when vexed. "I almost lost her the last time and I will not risk her again."

A jumble of emotions raced across their bond, and Lauren staggered under the weight of fear, regret, frustration, and grief flooding her soul. She quickly sat down; worried she might faint, as Alex's emotions hammered at her.

Merilyn pointed a finger to emphasize her idea. "We must find the additional traitors and quickly. We cannot wait until they show themselves. McLaran and I agree we must keep the pressure on. If we wait too long, they will crawl back under their rock and hide in the dark. Then we will never find them and never have peace." Merilyn pointed at herself, and then swept her arm in a gesture which included the two soulmates. "I do not want to continuously look over my shoulder, waiting for the assassin's knife to slip between my shoulder blades. Nor do I wish to continuously worry about when the next coup attempt will arise. This should be a time of great joy for Terra. Our children have been returned to us. Our Ruler has found her soul's other half. A great technician is now among us, which means enhanced growth of our science. And Clan Fraser lives again." Merilyn moved around the table and reached out to Alex. She dropped to one knee as she took Alex's right hand in hers. "Please, Your Majesty, let us act now, and act decisively. We must take and maintain the offensive in this war. We have neither the time nor the resources to fight a protracted defensive struggle."

Lauren listened to them spar. She recognized Alex's reticence to act using her as a weapon, and frankly she wasn't keen on being used that way either. But she saw the benefits and knew Merilyn was right—time wasn't on their side. If they didn't find Gwenhwyfach's accomplices now they never would. Alex shook her head, but Lauren felt her mentally pause and start to objectively consider the idea. *That's a step in the right direction, at least.*

"It's okay, Dearest, I can do this."

"I do not doubt you can do this. However, it is not fair we continually ask you to."

"But Merilyn is right. We don't have time. We only have four weeks, and part of today's agenda is to complete the ratification of the Letters. With that and me wearing the Doouglas plaid, we'll light a fire under someone. Let's see what happens."

"I will not use you." Alex stomped her foot again.

Merilyn rose, releasing Alex's hand and stepped back, as Lauren placed a gentle hand on Alex's shoulder. She spun Alex around, when their gaze locked their psychic connection strengthened. *"Hey, if I volunteer, you're not using me. I only ask you forewarn MacDonald and the others. They have to be prepared if things get out of hand."* Lauren felt resignation, and then a grudging acceptance from Alex.

Turning, Lauren bowed to Merilyn. "Your Grace, I accept this amazing gift. I pledge I'll honor Clan Doouglas, as I've pledged to honor Clan Fraser. I also accept the role of instigator in our investigation."

"Very well. Let it be done." Merilyn clapped her hands once.

Alex grumbled and pouted as they stood before the Council chamber doors, waiting to be announced. Although MacDonald took the plan in stride, Newkirk and McLaran the Younger reacted as Alex had. It took over an hour to convince them Lauren should be used in this fashion. They all agreed something had to be done, but this wasn't the something they had in mind. Snow was the most vocal of all in her objections, stating how she and Ice would be able to smell the traitors' fear and duplicity once the questioning began and Lauren need not be placed in harm's way. But in the end, they all agreed there wasn't enough time for anything else.

With such a full agenda, Lauren knew they would spend the rest of the day and perhaps into the evening in this meeting. If it devolved into an open conflict, preventing them from accomplishing everything needed for the Investiture, the ceremony would be in jeopardy. *In jeopardy? Wait a sec. What if that's what the accomplices want?* "Alex?"

"Hmmm . . ."

"Have you thought about the Investiture?"

Turning to Lauren, Alex lifted a single eyebrow in question.

"What I mean is, what if the traitors want to stop the Investiture?" Alex frowned in confusion but Lauren could tell she was listening intently. "What would they do to accomplish that? I mean, if they wanted to stop the ceremony, they might try and use this meeting and its lengthy agenda to keep the Letters from being ratified. What would we do then?"

Now both of Alex's eyebrows rose, disappearing into her bangs. She hesitated for several heartbeats, searching Lauren's eyes, and then deeper still, searching her soul. Suddenly, she grabbed Lauren in a great bear hug and lifted her off her feet. Spinning around in a circle, she twirled the pair. "What would I do without you, Dearheart? You have figured it out. You are the genius who will forever protect Terra and her future!" When Alex set her back on her feet, Lauren swayed. Alex grabbed her upper arm. "Are you all right?"

"Yeah, I think so." She waved her hand. "Dizzy."

Ice, Snow, and the rest of their allies arrived at the Council doors, and Alex immediately addressed them. "Seneschal, please tell the Council We will be delayed and the meeting will start mid-afternoon."

Merilyn stepped back and her eyebrow rose higher than Alex's had. "Alexandra, we will not be able to complete all that is needed if we delay the meeting that long."

"The meeting will not be long. The agenda will contain only one item—the ratification of the Letters Patent. There will be no discussion, nor a solicitation of additional agenda items in this meeting. The Letters will be read by you." Alex nodded down at Merilyn, and then she placed a hand on Lord McLaran's broad shoulder. "And then McLaran the Elder will call for a vote of ratification. Once the vote is taken and tallied, we will know whom to focus our efforts on to ferret out the additional traitors."

Lauren smiled as she watched Alex assign tasks. She was Queen of Fuar Ćala, of that there was no doubt. Everyone listened with rapt attention. Then Lauren paused. No one seemed to be agreeing. They were simply listening, going along with her, no questions asked.

"Ah, Dearest?"

Continuing her assignments, Alex didn't hear Lauren's mental query.

"Dearest, you may want . . ." Still no reply. *I'm not getting through. She's on a roll.*

"Alex!" Lauren shouted over their bond.

Alex physically started, jumping at the mental shout from her soulmate.

"What?"

"You may want to share a bit of an explanation with them about why you're making these drastic changes at this late time. We're standing at the Council doors. The meeting starts in a couple of minutes but you're throwing all that out. They don't get **why** *you are doing this."*

"Why We are doing this."

Lauren nodded up at Alex and tapped her on the chest with a finger. *"Fine, We. But this should come from you."*

"Okay—"

"So, tell them what you're thinking and why you're making these changes. Get their buy-in, not their blind obedience." Alex nodded and turned back to her group of friends. She explained her reasoning behind these wholesale changes to the meeting. Lauren placed her left hand on Alex's right arm and smiled as her Ruler led her compatriots through her thinking.

Mid-afternoon found the group at the Council doors once again. Merilyn grabbed the golden boar's head and dropped it three times onto the knocker plate. Lauren turned to Alex and watched her become Her Royal Majesty right before her eyes. Standing to her full height and squaring her shoulders, Alex reset her plaid away from the hilt of her sheathed broadsword which rode low on her right hip. Sun shone through the giant oculus in the ceiling of the grand hall and glinted off the large wolf brooch on Alex's shoulder. Lauren faced back to the doors and straightened her own spine, standing tall at Alex's right shoulder.

The great oaken doors swung open and Merilyn strode into the Council chamber. Raising her staff above her head she announced, "Rise, all Councilors, to give honor to your rightful Rulers." She waited until everyone was on their feet.

"I present Her Royal Majesty, Alexandra Regain Rìoghachd Fuar Ćala. I present Her Royal Majesty, Lauren, Cáraid Rioghail Fuar Ćala, soulmate of Alexandra, daughter of Clan Fraser, healing technician, nexus traveler, Captain of *Ruadh làn-damh*, Savior of All Terra." Merilyn turned to the pair and bowed deeply, swinging her staff to the floor in a graceful arc. She held the bow for ten heartbeats. Standing, she swung her staff up and struck the floor three times. "This meeting of the Terran Council is called to order. Be seated, and hear your Ruler."

Alex moved to her clan's side of the great thirteen-sided tree table. Before she sat, she took up her tartan from the back of her chair and swung it into place around her shoulders. She was careful to leave her sword hilt free. An action no one could ignore, as several Councilors stiffened and freed their own swords from any obstructions. Lauren felt the tension in the room ratchet up. She wondered, *who would attack first?* Alex sat and all the Councilors followed suit. Lauren was seated at her right hand, with Merilyn on her left. Lord McLaran, Chief Guardian, sat next to Merilyn. Snow sat between Merilyn and Alex, while Ice sat on Lauren's right, leaning slightly into her chair. She dropped her hand into the wolf's furry ruff and gently squeezed. Settling into their chairs, the representatives of the twelve clans turned to Alex.

"Be ready, it should not be long before someone gives themselves away. Merilyn's introduction raised a few eyebrows," Alex projected.

Lauren sat forward in her seat and focused on each of the Councilors in turn, resting her elbows on the great tree table. She could hear her mother admonishing. "Sit up straight and get your elbows off the table." Lauren sat back in the tall chair and placed her forearms on the carved armrests.

"I welcome all to this most important meeting," Alex stated aloud. "Today, this Council will hear the Letters Patent read. A vote of ratification will be taken. Ratification will complete the preparations for the Investiture of Lauren Beckwith as adopted daughter to Clan Fraser, and as Royal Consort and Co-Ruler of our Country of Cold Harbour."

Lauren started, in shock, with the introduction Merilyn had made and now the way Alex was driving of this meeting. *What a pair! And to think I'm marrying into it.*

"Seneschal, the Letters."

Merilyn rose from her chair and looked around the table, meeting the eye of each Councilor in turn. She pulled a rolled parchment from her sleeve, unrolled it and began to read. Lauren sat rigid in her chair, concentrating on the burble of emotions swirling around the room as Merilyn read the formal decree aloud.

"On behalf of our Ruler, I, Duchess Merilyn Arrin Cian Fionna Fraser Doouglas, Seneschal of Fuar Ćala, Guardian of our Ruler, present the Letters Patten:

Alexandra Aoeron Aonwyn, nighean mhic Fionnaghal, and Her Thirteen Foremothers before, of Terra Prime and all her Satellites, and at present of Terra and her Satellite Luna and of Our other Realms and Territories, Queen of Fuar Ćala, Defender of the Thirteen Clans and all Our Subjects whatsoever to whom these Presents come, Greeting!

Know Ye that We of Our especial grace and with certain knowledge and with mere motion do by these Presents appoint Our Lauren Beckwith, Soulmate of Alexandra, Healing Technician, Nexus Traveler, Daughter of Clan Fraser, Captain of Ruadh làn-damh to the dignity state of Citizen of Terra, and decree She to be Consort to the Queen."

Lauren saw several Councilors frown. *What's the problem? It's a marriage. Geez, I'm not taking over the world here.* Clan Campbell's chief folded his arms across his chest, body language a clear indicator of his disapproval.

"Further, We of Our especial grace and with certain knowledge and with mere motion do by these Presents also name Our Lauren Beckwith, Soulmate of Alexandra, Healing Technician, Nexus Traveler, Daughter of Clan Fraser, Captain of Ruadh làn-damh with the dignity title and do decree Her Cáraid Rioghail of Fuar Ćala, Co-Ruler of Cold Harbour.

And for Us, Our heirs and successors, do appoint, give, and grant unto Her the said name and dignity honor title of Her Royal Majesty."

More Councilors joined Campbell in obvious disapproval.

Lauren sent a brief thought to Alex. *"What's up, Alex? I thought we agreed we would hold back on Co-Ruler."*

"I wanted to place everything in the open. This should be one more stimulus for getting a reaction from the traitor's co-conspirators." Alex turned toward Lauren, a sheepish look on her face.

"Next time, a little warning, please."

"And by these Presents do dignify, invest, and ennoble her, by giving into Her hand a rod of electrum to show all Her wisdom and intellect with which to serve and protect all of Terra, Terra Prime, and Her Realms.

By placing a coronet of gold upon Her brow to show Her position and duty as Co-Ruler of Our Country of Cold Harbour.

By putting a plaid of her clans—Fraser and Doouglas—about her shoulders to show her membership of sorority with All subjects of Terra, Terra Prime, and Her Realms.

By girding her with a sword with which to defend Her Royal Majesty the Queen and All of Terra, Terra Prime, and Her Realms in need or deed.

And to have and to hold the said title and honor of Savior of Terra and Satellite Luna, and Her Realms unto Her and Her heirs of Her body lawfully begotten and to be begotten.

Willing and by these Present granting for Us Our heirs and successors that She and Her heirs and every one of them successively may have, hold, and possess a place and voice of counsel, within Our Terra and Satellite Luna and beyond, for always amongst this Council of the Clans."

There you are. While some Councilors disapproved, more than half had small smiles on their faces, and two—McLeod and MacDonald—were nodding in approval.

"That She may enjoy and use all the rights, privileges, pre-eminences, immunities, and advantages associated with the titles of Consort and Co-Ruler, and Savior duly and of right belonging, wherever within Our Terra and Satellite Luna, Terra Prime, all Her Realms beyond.

In Witness whereof We have caused these Our Letters to be made Patent. WITNESS Ourself at Council of the Clans on this the Siathamh day of An Céitean in this year of Our Reign."

Merilyn re-rolled the parchment and replaced it in her sleeve. She turned and bowed to Alex and then to Lauren. They rose as one from their chairs and returned her bow. Sitting again, Lauren felt Alex shift her position several times, attempting to get comfortable. Lauren felt her discomfort, her tension. She knew Alex was waiting for someone to act. She sent a quick burst of love and reassurance along their bond.

Lauren tried to 'feel' the undercurrents, waiting for the next part of the meeting. Alex had divided the 'listening' among her group before the

Council meeting. She didn't want to overload anyone and thereby miss something. So, Alex, with Newkirk and MacD, focused on the physical reactions of the Councilors, while Merilyn and Lady MacDonald were assigned the task of watching the Councilors' auras. Lord McLaran was directed to use any response needed if violence erupted.

"I've got nothing. Ice? Snow?" Lauren asked the wolves.

"No, Lauren, we do not hear anything or smell anything," Snow answered and both wolves whiffled in frustration.

Lord McLaran rose and bowed to Alex and Lauren before speaking in his deep baritone. "Your Majesties, with your permission, I ask these Letters Patent be affirmed and ratified by this Council. That this Council shall do so in one vote by written ballot. That those ballots shall be held in private individually, but the results of the vote be made public collectively. That the number of Ayes and Nays be said aloud. That all shall be recorded within the records of this august body on this day."

Alex slowly scanned the faces of each Councilor. "Aye, McLaran. I accept and approve a written ballot be used to ratify the Letters Patent. Distribute the ballots, please." McLaran took up the stack of paper before him and handed it to his son at his right shoulder.

Young McLaran walked around the table, placing one sheet before the chief of each clan by reaching around their left side. The last ballot he placed before Alex, reaching around her right side. He glanced at Lauren. "I am sorry for turning my back to you, M'lady, but I must not block Her Majesty's sword arm," he whispered.

"No worries, Robert." Lauren jerked upright as she felt something. *Was that anger?* It was getting stronger, but she couldn't pin down where or from whom it was originating. *"Ice, where's that coming from? I can't get a fix."* Lauren scanned the Councilors one by one. Only Hamish McLeod and Síobhan MacDonald met her gaze and acknowledged her glance with a nod. All the others were either busy reviewing their ballot or purposefully not making eye contact. But she still couldn't feel where the building anger was coming from.

Ice rose from the right of Lauren's chair and circled the table. The wolf paused behind each of the clan chieftains' chairs and sniffed loudly. Snow moved in the opposite direction and paused before the Councilors' aides, seated around the circular outer wall of the chamber. They hadn't made it halfway around the room before the Chiefs of Clan Buchan and Clan Stuart rose as one.

"Your Majesty, we object. This Council had a full agenda, which you have dismissed out of hand. Granted one item was to hear the Letters Patent read, but to have them forced upon this body without preamble is an affront. The more important agenda item was the discussion of the exile of Clan Cador and the implications of this exile for all its clan members. You cannot summarily discount an agenda and then delay the meeting's start without explanation." Stuart was a tall man, broad shouldered, with graying black hair. A full beard covered his face, his mouth hidden behind drooping mustaches. When he spoke only the mustaches moved. The color of his face matched his bright red plaid which was draped over a black shirt.

"Chief Stuart, I can change an agenda when the need arises. And the most important matter before this body is the Letters." Alex sat forward and tapped the tree table. "The exile and all the other agenda items will be discussed in our next meeting."

Buchan pointed at Lauren. Where Stuart was tall, Buchan was short and whippet-thin. He wouldn't come up to Lauren's shoulder. "And we wholly object to this alien being named to any position within our society. She is neither worthy, nor is she one of us."

Lauren felt Alex's rage surge along their bond and she placed a calming hand on her arm. *"Easy, Dearest. Let's hear what else they've gotta say before we jump into the fray. We don't know enough yet."*

Stuart picked up Buchan's objection. "Though we acknowledge she may have contributed to the children's cure, it is our belief Newkirk the Younger was the one who actually discovered the cure. We do not believe an inferior creature," he pointed at Lauren, "could know anything of us. Let alone understand our physiology." He then turned a laser glare at Alex. "And we are not impressed by the allegations of treason levied against Clan Cador. You and your witch, Merilyn, could have made the tree and blade speak. It was a good show and we grant the Lady Cador had no right to fire on Beckwith—"

He couldn't complete his sentence for Newkirk the Younger was at his back, blade drawn. Alex stiffened at Newkirk's rash reaction. Physical confrontation was not part of their initial plan. "How dare you speak of Lady Beckwith in this manner! I challenge you here and now."

The muscles beneath Lauren's hand were taut. Anger rolled off Alex in waves of white-hot fury. It took all Lauren's mental strength to calm her down and help Alex hold her anger in check. Alex was as volatile as Newkirk when this angry. *"Let him aggravate them. They'll give themselves away."*

Stuart spun in place, hand on his hilt, and sneered. "Really, boy? You wish to challenge me? You had better think long and hard before you act."

"You have nothing I am afraid of. You know nothing of the sacrifices Lady Beckwith has made for Fuar Ćala and its citizens. Nor do you understand the genius behind the cure she discovered and created. You will apologize, or face my blade." Newkirk took another menacing step forward and towered over the clan chief.

Lauren now recognized the emotions she felt earlier were coming from Clan Stuart. All three Councilors on the Stuart clan's side of the table radiated anger. And something else, a need to hide something. *What could they be hiding?* She sent a burst out to their group. *"All of the Stuarts are angry and the Buchans not far behind."*

Buchan turned to Alex. "Alexandra, you must stop this."

Merilyn sprang to her feet. "You will show proper respect and honor to your rightful Ruler and Queen. Apologize or relinquish your seat to your second."

McLaran the Younger had completed his task of distributing the ballots, now he moved to stand behind the diminutive Merilyn, a shadow of strength in the steel of his drawn blade. Lauren saw Lord McLaran make a small hand gesture, which brought MacD out of his chair. He drew his blade and moved to meet Buchan. The meeting was devolving into chaos and something needed to be done.

"Enough. Sheath your weapons, and sit down, all of you." Lauren's voice rang through the chamber though she didn't raise her voice. Her command startled the combatants. When no one moved, she stood and slapped an open hand on the tree table. "I said, sit down." She drew each word out as she let her anger roil through her.

Once they were all seated, Lauren called the wolves to her. Flanked by the pair, she spoke. "I didn't ask to be drawn to your reality. But now that I am here, I wouldn't give up coming here for anything, for I met my soulmate." She moved a hand to Alex's tartan-covered shoulder and squeezed gently. "I'm glad I was able to help heal our children, but as I've said, this does not make me a savior. And it is true I couldn't have discovered an antidote for the Comin weapon without Newkirk's aid." She smiled at Newkirk.

"I accept the honor of being Consort to the Ruler because Alexandra is my one true love. I would give her everything I have, including my life." She drew herself to her full height and leaned slightly forward toward the Councilors. "No one can destroy our bond. However, I'll not stand idly by and see our society torn asunder because of something so precious. What we share can't be taken away or made less, but it can be tainted and soiled, with the regret of injury done."

Lauren's hands again found the ruffs of the two wolves at her sides and she drew strength from them. The two leaned against her legs offering their physical support. "If my being named Co-Ruler of Terra is such an affront to members of this Council then I formally reject the position." She felt Alex's anger shift focus on to her.

"What are you doing, Lauren?" Lauren ignored Alex's question

"However, the discord within this Council began long before I entered your reality. In fact, it began with the First Foremothers, did it not?"

A collective gasp ran around the table at Lauren's pronouncement. The Councilors were so taken aback by her allegation she could hear snippets of their thoughts, especially from Stuart, whose thoughts, still fueled by his anger, were the loudest of all.

"What can this upstart alien know? We have waited for the proper time. Waited for our turn. It's all that Doouglas' fault. Had Altair Doouglas not blamed Clan Cador—"

Merilyn interrupted Lauren's eavesdropping and she lost Stuart's thoughts. *"It always comes down to fear of someone or something different, does it not, Lauren?"*

"Yes, Your Grace, I'm sorry to say it does. Throw in some greed and you've got a volatile mix. I think you've got your co-conspirators." Merilyn gave a slight nod.

Lauren spoke to the room. "Again, Esteemed Councilors, I gladly accept the title of Consort as spelled out in the Letters Patent, but I do not accept a title which will fuel discontent in this society." Lauren paused and again squeezed the wolves' fur. "Be clear, however. I am stepping aside because it is the right thing for Terra, not because some of you think you've bullied me and won. We will not be bullied. We will always place Terra and Her needs before our own."

Lauren took a deep breath to clear her mind. She met and held Stuart's gaze and again tried to hear his thoughts but he had shielded them. Or someone had shielded them for him. She sat down, continuing to stroke the wolves' long necks. Lauren felt Alex's shock. *"It's okay, Dearest. We got what we set out to get. You know where to focus your investigations. And you know I wasn't comfortable with the Co-Ruler thing, anyway."*

No one spoke. No one moved. Silence reigned over the Council. Finally, Siobhán MacDonald rose from her chair and turned a baleful gaze on the Council and folded her hands within the draped sleeves of her purple tartan robe. "Know this, Council of Terra, I am most embarrassed to call myself a member. You sicken me with your petty grievances and demands for power. You bring shame on your clans by allying with others more greed-driven than yourselves." Her eyes rested on Stuart and his two seconds. "Lady Beckwith is a protector and a savior proven. She holds the heart and soul of our Ruler in her gentle hands. The bond they share has not existed since our First Foremothers, and we are blessed it has reappeared at a time when we most need it." She paused and Lauren thought a Shakespearean actor couldn't have commanded the room better than this tiny woman did.

"Know this, Council of Terra, Lady Beckwith is Consort by right of a soul-bond so deep, its true nature is not yet fully known. She is Co-Ruler by right of holding Terra's needs before those of herself. Her words today prove that, and her actions since her arrival prove that. You will not disparage her in any way." Lady MacDonald turned to Alex and Lauren and bowed deeply.

She kept her head lowered. "Please accept my humble apologies for the anger and selfish actions shown by those against you this day." She stood straight and again scowled at her fellow Councilors. "I ask the Council vote now and the Letters Patent be ratified without delay. For if that does not happen, Clan MacDonald will remove itself from membership of this Council. We will then ask all of Terra and Luna Keep that this Council be disbanded." An astonished gasp ran around the great table. "We would further ask that Alexandra Aoeron Aonwyn and Lauren Beckwith rule Terra together, without a Council, as they see fit, as our First Foremothers did."

Out of the corner of her eye, Lauren could see Alex's eyebrow climb into her bangs again. Alex drew a deep breath to speak, but Lord McLaran beat her to it. "The ballots are before you. You have thirty minutes to mark your ballots and give them to the Seneschal." Merilyn reached out and turned on a timer which began to count down, the time remaining shown on the main viewer panel in large green numerals.

McLaran removed a stylus from his pocket, marked his ballot, and folded it in half. Pushing his chair back, he marched around the table and dropped the ballot into the basket before the Seneschal. He then spun on his heel and left the chamber, his two aides following in his wake. Other Councilors quickly followed suit, and soon the Council chamber was empty except for the members of the Stuart and Buchan clans. Merilyn sat quietly, as did Lauren and Alex. MacD stood to Lauren's right, blade drawn. Newkirk stood between their two chairs, watching the remaining clan leaders closely, gripping his unsheathed blade in his right hand. The Doouglas ballot sat untouched before Alex, as did the Fraser ballot before Merilyn.

"Ten minutes." Merilyn reminded the men of their time deadline. "This is not hard. You have three choices: Aye, Nay, or Abstain."

Grunting, Buchan scrawled a vote and folded his ballot. He gathered it up and threw it in the basket before leaving the room. Time counted down. Lauren felt the tension ratchet up among the three remaining clans.

Merilyn began to fidget in her seat. *"Easy, Your Grace. He's struggling. I can feel his rising unease. It's almost as if he's torn between two things—what's right and what's being demanded of him. He's being used, much as Oswein was."*

"Five minutes, Stuart."

He marked his ballot as the timer ticked down under one minute, crumpling the paper and throwing it at Merilyn. The wad bounced off the table and landed in front of Alex. She left it where it lay. "We will see how this charade goes, Your Grace. Alexandra may be a puppet to your whims, but we will cut her strings soon enough."

Neither Alex nor Merilyn rose to the bait, and Stuart stormed from the room. He seemed to take all the air with him. Merilyn slumped in her chair once the door closed. Alex pulled the Doouglas ballot to her and marked it. She leaned over and placed it in the basket. "Your Grace, the ballot," Alex gently reminded her Seneschal.

Merilyn shook herself and reach for the ballot. She quickly marked it and placed it in with the others. Alex tossed in the Stuart ballot. Merilyn closed the basket with a walnut lid, tying it shut with a leather cord. "It is done. One way or the other, it is done."

Lauren stood at the rampart above the eastern solar watching the immense crowd gathered around its base. "Alex, you gotta see this. Absolutely everyone in Terra must be down there." The crowd was packed shoulder-to-shoulder and covered the boulevard as far as Lauren could see.

"As well they should be, Dearheart. This is the most important announcement the Herald has made since we announced the success of the trials to heal the children." Alex leaned over the granite rampart and smiled at the Terrans below. It truly was a gigantic crowd. Lauren could only hope the news the Herald shared with them would be as happy as his prior announcement.

Feeling Alex's troubling thoughts roil along their bond, Lauren smiled up at her love. "Rest easy. It'll be all right, no matter what the results. And besides, no one can come between us or our bond."

The entrance door of the eastern solar opened and the Herald exited behind a bagpiper. Dulcet tones moaned over the gathered crowd, and the crowd fell silent as the notes died away. The Herald was dressed all in white, and wore a large drooping hat. His only adornment was a large golden, leather satchel he carried slung over one shoulder. He opened the satchel and pulled out a parchment, breaking the seal and unfurling it in one fluid motion.

"Hear my words, Terra. Today, I bring you the results of the vote on the ratification of the Letters Patent, written by Her Majesty, Alexandra Aoeron Aonwyn, Queen of the Country of Cold Harbour." He paused as the murmur of the crowd began to swell.

Lauren understood only Steward, the Seneschal's Chief of Staff, knew what was written on the parchment. As McLaran had stated, the results of the vote would be read as a total—the number of Ayes, Nays and Abstains—but not who voted which way.

Lauren and Alex leaned farther over the rampart, waiting for the Herald's next words. "Terra, your Council has voted as follows: Ayes—nine; Nays—one; Abstain—two. This vote of the Council ratifies the Letters Patent. The Investiture of our Royal Consort to the Queen and the appoint of her as Co-Ruler of Fuar Ćala will occur as scheduled on the dawn of the summer solstice." He bowed to the crowd. Rerolling the parchment, he placed it back in his golden satchel. "Terra has heard these words." He turned and reentered the solar. A cheer rose from the crowd, and Alex leaned farther out and waved to the upturned faces, a huge smile split her face.

Lauren wasn't smiling and she didn't wave to the massive crowd. Her stomach clinched in anxiety and she could barely speak, her throat constricted in fear. She turned to Alex and gripped her shoulder, "Three?"

"Three, what?" Alex tilted her head in question.

"One nay, that's Stuart for sure. But two abstains? We know one is probably Buchan. Who's the other one?"

Chapter Twelve

All the preparations were complete, and now Lauren had only one more day to wait. The most difficult thing she ever had to do was wait. She hated waiting. She tried to distract herself by reviewing her Terran history. Learning fifty-four millennia of history had been a daunting task, and because history wasn't her strongest subject, she had to find a way to learn all of it and retain it. So, she built a three-dimensional data matrix: time versus political events versus art/literature/scientific discoveries for each of the major dynastic eras of Terra Prime. If she could 'see' the history in a format she was familiar with, she'd be able to remember all the events in their temporal sequence.

Curled up on the red leather sofa, Lauren reviewed her matrices. The warm summer breezes floating into her solar carried the hint of wildflowers from the meadows beyond the Keep, but the aroma of open-pit cooking nearly overwhelmed those floral scents. Huge outdoor cooking areas had been built over the last week. Now a variety of foods was being prepared for the festival scheduled after the ceremony tomorrow. *They'll eat, if I don't blow it and fail the Investiture challenges.*

"What have I said over and over?" Alex's question came up the stairs before her ebony head appeared above the bannister.

Lauren laughed despite her growing uncertainties. "I know. Stop with the self-doubt. I got it. But, Alex—"

"But, Lauren," Alex mimicked and they both laughed softly. "I have dinner with me, and the boys will be here soon."

Lauren smiled at her love, as she watched Alex arrange the large dinner trays on the low table between the two sofas. The smell of perfectly roasted venison and broasted vegetables made her mouth water. "I'm glad we'll all be together. The more time I spend alone, the more nervous I get."

"What is all this?" Alex swept her arm around the room. Large printed sheets covered every square meter of wall space in Lauren's solar.

"These are my flash cards." She laughed again as she saw the room through Alex's eyes, the room's image projected along their bond.

Waving her arm again, Alex asked, "What are flash cards?"

"Remember when MacD was trying to explain his hypotheses on how someone like me," Lauren pointed at herself, "could take on a skilled swordswoman," Lauren pointed at Alex, "and win?" Alex nodded. "I asked him to show me, not tell me how to do things. I'm a visual learner. So, I took the millennia of Terran history and divided the information into eras by ruling dynasty. Then I grouped all the major learnings from those eras around critical temporal events."

Alex nodded as she studied the matrices. "I am most impressed, Dearheart. Has Lady MacDonald seen your summations? I am sure she would love to include these 'flash cards' in her written histories."

Blushing, Lauren shook her head. "Nope, I haven't shown her these, nor will I. These are so I can try and remember everything I need to, so I can be successful tomorrow."

"Why do you think you will fail?" Another voice floated up the stairs. "Failure is not in your DNA, M'lady." Newkirk and the two other boys stormed up the stairs and piled into her solar. They grinned at Alex and Newkirk bowed to Lauren.

"She cannot fail because she has her flash cards." Alex spoke with authority as she indicated the wall coverings around the room. "All fifty-four millennia of our history summarized on these walls."

Young Robert McLaran hummed as he spun around, taking in all the diagrams. "I wish I had these back in our school days." He nodded at his cohorts. "I would not have had such a hard time completing history."

"Having these would not have helped you, my boy. You were too focused on swordsmanship and sailing the stars rather than on your classroom lessons to give a fig for our rich histories." The Lady MacDonald joined the room's occupants and a blush painted young McLaran's cheeks. Lauren blushed along with him. It seemed the Lady MacDonald would in fact see her matrices.

Bowing low, he acknowledged her observation. Lauren had heard all about Alex's school day exploits, and how the 'four terrors,' as they were called, did everything they could think of to get out of the classroom. She could imagine what their instructors had to go through to get them to sit still long enough to complete a lesson. She was sure they sat still for their riding, weapons, and flying lessons, but not so much for language, history, literature, and art.

In some ways, they were a lot like she was. All that mattered to her was science and math. Lauren didn't spend any more time than she had to on the 'fluff,' as she called all the other academic subjects. She shook her head. *But I was so wrong. Life is a balance—science and art entwined. We may learn more about how things work but what creates humanity is her arts.*

Lauren smiled to herself as she remembered arguing with her grandmother about why reading poetry was not more important than solving differential equations. *The hubris of youth.* She shook her head. Now she wished she had read more poetry or spent more time studying a flower long enough to capture its essence in a watercolor.

"Where are you, Dearheart?"

She glanced up at Alex. "Here, with my love, my friends, and my family."

"Not really. You were a long way off somewhere."

Shaking her head again, Lauren knew she couldn't dissemble. "I was thinking of Grandmommy and her love of poetry and art and literature. How she tried so hard to get me to put aside my science long enough to stop and smell the roses. I missed so much." Lauren paused, again caught in her bittersweet memories. "I was so focused back then."

Alex wrapped her in a warm hug. "If we do not focus on dinner there will not be any left for us."

"I know what you're doing." Lauren pinched Alex in the side. "You're trying to distract me."

"Is it working?"

Lauren laughed. "Yes, it's working, and thank you. You always take such good care of me and know what I need." Lauren returned the hug and sent her love along their bond. "Sometimes, even before I do. That's one of the joys of our bond. Knowing what the other one needs."

Once Merilyn, Lord McLaran, and the wolves joined them, the group settled down to their evening meal and a discussion of tomorrow's activities.

The sky was inky black with no sign of the coming dawn to paint the horizon. Lauren rolled on her side and surveyed the dark sky through the octagonal window above her bed. The only light in the room was a small glow from the dying embers in the copper-flued fireplace.

"You have not slept, Dearheart." Alex's warm arm wrapped around her and a hand lightly rubbed her belly in small circles.

Lauren grasped Alex's forearm and squeezed in thanks for her ministrations. "I know, and I'm sorry I'm keeping you up, but I can't quiet my brain. I seem to be caught in a mind-loop. I keep thinking about all the things I need to know and do and say, and where to stand, and when to kneel, and how to act—"

"Enough." Alex rose on her elbow and peeked over Lauren's shoulder. "You are making my head swim and all I have to do is ride in and sit regally. But if I do not get some rest, I will fall asleep in the middle of your ceremony. How would that appear?"

"Oh, I can imagine what Merilyn would do. And Lady MacDonald would have your hide if you fell asleep. And then where would I be? All alone."

Pulling Lauren over onto her back, Alex gazed down at her with love-warmed eyes. "You are never alone. Even when we sleep, we are in each other's minds, our souls entwined. I do not think even physical distance could keep us from each other."

"That's not gonna happen, being apart I mean. No being apart." Lauren emphasized, as she reached up and cupped Alex's right cheek. "I love you."

Alex's smile widened, and she lowered her head, and kissed Lauren. A statement of agreement and confirmation. But then she deepened the kiss, and Lauren's heart rate increased.

"Hmmm—" The sound rumbled in the back of her throat. *Ah, gawd, she's so good at that.*

"It takes two. Relax and let me do the work for a change."

Lauren didn't argue. She couldn't argue because her brain had shut down, along with every other higher function. Her body relaxed, and she submitted to Alex. The dance began. Alex led Lauren through the moves as expertly as ever. A kiss, a touch, a pinch, a lick, a caress, a stroke, a slide, a rhythm, a pull, a push! There! Synchrony burst over the two as music only they could hear played in their heads. Soaring together, always together.

"And I love you," Alex said into the silence, as their bodies fell back to Terra and they reconnected with their physical world.

"How can those simple words mean so much?"

"I do not know. I only know I do and you do, and together we are more than apart."

"'The whole is greater than the sum of the parts.' Aristotle had that one right, but I doubt he ever felt something as wonderful as this." Lauren watched a smile of such beauty and joy spread across Alex's face that tears slipped from the corners of her eyes. "No way, no how," she choked out. And then she was enfolded in the arms of her beloved, who knew these were tears of happiness, joy, relief, anxiety, and anticipation all rolled into one overwhelming bundle of emotion.

"Easy there, Dearheart. I have you. Rest a bit. We have time. Let us enjoy this moment."

"Always, Dearest."

Chapter Thirteen

The first ray of dawn pierced the horizon as the dual tones of a bagpipe shattered the silence. Lady MacDonald stood, head bowed, behind the altar at the center of the standing stones, resplendent in robes of a purple so deep it appeared black, sewn with gold and silver thread. She raised her face to the rising sun and waited. The growing light caused the threads of her robe to glow and send tracers of multicolored light around the stone circle. The dawn light turned her red hair a burnished copper.

Lauren stood alone at the foot of the Grand Approach, a linear path which bisected the large crowd and led through the standing clan stones, directly to the altar. She had no idea how a crowd of so many could be so quiet. Not a sneeze nor rustle of clothing or murmur could be heard. The crowd stood still as mannequins. Only the drone of the pipes could be heard.

Lauren watched in fascination as the chiefs of ten clans marched in unison into the circle, each entering from behind their stone. Their formal tartans aglow in the rising sun. Sharp, glittering reflections arced from the pommel-stones of their broadswords, carried at their side or across their back. *A flock of peacocks, each preening, trying to outdo the others.* Lauren chuckled to herself. No clan entered before or after the other. All—Buchan, Cameron, Campbell, Graham, MacBain, MacDonald, McLaran, McLeod, Newkirk, and Stuart—arrived within the circle together.

Each trio—chief and two subordinates—entered the circle and took their places before intricately carved wooden chairs placed in front of their stone. Facing into the center of the circle, each chair was draped in the formal tartan of their clan. Three of the clans were not represented before their stones. Alex—chief of the Doouglas Clan—would not sit at her stone. In fact, only one of the three chairs of the Doouglas stone would be occupied by the Terran Seneschal. Merilyn would lead Lauren into the circle and then take her place before the Doouglas stone. Alex would enter the circle after Lauren and take her place on one of the two stone thrones behind the altar. The MacDonald Clan would be represented by the two clan subordinates, as Lady MacDonald would conduct the ceremony and not sit at her stone as chief.

The newly erected Clan Fraser stone—the thirteenth stone which now completed the circle—had only one chair before it. That chair would sit empty, until after the Letters Patent were read and accepted, and Lauren's adoption was formally recognized by Terra. Then Lauren would sit in that one chair, before her clan stone and face her challengers.

Clan Cador was not represented and no member of the clan would be present for the Investiture. Their huge monolith was shrouded in black crepe. The three chairs before the stone were overturned and faced away from the center of the circle.

The bagpipe reached a crescendo as the sun crested the horizon and lit the long path before Lauren. Her shadow stretched before her, down the Grand Approach. She would walk into the circle as if walking out of the sun, newly born of heat and fire—representing eternal life. As the sun supported life on Terra, so she would walk out of the sun to support and protect the lives of the Terran people.

The last note faded into silence and Merilyn, dressed in the formal tartan of Clan Doouglas with a plaid of Clan Fraser across her chest, stepped out of the crowd to stand before Lauren on the path. Lauren felt like an ugly duckling following her fully-fledged parent. She was dressed in a simple open-necked, white shirt, sleeves rolled up to her elbows. A Fraser hunting tartan kilt of muted browns, greens, and cream was draped around her waist. Her kilt was held in place with a two-inch-wide brown leather belt. An empty scabbard of deep red leather, tipped in gold, hung from it. Low brown leather boots laced to above her ankles, the soles covered in non-slip crepe. She carried nothing else into the circle. She wasn't unprotected though, because beneath her kilt and shirt she wore a suit of the lightest body armor she'd ever seen. It was a gift from Alex the night before. Always one to be prepared, Alex had said she would protect her soulmate as her soulmate protected Terra. The suit fit like a glove and moved freely as she did. Only her head, forearms and lower legs were left unprotected.

Merilyn reached the altar and bowed to Lady MacDonald as Lauren knelt behind her and lowered her head, eyes fixed on the inlaid stones of the path. “M’lady, may I present Doctor Lauren Beckwith, healing technician and nexus traveler, daughter of Clan Fraser, Captain of *Ruadh làn-damh*, soulmate of Alexandra, Regain Rìoghachd Fuar Ćala, Our Queen of the Planet Terra, Bhean cheile agus comh-rialoir, and Savior of Terra.”

Lady MacDonald said, “Your Grace, why do you present this person before us today?”

“To invest Doctor Lauren Beckwith as Consort to the Queen of Fuar Ćala and crown her Co-Ruler with Her Majesty of the Planets Terra and Terra Prime and all her realms beyond. That her deeds and sacrifices for the people of Terra and our Queen be read into our history and acknowledged. That her adoption into Clan Fraser be accepted so Clan Fraser will live again.”

As Merilyn spoke, Lauren shivered. She had studied and prepared, but the magnitude of this day’s events wasn’t real until now.

“Why do you believe Doctor Lauren Beckwith deserves these titles, styles, and the honor and privilege of such a state?”

“Her deeds and sacrifices alone are enough to warrant these honors and privileges. But it is the existence of a bond of such strength she and our Queen are one, for she holds the heart and soul of our Queen within her gentle hands. This alone proves her worthy of these titles.” Lauren smiled as her bond sang. She raised her head.

Lady MacDonald bowed her head in acknowledgement of these attributes. “Those are truly worthy reasons to name Doctor Lauren Beckwith as Consort and Co-Ruler. Has the Council of Clans recognized her deeds and sacrifices?”

“Aye. They have.” Pulling a rolled parchment from her sleeve, Merilyn placed the document on the altar atop a golden platter. “I, as Seneschal and Guardian of Her Majesty, Alexandra Aoeron Aonwyn, present the ratified Letters Patent.” She bowed her head and stepped away from the altar, moving to stand behind Lauren where she knelt. Lady MacDonald picked up the parchment, broke the purple dragon seal, and unfurled it. Lauren shivered again, as Merilyn placed a small warm hand on her back.

"This document, signed by our Queen and ratified by our Council of Clans, reads as follows—" As Lady MacDonald read the Letters Patent, the Regalia of State were brought before the altar.

"—By giving into Her hand a rod of electrum to show all Her wisdom and intellect with which to serve and protect Terra, Terra Prime and all Her Realms—" Lady MacDonald paused.

Glowing red-orange in the rising sun, a pair of white wolves walked down the path. They carried an electrum rod in their mouths, approached the altar, and dropped to their knees. Lord McLaran rose from his seat and stepped to the altar, where he took the rod from them. He turned and placed it in the center of the altar, bowing first to Lady MacDonald and then to Lauren and Merilyn. The wolves moved to sit on either side of the kneeling Lauren.

The reading went on. "—By placing a coronet of gold upon Her head to show Her position and duty as Co-Ruler of Our Country of Cold Harbour—"

Next came Angus Newkirk, Lauren knew he carried a red silk pillow in his hands. A coronet of platinum and gold rested upon it. She had not seen the actual coronet crafted by Clan MacDonald, only the drawings made by Hamish McLeod. She knew the coronet was an open circle of platinum, one end adorned with the head of a golden owl, the other with the head of a golden wolf. *Wisdom and cunning.*

As Newkirk approached the altar, a murmur rose from the crowd behind her. This was the first sound the crowd had made, and Lauren snuck a peek to see what caused such a reaction. Newkirk was dressed head-to-toe in a black armored body suit, his face covered by a tinted pneumatic membrane face-shield. His clan represented only by the plaid he wore about his shoulders. The armor absorbed the dawn light, which only accentuated the reflection off the large golden clasp at his shoulder—an open book, encrusted with rows of diamond letters. But Lauren knew the crowd was reacting to the phased-blaster pistols which rode low on his narrow hips. *Whoa, I get the whole power in knowledge thing. Newkirk is as big a book-nerd as I am. But to make a statement like this, overlaying that power with the leashed power of a primed blaster pistol.* She stifled a chuckle. *Gotta love it. Not much subtlety there but definitely appreciated.* She couldn't keep from shaking her head slightly.

Newkirk placed the pillow next to the rod and stepped back, moving to stand behind Merilyn along the path.

Lady MacDonald read on. "—By putting a plaid of her clans—Fraser and Doouglas—about her shoulders to show her membership of sorority—"

Robert McLaran the Younger came next. The formal tartan kilt of Clan Fraser and the rich tartan of a Clan Doouglas plaid rested one atop the other in his strong hands. He placed his burden down next to the coronet and stepped back to stand behind Newkirk.

"—By girding her with a sword with which to defend Her Royal Majesty Our Queen and All of Terra, Terra Prime, and Her Realms in need or deed—"

Last up the Grand Approach, between the stones, came Tavish MacDonald, resplendent in his formal tartan of black, white, and red, with a plaid of red, white, black, and blue over his right shoulder. It was held in place by a platinum clasp of crossed swords overlain by a golden starship. He carried a deep purple pillow across which lay Lauren's sword. The green diamond pommel strobed a slow steady beat in the day's dawn light. He stepped to the altar and placed the pillow and sword down on the altar's top stone. Bowing low, he stepped back to stand behind McLaran.

Lauren felt the strength of the companions as they stood behind her. Their support, love, and respect flowed along her bond. Her heart beat sped up.

Lady MacDonald finished reading and re-rolled the parchment. She held the document up to the clans and crowd. "Do you, in witness to these ratified Letters Patent, accept their word and thereby accept Doctor Beckwith?"

A roar of "Aye, M'lady, we do!" rose from behind Lauren, so loud it shook the ground beneath her knees. Lauren was humbled by the swell of acceptance and approval.

Above the roar of the crowd came the steady beat of hooves. Two black horses of immense size galloped up the path and passed on either side of Lauren and her companions. Ffrwyn carried Alex. Gríobhtha, Lord McLaran's companion, carried a large silk-wrapped package in his empty saddle. The two horses stopped at the foot of the altar and bowed, one foreleg straight before them, the other bent beneath.

Alexandra was dressed in the formal military uniform of the Black Guard. Her red wool overtunic jacket was festooned with her ancestral badges of power. A starched white shirt collar peeked from beneath the tightly fitted high-collared jacket. White riding breeches covered her muscular thighs and disappeared into over-the-knee black boots, polished to a bright luster. An ermine-collared cape of purple wool, lined in red silk, hung from her throat held closed with a clasp of two facing loons. The cape covered Ffrwyn's flanks and hung nearly to the ground on either side of the tall horse. Upon her head rested the golden coronet of state. Embedded around the circle of gold were thirteen square-cut diamonds—one for each of her Foremothers. Her blade rested in its red leather scabbard and hung from the saddle dees at her right knee. The large sapphire pommel glinted in the morning light, giving off rays of blue and green, beating with a double pulse.

"Your Majesty," Lady MacDonald came from behind the altar and sank into a low curtsy.

"M'lady, you have summoned me here this day. Why?" Alex asked from Ffrwyn's tall back.

Never rising or lifting her eyes Lady MacDonald, the Terran Lady of the Ancients, answered, "I summoned you here this morning to formally bestow upon Doctor Lauren Beckwith, the titles, privileges, honors, and dignities as enunciated in the Letters Patent, drawn by your hand, ratified by the Council of Clans, and accepted this day by the populace of Terra. That she has rightly and truly earned these through deed and sacrifice. That there exists between you a bond of such strength you hold within you the other's heart and soul, whereby, the whole is greater than the sum of your individual parts. That henceforth, Doctor Lauren Beckwith shall be daughter to Clan Fraser and known as Lauren Beckwith Fraser. That she shall be Consort to the Queen and Co-Ruler of Terra and her satellite Luna, Terra Prime and her satellites, and all her realms beyond, and be known as Her Royal Majesty."

Alex stood in the stirrups, spun her cape off her right shoulder, and swung from Ffrwyn's back. After removing her sheathed blade from the saddle, she took four strides to stand before Lady MacDonald. She placed her right hand on the lady's bowed head. "Rise, and let us see if this person is who you say she is." Alex turned to the clans and the crowd beyond. "As is my right and in the manner of all my Foremothers before me, I say Lauren Beckwith must stand to the Challenges of Investiture."

Lady MacDonald turned to face Lauren and her companions and nodded. Her gaze shifted to the massive crowd beyond the clan stones. "Hear me, Terra. Our Ruler has spoken. This day, Lauren Beckwith will face the four challenges of Investiture. She must prove her intelligence and ability to augment Her Royal Majesty's wisdom. She must swear her loyalty to our Ruler and prove her willingness to obey all orders of her Ruler and clan, and uphold the law of Terra. She must demonstrate her knowledge of our culture and heritage, supplementing our history. And most importantly, she must prove her ability to protect our Ruler."

Alex nodded and marched around the altar to sit in one of the two stone thrones, her purple cape billowing behind her.

The crowd roared again, and once quieted, Lady MacDonald said, "Rise, Lauren Beckwith and prepare to meet these challenges." Lauren rose to her feet and squared her shoulders. "Her Royal Majesty has spoken. You will be tested by four of our Terran clans. Are you prepared to meet these challenges?"

"I am." Butterflies swirled in a chaotic pattern within her stomach but her tall stance never wavered.

"Then be seated and await the first challenge from Clan McLeod." Lady MacDonald motioned to the one empty chair within the circle.

Lauren moved to the Fraser stone and sat in the single chair, facing the center of the circle, forearms draped over the ornate chair arms, hands gripping the carved stag heads. Snow and Ice moved to either side of her chair and settled on their haunches. *"Thanks, guys."* The other companions moved to stand next to the Chiefs of their respective clans, before their clan stones.

"We will always be here to support you, Lauren. We know you will do well today," Snow said encouragingly.

"Yes, and then we can eat."

"Ice, some day you and your stomach are going to get us in trouble." It took all her effort to keep from laughing aloud at the grinning wolf.

Lauren had barely settled before Clan Chief McLeod stood and strode to the center of the stone circle, his unique gravity suit visible beneath his kilt. He bowed to Alex. "Your Majesty."

He turned to Lady MacDonald. "I have been elected by my clan to test the Lady Beckwith's intelligence and ability to augment our Ruler's wisdom. May I begin our challenge?"

"Proceed, M'lord."

He faced Lauren, "Doctor Beckwith, I am Iain McLeod, Chief of Clan McLeod, Spacing and Engineering Technician, Admiral of the Terran Intragalactic Fleet, and Chief of Luna Keep. I am chosen to test your intelligence."

Lauren inclined her head to McLeod but remained silent.

McLeod smiled at Lauren. "Let us begin. As you know, the thirteen standing stones around us are made of anorthosite, quarried from the surface of Luna by each of the clans. Do you know the origin of this rock?"

Lauren stood and bowed deeply to McLeod. "M'lord, anorthosite is an igneous rock, formed by crystalizing from a magma or melt. It is one of the most ancient rock types known. It is unique because it has not been formed since the earliest days of this planet's history. Its primary constituent is Labradorite plagioclase, a calcium-aluminum tectosilicate mineral. These giant crystals are what create its blue-tint. Anorthosite makes up the light patches one sees on the lunar surface, when we observe Luna from Terra."

McLeod nodded. "And?"

"It is also important because though the clans quarried these megaliths on Luna, it didn't originate on Luna." Lauren paused as she watched McLeod's eyebrow rise a few millimeters. *Here we go. This is something we're still arguing about.* Lauren heard her grandfather's voice, "*Answer the question from your point of view, using your data and understanding of the problem, even if your answer flies in the face of current theory. Stand tall. Be your own person. Tell them what you think.*"

Lauren cleared her throat. "Even though the stone was brought from Luna, the anorthosite originated here on Terra." The crowd murmured at this revelation. "During the earliest days of the formation of Terra, the proto-planet was struck a glancing blow by numerous objects, each approximately one quarter Terra's total size. These collisions sheared a large mass of material from Terra's crust and upper mantle. This material was retained in orbit about early Terra, caught in the new planet's developing gravity well. Ultimately, it coalesced into its own planetary body. We call that body Luna. We know this is true due to two observations. One, the lunar anorthosite making up these standing stones is chemically identical to the anorthosite found on Terra." Lauren turned a full-circle indicating the megaliths around her. "Two, a planet the size of Terra doesn't have a large enough mass and thereby doesn't create a deep enough gravity well to capture and hold a satellite the size of Luna by grabbing a passing meteor or other body from a random orbit."

Lauren paused again and waited. McLeod finally nodded as if he accepted her explanation. "And why is this important to Terra?"

"It is important to Terra because this collision event created the Terra we know and produced a planet that could and does sustain life. All life, including Terrans."

"Because?" McLeod probed.

Lauren smiled at him. "Because the initial collisions tilted Terra's axis of rotation over to the twenty-two degrees it has today. This tilt creates the seasons Terra has. The existence of a body as massive as Luna is responsible for the tides. It also drives the global climate. The existence of this large, relatively massive satellite slows the rotational speed of Terra and stabilizes her movement. Without Luna, Terra would spin faster and have shorter days. The planet would wobble uncontrollably about its axis and this erratic motion would cause disruption of the planetary surface. Without Luna, Terrans would not have been able to settle here." McLeod smiled at her and nodded in acceptance of her explanation.

"Thank you. The second part of this challenge has to do with your ability to augment the wisdom of our Ruler." McLeod turned away from Lauren and faced Lady MacDonald. "M'lady, Clan McLeod feels Lady Beckwith has already demonstrated her perfect complement to our Ruler's wisdom through her discovery of how the Comin bio-weapon worked and in the creation of a successful antidote, which saved our children and the future of Terran civilization. She did this by using the data Her Royal Majesty recovered from the Comin homeworld in a singular act of bravery. Together they saved us."

The roar of agreement and approval from the crowd almost drowned out his next comments. "We are all familiar with Her Royal Majesty's skills in tactics, her demonstrated leadership in our escape from Terra Prime, and our successful relocation here on Terra, and also in her engineering and architectural skills as demonstrated by the Keep around us." He pointed at the massive granite edifice standing around the stone circle. "And in the design and building of Luna Keep, Lady Beckwith's healing and scientific knowledge and abilities are perfect complements to Her Majesty's demonstrated skillsets. Therefore, we have no further questions."

Lady MacDonald turned to Alex. "Your Majesty, are you satisfied with Clan McLeod's challenge and Doctor Beckwith's answers?"

"Yes." Alex nodded. Lauren felt a burst of discomfort color the emotional agreement along their bond. She knew why. Alex was uncomfortable. She wanted to sit with her legs thrown over the chair's arm, but propriety kept her from it.

Turning to the clans, Lady MacDonald asked, "What say you, chiefs? Has Doctor Beckwith demonstrated her intelligence?" Lauren watched closely as they replied. Clans Buchan and Stuart did not reply, merely nodded their assent. The others answered with enthusiasm. "Very well. The Clans concur. Doctor Beckwith has successfully passed this challenge." The crowd again roared their approval.

Clan Chief McLeod stepped up to the altar and picked up the electrum rod. He turned and moved to stand before Lauren, where she stood before the altar. He held the rod out to her. "I place this rod in your hands as a symbol of your intelligence and wisdom. By holding the rod, you are committing yourself to augmenting our Ruler's wisdom with your own. In making decisions for what is best for Terra in her absence. For providing counsel and advice when asked. And most importantly, for giving counsel and advice when it is needed even if it is not asked for. Do you accept this?"

"I do."

"Then I place this rod in your hands." Lauren reached out and took the rod in her left hand. "Be wise, Lauren Beckwith." McLeod took two steps back and bowed, turned, and walked back to his chair.

Lauren returned to sit before the Fraser stone. The first challenge complete. Lauren felt her taut muscles relax a fraction.

Once the crowd settled down, Lady MacDonald picked up the red silk pillow. She presented the pillow to Alex with a bow, and said, "Your Majesty, are you prepared to hear and accept Doctor Beckwith's oath of fealty and place upon her brow this coronet?" She raised the pillow up.

"I am prepared." Alex rose from her throne and walked to the front of the altar.

Lauren stood and placed the electrum rod in her seat. She walked to the altar and stopped before Alex, kneeling, and clasping her hands together between her knees, she bowed her head.

"I, Lauren Beckwith, do swear that I will be faithful and bear true allegiance to Her Royal Majesty, Queen Alexandra Aoeron Aonwyn, her heirs and successors, according to all Terran law. I further swear to uphold, support, protect, and defend all citizens of Terra and her satellite Luna, Terra Prime, her satellites, and all her realms beyond. I will defend her to the utmost of my power against all conspiracies and attempts whatever, made against her person, crown, or dignity; and I will do my utmost to disclose and make known to Her Royal Majesty, her heirs and successors, all treasons and traitorous acts which may be formed against her or them." Lauren heard Alex inhale sharply. Obviously, she hadn't known about the change Lady MacDonald had added to the Fealty Oath.

Alex placed her hands on Lauren's head, "Will you solemnly promise to govern all citizens according to our laws and customs?"

"I solemnly promise to do so."

"Further, will you execute all your judgments with mercy and cause justice to prevail?"

"I will." Lauren felt warmth spreading from Alex's hands as she spoke. *I love her so much.* She smiled, feeling Alex's matching emotions hum through their bond.

"Will you do your utmost to maintain and allow our culture to grow, encouraging all facets of the arts and branches of the sciences, to improve the life of all Terrans?"

"I will." Lauren was most comfortable with this part of the oath.

"And will you also swear to uphold each individual, no matter how unique or different from yourself, such that those persons may thrive and contribute in their own way to the improvement of Terra, through idea, deed, or action?" She and Alex had discussed this part of the oath at length. She had shared some of the discrimination people of Earth faced and knew this should be part of all oaths, heads of government swore in her reality.

"I do swear to perform all these duties to the best of my abilities, today and forever."

Alex turned and lifted the coronet from the silken pillow, Lady MacDonald held. Facing forward into the center of the circle and the crowd beyond, she held the coronet above Lauren's head. "Terra, I present unto you Lauren Beckwith, your Consort to the Queen. Henceforth, to be known as Her Royal Majesty. Are all who come this day, willing to do homage and service unto her?"

"Aye." Rumbled from the crowd and the Clans around them.

"To follow and obey her word and judgment?" Alex's voice rose in volume.

"Aye." The sound swelled.

"To follow her to preserve and better Terra for all her citizens, today and forever more?"

The crowd roared their final approval with a united, "Aye." That acknowledgement seemed to shake the standing stones to their foundations. And under the human voices could be heard the baritone rumble of the *Hyper-arborea sempervirens,* as the trees of the sacred grove surrounding the standing stones added their approval and acceptance.

Alex lowered the coronet and placed it on Lauren's bowed head. "From this day forth, Lauren Beckwith will be Cáraid Rioghail Fuar Ćala. Rise, Your Royal Majesty, and accept the respect and homage of your peers and citizens."

Lauren stood and turned to face the center of the circle. She took one step to her right, as Alex stepped forward to stand at her left shoulder. Sunlight glinted off the platinum coronet. Cheers crashed over the pair as they stood in the center of the circle within the sacred grove. They represented the continuance of Terran culture, and all Terra rejoiced in this moment.

Lady MacDonald moved to stand before them and bowed low. "Your Royal Majesties, the people of Terra, and the sacred trees of our Homeworld acknowledge and accept the Consort. With your permission, we will move onto the third challenge of the Investiture."

"Let it be so." Alex turned to sit back on her throne, while Lauren stepped down to sit at the Fraser stone.

"In the third challenge, Her Majesty Lauren Beckwith must prove her knowledge and understanding of our culture and heritage. In so doing, she will be accepted as a citizen of Terra and a member of her adopted Clan Fraser. She will walk among us as Terran. Who will be the tester in this?" Lady MacDonald asked the clan chiefs seated around the circle.

"As her adopted mother and sole member of Clan Fraser, I will do the asking." Merilyn rose from her seat before the Doouglas stone.

A shiver ran down Lauren's spine as she watched the diminutive Seneschal move to stand before the altar. *I've never felt this much love for my birth mother. How could this woman come to mean so much to me? And in so short a time.*

"Because of who you are to her. It is a relationship of mutual love and respect you share," Ice explained. Lauren reached out and laid a gentle hand on each of the wolves. *"When did you get so smart?"*

"I have always been smart, although not as intelligent as Snow." Lauren felt the other wolf start at Ice's compliment. *"But I see feelings very well."*

Snow growled in agreement and a wolfy grin graced her face.

"Focus, Lauren. If I know Merilyn, this will not be easy." Alex's admonishment was the first time they shared conversation across their bond today.

Lauren didn't have time to answer Alex before Merilyn spoke. "Your Royal Majesty, will you please describe the Age of Tribulation and list its underlying causes."

Clearing her throat, Lauren rose and walked to the center of the circle. She bowed to Merilyn. "There have been four Ages of Tribulation in the enduring and rich history of the Terrans. Would you please tell me which age you are asking about?"

A small smile crossed Merilyn's face, and she inclined her head in acknowledgement of Lauren's question. "I am asking of the second age."

"The second Age of Tribulation was a time of great strife within Terran history. Terra Prime was divided into any number of fiefdoms, each ruled by a chief who held the position through blackmail, treachery, and even murder. Only those supported by the black priests were able to hold their positions for any length of time. If I were to compare it to the history of my reality, I would call it the Dark Age of Terra Prime.

"All learning and growth were suppressed by a religious order based in superstition. Alchemy was the leading science of the time. The bulk of the Terra Prime population was illiterate and lived in poverty, caught between warring liege lords."

Merilyn slowly nodded in sad agreement. "It truly was a time of great strife. What allowed the Terrans to survive?"

Lauren took time to organize her thoughts. So many factors led to the overthrow of the fiefdom system and the birth of a Terran renaissance. She started to answer and then paused again. *Why would Merilyn ask such an open-ended question? She never speaks without thought and purpose.* Lauren thought hard and then smiled. *Of course!*

"It started as a small thing because of a large thing." Merilyn nodded, a motion so small Lauren was sure only those at the altar could see. "A plague was ravaging the population of Terra Prime. The black priests, who blamed the sickness on the evils of the liege lords' debauchery, may have actually been the ones who spread the plague." A hiss rose from several of the seated clans. *Didn't they realize the plague was probably a highly infectious bacterial disease, maybe Hanson's disease?* "That infection could linger without symptoms for many years in its host. So, the priests would carry the bacterium from settlement to settlement and not know they were the host."

Lauren ignored the clans' reaction. "As the plague spread across the Terra Prime lands in the south, a small band of seafolk lived and thrived on the far northern islands. Not many of the black priests journeyed across the northern ocean, so the plague wasn't known there. The people of these northern islands honored learning, family, ancestry, and nature. They had their own language, culture, and forms of worship, as indicated by the large circles of standing stones they built. The few priests who did arrive on their islands were expelled quickly."

"Aye, and what did the seafolk do?" Merilyn winked at Lauren, causing Lauren to struggle to control her laughter.

"There were numerous families scattered about the many islands. They were sailors who discovered and excelled in the intricacies of stellar and solar navigation. So, they ranged far across the northern ocean, in quests of discovery. The sailors brought back foodstuffs, spices, rare metals, precious stones, and most importantly, ideas and knowledge. Those that didn't go to sea stayed home and shepherded herds of native sheep and goats. The families were master weavers, who utilized the wools from their herds and dyes from the land and sea to create threads of bright colors." Lauren paused and tried to choose the proper words to complete her answer. "While these families thrived and learned and grew, the fiefdoms in the south failed, one by one. After four hundred years, only a few disparate gangs of survivors roamed in the south. When the families of the north finally came south to the mainland continent, they found a land rich in natural resources, and they settled the coastlines, ignoring the mid-continent."

Merilyn asked carefully, "Do we know these families?"

"We do." Lauren affirmed and turned in a full circle, meeting the gaze of each of the clans. "They sit here, dressed in the bright fabrics of their familial tartans, now as navigators of the stars not the seas, prizing learning and clan growth. Still thriving." She swallowed hard, as her voice threatened to break. "Still conquering all challenges thrown before them, whether from within or without."

The silence deepened and no one seemed to breathe for a handful of heartbeats. Then it began, a slow clap, clap, clap rhythm. The cadence sped up and soon all Lauren could hear was a cacophony of sound. She picked out the stomp of horses' hoofs and the howl of wolves. Lauren had successfully reminded the clans of their origin, of the honor of their heritage, of their successes, and of their ability to overcome anything. All because they did it together, as family and clan.

"Well played, Your Majesty," Merilyn's mind-voice tickled her bond. Lauren could feel her pleasure as well as how proud she was of Lauren. *"Let us see how they handle that."*

Lady MacDonald raised her arms and slowly quiet again filled the grove. "What say you, chiefs?" She turned first to Clan Cameron.

"M'lady Beckwith." At Lady MacDonald's scowl, he corrected himself, "Your Royal Majesty, you summarized our birth as clansmen correctly. You remind us how together we are successful no matter the challenge, a learning we best remember if we are to thrive and overcome."

Lauren watched as Lady MacDonald solicited input from each of the clan chiefs around the circle. Each had a positive and approving comment, until she came to Clan Stuart. The clan chief glared at Lauren and then turned to the Lady Macdonald, shaking his head in the negative. "Very well, Clan Buchan?"

The Buchan chief rose to his feet. "M'lady." He bowed to Lady MacDonald, his back to Lauren. "My clan honors our heritage and teaches our children about their beginnings. However, we do not need to be lectured about our origins by an alien imposter." He turned and pointed at Lauren, but she couldn't hear the rest of what he said. Nine clans rose as one and shouted him down. The crowd heard his initial words, repeated on the monitors scattered about the grove, and added their voices to their clan chiefs' protest.

Buchan shouted to be heard above the roaring din, but his words were lost. Lady MacDonald tried to stop the shouting, but she couldn't be heard either.

Alex stood from her seat, a scowl on her face. Her blue eyes, black with anger.

Lauren felt Alex gather the strength of the companions to her and she freely added hers. Alex sent out a mental shout filling the minds of all in the grove. "*Silence!*" The quiet was more deafening than the roar as the crowd settled.

Lady MacDonald's voice rang in the silence as she spun on Chief Buchan. "You speak of educating your children as the duty of your clan. But who would you educate if you had no children?" The gasp of a collective indrawn breath split the grove. Lauren knew nothing was more sacred to the clans than their children.

"Our children are not in question, M'lady. This alien is."

"This alien, as you call her, saved your children so your clan has someone to educate and has a future. Without her selfless contribution, we were doomed with this generation, and Terra would cease to exist. You would be wise, M'lord, to remember that."

She bowed to Lauren. "Accept my apology for this affront, Your Royal Majesty."

Lauren nodded her acceptance and turned back to her chair. Lady MacDonald turned to Merilyn, "Are you satisfied with Her Royal Majesty's response to your questions, Your Grace?"

"I am."

"Then I confirm Consort Lauren Beckwith Fraser a citizen of Terra and her adoption into Clan Fraser as requested by our Seneschal is recognized. Her deeds and contributions will be added to our history for all future generations to know what she did to save Terra. Further, I mandate that from this day forth, the records will show she has earned the title, Savior of Terra."

Merilyn picked up the folded kilt and plaid from the altar and moved to stand before Lauren. "Rise, daughter and don the colors of your clans." Lauren stood and pulled off the muted kilt, replacing it with the kilt in formal Fraser tartan. Merilyn draped the Doouglas plaid around her shoulders, fastening it in place with a golden brooch in the shape of a tree bisected by a platinum blade. Then she completely stunned Lauren as she gathered her in a tight hug and held on. "I am so proud of you, my daughter. You are a great addition to our Clan Fraser." Merilyn's tears soaked through the fabric of Lauren's shirt.

"The first three parts of Investiture ceremony are complete. We will take a two-hour respite to refresh and gather ourselves before the fourth and final challenge." Lady MacDonald bowed to Alex and then to Lauren before exiting the circle of standing stones.

Lauren sat in her chair beneath the Clan Fraser standing stone, waiting. This was the part of the Investiture she feared most. The boys kept trying to tell her the challenge was a challenge in name only. No Foremother's consort had fought a challenge since the Fraser did in her Investiture. Foremothers after that were either married when their partners were crowned Queen or their partners weren't made Consort. None of which made Lauren feel any better, though, because nothing about Lauren or Alex or their bond was normal or fit into the standard of prior history.

Lady MacDonald reentered the circle, and took her place behind the altar, saying to the clan chiefs and crowd alike, "If any person, of any station, deny the right of our Queen to choose a Consort, deny the bond of our Queen and her Chosen, or deny the validity of this Investiture, I say on behalf of Her Royal Majesty Alexandra that she lies and is a traitor to the Crown. And in saying she is traitor, here is her Champion—Her Royal Majesty, Lauren Beckwith Fraser." Lady MacDonald pointed at Lauren. "She is ready to combat this person and will do so with the sword placed around her waist by the Queen."

Lauren stood and approached the altar where she waited for Alex to take up her sword and sheath it in the empty scabbard on her left side. Once the sword hung from her waist, Lauren picked up a leather glove off the altar and held it high above her head. "I throw down this gauntlet and challenge any and all traitors to my Queen and the Sovereignty of Terra and her satellite Luna." She threw the glove to the ground at her feet and waited to see if anyone would take up the challenge.

She didn't wait long. Those standing at the altar heard the murmur build as a challenger separated himself from the crowd and approached the standing stones from behind the Campbell stone. He stepped into the circle. Nine clan chiefs leaped to their feet and one cried out, "No, this is not right!"

Stewart McGuiness strode without pause to the base of the altar where he picked up the glove. "I will not stand by and allow one such as this, to disgrace our history. It will not be done. I am SwordMaster of Terra and Champion of the People. I will stand and uphold the honor of

Terra and her people. I call the Queen traitor for allowing this to happen." He threw the glove back down at Lauren's feet. "I accept this challenge and say on behalf of my family McGuiness and my Clan Campbell, you will not be successful."

Lauren stood frozen in shock. *"You must pick up the glove, Lauren, or the challenge is forfeit and the challenger automatically wins."* Ice's growl cut through the rigor in her muscles.

She picked up the glove and took a step forward. "You will lose and will never again be called Champion. For your title will forevermore be Traitor."

A growl built deep in McGuiness' chest. It resonated within the circle, spiraling outward to rumble over the crowd where an answering growl built and was reflected back into the circle.

"The Terrans are with you, Lauren," Snow said, as she and Ice moved to stand beside her.

"Do not distract her, Snow," Alex said. *"She must do this alone without our help or interference."*

The boys were not privy to the conversation going on among the wolves, Lauren, and Alex. They moved forward from their positions at their clan stones, blades drawn.

"I am Her Majesty's Guardian and Protector, it is my right to stand against this challenger," MacDonald shouted.

Lauren laid a gentle hand on his arm, and smiled. "No, Tavish, this is my challenge. You may be my Protector, but I'm Alex's. It'll be okay. You've taught me well. Believe in that." She turned to face the challenger and her blade sang as she drew it from her scabbard. She sent a quick message to Alex.

"Should I fail you, you now know who abstained and who the third party to the Hebridean's acts of treason is. Make them pay!"

There was a long pause but finally Alex replied, *"I swear on all that I am, they will pay and their clans will cease to exist."*

Lauren glanced at Alex, who again sat stoically on her throne, glaring at McGuiness. *"Be wise, Dearest. What happens today will rend the fabric of our society for millennia if not handled properly. Do not act in haste. Gather your allies, and protect Terra and her future."*

"I will, Dearheart." Lauren felt how hard this was for Alex—to watch Lauren fight—but Lauren knew this was her duty, and she would do her best. And then she felt it, the strength of Alex's love sang along their bond, strong enough to stiffen her spine and settle her resolve.

Chapter Fourteen

Lauren returned to her chair and removed the Doouglas plaid from her shoulder. She folded her tartan, laying it on the chair, carefully placing the golden tree and blade brooch on top. The wolves sat on either side the craved chair.

"Everything will be all right, Lauren." Snow tried to reassure her.

"Perhaps, Snow. But he is Champion. And moreover, he's gigantic," Lauren replied distractedly. She swallowed hard, fear nearly freezing her muscles as she fumbled to remove her leather belt and scabbard.

Ice whiffled. *"That is true. He is gigantic, but size reduces quickness and grace. And more importantly, his small movements are exaggerated because he uses an immense blade. In fact, when he was tutoring Alex and the boys, he made them use a copy of his blade to build their upper body strength. You will win and win quickly."*

Lauren turned toward Ice and realized the wolf was offering her tips about the challenge. She knelt before Ice and gathered her in bear hug. *"You're the best, you know that?"*

"Oh, she knows she is the best, but if you keep telling her, she will not fit through the solar door because her ego will be so large." Snow's observation could have been taken as an insult had Lauren not felt the teasing glow along their bond. She laughed and reached out to pull the other wolf into their group hug.

A gong sounded, pulling Lauren out of their hug. Rising, she turned to the center of the circle and saw McGuiness. He had also removed his plaid and rolled his sleeves to above his elbows. His kilt ended at his knee and met the top of his tall black boots, where a bone-handled dirk peeked out. But it was his broadsword which captured Lauren's attention. The hilt peeked over his left shoulder while the end of his scabbard hung nearly to his knees. *Gawd, that blade has gotta be a meter and a half long.*

"Combatants, please step forward and meet in the center." Lady MacDonald stood in the center of the circle, a thirteen-sided paved area before the altar. This area was thirteen meters across, formed from the intersection of the radii originating at each of the clan stones. "This challenge will be fought within the central area of the circle. If either combatant steps out of the area, that person forfeits the challenge. The bout will continue until one of the combatants can no longer lift their blade due to fatigue or is unable to lift their blade due to injury." Lady MacDonald's instructions were interrupted.

"M'lady, Clan Stuart demands the challenge be fought by the Rules of Llewellyn." Arrogance laced the chief's deep voice.

Lady MacDonald turned toward the Stuart stone, where the chief stood. "This is a challenge of Investiture, M'lord. There has been no insult to clan. A Llewellyn challenge does not apply here."

"I beg to differ, Lady MacDonald. An insult has occurred. Clan Stuart, with the support of Clans Buchan and Campbell, hereby file a formal Writ of Damages against the Clan." He moved forward and held out a rolled parchment. Lauren was stunned. *What was he talking about?*

Lady MacDonald pushed her arms deeper into the sleeves of her robes, refusing to accept the document.

Alex answered Lauren's mental question, anger dripping from her thoughts. It was her underlying fear that scared Lauren, *"A Llewellyn challenge is a fight to the death."*

Stuart held the writ out. "You do not have to physically take the writ for it to be valid, M'lady. A copy is being delivered to the Seneschal's Chief of Staff as we speak."

"As I said." Lady MacDonald gathered herself and seemed to grow in stature as she glowered at the clan chief. "No harm has come to you or your clans. Without harm, or proof of harm, this writ is invalid."

"But harm's been done not only to my clan, but to all of Terra." He pointed at Lauren. "This alien comes to us from an unknown place, without providence or ancestry we can validate. She comes bearing alien technology. We do not know what these devices could do to us in the future. But most grievous, she has clouded the mind of our leader, through trickery or poison or mind-control, we know not. You claim they have a bond, but we have no proof of it being mutual. This is the harm we claim."

Merilyn rose and began to make her way toward the center of the circle, but Lauren stopped her with a raised hand. "No, this is my challenge." Lauren's fury snapped, fueled by Alex's anger. *How many more times must I tolerate being called alien?*

Lauren turned to the crowd and spoke into the silence. "Hear me Terra. As I said in Council, I did not seek out your reality. I was drawn here without any desire or action of my own." Lauren slowly spun, engaging the crowd at the edge of the standing stones as she spoke.

"It is my sworn and moral duty, as a physician, to aid those injured or ill. And I did that to the best of my abilities. I healed Alexandra and then your children. I accepted my bond with Alexandra, with the swords, and with her companions. I am recognized by the tree and blade of your world, and by the dragons of the First Foremothers." Lauren pointed her blade at McGuiness. "But I will not stand idly by and see a band of traitors, who do not respect your history or culture, tear our society apart." She turned to Lady MacDonald. "As Protector of our Royal Majesty Alexandra and Defender of Terra, I will fight this challenge by whatever rules are demanded. For I fight for Alexandra, I fight for Clan Fraser, I fight for Clan Doouglas, I fight for Terra!" She raised her blade high and sunlight flashed through her diamond pommel. The crowd cheered and stomped.

McGuiness drew his massive broadsword and roared, "Come on. You are mine and will die on my blade."

This fight hasn't even started yet. Lauren dropped her blade to a forty-five-degree down angle and waited. MacD's words filled her head. '*Patience. Make the challenger come to you, force him to make the first move, watch and learn how he gives himself away. Then fight your fight. You have all the advantages with your blade.*'

Without warning, McGuiness took a quick step to his right, turning himself away from Lauren's blade, feigning exposure of his left side. Lauren didn't react and he quickly reversed his step and brought his blade back around in a two-handed stroke parallel to the ground, swinging toward Lauren's midsection. Lauren leapt back as the blade whistled past her. The tip caught the front of her shirt and slashed it open. Sparks flew off her body armor and a blaze of blue and green energy was released as the blade grazed its surface. She kept her balance, and when the momentum of his stroke put most of his weight on his left foot, Lauren lunged under his guard and into his open right side. A flick of her wrist and the point of her blade opened a bloody line beneath his right arm.

His roar split the silence. "Lucky blow, alien. That will not happen again."

Lauren didn't waste her breath replying. Instead, spinning in a circle on the ball of one foot, she cut him on his left forearm above his wrist as he gripped his sword to reverse his stroke. The spin lowered her center of gravity, and McGuiness' next stroke passed over her head. She lunged upward, standing to her full height, and drove the diamond pommel up into his throat, hard. He drew a ragged breath and staggered backward. But Lauren wasn't quick enough to get out of his reach as she reversed her blade. He grabbed her by the back of her neck with his free hand.

Lifting her off her feet, he shook her like a wayward cat and tossed her to the pavement. She smashed down into the pavement and landed awkwardly on her right shoulder. The joint failed, pain shot down her arm, and her hand went numb. She lost the grip on her blade. McGuiness lifted his foot to stomp on her head. Rolling away, she grabbed up her blade in her left hand. As the hilt re-formed to accommodate a left-handed grip, she continued her roll until she came up on her left knee, right arm dangling uselessly at her side. As the challenger's foot hit the pavement, she lunged forward off her knee.

MacDonald had said her blade was a thrusting weapon not a slashing weapon, so she thrust upward, the tip of her blade sank deep into McGuiness' upper left thigh. Unfortunately, her uncoordinated lunge made it impossible to stop her forward motion. Lauren crashed face-first into McGuiness' knee. Glancing off, she fell toward the edge of the paved area, stunned. The sideways momentum of her fall pulled her blade free and a thick stream of bright red blood pulsed from his wound.

In the distance, Lauren heard the howl of wolves and the cheer of the crowd but all she saw was McGuiness staggering forward. He hovered above her, flipping his blade—point to the ground. He lifted the hilt above his head in a two-handed grip. The point aligned with the middle of her chest. "I have you now, and then I will have Alexandra."

Lauren lay paralyzed with fear, all she could see was the point of his massive blade hanging above her chest.

"You are at the edge!" Ice's frantic cry ripped through her terror.

Lauren glanced away from the upraised blade and saw they were less than half a meter from the edge of the pavement. Turning back, Lauren saw McGuiness bunch the muscles of his forearms in preparation for driving the blade downward, then he took a half step closer to her prone form and she saw her chance. She rolled into his shins.

McGuiness' blade plunged downward and impaled Lauren. The point embedded into the underlying pavement. He tripped over Lauren's tumbling form. His forward momentum caused him to fall out of the paved area. But, Lauren was trapped on the impaling blade. Pain radiated from her side and her impinged shoulder screamed in agony. *I'm going to die! Alex, I love you!"*

Merilyn's voice rang through the circle. "The Champion has stepped from the circle and has forfeited the challenge. Her Royal Majesty Lauren Beckwith Fraser is the winner. She will forevermore be Protector of Our Queen."

The Seneschal spun and glared at Clans Buchan, Campbell, and Stuart. "Due to your actions and malice against our Rulers, your Writ of Damages is declared null and void. Your chosen champion has failed. Remove yourselves from this venue and prepare to hear your Ruler's judgment. You will be held under house arrest until such judgment is prepared. Be gone from this sacred place." A cadre of Black Guards entered the circle from behind the thrones at Alex's back and escorted the three clan chiefs and seconds from the sacred grove.

Lauren floated in a haze of white-hot pain, face pressed into the paving stones, unable to move. She could hear someone speaking, but it was far away. The indecipherable words pounded in her head with the beat of a drum, trying to split it open.

Chapter Fifteen

No one moved following the Guard's departure. The only sound was McGuiness' ragged breathing as he lay in the grass, blood pumping from the wound in his thigh. Lady MacDonald's voice rang out. "Call the healers, now!" Lauren saw McGuiness out of her left eye, lying motionless in the grass beyond the circle, a growing puddle beneath his left leg. *He needs help.* She struggled to get to him, pushing her pain down.

"Lauren can you hear me?" Snow's mental shout went unanswered, as the wolves rushed forward. Lauren twisted. *Gotta get to him, he'll bleed out.*

Ice skidded to a stop at Lauren's side. The scent of blood hung heavy in the air. She circled and stopped near Lauren's head. Leaning forward, the wolf swiped her tongue up her cheek.

"Argh—stop. I hate that." Lauren twisted again, arm and legs whirling, but she couldn't move her torso. The massive broadsword had pinned her to the pavement. She could feel the pinch of the sharp edge against her chest where it rubbed against her body armor as she struggled, but she didn't feel it had injured her.

"Dearheart, are you okay?" Alex knelt next to Ice.

"Yeah, I think so, but I can't move. The blade's got me trapped." Lauren replied through gritted teeth. Her answer was muffled due to her facedown position.

A healing technician arrived, a large blue medkit thrown over one shoulder, his robes billowing as he kneeled. "Your Majesty, where is the pain?"

"I've got a separated shoulder and I may have cracked my jaw when I hit his knee. But other than that, I'm okay. I need to turn over. First, you've gotta help Stewart. His femoral artery is cut." The healing technician hovered over Lauren's prone body.

Alex brushed Lauren's hair aside. "We will get you up as soon as we can." Alex stood and grasped the hilt of the challenger's blade. She tried to pull the sword loose. Lauren screamed as the blade rasped against her armor. Alex couldn't budge the blade. Leaning down again, panic laced her voice as she said, "I'm sorry, Dearheart. The blade is stuck and I do not want to risk injuring you by pulling it free from the pavement."

MacD leaned over Alex's shoulder and handed her a dirk. "Here, use this and cut away her shirt. Let us see what has her trapped."

Carefully, Alex cut away Lauren's white shirt, exposing her body armor. The edge of the broadsword would have cleaved her side open had the armor not deflected the blow. But in so doing, the armor was now fused to the blade. Alex looked at MacD. "Now what?"

Lauren watched through one eye, as MacD stroked his chin, deep in thought. "We cannot cut through the armor. It will only absorb more energy from our efforts and deepen the fusion with the blade. Can we release the armor and peel her out of it?"

"We are not going to be able to do that. The armor is fused over the seam." Alex pointed to a spot beneath Lauren's left arm.

"I don't think my shoulder is going to be very happy with any movement, guys." The white-hot pain morphed into a bone-deep agony radiating up into Lauren's neck, her muscles were rigid as she tried to fight the mounting agony.

Ice knelt next to Lauren and grinned her wolfy smile. *"Well played, Lauren. I am truly amazed at your speed and grace. The challenge was over in mere minutes. The Champion is defeated and you have successfully completed the four challenges. MacD was correct. A rapier can defeat a broadsword easily when the SwordMistress fights her own battle, by her own rules."*

Lauren knew the wolf was trying to distract her. *"Thanks, Ice, but it felt like hours."*

"It truly ended quickly." Lauren saw movement around McGuiness' body, as healers finally swarmed over him.

"Is Stewart all right?" Lauren's physician's instincts again overrode her pain. She knew if he didn't have medical care, he would die.

"He is being removed from the circle. The healers will repair the artery. Your weapon left a clean through and through injury, and I doubt he will have much muscle damage. But the femoral nerve appears to have been severed also. His leg is nonresponsive." The healer explained, as he knelt near her head.

"Then get me up now, Alex. I can repair that nerve." Lauren knew her trauma skills were needed. The Terran healing techs would try to heal the nerve systemically. Lauren would repair it surgically. And time was critical with nerve injuries. Lauren struggled against the broadsword again. Blue and green sparks flew as her armor rubbed against the blade.

Newkirk moved into her field of view. "Stop moving. You are only making it worse." She watched him turn back to the others. "I recommend we break the blade and lift Lauren off it."

"How are we going to do that?" MacD asked. "You know this blade and how it was forged. We cannot break it."

By now others had gathered around Lauren. Lord McLaran placed a warm hand on Lauren's back and leaned over her body inspecting her side. "You are fortunate to have had the armor on, Your Majesty. This was a death blow." His voice was matter of fact, but Lauren shivered at his statement.

"That nerve injury isn't going to wait, guys," she said, trying to distract herself from the knowledge of how close she came to dying. "The longer we wait, the poorer the result we'll have with a repair. Get me up. I don't want to see Stewart have a permanent disability."

"Young Newkirk is correct." Chief McLeod agreed as he too knelt and inspected the fused armor and blade. "We must break the hilt off and lift her up. This blade was constructed by folding the metal on itself as a tempering process. I suggest we freeze the blade. Freezing the metal will cause the blade's layers to separate so it will become brittle and should shatter when struck."

Alex rocked back on her heels. "All right, we have a plan."

"We have a supply of liquid nitrogen in the engineering laboratories. Let us retrieve a tank and get to work," Young McLaran said. He and McLeod rushed away.

"Alex, don't leave me, please." Lauren sent a whispered mind message along their bond.

She didn't know if Alex would hear her with all the shouting, or through all the people crowding around. *"Of course, I heard you, Dearheart. I will always hear you."* Alex knelt beside her. *"I am right here.*" She placed a hand on her shoulder. Warmth infused Lauren, but she shivered hard.

"She is going into shock." The healing technician laid a gentle hand on her forehead. "Please be as still as you can, Your Majesty."

Lauren shivered. "Shock, cold." She said through gritted teeth. The pain mounted, every movement driving it deeper into her bones. But Lauren knew the penetrating cold was the first indicator of the shock to come.

The healing tech turned to the group crowded around her. "Get back everyone, please. Give us some air here. I need blankets."

"We will be your blankets, Lauren." With Snow's comment, Ice lay across her bare legs and Snow stretched out along her back. Their combined body heat slowed Lauren's shivering. Lauren struggled to stay conscious, fighting the pain. *"Focus on us, Lauren. They will be here soon."*

"I'm trying, Snow," Lauren said through chattering teeth. Blankets were retrieved from somewhere, and these now covered Lauren and the wolves.

Four engineering techs rushed down the Grand Approach of the circle with a large tank. McLaran followed with a large silver tarp in his arms. McLeod moved fastest of all taking giant leaping strides, thanks to his gravity field generator. He knelt beside Lauren. "Your Majesty, we need to cover you in a thermal blanket to protect you from the liquid nitrogen. Also, you must keep your eyes shut at all times." Lauren nodded slowly. "But even with all of these protections, I am afraid you are going to get cold. We will go as quickly as we can." Lauren nodded again.

The techs attached an insulated hose to the tank and they handed the nozzle to MacDonald.

"All right, my boy," McLeod said, "given your smithing knowledge, you better than anyone know how to do this."

MacD walked around to stand behind Lauren's back. He focused the nozzle across the base of the hilt and away from Lauren. McLeod was correct. The liquid nitrogen sank, covering the silver-shrouded Lauren and wolves in a dense white cloud of expanding gas. She watched their actions through her bond with Alex. Her shivering increased, pain tore through her injured shoulder with the movement.

"Cold. It's so cold. Alex, I don't know if I can stand much more."

"Hang in there, Dearheart. We are almost done."

Turning off the nozzle, MacD stopped the flow of liquid across the frosted hilt and took a sledge from one of the engineers. "Stand clear, please."

Alex removed the thermal blanket from Lauren's head. "We are going to strike the blade. Be ease, Dearheart, it will not be long." Lauren tried to smile but it came out as a grimace.

Swinging the heavy hammer in two hands, MacD struck the hilt, but the hammer glanced off in a ringing blow. McGuiness' broadsword vibrated, and colored sparks erupted from Lauren's body armor. Lauren screamed, barely clinging to consciousness. The vibration amplified her acute pain. He took another swing and struck the blade below the hilt. The blade shattered and the sound of rending metal echoed around the circle. Metal shards exploded as the hilt broke off.

Alex knelt at Lauren's side again. "Open your eyes, Dearheart, the nitrogen has dissipated." Slowly Lauren opened her eyes. Shards of metal were scattered about the pavement within her field of view. "I am afraid this is going to hurt. We will do all we can to minimize that. We will get you free."

The wolves stood up and moved away, as Alex slid her arms under Lauren's torso. The healing tech slid his hands under her shoulder to stabilize her injured joint and neck. Newkirk gathered her legs together and MacD slid his large hands under her hips. McLaran held her feet. "Everyone ready?" Nods all around answered the healing tech. "All together please, in one, two, three. Stand up."

Lauren's scream tore through the circle as the group lifted her off McGuiness' blade. They tried to keep her body level but it wasn't possible and the pressure on her injured shoulder caused agony to rip through her chest. Panting, Lauren realized she was free from the blade. They moved away from the edge of the circle and slowly lowered her to the grass. As she touched down, she rolled over on her back. Tears streamed from the corners of her eyes.

The healing tech grimaced. "I am so sorry, Your Majesty."

Lauren tried to smile at the tech. However, the pain lancing through her shoulder and neck, prevented her from smiling naturally. "I'm glad to be off my shoulder."

Alex wiped her tears away. "We did not mean to cause you more pain, Dearheart."

" 'S okay. Give me a sec to get my breath back and then I'll go see how McGuiness is. We should probably fix the nerve at the same time as the arterial repair." Lauren struggled to sit up. "A hand here."

Newkirk and McLaran jumped in to assist her to a sitting position, supporting her back. "Thanks, guys." Her right arm dangled at her side but sitting up helped reduce the pain.

"Your Majesty, we need to put your shoulder back in. If it stays in a dislocated position, you could have tendon damage. The pain will also lessen if it is repositioned."

"I know. I've dislocated it several times, and the tendons are chronically weak. Can you help me to my feet? From there I can pop it back in." Lauren saw Newkirk grimace. "It's okay Angus, I've done this before."

Alex steadied her once she was on her feet. Lauren tried to reach out to the healing tech but couldn't lift her arm. "Please take my hand and hold the arm at the wrist and elbow. Keep it from adducting. I'll rotate it back into place." The tech gently took her arm and nodded. "Okay, here we go." Lauren twisted to her left and rose on to her toes in one quick motion. Dropping back down her arm popped back into place with a resounding snap. Relief was instantaneous. "Better. Not great, but definitely better." She carefully shrugged her shoulder, testing the joint. It was back in place but she could feel how weak the tendons were, they may even be torn through. She knew she couldn't raise her arm above her waist.

Using her left hand, Lauren tucked her right hand into the belt of her kilt to take the weight off her shoulder joint. "All right, let's see to McGuiness."

Lady MacDonald stepped forward and blocked her path. "Your Majesty, we have one small thing to do to complete the Investiture. If you would come forward please, we will complete the ceremony.

"We don't have time for this. I need to see to that nerve."

"I understand, but this must be done," Lady MacDonald insisted.

"Dearheart, I understand your haste. However, if the Investiture is not completed properly, others could claim it never was done in the first place."

Lauren blew out a small breath and reluctantly followed Alex back to the altar. With Alex's help, she knelt carefully and bowed her head. Lady MacDonald picked up the coronet and placed it on top of the folded package Gríobhtha had carried into the circle. She turned to Alex and bowed. "Your Royal Majesty."

Alex picked up the coronet and placed it on Lauren's head, and then unwrapped the package. She lifted the folded material free of its silken wraps and shook out a red wool cape. The cape had a broad, white ermine fur collar, which was decorated with Lauren's badges of honor: twin loons for Alex's mother, the golden stag of Clan Fraser, the platinum crossed swords and orb of the right to rule, a caduceus in acknowledgment of her medical expertise, a fly rod in honor of her grandfather, and the tree bisected by a golden sword in recognition of the First Foremothers. Alex swept the cape over Lauren's kneeling form and gently settled it about her shoulders. She fastened it in place with a diamond brooch—a double helix held within the body of a nanite, in recognition of her cure for the children.

"Rise, your Royal Majesty, and take your rightful place beside me." Alex helped Lauren stand and adjusted the weight of the long cape off Lauren's right shoulder. Turning, Lauren and Alex bowed to the clans. Lauren struggled to remember the vow as the roar of the crowd enveloped them.

"From this day forth, I, Lauren Beckwith Fraser, will guide, encourage, steward, govern, and protect Terra and her satellite Luna, Terra Prime and her satellites, and all our Realms beyond. I will stand as our Queen's Protector and Guardian. I will protect and defend her against all enemies who arise from within or without. I will rule in a just manner and facilitate her Majesty's rule in all things, from this day forward and forever more."

Cheers rose from the crowd. The sound beat at the pair standing before the altar. Each of the clan chiefs bowed to them, and they returned the bow as one. The crowd roared, and the baritone of the trees grew louder. *"Alex, look."* Mind-voice was the only way to be heard over the din. Alex swung around in the direction of Lauren's tipped head. The crowns of the mighty sacred trees were bent in homage, bowing toward them. As the crowd started to notice the trees, they slowly fell silent in awe.

"As the children of the sacred grove on Terra Prime, we honor Her Royal Majesty, Consort to the Queen and Co-Ruler, Lauren Beckwith Fraser. As representatives of the First Foremothers, we recognize her rightful place beside Alexandra Aoeron Aonwyn and sanctify their bond."

The mind-voice of the trees projected outward through Terra Keep, around the planet Terra, and upward to be heard in Luna Keep.

"No one shall come between them. They are the rightful rulers of us all."

Chapter Sixteen

"How's he doing?" Lauren rounded the corner of the central nursing dais in the trauma unit. The trauma unit was a large white circular room. The outer circumference of the circle was divided into individual patient rooms, separated from the nursing dais by glass walls. A bank of monitors ringed this elevated work area. Indirect lighting highlighted the work area, leaving the patient area in a dim warm glow. She dropped into a chair in front of a health analyzer. Dipping her left hand into the gelled-surface, she pulled up Stewart McGuiness' chart. Her right arm was strapped tightly across her abdomen and totally useless, and it would be until the tendons healed. In the last two weeks, the bruise on her right cheek had morphed into a blotch of deep purple, shot through with red streaks, and her right eye was still swollen and only partially open.

The blue-robed healing technician turned toward her and frowned. "Physically, he is improving with each day, but he still refuses to speak. Today, he refused his physiotherapy. We are beginning to be concerned about his mental health."

"Yes, that's always a concern. Especially after trauma and major blood loss," she replied as she read through his medical data. "Do you have a feeling why he won't talk to anyone?"

"No. And we are worried when the feeding is stopped, he will also refuse food."

Lauren tipped back her chair and looked up at the circular lighting fixture, its burnished bronze tones contrasted sharply with the white ceiling. "Has his family been in to see him?"

"No, they have not. He is in exile from everyone." A soft guffaw brought all four legs of her chair back to the floor. The young healing tech shook his head. "You truly deserve your reputation as an epic healing technician. You always think of the whole person." He said ruefully. "Some of our technicians forget the most important point of healing is we treat a person not just a disease or injury."

"We'll see if that's true in this instance. Shall we see to our patient?"

"Is that a wise choice, Your Majesty?" The technician cautioned.

Lauren turned a confused look to the technician. "Why not? I'm his surgeon. Why shouldn't I see how he's doing?"

"It may be you are the source of his depression." Lauren saw the technician wince. "I am sorry, Your Majesty. That was inappropriate. I beg your pardon and ask forgiveness."

"Gavin." Lauren placed her hand on his narrow shoulder. "When I'm in the healing center, I'm Lauren, Doctor Beckwith, or Doctor Fraser. The most important thing is the patient and his recovery. Let's focus on that and not on a title. Okay?"

"Oh no, I could not do that Your Majesty. That would not be right." Gavin hung his head, "My clan chief would be most disappointed in me."

"Then, I'll have to have a word with your clan chief, won't I?" She squeezed his shoulder. "Let's go see our patient."

The room they entered was dark, the curtains drawn and the lights off. All Lauren could see from the door was a large lump in the bed. The technician activated the room lights, and a soft glow bloomed from wall scones. Lauren stood inside the door and waited as the Gavin moved to stand beside the large, tartan covered bed.

The lump grunted and rolled away from the door. "Stewart, Her Majesty is here to see you and examine your leg." Another grunt. Flipping on the over-the-bed lights, he scolded, "That is no way to greet your Royal Consort, Stewart."

A muffled growl was the only response. Gavin groaned and shrugged his shoulders. "This is how he has been since he woke from his surgery."

"Let's examine his leg. I want to check his peripheral nerve response in his foot and ankle." Lauren felt remorse for being the cause of his injury.

"Stewart, I am going to remove your cover so we can examine your leg." Gavin grasped the edge of the blanket and began to fold it back, exposing a bandaged thigh and hip.

Lauren stepped up to the bed and placed a gentle hand on Stewart's knee. "Can you roll onto your back for me? Please, Champion, I'm going to check your nerve function." Stewart kept the blanket over his head but complied and rolled over.

Her exam would test nerve response from the injury site in his groin to the peripheral nerves in his shin and foot. These nerves were critical for standing, walking, and running as they control the muscles from the thigh down to the tendons of the big toe. Lauren pulled a metal probe from her pocket. "Okay, Stewart, here we go. Let me know when you feel something."

She began to gently prod the nerve track along his inner and frontal thigh with the metal probe. She watched for any involuntary muscle reflex, and how he responded. His muscle was unresponsive as she tested peripherally down his thigh. Once she tested down to the knee, she looked at Gavin and shook her head. *Damn, he should have some feeling by now. The nerve was only partially severed. Some of the function should have been preserved as the repair healed. Maybe the swelling around the injury is impinging the nerve root.*

Moving to his foot, Lauren pulled the top off her probe, exposing a pin. She pricked his skin from the point of his big toe across the top of the foot to the top of his ankle. When she moved the pin to the bend of his foot and up his shin, he flinched.

"Do you feel that?" Lauren re-pricked the spot above the bend and again he flinched, as the muscles in the top of his foot bunched. "All right, we've got peripheral response in the infrapatellar branch of the saphenous nerve. Something's getting through the patellar plexus, but it could be innervation from the sciatic nerve."

She pulled a puffy, white eagle feather from her pocket and traced it down the outside of Stewart's thigh, the muscle bunched and goosebumps rose on his skin.

Gavin leaned forward. "The lateral femoral nerve is responding."

Lauren nodded absently, focused on Stewart's leg. She stroked the feather over the top of the thigh and watched the muscle shiver. Stimulation that moved from the lateral to the anterior side of his leg activated the thigh muscles, but stimulation from the groin down to the knee did not. Lauren placed the feather on the bedside table. Signaling Gavin, they stepped away from the bed.

She turned her back to the bed and whispered, "He's guarding." Gavin's eyebrows rose in confusion. "He knows or sees what we're doing, and he's controlling the muscles. Did you see the goosebumps?" Gavin nodded. "That indicates the sensory nerves to the skin are functioning. Those impulses are carried in the afferent nerve fibers on the outside of the nerve bundle and some were probably left intact with a partial injury. The efferent nerve fibers, those carrying impulses to and from the muscles, are within the nerve bundle, and were the ones severed in his injury. I'm going to try something different, but I can't do it myself with only one arm."

"How may I help, Your Majesty?" Gavin smiled gently at her.

"I need you to rub the feather over the lateral side of his thigh. Once we get the peripheral nerve response again and know the nerve is firing, I'm going to push down on the femoral nerve track below the repair. I want to see if we can override his conscious control and get a deep response. This is going to hurt him, probably a lot. So, expect him to recoil," Lauren looked into Gavin's soft blue eyes and knew he understood. She nodded and put a hand on his shoulder. "Thanks, Gavin. You're a great healing tech, and I appreciate your help."

"As you say, Your Majesty, no worries." They both smiled and turned back to complete their exam.

Lauren impinged Stewart's femoral nerve and he roared, rearing up, blankets flying. Lauren leaped away and avoided being hit in the head by a flying arm but Gavin wasn't as quick. He caught a knee under the chin and was thrown backward into the wall.

"Stop! That hurts!" Stewart commanded.

Lauren helped Gavin to his feet. "You okay?"

"Sorry, Your Majesty. I did not expect quite that large a reaction." He rubbed his chin and grinned up at her even as a bruise began to bloom on his skin. "At least you got him to talk."

"Yeah, we did, but at what cost?"

Laughing, he answered, "No cost is too great to pay if the patient improves."

"Once a healer, always a healer, I say." Lauren joined in his laughter.

"I am not healed. You should not be laughing." Stewart growled from his bed.

Lauren remembered Alex saying almost the same thing to her. “No, you aren’t healed. For that, you will need time and lots of work.”

He scowled back at her.

“Oh, no you don’t. We know you can talk, so we’re going to proceed with that.” She gave Stewart her ‘doctor knows best’ glare and tapped her foot on the floor, waiting.

“I do not want or need your help. You are the reason I am here.” He glowered again. “It should be you here in this bed or better, already on the funeral pyre.”

Gavin stepped up to the bedside and scolded. “You are out of line.”

“Have I not spoken the truth? She won the challenge with an illegal weapon. I am justified in my rebuke,” Stewart countered and crossed his arms over his massive chest.

“She is your healer and the one who saved your leg and your ability to walk.”

Stewart scoffed. “Our healers saved my leg.”

Gavin replied, “Our healers may have saved your life by repairing your femoral artery but Consort Lauren saved your leg and future mobility. Without her knowledge of nerve repairs and her quick surgical intervention, you would not have felt what we did, let alone be able to knee me in the chin.”

Stewart dropped back down onto his pillows, glaring at them.

“Your leg will heal, but it’s a slow process. You’ve got about three and a half years for full nerve regeneration. You have some function already. My best prescription is to begin physiotherapy now and maintain as much muscle mass as possible.”

“I will fight again?”

“Yes, Stewart, you will, but not without a lot of hard work. The new nerve fibers will need training.”

He frowned. “You called me Champion. I am not.”

Lauren knew where this was headed and she knew what she said would have a direct impact on his recovery. “You are and always will be Champion of the Terran People. You have not relinquished that title.”

Stewart turned a rueful gaze on Lauren. “No, you called me traitor.”

“I said if you lost you would be a traitor.” He huffed. “You didn’t lose. You forfeited. You stepped outside the central circle of stones. The Rules

Llewellyn are quite clear. Ours was a challenge to the death, and neither of us died. Both of us live, with some injuries, but we still live. Therefore, you are still Champion. No one would argue that."

Stewart didn't comment. His eyes lost focus, as he seemed to consider her explanation.

"Champion, my work is done here. It's all up to you and your therapists from here on. But I challenge you to another bout, not a bout to the death but a sparring session, where you can learn the advantages of a blade like mine. Do you accept?"

Lauren knew Alex would be pissed when she heard about this, but she couldn't think of another way to give Stewart a goal to focus on to get better. She still didn't know how Alex was going to punish the three clans who were complicit in the Hebridean treason, but she did know she had to put herself out there for her patient. And maybe she could shed some of her guilt at causing harm, at the same time.

"Your Majesty—" Lauren made a small hand gesture and silenced Gavin.

"You must have time to heal. Unless you are as accomplished with your left arm as you are with your right." Stewart nodded at her strapped arm and bruised face. "And I do not have a blade with which to fight."

"Nope, not ambidextrous. And you're right. I'll need time to heal as well. It will be months before this shoulder will be healed enough for me to lift my blade again. As to your blade, I suggest I replace your blade, with a blade like mine, a rapier. You will use this blade in your therapy." Stewart frowned and started to speak. Lauren silenced him with a raised hand. "No, as therapy for my shoulder, I will use a broadsword like yours." Lauren knew using a rapier and learning to lunge would be a great therapy technique for strengthening his injured leg. And she could use the weight of a broadsword to strengthen her shoulder.

Stewart reared back in his bed as if slapped. But then he paused, obviously thinking about her challenge and he smiled a sly smile. "Then perhaps we will meet in the therapy room, as each of us prepares for our next bout." Stewart reached out with his right hand and shook Lauren's left in agreement. "I look forward to showing you the proper use of a proper blade." Stewart paused and a small smile crossed his face as he winked at Gavin. "Your Majesty."

"She did what?" Merilyn shivered as Alex's anger skyrocketed when she explained what was being said around the healing wards.

"She challenged the Champion to another bout."

"Let me tell you, that is not going to happen. The next weapon he will face will be my broadsword. And he will feel its point all the way through to his spine."

Merilyn shook her head. "Do you not see what she did?"

"Oh, I see all right. She gave that overgrown, muscle-bound, thick-skulled traitor another chance," Alex raged on.

"No, she did not." Merilyn's tone sharpened while the volume of her voice decreased. "She gave her patient the incentive to get well and thrive. The healing technician who was with her in the room, said Stewart not only responded but now is improving daily and pushing himself and his therapists to the limit. They cannot keep him down long enough for the arterial-neural repairs to fully heal before he demands more of his rehabilitation."

"He and his clan are traitors and will be banished if I have anything to do with it."

"We do not know enough to bring those kinds of charges, Alexandra. All we know is they are complicit. The Council will hear each of the three clans' testimony, under psi-examination. And with this information, the Council will decide their guilt and associated punishments."

Lauren burst into Merilyn's rotunda. "What's going on in here? I felt your anger all the way in the far hay barn. My dragon is pissed and spewing flames."

Merilyn knew Alex was caught between concern for her soulmate and the reason of her Seneschal. This was not the time for hotheaded reaction. This was a time for patience. And if Merilyn were honest with herself, she had to admit how amazed she was at how Lauren saved the Champion from his depression by couching his defeat in terms of forfeit.

Merilyn felt their bond swell as Lauren sent a burst of love and warmth along it to quiet Alex's anger. Alex smiled down at her heart's other half, visibly relaxing as Merilyn felt their souls sing in unison.

"That's better." Lauren patted her side and turned toward Merilyn. "Now, what've you done to piss her off?"

"Alexandra must calm down and take a step back from the treason investigation. Allow Lord McLaran and his Black Guard to finish their work. Once all the evidence is collected, we will have Lord Newkirk and some of his strongest shield technicians perform a psi-examination on the guilty members identified from each of the three clans."

Lauren eased Alex over to the two chairs fronting Merilyn's large parchment-covered desk.

She gently pushed Alex down. "Sounds good. Any ideas on what you're going to learn?"

Merilyn was amazed at how easily Lauren could calm a situation by simply being herself. She turned a conflict away from the person and toward the problem. Lauren glanced again at Alex. Merilyn caught the conversation due the strength of Lauren's projection. *"You need to breathe, Dearest. Let someone else take the lead once in a while."*

"You are correct, and in this instance, I am going to step back and allow the Black Guards to finish up."

"I bet when it's completed, you'll find only a few of each clan were involved, for greed or power or position or whatever promises were made. I doubt the entire clan was aware of how their leaders were supporting Clan Cador's actions."

Alex growled at the mention of the traitor's clan name. *"We shall see. But we will try and minimize the damage to our society."*

"Let us do our jobs, Your Majesty," Merilyn interjected, giving up trying to reprimand them for their silent conversations. Perhaps we are all growing and changing.

"Lauren is such an amazing influence on us," Alex stated.

"Just doing my job as a doctor and a Consort."

The three smiled at each other, knowing another hurdle was topped. Now all they needed were the results of Lord McLaran's investigation.

Chapter Seventeen

Alex relaxed into her chair and snuggled deeper into her tartan. So far, the council meeting had lasted six hours, and they still were not done listening to the results of the Black Guard investigation. A break had been called, and she was left alone in the chamber. Not alone. She felt the other presence in the room. The tree had not been awake when the meeting started, but Alex felt its awareness grow as the meeting progressed. Now, it was pensive but obviously waiting to also hear the results of the investigation.

"We are making progress. It seems only the Stuart and Buchan Clans are actively involved in this treason. How deep it goes is not yet determined," Alex mused aloud.

A rumble filled the room. *Acknowledgement, perhaps?* Alex didn't know what it was, but she felt encouraged they were on the right track. A feeling of support filled her. The two clan chiefs and their subordinates were in psi-isolation, pending the results of the completed investigation and decisions of this Council. She was sure the Council would vote to permanently exile these groups, but one couldn't exile only the clan chief and not her family and their families, and so on. It was all so intertwined, much like an intricate spider web. Pull one strand and many others move as well. *Maybe it would be easier to exile the entire clan.*

"That will not aid you." A deep basso mind-voice jarred her from her thoughts.

Alex sat bolt upright and laid both hands flat on the tree's warm table-top. "How is that not going to help?"

"Our society would not survive a rift so great. The clans are interwoven. You cannot remove one entire clan without damaging all others. This would create tension and anger among those left behind. You must find a way to unite not divide."

"Easier said than done. How will we build trust again after we see how deep the treason goes? How will I trust again?"

"We thought healing the children would unite the clans. That was not enough. Then we thought the Investiture would complete the unification. That was not enough, either. Perhaps, the healing needs to start with you."

"With me?" Alex spluttered.

"Yes. You cannot build trust in others, if you are not trustworthy yourself."

"What the?" Alex's anger spiked and she stood from her chair, leaning over the vast table-tree. She visually traced the tree's growth rings, trying to control herself in the face of this challenge from this ancient entity. "How dare you accuse me of being untrustworthy." Her voice was almost as deep as the tree's, and it reverberated around the circular room. She was wounded by the tree's accusation.

"Think, Alexandra. You left this world to go to the enemy's homeworld without informing others. Your actions were based on a noble quest, but it was done in an underhanded and secretive manner. You admit even your own companions were angry."

Alex sat back down with a thump. Her anger bled away. But her people had needed her. Needed those data. Without the data there would not have been a cure, and the children would have died. She had to do what she did.

"And you brought an alien back with you. One with whom you claim to have a bond."

"But—" Alex felt whiplashed as the great tree forced her to reconsider actions she thought justified.

"You and she are what you say you are. The Consort did heal the children allaying the fears of most. But you are asking a lot on faith alone. In fact, you never asked, you decreed." The tree paused as if to gather their thoughts. *"Some do not understand or recognize your bond. Some are afraid of it. They worry Lauren could use it as a tool to influence and undermine our world and you from within. Is she an enemy spy?"*

"But . . . Lauren is not . . ." Alex's emotions roiled at these accusations. She was becoming more distraught as the tree continued.

"Lauren has not touched all Terrans as she has touched you, and us. There are those who see this uncertainty as an opportunity to exploit people's fear to further themselves. To get their propaganda listened to and

believed in. Others simply like to gossip, and then distort it in their own way, for their own gain."

"Lauren would never—" Alex had to defend her Love.

The tree rumbled.

"Do not laugh at me," Alex admonished.

"We are not laughing. We are amused you only now realize what we say." The tree's mind-voice became stern. *"You must consider your own actions, Alexandra. You precipitated a physical confrontation in a Council meeting that resulted in bloodshed. This has not happened since before the last Age of Tribulation."*

"But I . . ." Alex sagged down into her chair and pulled her tartan more closely around her shoulders. She was thrown completely off balance, but she squared her shoulders and stood to face her accusers. *Or were they accusing?* It seemed they were intervening to help her once again.

"You face the same challenges the First Foremothers struggled with. This is why they kept the true nature of their bond hidden. Perhaps it was a mistake to hide a gift so great. Neither of you realize the impact of your actions. You are natural leaders, you and the Doouglas, but your way is not always the right way. Trust others, and lead by consensus not by decree. Let others lead when needed. You do this with the Consort. Her ways are different from your own."

Alex rocked back on her heels and shook her head as if struck. The tree had shaken her to her core. Challenging all she believed in, challenging all she was. She paused and let her anger fall. *Or did they? What is the tree asking of me? What is the tree saying?*

"We are not asking you for anything you do not already have. Think long and hard on this. Watch and learn from your Consort. She is your counterpoint."

"I know that! She is not I." Embarrassed, Alex's anger took hold of her once more.

"No, she is not. Look how she managed the Champion." The tree rumbled again, this time in a rueful tone. *"Even we could not have done better in that situation. She is clever."*

Alex had to agree. "But as she says, she is just Lauren."

"Perhaps, but wiser than you."

This stopped Alex cold. "What did you say?"

"Put your ego aside, Alexandra, it is unbecoming to always be right." The tree paused before continuing more quietly. *"Use the resources around you. Let others shine with your support. Let others show how trustworthy you are through the trust you place in them."*

That admonishment stunned Alex into silence, and in truth she felt like a wayward child being reprimanded by her tutor. But what the tree said made some sense. *What did Lauren say about the philosopher from her reality? Ah yes, 'the whole is greater than the sum of the parts.'*

"She is wise beyond her years. Think on what we have said, Your Majesty. Let your Consort lead."

When Lauren reentered the Council room for the remainder of the meeting, she found Alex still sitting where she'd left her. Leaning down, she kissed Alex on the temple. "Hi, Dearest. I missed you at dinner."

Alex didn't respond, so Lauren leaned over her shoulder to see her eyes. "You okay?" Lauren also sent a query along their bond, but she hit an unusual wall. *Is Alex blocking me? What's up with that?*

"Hey, Alex." She placed a firm hand on her soulmate's shoulder and leaned farther over. Now Lauren view of Alex was skewed by her upside-down position with her head hanging over Alex's broad tartan-covered shoulder. "What's going on? All we did was have something to eat. You gotta admit six hours is a long time to go without food. As hungry as I was, you must be starving. Shall I have Merilyn's steward bring something in for you?"

Slowly, Alex blinked her eyes, as if waking from a trance, and a slow smile spread across her face. "Dearheart, I hear you and would never block you in anyway. I was lost deep in my thoughts. I am sorry I did not respond. And I am not hungry."

"What had you so lost in thought you didn't hear me?"

"I heard you, but I needed to finish sorting my thoughts. The tree gave me much to think about."

Puzzled, Lauren asked, "The tree?"

"Aye, the tree. Seems they are not happy with how I have been leading Terra." Alex frowned. "And after thinking about what they shared, I would have to agree. I have not been the best leader I could be."

"How's that? You're a great leader." Lauren frowned and searched Alex's sapphire eyes. "You always think of others and what's best for Terra. You balance problems and reach the best solution. You don't favor the individual over the needs of the group."

Alex laughed and pulled Lauren around into her lap. "That may be true, but I do not ask for the input of others in making those decisions. And you must admit I do have a temper."

"A temper? I don't know. Sometimes you gotta do what you gotta do." Lauren paused, recognizing she was trying to soothe Alex's feelings. She felt a burst of uncertainty and self-doubt creep across Alex's psyche.

Lauren placed a gentle hand on Alex's cheek, she searched her soul for the source of her discord. "What's causing this self-recrimination? You're usually comfortable in your leadership, and in yourself. What'd the tree say that has you so upset?"

Alex leaned into her palm and smiled. "The tree said that to build trust, I must be trustworthy myself. That my recent actions indicate I am not trustworthy, and that we need to unite the clans, not divide them."

"What's that supposed to mean?" Lauren's anger flared as she questioned the trees' veracity.

"Seems I need to follow your lead. Learn to use consensus in decision-making. You are better than I am at that."

Lauren dropped her hand and cuddled deeper into Alex's arms. She smiled. "Not better, Dearest. Maybe different, is all. Everyone comes at problems from a different angle. Their solutions are created from current needs as well as their own life experiences. No two people have the same experiences, so of course their solutions will be different." Lauren leaned back. "So, different, not better or worse. It's not a contest."

"When did you become such a diplomat?" Alex asked with a small smile.

"Oh, I don't know. When I became Co-Ruler with the Queen maybe?" They both laughed. "You gotta admit that's jumping into the deep end of the pool without floaties." Lauren watched as various expressions raced across Alex's face and felt different emotions trace along their bond. She knew what Alex's next question was going to be and it didn't have anything to do with her uncertainties. "And don't ask. I'll tell you what they are later. Right now, your Consort says you need to eat something or we'll never hear the rest of Lord McLaran report over the sound of your growling stomach."

Chapter Eighteen

Lauren knew Alex wasn't comfortable with all the tree had said to her. She felt her unease and distraction. *Maybe I can take some of the pressure off her?* The meeting droned on. Darkness had settled over the Keep long hours ago. McLaran's report was incredibly detailed, almost a verbatim recounting of the interrogations. Lauren settled back in her chair and rubbed her nose. *Why?*

Still lost in her thoughts, she missed his last comments, but she felt Alex stiffen in the chair next to her. Refocusing on the meeting, she realized McLaran had moved on to yet another interrogation summary of yet another clan member. He had paused to take a drink of water and organize his notes for the next part of his report. *I wonder?*

Lauren spoke up. "M'lord, would you give us a summary of all your interrogations, please?"

"A summary?"

"Yes, a summary of your impressions. I'm sure you've developed impressions after completing all these interrogations. Is there a common thread with each person interviewed? Is there one theme or central idea the clan leaders are trying to force on others? In fact, are there leaders and followers?"

Lauren could see she caught McLaran off guard with her questions. He blinked at her in confusion, but she had to find a way to move the meeting along. She strongly suspected this enormous amount of detailed information was being reported because he felt Alex would need it to make an informed decision. Alex's decision, not McLaran's or the Council's.

McLaran shuffled his feet. Out of the corner of her eye Lauren saw Alex nod ever so slightly. He stood for long minutes, clearly reordering, and rethinking his report. Then he cleared his throat. "Yes, Your Majesty, I can give a summary."

"Very well." Lauren swept an open hand outward. "Please. I'd like to hear it, and I'm sure the Council would too." The other Councilors gathered around the table let out a collective sigh and relaxed back in their chairs. Lauren felt Alex's hand rest lightly on her thigh and squeeze. No one else could see the gesture as it was beneath the table, but she felt a jolt of thanks in her touch.

"After interrogating two-hundred and seventy-four members of Clans Stuart, Buchan, and Campbell." McLaran glanced at the three empty sides of the great tree-table and his frown deepened. "It seems few are actively involved in any collusion with Clan Cador."

Alex's arm stiffened and her grip on Lauren's thigh tightened at the mention of Cador.

"Easy, Dearest. Let him continue." Lauren placed her hand on top of Alex's.

"In fact, I would say only nine clan members are fully involved. The rest are unknowing accomplices or dimwitted dupes." A small gasp went around the table. Lauren noticed several clan chiefs leaned forward, again actively listening to McLaran.

McLaran waited for Lauren to nod before he continued. "Did the accomplices actually not know what was going on?"

"Almost to a one, Consort. The plot seems to have been compartmentalized. Each part directed by an individual, who knew only his part of the plan and to whom he reported. The minions below this individual knew nothing of the plan at all and had only one task or duty to perform. In most instances, these tasks were normal parts of their everyday duties and not questioned when they were asked to perform them at a specific time or in a specific way." A deep line of worry creased his brow. "The entire plan was well conceived, and it does seem to reach far back into our past." He hung his head. "I would have to say Your Majesty was correct."

Everyone at the table turned en masse to stare at Lauren, as if waiting for her to clarify what she was right about. Lauren sat straighter in her chair and placed both hands on the tree-table. "Excuse me, M'lord. I don't understand."

McLaran raised his head and looked her straight in the eye. "Perhaps it was the result of your recent and thorough studies of Terran history. Or maybe your summary matrices helped you see central themes running through our history?"

Lauren could feel Alex's confusion streak along their bond. *"What is he getting at?"*

She was as confused. *"I haven't a clue."*

Lord McLaran stood tall and drew a deep breath. "This is a plot of treason." This time, the collective gasp was louder. "And it is a plot set in place before our First Foremothers united the clans and established this Council. Our Consort recognized this and pointed it out in our last council meeting. Her Majesty said the discord we are now experiencing was set in motion at the time of the First Foremothers, and our investigation proves her correct." Lauren fell back in her chair shocked by his revelation, but Alex stiffened and leaned forward.

The clans seemed stunned into silence, but McLaran filled the silence. "It seems a plot was initiated by Clan Cador millennia ago, and we are simply pawns. Their plot was designed to eradicate Clans Fraser and Doouglas and take over the rule of Terra Prime. And they almost succeeded."

The clan chiefs suddenly spoke up at once, shouting over each other and arguing with McLaran that such a plot was impossible. They were incredulous a plot, if it existed, could be set in motion so long ago but only now be acted upon. That they could be duped in such a way.

"Clan Fraser had only one surviving representative, the Seneschal," McLaran shouted to be heard and he pointed at Merilyn. "Had she not adopted Lauren and this adoption been recognized by Terra, Clan Fraser would have ended with her death. Clan Stuart, at the instruction of Clan Cador, coerced Clan Campbell to put the Champion up as the Challenger. Had he killed Her Royal Majesty Lauren Beckwith Fraser, again Clan Fraser would have ceased to exist with the Seneschal's death. Clan Campbell knew nothing of the Cador plot and agreed to this nomination due to the comments the Champion himself made about the Consort's unconventional blade and how its use was an affront to our traditions. They were unknowing dupes, trying only to preserve our ways. Their only crimes were inflexibility and their unwillingness to recognize all cultures must change and grow to survive."

An enormous feeling of dread grew within the room as McLaran outlined what he had pieced together from his interrogations. "Since the Consort and Her Majesty are bound by a bond of such enormous strength, Clan Cador knew if Lauren was killed, Alexandra would have followed her in death. Clan Doouglas would be without a chief, and Terra would be without a ruler. Fortunately, the Consort won her challenge, protecting the future of Clans Fraser and Doouglas. Again, Lauren Beckwith Fraser is our Savior." McLaran swept a deep bow to her, and then the other chiefs rose one by one and did the same. Shock and grief etched their faces with this information but they gave Lauren her due.

She rose and acknowledged their bows. "No, M'lords. I didn't recognize this plot. Granted there were hints in the Foremothers journals, but I simply did what my heart and soul said I must." Lauren knew no one listened to her words.

"Further, I believe even Clan Cador is a pawn to this immense plot, for they were only acting on directives left for them by their ancestors." He paused and shook his head. "The plot was not to be initiated until such time as one of the clans was weakened, or a Doouglas was not chosen as the next leader." McLaran wiped his brow and again nodded at Lauren. "When Gwenhwyfach realized Clan Fraser had only one surviving representative, she activated the plot. What she did not know was that Alexandra would act alone to retrieve the bio-weapon data from the Comin homeworld, and no one could have predicted an alien would arrive in this reality, heal her, and then heal the children."

Lauren grimaced at his reference to her as an alien.

McLaran shook his head yet again. "We are all incredibly fortunate these disparate events happened. For without these fortuitous actions, this Council would have been disbanded, and a traitor would now be ruler of Terra."

McLaran bowed again to Lauren and Alex. "I have nothing else to report, Your Majesties. All I can say is Clan Campbell is innocent of treason and should not be punished. Clan Buchan's chief and his two subordinates are complicit in this plot in so much as they acted as agents for Clan Stuart. They had to know what they were doing was wrong and know they were participating in a plot to overthrow our Council. Clan Stuart is as guilty as Clan Cador as they were the primary agents to complete the plot, once the chief of Clan Cador was exiled and the remaining clan placed under house-arrest."

He shrugged his shoulders and frowned deeply, and gave his final conclusion. “But none of this would have happened had Clan Chief Robert Bruce Cador not failed to take over Clan Doouglas when he assassinated Atair Doouglas.” The Council members recoiled in shock from this pronouncement. “Robert Bruce Cador did not believe Clan Doouglas would elect a woman chief following Atair’s death. They did, though, and Clan Doouglas has been ruled by a woman ever since.”

A small smile softened his stern features. “As has Terra, as our line of Foremothers illustrates. We would have been doomed on Terra Prime and her satellites had not three of our Foremothers acted as they had and two of them died from their brave acts to protect and save as many Terran citizens as they did.”

Lauren had suspected some plot or other was behind Atair Doouglas’ death, but she knew from reading the journals assassination was a common practice during that time on Terra Prime. The Doouglas could never prove who killed her father, or even if it was nothing more than an accident, and therefore, she never took direct action against Clan Cador in her time. But in her heart, the Doouglas did know her father was murdered, and his death haunted her. As the Cador plot haunted Lauren and the Terrans now.

From the Journal of the Doouglas

It has been proven. My *Eponá* was sabotaged by one of the technicians at the Space Port. Packets of sodium azide were placed around the strut brackets of her stabilizer fins. It took Father this long to determine the guilty party because he had only paper trails to follow. My recovery was a long and arduous journey, and he chose to focus on that instead of on the wreckage.

However, he was able to trace the sale and purchase of the chemical and the unique material used to construct the packets once we received samples of these materials from the fins.

Shamus Cador was the technician who placed the packets within the *Eponá*. We have vid-documentation of his working on the fins of my ship from the Space Port authorities. We have sales receipts from the various suppliers of his purchase of the chemical and the fabrics. We also have microscopic evidence. Fibers of tartan were recovered from the framework bolt heads within the hatchway to the fin brackets. Cador had no reason to access that entry hatch nor be anywhere near the *Eponá*. He was only assigned to work on his clan's ships on the other side of the port.

Although, this evidence could be seen as circumstantial, Father will present his case to the other clan chiefs. Then, he will recommend exile.

From the Journal of the Fraser

My Doouglas' sire presented his case for exile of Clan Cador this day at the solstice clan gathering. He received mixed responses. However, the majority of the chiefs agreed with his recommendation, and Clan Cador has been exiled back to the Hebrides, on our satellite Cailleach Bhéarach. The exile is to last for twenty rotations.

Although I agree with this punishment and am pleased to see the clans working together, I worry this will begin a cycle of retribution between these two powerful groups. This potential feud could have ramifications for years to come. The Doouglas and I have spoken often on how to stop the ongoing feuds. Terra is stronger united than divided. But time will tell what this latest tragedy will cause. However, we now focus on continuing our effort to bring the Clans together and setting Terra Prime on a path of unity. We hope to build a Council of clan chiefs to govern Terra Prime and her satellites together.

Lauren's shock slowly wore off and her mind raced to integrate all McLaran had reported with what should be done next. Lauren felt Alex's resolve harden. She placed her hand on top of Alex's forearm where it rested on her chair. *"Take a deep breath, Dearest. This is a tremendous shock to everyone. What is done next will impact the entirety of Terra and her future."*

"I know, but something must be done. We cannot punish someone who has been dead for millennia. And most of Clan Cador are innocent. They are oblivious of the machinations of their chief."

"True. Perhaps, McLaran has a feel for how many of Cador knew or participated?"

Alex nodded at her Consort and spoke for the first time since McLaran concluded his remarks. "M'lord, do you know how deep the conspiracy goes within Clan Cador?"

McLaran took a small step back, reluctant to answer. Lauren asked another question to give him time to think about Alex's question. "If the plan was compartmentalized and kept from the other clans who were co-conspirators, was it also compartmentalized within Clan Cador?"

"Yes, it was, only a few of Clan Cador were privy to the plan. Though, it does go deeper there than in the other clans. We have identified thirty-one individuals within Clan Cador who are directly involved, but only four who knew of the entire plan. At the onset, only the chief knew the entire plan. However, once she was exposed in the council meeting and exiled, she had to pass on her knowledge of the plan and give over control of its execution to others."

Lauren rubbed her nose. "You've identified the conspirators?"

McLaran nodded.

"Therefore, we can take action against those involved?" Again, he nodded. Lauren turned to Alex. "What do you think, Your Majesty? Given what Lord McLaran has discovered, can the Council define the steps needed to protect Terra and our clans?"

Alex sat quietly with a far-off look on her face. McLaran began to speak but Lauren shook her head. She felt the councilors' pensiveness rise as they waited for Alex to make a decision. But Alex surprised them. She didn't decide. She made a recommendation instead.

"First, I wish to thank McLaran and his Black Guards for their efforts. The report was thorough and provided us with the information this Council needs to develop a plan of action. My gratitude goes also to Lord Newkirk and his psi-engineers." She nodded at the Newkirk clan. "We recognize how difficult it is to conduct these examinations, how tiring, and how dangerous it can be for the examiner when the defendant is blocking their efforts. Their work provided the facts McLaran used to identify those to investigate further."

Lauren remembered what Alex had shared about the tree's concerns. *Could she start now, with something so important to the future of Terra?* Lauren sent a burst of encouragement along their bond. She felt Alex struggle against her instincts. Instincts which told her to act, but Alex pushed those down. *Come on Alex, you can do this.*

Alex purposely looked at each clan chief in turn. "We are at a crossroad, Councilors. One not seen in many generations. What we decide today will impact our society and set the course for our future. So, I ask each of you to carefully consider what you have heard as we move toward a decision on how to proceed."

Silence reigned in the Council Room. "What are you saying, Your Majesty? I do not understand," Lady MacDonald asked quietly.

Alex smiled, and Lauren realized Alex was trying to get the Council's buy-in. Hopefully, she would be able to get everyone to participate in the decision process and not abdicate the decision to her.

"I think Her Majesty is giving us the latitude to determine how we proceed," Hamish McLeod answered. "I believe we should create a plan which will allow us to punish the conspirators, but also allow us to educate all of Terra about what has happened and explain why we did what we did."

"Well said, McLeod. I suggest once we decide on a course of action, we consider presenting our plan to Terra and allowing the populace to have a say, prior to punishments," Lady MacDonald said. Alex sat back and tried to relax as the discussion swirled around her.

"How will that work? We have no process to allow Terra to weigh in on a matter the Council is considering," Chief Graham questioned.

"But we do, M'lord," Lauren said. "We instruct the Herald to give the news and then we have you." She pointed at the chief.

"Excuse me?"

Lauren saw confusion on more than one face but a few were beginning to understand.

Alex smiled and interjected. "Let our Consort explain." And she turned to Lauren encouragingly.

"You, M'lord. Each of you and your clans. Each of the clans has ways to communicate directly with their members. Use that ability to quickly spread information through your clan. Use your family. As I understand it, Terran word-of-mouth is fast. I've experienced the speed of that communication system myself." A chuckle rolled around the table. "If we augment that with a general information blast through the analyzer network, we should be able to keep the news consistent and not allow it to morph as it spreads. We wouldn't want to play a game of telephone about something as important as this."

Everyone turned to her. *"What'd I say?"* Lauren asked Alex through their bond as she saw all the questioning looks.

"I think you used another alien term, Lauren. You had them until you mentioned a game and a tele-something," Ice interjected.

Lauren understood her mistake, "Sorry, everyone. I recommend we share the plan in its final form, in a format which everyone can read firsthand, because word-of-mouth can change shared information as it spreads. I believe we want a consistent, concise message."

"Well stated, Consort. I agree." McLaran sat down and relaxed back into his chair.

"All right, if everyone is in agreement, let us develop our plan and move forward." Alex again stepped into her leadership role.

It didn't take long for the Council to reach consensus on the next steps. Lauren watched as Alex led the meeting but didn't dictate her demands. Everyone had a voice and if someone didn't speak up, she or Alex solicited input from that person. She was so proud of Alex, knowing how difficult it was for her not to act immediately when she saw a need.

The Council decided those directly complicit with the Cador plot would face exile without possibility of parole. Those who acted, whether with prior knowledge or not, and whether their actions caused harm or not, would face censor and be banned from a voice on the Council.

Of the two-hundred and seventy-four investigated, the Council decided Clan Chief Stuart and his two subordinates would be exiled. They would join the leaders of Clan Cador and be isolated on individual islands within the western ocean archipelagos.

The Council also decided to recommend censor against Clan Chief Buchan and his two subordinates. The Council would ask Terra to decide on the length of punishment, with the stipulation they would not be allowed to hold a leadership position again, nor would the Council recognize them in the future.

The names of the remaining two-hundred and sixty-five clan members interviewed by the Black Guards would be published, as would the complete transcripts of those interviews. Each clan would then be allowed to make their own decision about next steps, punishment or not, on those within their clan who were deemed complicit. It was hoped with full disclosure of this information and the recording of this information in the histories of Terra, future generations would learn a valuable lesson and hopefully not err as their ancestors had.

Lauren was pleased with the decisions. *"What do you think, Dearest?"*

"I feel, we are poised on the precipice of great things to come. This Council will rule together, and we will be able to achieve everything we want and need."

Lauren's heart sang with hope for their future at Alex's answer.

Part Two

Mt. Zirkel Wilderness, Routt County, Colorado, Earth

Not only is the Universe stranger than we think, it is stranger than we can think.

~Werner Heisenberg

Chapter One

Jamie Gilchrist, Lauren's co-worker from GeoDynamics, stood on the icy shore of a small alpine lake and watched the rising sun glint off the partially frozen surface. A light morning breeze ruffled his long blonde hair. The day dawned surprisingly warm for this altitude and this early in the spring. He still couldn't believe it had been over a year since he last saw Lauren. A year of searching. A year of sadness and disappointment. A year of heartbreak. A year now over. He knew he had to face the fact—Lauren really was gone.

They were back at the site of Lauren's disappearance to honor her memory and formally stop their search. He had a pair of gray outer gloves in his hand, their red draw strings swinging gently in the breeze. *How is this all we've found? All we have left of the vibrant, intelligent, amazing woman?* Turning away from the sun, he gave his friends a small smile. "I guess this is it?"

The wan smiles he got in return seemed tainted. Doctor Susan Stanley, her large muscular frame diminished with grief, knelt in the snow, her arms around a small black, tan, and white Pembroke Welsh Corgi, her face buried in his neck. Her tears were lost in his coarse outer fur. Boscoe had been their best searcher. He was the one who found the gloves Jamie held. A lucky find. Had they not been frozen into the surface of the lake ice, they would have been lost in the storm. And they were the only clue Lauren had come and gone. Well, that and the fact the monitoring station was up and running. Once Bosco found the gloves, he led them off to the northern cliff and its caves, but they didn't find anything else.

Jamie knew Lauren was a well-trained survivalist. She would seek shelter, especially with the blizzard. The caves were an ideal place to wait out the storm. The blizzard had kept Jamie pinned down for four days in their base camp outside the basin. He was able to call for a search party and notify Susan and Sharon that Lauren was missing.

Sharon Frasier was a different story. He knew that the diminutive redhead would never give up. She was angry at them for having this memorial. *Was that what this was? A memorial? Permission for them to stop searching without guilt? Closure?* No, it wasn't closure and Sharon knew it. She was adamant about not having this memorial and was here under protest. She only came to support her partner, Susan. In his heart, he knew she would search until her last day. Sharon carried an additional guilt neither Jamie nor Susan could dissuade. Sharon had shamed Lauren and ridiculed her work when they were last together. Now, she constantly worried her words forced Lauren push past safety to ensure the monitoring stations would gather the best data. That she drove Lauren into the storm, and it was her fault Lauren had vanished.

Jamie knew this wasn't the case. Sure, Lauren had a Type-A personality and she was a perfectionist to boot, but they had talked of her rising concerns about GeoDynamics and the conflicts between her personal ethics and the corporate values of the company. Sharon's words hadn't helped, given Lauren's existing inner turmoil about the Zirkel project and the direction her professional future was headed, but Lauren would have set that last station regardless. Lauren's science came before anything else. She would never compromise her project for a little snow. But it wasn't just a little snow. That blizzard broke records in the Yampa Valley. Northwestern Colorado was buried under six feet of snow in three days, with winds building drifts more than seventeen feet high in places.

Once the storm abated, crews got snow machines up Tree House Road to Jamie's base camp, then the search began. More than fifty people searched over the last fourteen months, regardless of the weather. The search party was a combination of US Forest Service personnel, Sharon's Steamboat Heritage staff, and Susan's friends from her veterinarian practice.

Sadly, no one from GeoDynamics participated. All the CEO was concerned about was how much a work-related, wrongful death would cost him. When Jamie had informed Peter Lauren was lost, Peter informed him no death benefits would be paid unless a body was recovered. If they never found her, the estate would have to wait for the missing person statutes to expire before payout. Jamie quit his job on the spot. He then spent the next fourteen months organizing search resources, coordinating the management of Lauren's estate, and grieving. Now the time had come to celebrate his friend and co-worker's life.

Lauren's parents weren't much better than GeoDynamics. All they wanted was Lauren declared dead, her will read, and all her assets transferred to them. Lauren was estranged from her parents and hadn't spoken to them in over ten years prior to her disappearance, so their attitude didn't surprise him much. Jamie worked with Lauren's attorneys to keep her parents at arm's length. In this instance, the seven-year statute for missing persons worked in their favor, with a defined legal procedure for declaring her deceased, and then initiating the disbursement of her estate. This allowed Jamie to put her parents off. His only requirement was to keep the courts informed on a regular basis. Once the three of them declared the search over, the seven-year clock on the missing person's statute would begin.

At this moment, all that seemed far away and completely ridiculous. This moment was for Jamie, Susan, Sharon, and even Boscoe. He smiled down at the little corgi who seemed to realize the significance of this moment, too. The dog whiffled and nodded. All right then. Time to be about this.

"We come to this place, at this time, to remember Doctor Lauren Beckwith. To acknowledge her tireless efforts to preserve our planet. To share our relationships with her as a doctor, a scientist, a human being, and a gracious and loving soul. To recognize her as our friend. To celebrate her life." Tears now flowed in a steady stream down his cheeks and threatened to close his throat.

"This place is where we lost her. She was doing what she loved best and believed in most. Trying to determine how corporate actions were impacting and destroying the world we live in. Actions that were actively damaging this fragile and pristine wildness around us." He waved his hand, indicating the towering granite arêtes standing guard over the fir and aspen treed basin. "We know from the data collected in this study she was correct. Airborne pollution from the coal-fired power-generation plants to the west was causing acid snow. Her data were used to halt the construction of new power plants. Her data are being used to force Colorado Power and Electric Company to convert the existing plants from burning coal to natural gas usage, eliminating dirty emissions." He smiled at Sharon. "The Sierra Club and Steamboat Heritage are now taking steps to prepare an application for UNESCO. In that application, they will request the entire eastern Yampa Valley be declared a World Heritage landmark site to preserve and protect this area for all time and for all future generations."

Susan's sobs interrupted his words, and he knelt beside her, placing a hand on her shoulder. "Do you want to say something?"

"I don't know what to say." Susan raised her tear-streaked face to the rising sun. "Lauren was special. We'd go months without hearing from her, as she jetted around the world doing her science, but I know if we ever needed her, she would always be there." Susan hiccupped and gathered herself. "When we met, we were in a pickle, in the middle of nowhere in the outback of Australia. Sharon was hurt and I couldn't manage her and all our gear alone. I knew our water wouldn't last. Then along comes this redheaded dynamo. She took charge. Loaded all our gear into her backpack, treated Sharon's injury as best she could with our combined medical supplies, carried all our stuff, and helped me carry Sharon back to the car park." A small smile crept across Susan's face at the memories.

Jamie squeezed her shoulder.

Sharon spoke up. "I know I'm a klutz, but that isn't the best story I have about Lauren."

This was exactly what Jamie wanted when he suggested they come to the Zirkels. He wanted Lauren's closest friends to come together and remember the fun times they had with her. Try and put some distance between them and the trials of an endless search. Sharon shared her story about Lauren, the rainbow trout, and the moose.

Jamie jumped in with a story about Lauren trying to buy panty hose for the male members of one of their expedition teams. "In the jungle, the only place to collect our samples is from the streambeds. There, the running water erodes the deep jungle soils down to bedrock and we can walk through the stream to collect our rock samples, but leeches live in the streams of most jungles. So, to keep the leeches from latching on, we would wear panty hose." Sharon and Susan laughed. "One of our team members was a weight lifter and over six and a half feet tall. Lauren had to explain to the shop owner in Manaus, Brazil, what size she needed.

Her broken Portuguese left a lot to be misinterpreted." Jamie shook his head at the memory. "I'm sure by the time we got out of the shop, the owner was convinced all Americans had kinky sex lives, but Lauren got our hose and no one suffered leeches on that trip."

Susan started to tell another story about a shopping trip, this one in New York City, when Boscoe growled low and deep. His hackles rose, and he spun out of Susan's grasp. Before the three could react, he was off across the snow toward the surrounding tree line.

"What the . . ." Jamie exclaimed. Susan jumped up and sprinted after the small dog.

"Come on! We've got to catch him, or we'll be out here searching for someone else." Sharon and Jamie took off after Susan.

Boscoe led them on a chase through the trees and out into the central part of the basin. He cleared a herd of elk out of his way, and headed to the granite wall.

"Where is that dog going?" Jamie panted.

Sharon stumbled in the thick snow, and Jamie helped her up. She glared at the dog's retreating behind. "I haven't a clue, but when I catch him, he's toast."

It took about three hours to catch the little corgi. They didn't so much as catch him as found him sitting near one of the cave entrances. He seemed to be waiting, but for what or whom, they couldn't figure out. Regardless, by that time, all four were exhausted.

"All right, Boscoe, you've had your fun. It'll be getting dark soon and we need to head back to the truck." Susan scooped the dog up in her arms. He tried to wiggle loose, barking his head off as they walked away from the granite wall, back toward the southern rim of the basin.

"I wonder what got him so excited?" Jamie couldn't see, or hear anything in the area around them, except for the large elk herd settling back into the center of the basin to forage on early grasses. Boscoe had stopped before one of the empty caves they searched early in their efforts to find Lauren.

As they made their way back the trailhead, Sharon stopped suddenly. "Look at these." Her whisper rang loud in the still, early spring air.

Jamie and Susan stooped to investigate at the line of tracks Sharon pointed to in the snow. "These aren't our tracks. There are too many.

These dog prints—they're huge." Jamie pointed at two parallel lines of canine tracks.

"Are those horse prints?" Sharon asked and Susan moved over see what else she'd found.

"Whoa, if they are, those are the largest hoof prints I've ever seen." Susan turned to Jamie, sadness coloring her voice. "Did the Forest Service say there would be others here today? I thought we had the basin to ourselves for our memorial."

Jamie scratched his chin. "They did. I mean, we were supposed to be alone." He bent down beside her. "All they asked was we call them when we got back to Clark on our way back to Steamboat. I haven't a clue what all this is." He pointed forward along the long line of prints, horse and canine.

"Is that a boot print?" Susan pointed off to the side. Jamie walked over to the marks she indicated.

Sharon joined them and crouched down. She placed her small hand in the indentation. "About a size ten, maybe a little bigger."

Jamie saw another. "That one's bigger yet. These aren't very old. The edges are still sharp and well defined. They had to be made today. Let's head back to the truck. We can report this when we call the Forest Service."

The trio, with Boscoe now on his retractable leash, made their way to the trailhead leading out of the basin. At the top of the ridge, Jamie stopped and turned to northeast toward the granite peaks. He walked a couple of paces off the trail to the edge of the ridgeline and dug a shallow hole in the soft earth. He placed the pair of over-gloves in the hole and covered them in dirt. Susan and Sharon stood on the trail, watching as he completed his small memorial.

Building a cairn of rocks over the small mound of loose dirt, he said, "I know we aren't supposed to do this, but I think Lauren would want her gloves. Wherever she is, she might need them." Standing back up, he walked over and rejoined his friends on the trail. All three had tears running down their faces.

The small group arrived in Clark as the sun was setting behind the western hills of the Elk River valley. Susan pulled the truck into the parking lot of the General Store, and Jamie hopped out. "I'll give the rangers a call."

"What flavor do you want this time? Butter pecan?" Susan asked as she lifted Boscoe from the backseat of the cab.

"That'd be great, thanks." He smiled. They were getting to know each other.

"Again? Don't you want to try something else? Butter pecan is boring when they have local wild blueberry and blackberry," Sharon said.

"Nope, butter pecan. But two scoops this time, please." Jamie dialed the ranger station number on his mobile.

"Hahn's Peak Ranger Station, Glasgow speaking." A voice answered his call.

"Hey, Ben, it's Jamie Gilchrist. We're back in Clark."

"Jamie, good to hear you're back. You had some great weather."

Jamie smiled faded. "Yeah, the weather was nice for this time of year. No wind. Not a cloud in the sky."

"Are you headed to the 'Boat or staying in Clark?"

"We'll head back to Susan and Sharon's. I've got an appointment in Denver tomorrow, and I need to get an early start from there."

"Sounds good. Glad it all went well today."

Jamie hesitated. *Did it go well?* He wasn't sure if well was the proper descriptor, but it went. "Yeah, it was nice. By the way, Ben, we saw a line of tracks on our way out. Some folks were up there with horses and some pretty big dogs. Do you have any permits issued for the basin this week?"

"Nope, you guys are it. Wonder what that's all about? Thanks for the heads up. We'll go up tomorrow and have a look around."

"Okay. Have a good evening. I'll call you next week and let you know how the Sierra Club meeting goes."

"Great. Thanks, Jamie."

Jamie's finger almost hit the disconnect button, when he heard Ben again. "What, Ben? I'm sorry, I didn't catch your last comment."

"I almost forgot, we had a message for you. Let me find it. Just a sec."

Jamie heard a *thunk* as Ben put the receiver down. *What could that be about? It better not be Lauren's parents again.* They seemed to be able to get a hold of him at the worst times and find him anywhere.

Ben came back on the line. "Here we go. A woman called this morning around 8:10. Her call was routed through the 9-1-1 emergency service from the sheriff's office. She asked if we had your mobile number. The ranger on duty said we didn't give out personal information, even if we had it. Seems she was okay with that, and she said she'd try your old number. Sally thought it all sounded kinda strange, especially as it came through the sheriff, which is why she left me this note. Oh, and, the woman wouldn't give her name."

"Weird is what I'd call it. I haven't changed my mobile number in forever, so if whoever it is has that, she can get me. I didn't have any messages on the phone or missed calls when I turned it back on this afternoon, though." Jamie felt a shiver trace up his spine. What was this all about? Were Lauren's parents trying an end around?

Ben sighed. "Okay, I'll keep an ear out for any other calls. Have a safe trip home."

"Will do. Thanks, Ben. Later." Jamie disconnected the call.

Susan drove the large SUV out of Clark and headed toward Steamboat Springs. The winding road meandered through the Elk River valley on their way south. Everyone enjoyed their ice cream in silence. Boscoe finished first and started looking for handouts.

"Sit down, you," Jamie ordered as the corgi tried to get a lick from his cone. "You've had yours."

"Be careful. He's an ice cream addict," Susan said from the driver's seat. She smiled in the rearview mirror at Jamie. *He's such a special friend. I don't think we would have survived this last year without him.* "Have you heard any more from Lauren's parents? They've been unusually quiet lately."

Jamie's voiced floated from the back of the vehicle. "They have been quiet and that has me a bit worried. Lauren's attorneys are confident they don't have a chance at getting their hands on any of her assets, but I'm not comfortable. I know her mother is going fight to the end."

Sharon shook her head.

"What, love?" Susan asked, and she stole a quick glance at Sharon sitting in the passenger seat.

"I don't know. If they're this quiet, they've got something going on. We've been told her father is focusing on his medical practice and ignoring the whole thing, but her mother is a pit bull."

"Hey, what have I said? You need to stop stereotyping that breed. Pit bulls are only as aggressive as their owners raise them to be." She shook her head. "But I agree with you, in this instance she is a pit bull. She isn't going to let it go."

Jamie sighed. "Maybe we put it all in a trust designated for charity. But it isn't a decision we need to make now. We've got time. My meeting tomorrow is to notify the courts our search is over and all we found were her gloves. Then seven years from now, we'll face the decisions that need to be made about her estate. I'll manage her affairs, with her attorneys and financial planners, until then."

"I hate this." Sharon spun around in her seat to face Jamie. "We still don't have any more information, even after all this time. I don't feel she's dead. I can't believe she is." She huffed, sounding a lot like Boscoe. "The next seven years are going to be interminable. I wish there was something we could do now."

Susan placed her hand on her partner's thigh. "Easy, love. We all feel the same but we've gotta move forward. Nobody wants to believe she's gone, but she is. It's our responsibility to protect her estate and do what we think Lauren would want."

Boscoe began barking and tried to paw his way through the side window.

"What, boy?" Jamie asked. Sharon leaned forward out the passenger window of the SUV. A herd of elk raced across the snow-covered field next to the road. "Looks like fun, doesn't it?"

Boscoe agreed with a happy yip.

Susan glanced back in the rearview mirror and watched Jamie cuddle the little dog. *We're going to have to get him a dog. He's all alone in Denver.* She turned her attention back to the narrow road and nodded to herself at her plan.

Soon they were headed up the winding drive toward Susan and Sharon's log home. It hadn't snowed in about a week and the days were warming as spring approached, making the drive a rutted, muddy mess. Susan handled the large vehicle was practiced ease, driving around the large house to the garages. She opened one of the bays with the remote clipped to the sun visor.

Sharon got out and disappeared through the interior door. Susan gathered their things from the cargo area, while Jamie helped the corgi down from the back seat. The dog went wild again, barking his head off. Susan came around and reached for him. "Now what's got you riled up?" Before she got a hold of his collar, he raced out the open garage door. "What's gotten into him? He's been on high alert since we left the Zirkels."

Just then, the little dog tore back into the garage, whimpering. If he'd had a tail it would have been tucked tight between his legs. He ran behind Susan and peeked through her legs toward the open door. His whimpering escalated into growls, low and deep. Susan felt his body's vibration through her jeans, and she bent down to comfort the dog, stroking his back to lay his hackles down.

Jamie shifted in front of the pair. "Er, Susan, we may have a problem here."

"What?" Susan looked up from the trembling dog and froze in place. A huge white wolf stood framed in the open garage door. "Stand very still, Jamie. Maintain eye contact and whatever you do, do not move."

Sharon popped her head out the kitchen door. "Come on, guys. I'm starved. Shall I throw some steaks—?" Sharon's voice stuttered to a stop. "Susan, why is there a wolf in our garage?"

"Stand still, Sharon. I mean it." Susan slowly bent down, never taking her eyes off the gigantic white wolf and scooped Boscoe into her arms. She tucked the now quiet dog under her right arm. "Sharon, please step slowly back through the doorway. Do not come out here." She slowly sidestepped in front of Jamie. "Take Boscoe." She felt Jamie gather the little dog to him. "Now, step slowly backward into the kitchen. Once there, close the door."

"But?"

"Do it!" Her quiet voice carried the whip-crack of authority.

Susan felt Jamie slowly move away, and then heard the soft click of the door. Susan had worked with wolves before. She had interned in Yellowstone National Park when wolves were reintroduced from Alaska. She knew she had to maintain her position as an alpha, show no fear to this animal. Control the situation.

She faced off with the white beast. "Okay, easy. We aren't going to hurt you. Back off. Go on. Head home." Susan took a step forward and slowly opened her arms, palms forward, trying to enlarge her silhouette.

The wolf didn't budge. It sat down and appeared to smile at her.

Her veterinarian instincts analyzed the situation. *What the heck? This isn't normal behavior. I wonder if the rabies epidemic is spreading into the large predator population.* She opened her arms expanding her size. She stepped slowly to edge of the garage bay and watched as the wolf tracked her movements with its ice-blue eyes. The animal never flinched. "Oh, come on, what's up with you?" As she stepped out of the garage, she heard a voice she knew was out of this world.

"Snow, where are you? We've gotta wait for them to come back."

Susan spun away from the wolf and gawked, as a person walked around the corner of the building. "No," she whispered. Her knees gave out, and she slumped to the ground.

Chapter Two

The wolves sat quietly while Lauren worked on Susan. She asked Snow. "Did she hit her head when she fainted?"

"I do not think so. She simply dropped to the ground." The wolf stepped forward and nuzzled the now unconscious woman.

"Well, then, she'll come around in a minute." Lauren turned Susan over to rest fully on her back and saw her eyes flutter. "Come on now. Wake up, you."

Lauren gently patted her cheek as Snow licked the other one. Susan opened her eyes and they widened in surprise. "No, this isn't happening. I'm dreaming, again."

Lauren smiled gently. "It's happening."

Susan tried to crab away.

"Easy there. Don't move too quickly. You might've hit your head when you fell."

"But I . . . you're . . . not supposed to be here. How?"

"That was a little jumbled. You might have a concussion." Lauren reached out to feel the back and sides of Susan's head, but Susan pulled away. "I want to see if you have any lumps."

"I'm fine." Susan smiled weakly. "No, not fine, shocked. That's it, I'm in shock." She pointed at Lauren. "You're dead."

Lauren countered. "Not really." Lauren rocked back on her heels. How could she explain what happened in a few minutes? She and Alex talked at length about this on their trip from the Keep to the nexus in the Zirkel Mountains. They couldn't come up with any easy way to reintroduce Lauren to her friends. She smiled. "Let's just say I've been away for a while."

Susan goggled at her before throwing her arms around Lauren and hugging her hard, and then stiffened. Pulling back, she saw Susan wasn't looking at her. She was looking over her shoulder. "Lau…ren," she drew her name out into two long syllables. "There are two wolves. Right there. Right behind you."

"Oh, them? That's Snow and Ice."

"They're wolves."

Lauren hugged Susan again. "Yeah, they are." Lauren motioned to the wolves. "Come here, guys, and let me introduce you to Doctor Susan Stanley. She loves animals. She's a veterinarian." Lauren put her arms around Ice as she came forward.

"I do not know what that is, but she has a wonderful aura. I imagine she has a gentle heart."

"Veterinarian is a doctor for animals. Like our animal technicians. And she does have a gentle heart. She is the one who taught me what furkids are."

Lauren realized she was ignoring Susan as she chatted with Ice. Susan was in shock, and if Lauren was being honest, this wouldn't be the last shock of the day. "This is Ice. She's a wonderful companion and a true friend."

Turning to the wolf, she said, "Ice, this is Doctor Susan."

Ice sat back on her haunches and held out a large paw. *"I am pleased to meet you, Doctor Susan."* Susan took the proffered paw and shook it gently, a huge grin on her face.

"Ice says she's pleased to meet you."

"I know. I can see her pleasure. I'm very pleased to meet her as well." Susan turned to the other wolf. "Then this one must be the beautiful Snow."

Lauren grinned. Susan had less of a problem meeting the wolves than she did with Lauren's apparent return from the dead. Snow bowed her head regally and then also held out a paw.

Taking this paw in her left hand, Susan held onto the two wolves and smiled.

"Ice is correct, Lauren." Snow whiffled. *"This one has a gentle heart and a generous soul. She is a true friend of furkids."*

Lauren laughed at Snow's summation of her friend.

"Do you think we should call the others up?" Ice asked. *"Doctor Susan appears to be accepting of us and of you."*

Lauren looked at Susan and Snow as they stared into each other's eyes. "Susan, we have some other friends with us you should meet. Shall we get Sharon or wait until you've met them first?"

Susan looked away from Snow and blinked her eyes rapidly, obviously considering Lauren's question. "Perhaps I should go in and get Sharon and Jamie."

"Wait, Jamie? Jamie's here?" Lauren was so excited she sprang up and started to go into the garage.

Susan scrambled to her feet. "Let me go get them while you get your friends. We'll meet you at the gazebo." Susan pointed absently to a small structure near the tree line and then she looked helplessly at Lauren. "I'll try and break the news, but I'm not sure what to say."

"Then let's do this. Bring them out, and I'll call in all my friends. All at once is a better way of introducing everyone." Lauren suggested.

"Okay, all at once." Susan nodded and then pulled Lauren into another hug. "I'm so glad to see you. You haven't a clue how much."

Susan came back out of the garage twenty minutes later, Sharon and Jamie in tow. Boscoe trotted along at Susan's heels. Lauren could hear their conversation from where she waited, Sharon's voice distinct in its timbre. "Come on, Susan. I'm starved. What's so important we need to go to the gazebo?"

"Trust me, okay. This is something you must see."

As the group approached the gazebo, Jamie stiffened. "What's going on, Susan? Who are these people?"

Alex stepped out of the group and bowed. "I am Alexandra. I am most pleased to meet each of you." She held out her hand. Her heavily accented English sounded stilted. "Lauren has shared many stories about you."

"How do you know Lauren? Who the hell are you?" Sharon stepped forward aggressively. "Lauren never said she had Scottish friends."

"They know me because I met them during my travels." Lauren clarified and stepped out from behind Newkirk.

Jamie's jaw dropped, and Sharon swayed. Susan reached out and steadied her partner. "Lauren isn't dead." She hugged Sharon. "You were right. She's not dead."

Jamie recovered first and walked over to Lauren. He looked her up and down. "If you are who you say you are, what was the name of our instructor at cold water survival school, and who'd that person work for?"

"Jamie, you're such a skeptic." She smiled at Jamie. "His name was Hans Olsen, and he worked for Global Marine. If I remember correctly, you didn't like that course much." Lauren cocked her head to one side. "Especially the part where we were flipped upside down in the cage of a helicopter cockpit into thirty-five-degree water and told to get out."

His eyes widened. No one but Lauren knew about his absolute fear of drowning. Had Lauren, his buddy for that exercise, not pulled him from his harness and out of the cage when he was paralyzed by fear, he would've died. She opened her arms, and Jamie fell into them. His bear hug nearly crushed her chest and her sternum ached in protest, but she didn't stop him. She hugged him back as hard.

"Where have you been? Why didn't you call? Let us know where you were? That you were safe and alive?" Sharon's string of questions beat at Lauren and hurt almost as much as Jamie's bear hug. She knew Sharon would be the one to take her disappearance the hardest. With how they parted and the difficult words they had exchanged before she left, she knew Sharon would carry a lot of guilt.

"We will answer all your questions as best we can, but may we go inside? I believe you said you were hungry and I would like to get the furkids settled for the night," Alex requested.

"Furkids?" Susan repeated. Lauren turned and introduced each of their animal companions.

"Susan, you've met Ice and Snow." The wolves stepped forward. The little corgi growled deep in his throat and took a menacing step forward, crouching low as if preparing to pounce. Jamie and Sharon however, took a step back as the two giant white wolves stood beside Lauren. Lauren dropped her arms around their ruffs and hugged them to her. "These two are the ones who saved me in the blizzard."

"Why does the little one make such noise?" Ice asked in irritation.

"He's trying to defend his territory. His name is Boscoe." Lauren glanced at Boscoe. Corgis were herding dogs, after all, and incredibly protective of their flocks.

Snow took a small step toward the corgi and dropped down to his height. *"Be still, Little One, we will not hurt you or your mistresses."* The corgi's growl cut off suddenly, and he took a tentative step toward the reclining wolf. When he was nose-to-nose with Snow, he licked her. And then he yipped a happy sound and lay down facing her, butt wiggling in excitement.

"Well, I never." Susan gaped at the dog's behavior. "Seems Boscoe's convinced everything is okay."

Next Ffrwyn and Gríobhtha came out of the shadows. The massive horses stood regally through their introductions, and then bowed their heads over bended knee. Susan stood stock-still, head tilted in contemplation as she stared at the horses.

"Susan, you all right?" Lauren watched her friend's strange behavior.

Susan didn't reply, totally focused on the horses. She surprised everyone as she stepped up to Ffrwyn and placed her hands on either side of the horse's large head. She rested her forehead on the broad brow. "You are not well, are you? When is your foal due?" She swept her hands gently up from the horse's jaw and onto her neck. "Let me have a feel. We'll see if we can make you more comfortable. I promise I won't hurt you."

Ffrwyn nodded.

"She knows you won't hurt her, Susan," Lauren said, shocked at Susan's diagnosis.

The group watched as Susan moved along Ffrwyn's left side. She ran her left hand along the horse's side and placed it on the horse's hip. "Easy now, big girl, easy." She placed both hands over one spot and rubbed in a circle. "There, I think?" Susan had her eyes closed, and she laid her forehead against Ffrwyn's side as she continued to massage that one spot.

Ffrwyn whiffled and dropped her head, eyes closed. *"Yes, there. That is the spot which has been paining me since we crossed the nexus."* Alex looked at Lauren, concern etched on her face.

"Ffrwyn, what she said? Is it true? Are you going to foal?" Alex asked along their bond. *"I would not have brought you along on this trip had I known."* She stepped up to the horse's head and captured her attention.

"I would not have allowed you to come without me, Alex. I am not to foal for months, yet. I am a bit sore, but this one has the hands of a healer."

"She is strong, Alex. She will be fine. It is muscle soreness as the foal stretches and moves," Gríobhtha said as he moved to watch Susan's actions.

"How would you know that? It's not like you've ever carried before." Lauren challenged him.

Gríobhtha huffed as he watched Susan massage Ffrwyn's side. *"I know what she tells me, but we all know how strong she is."*

Susan opened her eyes and slowed her ministrations. Ffrwyn turned her massive head toward Susan and nodded. *"Thank you. That is much better."*

Lauren said, "She says thank you. She feels much better."

Susan placed a gentle hand on the horse's brow and smiled into her large mahogany eyes. "I know she feels some relief. Her muscles are relaxed. That will help for a while, but I will need to do an ultrasound to see how the foal is progressing." Turning to Lauren, she frowned. "How could you travel with this one in distress like this?"

"We didn't know." Lauren cringed at Susan's angry scowl.

Susan threw her hands up. "Didn't know! What's up with that? Are you blind? You can see the outline of the foal through her side." She pointed at Ffrwyn's side. "It's turned and is hoofing her. We need to get her to my office."

"I am Robert McLaran. It is my fault Ffrwyn made this journey. When Alex and Lauren told us where they were going on their mating trip, we knew we had to go along." He nodded at Alex and Lauren. "These two seem to attract trouble, and Ffrwyn would not leave without Gríobhtha, for they are a bonded pair too."

"Bonded pair?"

Lauren jumped in at that point. "Let me introduce the rest of our party, and then we can take this inside. Obviously, we've got a lot to share with one another." Lauren placed a hand on McLaran's forearm. "This one has already introduced himself, Robert McLaran. This is Angus Newkirk." She pointed at the tall, lean Terran. She turned and smiled, "And this is Tavish MacDonald." Lauren gripped the other man on his broad shoulder. "Alex and I are on our honeymoon. The boys wouldn't let us come back without an escort. So . . . here we are." Lauren smiled sheepishly at her friends.

"Right, honeymoon. Seems you do have a lot to tell us." Jamie frowned at Lauren.

Susan stroked down Ffrwyn's long nose. "Come on, girl. Let's get you settled with your partner in the barn." She cast a glance at Gríobhtha. "We'll take good care of you, regardless of what these others say. Okay?"

"A warm barn, oats, and some soft straw sound marvelous. Thank you, healer," Ffrwyn answered.

"She says thank you," Lauren said.

"Of course, she does. She's a smart one, this girl, and polite, too," Susan added absently, as she turned and led the horses around the gazebo toward the barn off the back pasture.

"Now that that's managed, I guess the rest of us will head inside," Sharon stated and moved off to the house. Lauren cast a worried glance at the small woman who stomped back toward the house. Her pace indicated her irritation, even though she seemed to be taking everything in stride Lauren knew better. Sharon was shaken to her core and hiding behind a veil of civility. Jamie was pissed. His cheeks were reddened, and he seemed to be physically chewing on the matter as his jaw worked back and forth. He turned and followed Sharon, leaving the Terrans alone.

Alex placed an arm around Lauren's shoulders. *"It will be all right, Dearheart. They are shocked, confused, and overwhelmed. We did pounce on them."*

"I know. I wish we'd been able to call, but with the sat line disconnected, we could only make an emergency call. That ranger didn't sound too pleased with me when I asked for Jamie's number."

Alex squeezed Lauren's shoulders. *"What did you expect? You have been missing for a long time. I am sure they were only just coming to grips with your death."*

"I guess so," Lauren thought dejectedly.

"We will take the time needed to explain what has happened. They are intelligent people and they obviously care about you. One step at a time, agreed?"

Lauren smiled up at her soulmate. *"One step at a time. Right."*

The group sat around the great room. The three boys sprawled comfortably in large overstuffed chairs, and Alex and Lauren cuddled together on a love seat. The wolves lay by the open hearth where a large fire raged. Boscoe snuggled between Snow and Ice, a happy doggie smile on his sleeping face. *He's so content.* She couldn't say the same for the other three, who sat on the edges of their chairs, waiting. *But for what?*

Over dinner, a meal of sandwiches, eaten in the large kitchen, Lauren had tried to outline what happened during the blizzard and after. She touched on the highlights but left out most of the details. Perhaps that was a mistake. Maybe she'd sold her friends short.

"I don't think I'm doing very well here," she admitted. Turning to Alex, she shrugged. *"What do you think?"*

"I recommend you start again, at the beginning. And this time don't leave anything out," Alex suggested.

"Are you two having a conversation?" Sharon asked, her head tilted as she eyed the pair.

Lauren snapped her head around and saw her friend's frown deepen across her brow. "Well, yeah, we are."

"Then, I suggest you tell us the truth this time. And don't edit the facts. It's obvious all of you are different," Sharon said, as she indicated the boys and the wolves with a jerk of her head. She pointed at Alex. "But you are at the center of all this. Why?"

Alex smiled a slow and easy smile. "Your friends are truly intelligent and observant. Perhaps, the Lady Sharon is correct. From the beginning, Dearheart, and do not leave anything out."

"But, Alex, this has direct impact on," Lauren paused, trying desperately to think of what to call Terra. "On our country."

"Do you trust your friends?"

"Of course, I trust them." Lauren couldn't believe Alex would question that. *She can feel what I think and feel about them through our bond.*

"Well then, you owe it to them to be totally honest. Tell them what has happened. Where you went and why." Alex turned to the three seated across from them and smiled. "Take them into your confidence, tell them about Terra."

Lauren saw her three friends stiffen reflexively at the unusual name. "It's not bad, guys." She stated ruefully. "Well, most of it isn't."

Angus Newkirk interjected, "This may take some time. Does anyone need additional refreshment?" he asked as he rose from his seat. "I know I will need another ale. Even though I lived these events, it is a long and thirsty tale." His attempt to lighten the mood of the room seemed to work, and Susan rose with him.

"Come on then," she said. "You and I'll get more for everyone, while Lauren decides how she is going to come clean."

"Clean? She is not dirty that I see," MacD noted. And that broke the tension in the room, as chuckles rose from the group. Lauren rolled her eyes.

Dawn painted the east-facing windows of the great room as Lauren finished her tale.

"Why do I feel like I've been dropped into a bad episode of *Stargate*?" Jamie asked Sharon and Susan.

Leave it to Jamie to make an esoteric reference to something from this reality. Now she'd have more to explain but to the Terrans instead of to the—Lauren's thoughts were brought up short. *What do I call my friends? Earthlings sounds weird.*

"Friends," Alex answered quietly in a short burst along their bond.

"Of course. Thanks, Dearest."

"You're doing it again." Sharon narrowed her eyes and scrutinized the two.

"What?"

Sharon pointed at them. "When you're talking to each other, you drop out of the conversation and kinda go all dreamy. I don't know how you do it, but it's rude not to include us in your conversation when we're sitting right here."

With a small smirk, McLaran said, "She sounds much like our Seneschal, does she not, M'lady?"

"She truly does, Robert. Obviously, some human traits are ubiquitous across any reality," Newkirk added noticing the brightening windows. "It has been a long evening that has stretched into another day.

Perhaps, we should all have a rest. Allow you some time to think on what Lauren has shared. Listening to their tale is overwhelming for me, and I was there." He smiled at the others in the room. "I cannot imagine how you must be feeling."

Jamie nodded. "Thanks, Angus, you're right. I'm exhausted, and I feel whiplashed. Yesterday morning, we had your memorial, and now here you are. This is all going to take some getting used to. But, I'm glad you're here and all right." He paused and tipped his head at the pair cuddled together. "Happy, too. That's the only way I can describe all this. You're happy."

Lauren snuggled deeper into Alex's chest. "You're so right, Jamie. I am happy."

"On that note, I'm going to check on the horses and head to bed." Susan turned to Sharon and held out her hand. "Why don't we take a little walk, love?" Sharon rose and took her partner's proffered hand. She cast a glance at Lauren. "Don't think we're done, yet. You've got a lot more to explain."

"I know." Lauren smiled sheepishly. "I'm doing my best here."

"And that's all we ask. And that you're patient with us as we absorb all this." Sharon turned to Susan. "Let's go, hon. Come on Boscoe. Walk?" The corgi heard one of his favorite words and bounced up, running across Ice's face to get to the door first.

"Hey, watch it, squirt," Ice growled.

"Look at it this way, Lauren. You've had fourteen months to integrate into Terran society, acclimate to their reality." Jamie shook his head. "That is so weird, another reality." Lauren frowned but Jamie quickly added, "But cool, very cool. Heisenberg is probably rolling over in his grave, and I can't begin to imagine what someone like Carlos Rovelli would think." He smiled again.

"Your point?" Lauren prompted. *Can't let Jamie go tangential, or we'll end up staying awake another day discussing parallel universes and loop quantum gravity. At some point, we will talk about all that but one step at a time.*

"My point is, you need to think about how you felt when you didn't understand anything, when you first crossed the nexus. We're as adrift as you were. And we thought you were dead all this time. You've gotta understand, we're overwhelmed. But we trust you, and we'll listen and try and understand as best we can. I'm damn glad you're back." He nodded at Lauren. "And what a trip you've had. It'd make a great book, but I doubt anyone would believe it. Have to be fiction."

Lauren frowned and dropped her head back on Alex's chest. "That's kinda the point I'm trying to make here, Jamie. No one would understand, and frankly I don't want anyone to know. I don't want a bunch of crazies running around, hunting for nexi or gateways. I want Terra to remain separate. They've got enough issues right now. They don't need to take on all of Earth's, too."

Lauren felt Alex draw her fear and concerns away, tightening her hug. When she glanced up into her love's face, Lauren saw her frown. "When we agreed to come here for our trip, Lauren did not want to come." Jamie was confused. "Here, I mean, back to this reality. Even though she has wished she could share all she has done and all she has discovered with you and this world. Lauren takes her responsibilities as Co-Ruler and Consort seriously. I know she will do anything and everything to protect Terra." Alex sat up, taking Lauren with her. As Alex straightened, her persona commanded the full attention of those left into the room. The boys reflexively straightened in their seats. "But I know she trusts you, Jamie. Trusts you to keep her secrets and protect Terra."

Alex placed her hand on Lauren's shoulder and squeezed. "You must know she loves you. This trip is important because Lauren wants closure, too. She also wanted to allay your fears about her disappearance. The three of you were constantly on her mind. When she was recovering from her blast injury, she was so torn about which reality she should be in—Terra or Earth—it was a constant distraction for her. But she has made her choice. Agreeing to be my Consort and Co-Ruler means she has chosen Terra as her home, but you will always and forever be her friends and closest allies. When Lauren gives her trust and love, she gives it forever. You must never doubt that."

Lauren could see emotions dance across Jamie's face. Happiness at her return, but then his eyes grew serious and a small frown lowered his brows. They had more work to do to help him understand.

Alex stood, and Lauren jumped to her feet with her. "We have time, Jamie, for each of you to be with Lauren. Time for each of you to understand what has happened and how important she is to Terra and to myself. How important Terra is to Lauren. Also, Lauren wishes to share some of her discoveries with you. We have discussed various ways for you to introduce those technologies to your planet. Introduce them without too much fanfare, but in a way this reality will benefit from Lauren's work. But that is for another day. Now, I think Doctor Susan is correct, we all must rest and recover."

"Well said, Dearest. I couldn't have said it better. You're amazing."

"Let us give them some time. If they are half the people you say they are, they will adapt and accept, and then you can share the rest."

Jamie seemed to shake himself from his thoughts, and Lauren saw his resolve settle, as he slapped his knees and stood. "Right then, let me show you up to your rooms. Lauren, yours is as you left it. And I assume, Alex will share with you?"

Lauren nodded and felt warmth streak along their bond. "Got that right." She smirked.

Jamie turned toward the broad staircase and motioned for the Terrans to follow. "I'll put the boys in the rooms down from mine. I'm still across the hall, where you put me before." As the three Terrans rose from their chairs, the wolves stood up and stretched, arching their backs and yawning wide enough to show teeth all the way back to their molars. "What about these guys?" Jamie pointed at Ice and Snow.

"They'll join us. As long as they can come and go through the house and be able to go out of doors at their pleasure, they will be fine," Alex explained.

Snow and Ice trotted along after Alex and Lauren. *"We will be able to access the woods through the kitchen door, but given the wonderful treats the healer has here, I doubt we will hunt much,"* Ice said.

"Susan is a wonderful cook and I'm sure she'll be glad to cook for you. And then, there's always kibbles." Lauren looked down at Ice. *"You've gotta ask Boscoe if he'll share."*

"Kibbles, what are those? Are those something I would like? They sound good," Ice asked, again her mind focused on her stomach and the possibility of new treats.

Lauren paused on the landing and turned to face the wolf. *"I don't think you'll like kibbles, and remember Doctor Susan is an animal tech, if she thinks you're too fat she will give you those to slim you down."* Lauren looked down into Ice's blue eyes and became serious. *"And it's probably a good idea for you guys to stay close. I don't want any of the neighbors seeing you and taking a shot at a wolf."*

Ice harrumphed loudly at Lauren's comments about her weight. But Snow growled at the danger of getting shot.

Jamie leaned over the balcony bannister. "Coming?"

"Yeah, on our way. Just discussing body image with Ice here." She took Alex's warm hand in hers and climbed the stairs, following Jamie to the third floor.

Chapter Three

Surprisingly, Alex was the first one awake later that afternoon. Lauren still slept soundly. She had thrown a warm arm and leg across Alex's body, partially pinning her in place. Alex could hear wolfy snores from the two chairs across the room, so the wolves slept as well. Late afternoon sun filtered in through the partially closed lace curtains. *This is such a beautiful dwelling. So different from buildings on Terra. We never tried to build personal dwellings in wood, I wonder why? I must ask Lady MacDonald when we return.* Alex visually traced the complex wood grains across the planks that paneled the room. Their large bed was covered in a quilt made from a multitude of colored fabric swatches. Lauren had explained that Sharon's great-grandmother had sewn it over a century ago.

Alex carefully slid from the bed and turned to her pack. She held up a kilt in Doouglas hunting tartan, a white shirt, and a plaid of black, gray and white. When they crossed the nexus, Lauren had them all dress in Earth-style clothing. She worried if they were seen in the Zirkel area or during their trip to this town they would appear out of place in their Terran kilt. Alex was not planning on going out, other than to check on Ffrwyn, and those ridiculous trousers or jeans or whatever Lauren called them made her uncomfortable. Still she knew they must be cautious, so she placed her Terran attire back in her pack, and pulled out a pair of jeans. Checking on Ffrwyn was her first priority. *How could that Horse hide this from me and the other companions? I mean, how could she endanger herself so? I am going to have a word with her.*

She smiled down at Lauren where she lay sprawled across the large bed. Leaning down, Alex placed a gentle kiss on her cheek. Lauren smiled in her sleep and rolled toward Alex. Though tempted, she would not crawl back into bed. Lauren needed her rest more than anyone else, and Alex wanted to go outdoors and explore more of Doctor Susan and Lady Sharon's holdings.

Alex stepped out into the hall and turned toward the large staircase. She hadn't gone more than a step when Boscoe rounded the corner with a yip of greeting. The small dog reminded her of similar ones her grandmother raised on Terra Prime. A momentary sadness at the memory tugged at her heart. "Quiet, Little One. Let us not wake our companions." The dog seemed to understand and sat down at Alex's feet, a smile gracing his cream and tan face. "Shall we have a walk to the barn and see how my horses are doing?"

"Yip!" was all the answer she got, as the little dog spun around and sped down the long hall.

"Well, all right then." Alex paused for a moment. "Merilyn is correct. I am sounding more like Lauren every day. Gotta love it." Smiling, she followed the corgi.

In the kitchen, she found a variety of baked goods and fruits set out, along with the fixings for tea. She could smell the aroma of that dreadful coffee Lauren drank on their journey to Fuar Ćala, and her nose wrinkled in disgust. Alex tried Lauren's coffee once, but that was one too many times for her. She was glad when Lauren's supply had run out and she switched to the tea Alex drank.

After making a mug of peppermint tea and selecting a piece of bread covered in a gooey tan sauce and liberally sprinkled with some type of nut, she and the corgi exited the kitchen through the garage and headed to the large barn at the edge of the fenced pasture. She could see Gríobhtha munching happily on a few sprigs of spring grass which poked through the thin covering of snow. As Alex approached, he raised his massive head and whiffled a greeting. "Good afternoon, Gríobhtha. How are you doing?"

"Doctor Susan is a true marvel." He trotted over to Alex and hung his head over the top rail. *"She is tending to Ffrwyn now. She also provides excellent feed. The oats were warmed and mixed with honey and some other odd yellow grain that was sweet. We should consider taking that back to Fuar Ćala when we return."*

Alex ducked through the split rails of the pasture fence and turned to face the horse.

"I am pleased you agreed to come with us, especially now Ffrwyn is indisposed. I know being separated from McLaran is difficult for you."

Alex rubbed his warm neck in long strokes, muscle rippling in pleasure beneath her hand. *"Once Lauren has all her affairs dealt with and we decide how we are going to share technologies, we will make all haste to return."*

"Ffrwyn's condition is why I knew I must come along. McLaran understood the situation, and we are fine. Although I can no longer speak with him directly, our bond is still active. It is ever present in my mind. Therefore, I know all is well in our realm."

Alex patted his shoulder. *"Good. You will let me know if anything seems amiss or you lose that feeling."* Alex asked gently.

"Of course, though I imagine Robert would also feel something is wrong. He and his clan have exceptionally strong familial ties."

Alex nodded and brushed across the horse's forehead, scratching between his eyes. *"Are you planning on having a run today? I would like to send Snow and Ice along if you are."*

"I believe MacD and McLaran are planning on exploring the surrounds of this keep today. I will go along. The furballs are welcome to join us."

"Furballs? Oh, Ice is going to love that moniker."

"If the geometry fits, you must wear it, as Her Majesty always says." Gríobhtha snorted in horsey laughter, while Alex grinned.

She patted Gríobhtha once more on the rump and went to find Ffrwyn in the large barn. Alex was amazed as she entered the large post and beam structure. Numerous stalls ran along each side of a broad central aisle. The aisle was covered in a thick layer of clean, sweet-smelling straw. Large transparent sheets in the roof allowed the waning afternoon sun in and the walls glowed a soft orange. As she walked past the stalls, curious horses put their heads over their half-closed stall doors. Alex stopped to stroke a nose here and pat a neck there as she walked deeper into the barn in search of Ffrwyn. *"Horse, where are you?"*

"Here, Alex, in the last stall on the left, and stop calling me Horse. I do not like it."

"Lauren calls you Horse all the time. You do not complain to her."

"She is Lauren, and she is my friend. I would not complain to her."

Alex laughed as she approached the last stall. *"And I am not your friend?"*

"You are my friend and companion. Lauren is my special friend."

Alex peered over the half-door. Her retort to that comment died on her lips when she saw inside the stall and heard her horse grunt in pain.

Doctor Susan lay on her left side next to the horse, with her head at her rump and her feet near Ffrwyn's head. "Hello. Is everything all right here?" Alex asked softly, she didn't want to startle Doctor Susan during her examination.

Turning only her head, Susan looked up at Alex. "I'm not sure if everything is all right or not. I'm doing a vaginal examination to determine the position of the foal. If it's turned sideways, I'll try to reposition it with massage over the next few weeks. I don't want it to become impinged in that position as it grows, and we can't turn it later."

Alex frowned. "Impinged?"

"Stuck in a breech position. Ffrwyn will be uncomfortable in the last stages of her pregnancy if that happens. The delivery of a breech birth would be hard on her."

Alex's concerns rose and she turned her full attention on Ffrwyn. The horse had her eyes closed, but Alex could see her jaw working in discomfort. "Is she going to be all right?"

"No real reason she won't be. But I do want to do an ultrasound and for that, we'll need to take her to my office in town."

Alex considered that for a moment. "How are we going to get her there? We cannot ride over, and I do not think Gríobhtha will allow her too far from him. He is very protective."

Susan laughed and rolled over, pulling her arm free from Ffrwyn. Her left arm was covered in a long latex sleeve that stretched from her finger tips to her shoulder and dripped a viscous fluid. Alex shuddered. "I know. It was all I could do to get him to go into the pasture and let me work. When he was here, he kept trying to see what I was doing. He's a big horse. One of the largest I've ever been around and his trying to look over my shoulder about crushed me." Susan got to her feet and pulled the sleeve off inside out. She rolled it into a ball and tossed it a plastic bin in the corner of the large stall. "But a bit of warm oats and honey, and he followed me out to the pasture. Typical male. Thinks of his stomach first." Susan laughed.

Then, they heard the crashing sound of hoofs against wood. Alex tilted her head as she heard another crash. "I do not think he will be kept out much longer. If you value your barn door, I would suggest letting him in."

"Alex, let me in." Gríobhtha had obviously heard Ffrwyn grunt and felt her discomfort following the examination.

"And there he is now." Another crash sounded into the large barn.

Susan pulled the stall door open and turned to make her way down the center aisle when the barn door was thrown open from the outside and Gríobhtha entered at a run, with Lauren on his heels.

"What's going on in here?" Lauren demanded, skidding to a stop in front of Susan.

Alex and Susan looked at each other and back at Lauren before breaking into laughter.

Lauren placed her hands on her hips, "Well."

Alex pointed at Lauren.

"What?"

"It is your hair, Dearheart. I have not seen this style before," Alex said between giggles.

Gríobhtha stood at the open stall door. *"You must come see this, My Heart. Lady Lauren is quite something."*

Ffrwyn stuck her head out the stall door and snorted. *"I agree, Lovey."* She rubbed her head against Gríobhtha's broad neck.

"Waiting, here," Lauren said, while her foot beat a rapid tempo on the wooden floor.

Alex began to get herself under control, and then made the mistake of looking at Lauren again, and lost it once more. Susan was no better and she put a hand over her mouth to quell her laughter.

Ffrwyn said, *"M'lady, I believe it is your hairstyle that has these two so caught up."*

"My what?"

"Your hair is messy. It is standing up in a row across the center of your head and down the back, much like a short-cropped mane," Gríobhtha said.

Lauren attempted to smooth out her wild hair. *"Guys, thank you for letting me know I'm a mess here."*

"Not a mess, a little untidy. I will always protect you, Lauren, especially from the others." The horse and her Consort snorted together.

Alex hiccupped a few times, her lip curling over in a pout. "Ffrwyn does like you best."

"Thanks, Alex. I know I can always count on you to throw me to the wolves. But Gríobhtha woke me with a cry for help, and when I got down here, he was through the fence and ready to knock the door down. What are you up to, anyway?"

"What do you mean he woke you?" Susan's mirth dissolved into disbelief and doubt.

"What she means is . . ." Alex stammered out an explanation but wasn't having much success. *"How do I explain this to her?"*

"She's a vet, and some would consider her a horse-whisperer. I bet she'll understand before the other two will." Lauren's words gave Alex some insight into her friend.

"A horse-what?" Alex frowned at Lauren.

"Whisperer. In this reality, there are some who can seemingly talk to animals. Susan has that ability, which is why she is such a good animal tech. I don't think she can speak to them as we speak to the companions, but she understands them so well it seems like she can. Animals have always been comfortable around her."

Ffrwyn added her feelings. *"Even though she cannot hear my words, she listens so well she does understand my needs. Alex, you need to tell her. I know she will accept this."*

Alex turned back to Susan. "Doctor Susan, Lauren and I can talk to our animal companions in the same manner we speak to people."

"I knew it!" Susan nodded enthusiastically and clapped her hands together. "Last night, I knew you and Lauren were actually having a conversation between yourselves. Sharon picked up on it, too. She even reprimanded you two, but you glossed over it, and then Angus changed the subject."

The barn door blew open again and Robert McLaran rushed in. He had his sword in hand and was dressed only in a cream and green tartan nightshirt over bare legs, knobby knees exposed. "What is going on here? I heard Gríobhtha yell, and it woke me from a deep sleep."

"So, you can talk to animals, too?" Susan demanded.

McLaran lowered his sword. "Err . . . no, I cannot talk directly to Gríobhtha. He is my father's companion. But it seems he can speak with Lauren and therefore with Alex. I think I heard his call relayed along my bond with Alex."

Susan stared at each of them in turn. "So that's how it is, is it? All you guys, can talk to each other along some kind of mental connection?" She pointed to each of the Terrans, shaking her head before taking a deep breath and smiling broadly. "That's gotta be so cool. I wish I could do that. I bet it keeps folks from having secrets, and some things are probably explained a lot faster, too."

Alex could almost see the wheels turning in Susan's scientific mind as she extrapolated all the benefits of a bond.

"And animals, oh how I wish I could speak with my patients. I could do so much good for them," she mused.

Lauren turned to Alex. "That's one down and two to go. Maybe Susan can help us with the others. She seems to grasp the concept of bonds pretty well."

"And she is not even concerned about speaking with animals." Alex was perplexed by Susan's easy acceptance.

"That's the easiest part of all this for her. She's always been more comfortable around them than around us."

Susan turned back to the pair of giant horses. "Miss Ffrwyn, since you can speak with these two," she pointed at the soulmates, "I'll expect you to give them daily reports on how you're feeling. Don't try and hide anything from me, young lady. I'll know if you're keeping something from me. You're entering a difficult part of this pregnancy and I'm going to have to place you in a high-risk category, because of the size of your foal. We'll have to head over to my office and take a closer look." She glared at the large horse until Ffrwyn nodded. "All right then. I'll be back with dinner soon. Rest, no activity, and no running." Susan turned to Gríobhtha and pointed at him. "That's your responsibility. You must see that she rests as much as possible."

"How are we going to get her to your office?" Alex asked, worried the trip would be hard on Ffrwyn.

"I've been thinking about that. Lauren can't go because everyone at my office knows her, and they know she is missing and presumed dead."

Alex shuddered at the thought of losing Lauren. "But I think you and I can take her in my rig. Do you think she'd agree to ride in a horse van?"

Alex tilted her head in thought. "I do not see why not. She knows we are trying to do everything to keep her comfortable and protect her foal." Nodding as the plan crystallized, Alex tossed a thumb over her shoulder at Gríobhtha, "We will probably have to take him, too. I doubt he will let Ffrwyn go anywhere without him."

"That sounds like a great plan. I'll need some time to talk with Jamie, and then I'll fix dinner," Lauren said.

"You're our guests, and guests don't cook in this house," Susan replied, hands on her hips.

"Since when have I been a guest?"

Alex saw a tiny frown mar Lauren's forehead, and she pulled her into her shoulder, placing a small kiss on the top of her head. She sent a burst of love along their bond.

"You're not a guest. You know that. You're a member of the family." Susan gathered the pair up in a group hug and squeezed.

Lauren smiled broadly. "Well in that case, I'll have dinner ready by the time you guys are back." She turned to Alex. "But I suggest you let Robert have time to dress. I doubt he'll want to travel into town in his jammies."

Robert looked down at his nightshirt. "Jammies?"

Chapter Four

Lauren sat on a comfortable stool at the gray and pink swirled granite island in the large kitchen peeling potatoes. “I don’t know, Jamie. Terrans have a number of technologies which would have immediate applicability in this reality. The question isn’t what to share, since Alex and the Council already approved us sharing them, the question is how to share them. We can’t make all of it public at once. Everyone would ask all kinds of questions: where it came from, who discovered it, how we got a hold of them?” Lauren waved her paring knife at him in emphasis.

“I know. I’ve been wracking my brain, trying to figure all that out.”

Dropping another potato in the pot, Lauren put down the knife and wiped her hands on a blue and green striped tea towel. “Maybe we’re going about this the wrong way. You and I are scientists, not patent attorneys or marketing specialists. We need someone with that knowledge. Someone who understands how a scientist takes a discovery from her lab, turns it into usable technology, and then sells it.”

“But that means telling someone, who we don’t know, about you.” He pointed at Lauren. “How’s that going to work? You’re supposed to be dead, or at least hopelessly missing.” Jamie frowned. Lauren knew he was concerned about introducing another person into the mix. But she could see the twinkle in his eyes. He was glad she wasn’t dead, happy to be sitting with her in this warm kitchen, cooking dinner.

Lauren reached out and placed a gentle hand on his shoulder. “Hey, it’s okay. I’m right here. I’m totally fine. Better than fine, in fact.”

“I know, but I still get chills when I think about all you went through and how lucky you were to survive.”

“I know, right? Best science fiction story I’ve ever heard.” Lauren laughed and squeezed his shoulder. “But I think we do know a few people who know me and can help us.”

Jamie’s eyebrows rose in question at her statement.

“My attorneys. They know me, they know what I do, and how I do it. They knew enough about my personal life to help me set up my estate to block my parents' interference. And they have to operate under attorney-client privilege."

Lauren watched the light come on in Jamie's eyes. He sat back, deep in thought. "Yeah, that might work. I had a meeting scheduled with them today but I cancelled it." He smiled sheepishly. "I thought staying here with you was more important than meeting with a bunch of stuffed shirts to discuss estate law."

"Pretty dry subject, I'll give you that, but my attorneys are stuffed skirts, not shirts." Lauren and Jamie laughed at her small but accurate joke.

"How's it possible you found a bunch of female attorneys, who are that beautiful, smart, and compassionate, but could care less about me?" He pointed at himself. "I couldn't get one of them to go on a date with me. What's up with that?"

Lauren snorted. "Oh, Jamie, I'm sorry to put a damper on your dating, but they are all lesbians." He looked at her in shock. "What would you expect? There's no way I was going to use any attorney, who wouldn't completely understand my need to protect myself and my assets from my homophobic parents."

"I'm glad you found them. They're amazing, and they've been pit bulls guarding the door against your parents." Nodding as if he made a decision, he said. "Let's call them and set up a meeting here. Hell, we'll fly them in to get them here faster. I'll rent a jet."

Lauren felt a smile spread across her face. "Alex and I spent hours and hours talking about what to do and how to do it. We struggled to find a solution. All we decided is we've gotta figure out a way to get the nano-technologies out there for use. They're an amazing discovery, with so many practical applications. And with Newkirk here, the three of us should be able to brainstorm any number of new uses for them."

"All right, I'll call your attorneys and organize a meeting for tomorrow." He stood, shaking his head. "We were supposed to talk about starting the seven-year clock and informing the judge we were stopping the search. This is going to knock their socks off."

"Hose, Jamie."

"What?"

"Knock their hose off." They grinned at each other and laughed.

Alex and Susan walked into the kitchen three hours later, as Lauren was pulling a large roast out of the oven. "How'd it go, guys?" Lauren asked, as she set the roasting pan down and prepared a foil tent to cover the meat to rest.

"The foal is breech, but we can manage that over the next few weeks. Most importantly, it's a healthy baby and appears to be developing normally. But, boy is it going to be a big one. After all, it is Gríobhtha's offspring. We'll need to keep a close eye on Ffrwyn." Susan picked up a carrot from the appetizer tray and munched. "I'm going to add some prenatal vitamins to her grains and adjust her diet to include more protein and plenty of hay. We'll watch her water intake closely. She needs to stay hydrated."

Lauren looked at Alex, who was unusually quiet. She placed a hand on Alex's stomach and rubbed gently. "You okay, Dearest?"

"I think so." Alex ran a hand through her hair, pushing her bangs off her forehead. "Ffrwyn took the trip better than I thought she would. Better than I did actually." She smiled down at her soul's other half. "They were amazing, she and Gríobhtha. Everyone wanted to know where we came from, and what kind of horses they were. They were all so curious. I know I could not have fielded all their questions, but Doctor Susan stepped in and put her patient first."

"They are an amazing pair." Lauren snorted at her understatement about the two giant horses.

"Yes, they are, but it illustrates your point. We must be careful. We are an oddity and do arouse suspicions." Alex draped an arm around Lauren's shoulders.

"I won't have to take her in to the clinic again, unless something happens with the foal." Susan pointed her carrot stick at them to emphasis her point. "I was planning some vacation anyway, what with the memorial and all, so me being out of the office won't raise any questions."

Lauren turned out from under Alex's arm and started to pull dishes from the cupboards for their evening meal. "That's great. I'll need your expertise tomorrow. Jamie and I decided we needed some legal expertise to finalize how we introduce and control the Terran technologies here on Earth."

Alex and Susan turned toward her. "How are we going to do that?" Alex asked.

Lauren explained the plan to them.

"I'm going to claim attorney-client privilege and have my attorneys come here, tomorrow. We don't know enough about how to do what we want to do to get it all done. I need to be sure we're protecting you all and the technology."

"We'll be all right, but getting your attorneys involved is a good idea. I think?" Susan seemed to lose her thought for a moment, concern crossing her face. "They've been great handling your parents, keeping your mother at bay has been a big job."

Lauren shuddered, remembering what a pain her mother could be. "I know she can be a real bitch, but I'd be more concerned about Dad."

"He's back to work, with a full surgical schedule, according to your attorneys. So, we've been focused on appeasing your mother." Susan turned back to the tray and selected a long strip of green pepper.

"He may be back to work and seemingly quiet, but that's how they work. It's a feint. One appears to back off while the other goes full on, but then you're blindsided by an end-around." Lauren noticed a frown dart across Alex's face. "Sorry for the sports analogy, Dearest. However, it's the best way to describe how my parents function. You know, we've talked about them." Lauren rubbed her nose. "Let's see if I can explain. In military terms, I would say, they're trying a flanking maneuver." She saw Alex nod slowly. "In sailing terms, I would say it's all about cutting off your wind."

"But an end-around, blindsided? Your culture truly has some interesting terms." Alex frowned perplexed.

"We do. You'll have to watch a football game while you're here," Susan added helpfully. "Then Lauren can show you what an end-around is and how the quarterback can be blindsided."

"That's a great idea. I'm pretty sure the boys would love watching football. Although after watching some of their Terran games, I imagine rugby would be more their style." Lauren transferred the steamed vegetables to one of the warmed serving bowls on the granite island.

"Back to the subject at hand here, who are these attorneys and what is privilege?" Alex sat on one of the stools and selected a slice of cucumber from the tray.

Lauren went on to explain to Alex who and what attorneys were and how client privilege worked, all the while continuing her preparations for their meal. Alex didn't seem convinced this would work out, but Lauren knew once she met her cadre of pit bull attorneys, she'd be fine.

Sharon burst into the kitchen as Lauren placed a pat of butter on the huge mound of mashed potatoes. "What's for dinner? I could smell it all the way to my office. I'm starved."

"So am I!" another voice added as the two wolves followed Sharon through the swinging door.

Lauren spun around to face the portly wolf, hands on hips. *"Ice."*

"I will eat in moderation, however, that meat smells delicious. I will have to have you cook for me back on Terra if you can make something that tastes as good as that smells," Ice said, drooling.

"Dream on, Furball."

"Well, I never. Furball, indeed!" Ice retorted. *"You have been spending entirely too much time with those hay-burners."*

Snow rolled her eyes at Lauren and Ice's ongoing bickering about the wolf's weight. She huffed and went to stand next to Alex.

"What'd I miss here?" Sharon asked, as she looked from one to another of her guests.

"I'll tell you later, love. Let's get this into the dining room. Lauren said she set the table while the meal was cooking. Wouldn't want it to get cold." Susan picked up two of the dishes and turned toward the dining room. Sharon followed in her wake with a platter of carved meat and the gravy boat.

Lauren sent Snow to get the boys from the back pasture where they were sparring. The trio arrived winded and damp with perspiration. "We should clean up before our meal. My mother would be aghast if I came to the table like this." MacD indicated his sweat-stained shirt and dirt-covered jeans.

"That's fine, Tavish, but don't take too long. Sharon and Ice will clear the table before you're back, if you don't hurry."

"Five minutes." The trio departed for their rooms at a run.

Lauren picked up the bowl of steamed vegetables and the basket of rolls. "This way, Dearest. I wasn't kidding about Sharon." Lauren tilted her head toward the correct door, and Alex preceded her to open it for her.

"If she is anything like Ice, we may starve before the evening is over," Alex agreed, as the pair bumped their way through the swinging door into the large formal dining room. "And I—"

Lauren turned to Alex standing just inside the door, her mouth hanging open. Lauren didn't know what caused such a reaction and she opened her bond fully to try and determine the source. She felt question, awe, astonishment, and what could only be described as disbelief coming from her mate. *"What, Alex?"*

"I do not know. I do not know what to say." She indicated the room before her with a wave of her arm. *"This is almost an exact replica of the private hall in the First Foremothers' Keep. Down to the formal Fraser tartans draped over the high-backed chairs. All that's missing are the stuffed animal heads on the walls."*

"How's that possible?" And then it dawned on Lauren as she took in what Alex was focusing on. *Oh, my gawd, Sharon's last name is Frasier.* Granted she spelled it differently, but she was a Scot from the Highlands. Lauren never made the connection before. Joy filled her heart. In some way, she and Sharon were now related.

Jamie, Susan, and Sharon stood behind their chairs at the long dining table staring at pair. Lauren's joy filled the room. "I didn't make the connection until now. Gawd, this is great!"

The moment was broken, as MacD, in his formal highland tartan, burst into the room through the door to the hall, a corgi hot on his heels. He froze. Boscoe, Newkirk, and McLaran slammed into his back and the four stumbled forward into the room.

Newkirk recovered first. "What is this? How can it be? Lauren, I do not understand. How can this tartan be here?" His questions tumbled one over the other, as the four had physically tumbled over one another when they entered the formal room.

"Okay, guys, you're scaring me here. What's going on?" Susan asked.

Lauren turned to answer Susan and saw Sharon gape at the boys, each of whom wore the kilt and plaid of their clan.

"What the hell is this?" Sharon demanded, pointing at the boys. "Where'd you get those outfits?"

"Lauren, perhaps we should complete our story of Terra and her clans this evening over your meal," Alex suggested gently.

"This is unacceptable. No one—and I mean no one—wears a tartan when they're not of that family," Sharon went on, red-faced and shaking.

Susan leaned over to her partner and placed an arm around her shoulder. "Let Lauren explain."

Alex spoke first. "I am in error and beg your forgiveness, Lady Sharon. Let me formally introduce my companions, please?"

Sharon nodded curtly.

"Lady Sharon, may I introduce," She beckoned to MacD. "This is Tavish MacDonald, my strength and right arm, the Protector and Guardian of my soul's other half." Alex smiled at Lauren, and Lauren felt herself blush. MacD bowed low in acknowledgement of the title and moved to stand beside Lauren. "This is Robert McLaran, my conscious and compass. His father is companion to the great Gríobhtha and chief of my Black Guard. Protectors of Terra Keep." Another low bow from McLaran and with a grin, he stepped away. "And this is Angus Newkirk, my wisdom and skeptic, one of the foremost scientific technicians of Terra." Newkirk moved around the table and knelt before Sharon.

"Lady Sharon, I am most honored to make your acquaintance." He took her tiny hand in his and kissed the back of it. "It seems Her Majesty is correct." He indicated Lauren with a tilt of his head. "Our realities have crossed before, in times past. For this could not be a coincidence." He indicated the room around them with a sweep of his other hand.

"Stand up, Newkirk. You're embarrassing her."

Newkirk rose, still holding her hand. "I would be most interested in hearing about your ancestors and how you honor your clan."

"I'd be glad to share my family's history." Sharon turned to Lauren, pointing at her. "But you have some explaining to do."

"Then allow me to formally introduce my soulmate and partner." Lauren took Alex's hand in hers. "May I present, Her Royal Majesty,

Alexandra Aoeron Aonwyn nighean mic Fionnaghal, Chief of Clan Doouglas, Rigain Rìoghachd Fuar Ćala, Queen of the Country of Cold Harbour and Ruler of Terra, Terra Prime, Luna Keep and all her realms beyond." Alex nodded with the pronouncement of her full title, and Lauren squeezed the large hand in hers in reassurance.

Alex turned to Lauren and bowed. "And may I present Her Royal Majesty, Lauren Beckwith Fraser Doouglas, Cáraid Rioghail Fuar Ćala, soulmate of Alexandra, daughter of Clan Fraser, healing technician, nexus traveler, Captain of the Ruadh làn-damh, Co-Ruler of Terra, Terra Prime, Luna Keep and all her realms beyond, and the Savior of All Terra."

"Thank you Dearest. I love you." She sent a burst of emotion along their bond to reinforce her words.

Silence hung heavy in the room as Lauren's three earth friends tried to understand what they had heard.

Jamie broke the silence. "Well, all righty then." He clapped his hands together. "Guess you didn't share everything last night. That's probably a good thing. I don't know if I would've been comfortable sitting with a queen and her retinue. Let alone understanding the animals. But man, Lauren, you gotta admit, you scored on this one." He smirked at Lauren.

Susan reached around and popped Jamie in the back of his head. "Shut up, Jamie. You're such a cretin. Don't you know how to act around royalty?" Susan turned back to the pair and bowed. "Welcome, Your Majesties. We're honored to have you here. Please join us for this meal, and let's get to know one another." Hints of a smile crinkled the corners of Susan's mouth.

"At least someone understands proper etiquette. But now, let us eat," MacD said taking a seat at the long table.

"Yes, I am hungry." Ice crowded up to the corner of the table next to Lauren.

"Why is it all you two can think about is food?" Alex asked, but she sat in one of the chairs too, and placed her napkin on her lap.

Sharon shook her head in disbelief, her earlier anger gone. "Wow, I mean?" She plopped down in her chair and reached for the bowl of mashed potatoes. "Wow."

"I know, right?" Lauren laughed and sat down next to Alex. "We all agreed full introductions would be too much to handle for everyone. So, we thought we'd try and introduce one thing at a time. Maybe, that wasn't such a good idea?"

"You married royalty. And Scottish royalty, no less." Sharon smiled slowly. "That's so cool."

"It is, but not as cool as having a soulmate and a love for the ages." Lauren smiled at others around the large table. "I pinch myself sometimes, because at times I can't believe it either."

Dinner was eaten as each of them gave a full explanation of their roles in the governance of Terra. They even shared some of the Investiture ceremony. The Terrans had agreed beforehand they wouldn't share anything about the treason plot, Clan Cador, or the challenges they faced with the traitors. These things weren't important in the greater scheme. All Lauren wanted was to ensure that her friends were fine. That they knew she was happy and well. And that they could share those Terran technologies applicable to Earth. She knew all this and had Alex's undying support. Alex knew for Lauren to be able to achieve peace, they had to travel to Earth's reality.

Chapter Five

The next day at mid-morning, Jamie traveled to the Yampa Valley Regional Airport and picked up the three attorneys. They had made the short flight from Denver to Steamboat Springs. On the drive back, they chatted about the spring weather, how good the skiing was with the warm temperatures, how the Sierra Club was progressing with their stay against the construction of the new power-generation plant, but not about the real agenda for their meeting. Jamie and Lauren agreed they would wait until the attorneys were at Susan and Sharon's home, after Jamie had reaffirmed their attorney-client privilege before anything else was revealed.

Jamie laughed to himself, he couldn't imagine how they would react to the news. All three attorneys were dressed in what he would call cowboy chic. *Or was it cowgirl chic?* Tight black jeans, form-fitting leather jackets, and boots made of various exotic animal hide. Though, he imagined they were faux-leather. None of the attorneys were the type to exploit animals. Another thing he liked about them.

Each wore a different color scheme—pastels, navy blues, and sage greens. The lead attorney sitting beside him in the front seat, dressed in a navy-blue outfit. He speculated, *Man, those jeans must be brand new, the creases would cut you they're so sharp. And probably cost more than I can imagine. They may be well off, but meeting royalty is going to throw them for a loop.*

He pulled Susan's large SUV into the open garage bay and shut off the engine. He turned in his seat to face all the vehicle's occupants. "Thanks for coming all this way. I know I threw a spanner into your schedules but I couldn't do this any other way."

Patricia, the senior partner in the firm, said, "We want what is best for you, Susan and Sharon, and Lauren's estate. I would like to have a complete plan in place to present to the judge when we ask her to start the clock." Patricia, or lead pit bull as he called her, held a burgundy leather portfolio on her lap, her initials stamped in gold on the lower right corner. He'd never seen her without it. Her salt and pepper hair was cut short in an asymmetric style.

"Hopefully, after today you'll have that plan. Or at least enough information for you to put a plan together. The three of us agree about how to proceed and I know Lauren doesn't want anything to go to her parents. Not after all they did to her when she was young."

Michelle, a striking brunette, cocked her head to the side, and Jamie watched her closely. Jamie had noted in their prior interactions that, although she never said much, she was the one who listened the best. *What'd I say to piqued her interest?*

"You're still talking about Lauren in the present tense. I know this is difficult for you, Jamie, but at some point, you need to move on." Michelle said.

"Sorry, I can't get my head around the fact she's gone." He opened the vehicle's door. "Let's go inside. Susan has brunch ready, and we can eat while we get the meeting started."

The attorneys entered the large kitchen, each smiling a greeting at Susan. "You know Patricia, right, Susan?" When she nodded, Jamie went on. "Great, and this is Michelle." He pointed at the tall attorney. She carried a large accordion briefcase in one hand and had a computer-case backpack over one shoulder. "She has an MBA, as well as her law degree. I'm hoping she can handle some of our questions today. Her specialty is patent law."

"We all have a lot of questions," Susan said.

Jamie turned to the third woman, a petite blonde, dressed in a sage green silk shirt with pearl buttons. "And last but not least is Grant. She's the firm's corporate-law specialist." He turned back to Susan. "You know we've wanted to find a way to meld Lauren's estate into a foundation and partner it with Steamboat Heritage." He glanced at Susan for confirmation.

"I know Sharon will like that. Anything which furthers her efforts to protect our environment will be awesome. And I'm sure Lauren will like that, too." Susan organized the cream and sugar on a small silver tray.

Jamie saw Michelle cock her head again, but he jumped in before she could ask anything. "Do you need a hand?" He asked Susan.

"Nope, all good here. The beverages are set up along with a brunch buffet in the dining room. Why don't you head in? I'll be along with the cinnamon rolls as soon as the timer goes off. Does anyone want an espresso drink instead of coffee?"

Patricia spoke up with a broad grin. "I'd love a no foam, quad shot latte, extra hot."

"Gees, Pat, why don't you have a little milk with your shot of caffeine?" Michelle teased as she followed Jamie out of the kitchen.

Susan laughed. "Right, I'll have that latte ready in a minute."

Jamie, Susan, and Sharon sat along one side of the long table with Patricia commanding the head of the table, and the other two attorneys across from the three friends. A scattering of empty plates and cups covered the center of the table, pushed there to make room for working. Each of the attorneys had large yellow legal pads in front of them. Michelle also had a variety of electronics scattered about her, a tablet, a recorder, and a laptop. Booting up his own laptop, Jamie thought Michelle must be the techno-nerd of the group, while the others were old school. Susan had a tablet in front of her, but Sharon didn't have anything. Seems she didn't need anything. She sat pushed back from the table, arms crossed over her chest. Jamie knew that posture. Sharon wasn't happy about something or someone, but he couldn't figure out what or who.

What could it be? Last night's meal started a bit stiffly after the formal introductions. As all the ribbing about royalty subsided, their evening ended well. He felt everyone was becoming more comfortable with Lauren's situation. Frankly, he didn't give a fig what anyone else thought. He was so glad she was here. He didn't care Lauren was royalty now, she was and always would be 'just Lauren' to him. He looked at everyone.

"Sorry, a stray thought." He waved his hand in dismissal. "Before we get into the heart of this meeting, we need to revisit our attorney-client privilege and ensure we have complete confidentiality in all we're going to discuss today."

Patricia glanced at her co-workers and raised an eyebrow, before answering him. "Of course, Jamie. Anything discussed between us, here or in any form of communication with our firm, is held in the strictest confidence. It cannot be revealed under demand or discovery. We have an ethical duty to protect our clients' information, whether that information comes to us from the client herself or from another source." The other two attorneys nodded, all with grave expressions.

"Do we need to request this privilege in writing? Or is our verbal agreement here today sufficient to protect the confidentiality of this meeting?" Jamie asked, as he typed a note into his laptop.

Michelle answered this question. "Everything we've discussed to date is covered by client privilege and our ethical responsibility. But should you need additional assurances, I suggest we draft a formal letter and record it in your client file."

Jamie turned to Susan and Sharon, and they both nodded. "Well then, let's do that. We would feel more comfortable proceeding under the strictest confidentiality we can put in place."

"Are you concerned we've violated our existing confidentiality, Jamie?" Patricia asked, concern lacing her voice. "Because, if you think that, then I feel we are not meeting your needs, and we should recuse ourselves and help you seek other counsel."

"No, we haven't had any concerns to date. However, some things have become reality—" Sharon snorted at Jamie's choice of words. He ignored her. "That we need to be fully protected going forward."

"Very well. If you would give us access to a printer, we can prepare a letter for all our signatures." Michelle said, her voice flat.

Jamie knew he was starting off badly, but once the attorneys knew everything, they would understand his caution. He hoped. It'd been Robert who provided the best thought last night. He said they should get on with it. If Lauren's attorneys were good at their jobs, then they were all wasting breath talking about something which was not an issue.

It took the attorneys ten minutes to prepare their letter. They provided spaces for the three friends to sign, and then added their signatures. "Since we all know each other, we needn't have this document notarized or confirmed in another manner," Patricia stated once the letter was executed. The document was scanned into Jamie's laptop. Patricia placed the executed document in her portfolio, closed it, and folded her hands on top, obviously not needing to say anything else.

"Okay, then I guess it's my turn," Sharon said. "As you know, we went to the Zirkels to hold a memorial for Lauren. It was almost fifteen months to the day of her disappearance, and given the machinations of her parents, we knew we couldn't continue the search any longer. We needed to allow the legal processes to start and enable you all to do your jobs."

Jamie watched the attorneys. They sat quietly, eyes intent on Sharon as she tried to set the stage. *Man, I'd hate to play poker with these guys. They don't give anything away.*

"When we got home from the wilderness area, we had unexpected guests." Michelle frowned at this piece of information and Patricia again crooked an eyebrow. Sharon hastily added, "One of whom you know."

Now all of them frowned. Sharon turned to Susan and shrugged. "Maybe we need to call them in?"

"Yeah, that's probably best. Rip off the Band-Aid," Susan said and Jamie nodded.

"Let me go get them." Before Sharon could rise from her chair, the kitchen door swung open and Lauren, in full highland regalia, walked in. Jamie started to rise as she entered, but she waved him back down. Since she'd entered the room behind Patricia, only the other two attorneys saw her, and their poker faces faded in shock.

"My god, Lauren. Is that really you?" Michelle recovered her voice first. Her question caused Patricia to spin out of her chair.

"Is it? It is you!" Patricia grabbed Lauren up in a bear hug. "I'm so glad to see you." She held Lauren out at arm's length. "But, how? Where? What?" Patricia was obviously at a loss for words, which Jamie knew was a most unusual event for the verbose attorney. "And other than the outfit, you look great."

Lauren laughed. "I'm very well. And glad to see you guys. From what I've heard from these three, you've been guarding the door against the wolves that are my parents."

Ice entered the room, also through the kitchen door and growled at the mention of Lauren's parents. Patricia jumped back at the sight of the large animal, and the other two attorneys tensed ready to climb onto the table to escape.

Lauren laughed and placed her hand around the wolf's ruffed neck. "May I introduce Ice. She's a big furball. No need to be afraid." Ice mock-growled. "Why don't we all have a seat?" She waved her hand at the long table.

The remainder of the morning passed quickly as Lauren shared a summary of her journey with the attorneys. They recovered from their initial shock and disbelief that Lauren was here and not only survived but thrived in her new world. The whole idea of another reality didn't seem to faze them. They seemed more intent on understanding Lauren was who she said she was and concern for her overall wellbeing. Once she finished her tale and began to outline what they needed in legal expertise, Susan excused herself to make a late lunch.

Lauren watched her leave through the swinging door. "Maybe Susan has the right idea. Now's a great time to take a break and have a bite to eat. Then we can get into the heart of the matter. And most importantly, you can tell us how we can put a stop to my parents. Preferably, once and for all." This mention of Lauren's parent brought another protective growl out of Ice. For most of the meeting she laid at Lauren's feet under the table, snoozing off and on, but this brought her out to stand beside Lauren's chair. Her deep growl rumbled around the room. Everyone froze at the sound. "It's okay. She's reacting to the mention of my parents."

After their break and a wonderful lunch, Lauren sat down at the head of the table. Ice sat beside her, leaning into her chair. Her hand instinctively went to the neck of the large wolf, and she let her fingers sink into Ice's thick fur. Lauren was always calmer with Ice near. And this was another time she relished in Ice's calming presence. Things were going to get more difficult as she tried to articulate what she and Alex wanted done with the Terran nano-technologies.

A lengthy discussion followed which included a complete technical discussion of the nano-tech and the uses Newkirk, Alex, and the boys had determined would be applicable on Earth. Lauren couldn't believe the depth of questions Michelle asked or her apparent understanding of

Lauren's answers. "I don't mean to pry, Michelle, but I gotta ask. What was your undergraduate degree in?"

Patricia and Grant laughed, and when Michelle glanced at Patricia in question, Patricia made a shooing motion. "Go on. Tell her. She'll be impressed. I know we discounted it when you applied for a position at our firm because we couldn't see a direct correlation to our legal work, but we may have been in error on that point."

"I have an undergraduate degree in molecular biochemistry from MIT. My parents wanted me to be a doctor, but I can't stand the sight of blood. So, I completed my undergraduate degree and then did an MBA, also at MIT, before going to Harvard for my JD."

Jamie whistled through his teeth. "Whoa, and I thought Lauren took the cake in amazing educational achievements. But that one tops her."

"Right, Jamie, as if your PhD from the University of Chicago is anything to sneeze at," Lauren said, and the group laughed at Jamie's blush. "Aren't you the one who skipped his undergrad program after only one year and completed his PhD in only four more? We all know what an underachiever you are."

Jamie didn't respond and Lauren prompted, "Well?"

"All right, I give. You're right. But, man, the weight of sheepskin in this room is a bit overwhelming to consider." He shook his head.

"We're going to need all of it and maybe more to address everything Lauren wants." Patricia's voice of reason sobered the others quickly. Lauren felt her worries resurface. They had discussed rewriting Lauren's estate plan documents, particularly since neither her parents, nor anyone else for that matter, had seen the first will. But because those were dated, notarized documents, they couldn't be changed without an explanation of the timing. Lauren obviously couldn't sign anything after the date of her disappearance.

However, the attorneys agreed that by using some of Lauren's liquid assets, they could create an exempt, private operating foundation. Her three friends would hold the officer positions, along with Michelle as general counsel. It would be based out of Denver from the address of Lauren's loft. It turned out Jamie loved his rented loft in Lauren's building so much he bought it, while maintaining her loft across the hall.

Once the foundation was recognized as a legal entity, they would give grants to scientists to study everything environmental: from global warming to cleaning up superfund sites, and for physicians to explore the use of the nano-technology in medicine. They knew this would foster the growth of environmental studies and further medical research in unimaginable ways. However, the question still remained—how to introduce the Terran technologies? They only knew they had to introduce them slowly.

Lauren asked, "How do we fund the foundation? And what do we do with the technologies?"

"If their use takes off and or we discover other uses or new related technologies, we could make a lot of money," Jamie said.

Michelle rubbed her chin. "We need to patent each of the existing technologies. Protect them from theft of intellectual property and establish their origin."

"Can a foundation do that? And for that matter, can a not-for-profit foundation make money?" Lauren felt herself getting lost in all the legal ramifications of their discussion.

"Perhaps, we need to establish a for-profit company?" Patricia answered Lauren's question and turned to her colleagues. "Could we embed the Terran technologies there as the seed? If we did, a place could be created for scientists, researchers, and physicians to work on additional applications of the technologies."

"If the researchers worked within a for-profit company, they would be protected from academic responsibilities and the need to fund-raise for grants, but then the company would own anything they discovered or invented. That's one of the reasons a lot of people don't want to work in that environment," Jamie said.

Lauren picked up his concern. "But, with that structure, we could create an environment to encourage the unrestricted growth of ideas. I don't know? Maybe create a mini-university without all the pressure of tenure and publishing to survive. Jamie would be great as a mentor to others. He was always the one leading the intern education programs at GeoDynamics."

"And what kind of education programs were you leading, Jamie?" Grant asked with an impish smile. "Trying to lead young minds astray?"

Jamie blushed a dark red. "Leave it, Grant. And for your information, I love teaching. It was my first choice of careers, but the offer from industry was too great to pass up."

"Come on, guys, Jamie is a great teacher." Lauren tried to refocus the meeting. "Maybe we could send all the net profits from the corporation to the foundation?" Lauren rubbed the side of her nose, and Ice whiffled at her gesture. "I know, girl. I'm always thinking and working, and this is supposed to be my honeymoon." Everyone around the table grinned at her self-recrimination. Her questions spawned another round of brainstorming and soon the group had an outline for a for-profit partner company in place.

Grant recommended they patent the Terran nano-tech one piece at a time. With a logical progression of development, it wouldn't be questioned where the technology came from, or how it was developed then. It would be up to Jamie with Lauren's help to break down the technologies into those logical pieces. They all agreed Newkirk would be needed.

"I think once we get the first piece out and hire some wiz-kids and docs with a natural curiosity, that would generate other applications and new ideas within the corporation," Jamie said enthusiastically, rubbing his hands together. "This is so cool. Everyone will want to work for us."

"You're right!" Lauren agreed. "And it might even work."

"Oh, it will work. This is a tremendous opportunity which will do amazing things for this planet," Patricia said. "What we need to do now, is complete all the work for the two entities, draw up the patent documents for each piece of technology, and set the clock ticking on your disappearance." The attorney stretched. "I don't know about you all, but I'm exhausted and we still haven't met your new bride. I want to meet the woman who took our Lauren Beckwith out of circulation."

Heat scorched up Lauren's neck and blazed across her cheeks.

"Patricia, I can't believe you're still carrying a torch for this one." Sharon crooked a thumb at Lauren, who was too stunned to speak. "You'll meet Alex at dinner, the boys and the other half of that one." She pointed at Ice and when the wolf snarled at her, Sharon snarled back. "I know you can understand me, so cut that out. We know you're just a big furball."

Chapter Six

Lauren's attorneys met Alex and the boys, and they all enjoyed a leisurely dinner. The after-dinner discussion quickly turned back to the work at hand. The group decided the attorneys would stay on in Steamboat and work from Susan and Sharon's home. That way, they would have access to Lauren and Newkirk for any technical details needed to complete the preliminary patent applications for the Terran technologies and provide input into the design of the for-profit company.

Once all was organized, the attorneys retired to begin clearing their calendars for the next three to four weeks. Lauren and Alex excused themselves and headed to their room.

"I am most impressed by your attorneys, Dearheart. They are an intelligent and compassionate group. I can feel their desire to do what is right for you." She smiled at Lauren. "I am confident they will be able to meet your needs and ease your distress about this reality."

"I agree, Dearest." Lauren cuddled into a hug, the physical contact making their bond spark and crackle. "But my parents are going to make life, for anyone associated with my estate, a living hell. Hopefully, isolating all the Terran technology in a corporation will help keep their hands off my assets."

Alex kissed the top of her head and tightened their hug. Light from the two Tiffany stained-glass lamps on either side of the king-sized bed cast the two in a warm multicolored glow. "I do not understand what their motives are. As you have explained and Patricia confirmed, they do not need the value of your estate."

"It's not about the money. It never has been. It's about control. Being the masters of all they survey. And unfortunately, it's also about forcing everything and everyone around them to conform to their value system. Remember when we were discussing the fealty oath for my Investiture?"

Alex nodded.

"Terran culture respects and values diversity in all its various forms and expressions. You even go so far as to include it specifically in your oaths. My parents don't value diversity in any form. And god help anyone who is outside their narrow view of what the world should be." Lauren brought their foreheads together, and her soul sang with their physical contact. She leaned back and sank into Alex's concerned sapphire eyes. "Had I not been able to escape from them, I wouldn't have survived."

"But you did survive, and you excelled at all you did." Alex tipped her head to the side in thought. "I wish I could have met your grandsire. I would like to thank him for all he did for you."

"I wish you could've too. He truly was my savior. He would've loved the boys." Lauren frowned, and she saw a matching expression flit across Alex's face in sympathy. "I think his one regret was, I wasn't a boy." Lauren paused as she listened to what she'd said. "But in hindsight, maybe that was my regret, because Granddaddy never treated me any differently." Lauren tried to step away from Alex as her thoughts darkened, but Alex only tightened her embrace more. "It was all my parents." Lauren tried to rationalize her parents. "My dad wanted a boy so badly, and when my mom couldn't have more children, everything kinda fell apart for them. I was my dad's greatest success and greatest disappointment all rolled into one."

"I think you are simply amazing. And I am looking forward to getting to know your friends more in the next few weeks."

Lauren laughed, and some of her dark thoughts dissolved. "Simply, huh?"

"You are simply everything to me and to Terra."

"Be that as it may, I know we have a lot of work to do and if I don't get some rest I won't be anything to anyone tomorrow." Lauren knew the concerns about her parents tainted her emotions. She didn't want to bring Alex down with her, so she started to wall them off. She stepped out of their hug and turned to her pack.

"Is that right? I have watched you go on very few hours rest, so do not try and use that as an excuse." Alex pulled her back around. "Do not hide from me, Lauren. I can feel all you feel. Our bond has strengthened to the point neither of us can wall off the other." Alex's worried eyes seemed to bore farther into her soul. “In fact, I suggest we try an experiment over the next few days.”

“An experiment?”

“Correct. I suggest we try to block the other. See if we can. And if we cannot, try to determine how much physical distance is required to stop feeling the other. Though, I do not think any distance will be far enough.” Alex stroked a fingertip down Lauren’s nose. “I spoke with Gríobhtha yesterday and he said although he could not speak directly with Lord McLaran, he can still feel him. And not only that, but he knew all was well in Terra.”

“Wow, that’s amazing. If he can do that, we do need to determine what we can do.” Lauren ducked out of their hug and began to pace the room at the foot of the large bed. “If that’s the case, we should be able to communicate at any distance. If not in words then in images or emotion-thoughts.”

“Emotion-thoughts?”

Lauren shrugged. “I don’t know what else to call them. When we were on Luna and headed to Construction Site Alpha, I could feel your discomfort and worry about our delay in returning to the Keep. That’s what I thought I felt . . . you being worried, I mean. I later realized I was feeling your anxiety about keeping me in the dark about the *Ruadh làn-damh,* and then I forgot about my mistaken interpretation of your emotions when the EVA went south.” Lauren grimaced as memory filled her mind, and her stomach rolled sympathetically. “But in hindsight, had I concentrated fully on you through our bond, I would’ve felt all the nuances of your emotions and been able to distinguish what you were actually feeling. For instance, if I concentrate on you right now.” Lauren put her finger to her temple and closed her eyes, a slow smile curling her lips. “You’re feeling love, concern, anxiety, amusement, and, wait for it, horny.”

“Lauren!”

Lauren opened her eyes, a thrill running through her at Alex’s blushing grin. “Don’t try and hide it, Alex, it’s okay.” Lauren stepped into Alex’s arms and snuggled into her long body, gathering her into a full-body hug. “Don’t be embarrassed either. This has been a strenuous trip for us, and then learning about what a pain my parents have been, not to mention Ffrwyn and her pregnancy. As usual, we've put ourselves last. Why don't we do something about your needs tonight? Then, I was thinking we could go to Denver in a few weeks, after Patricia and her pit bulls make some progress in their work. We can stay at my loft, and be by ourselves. What do you say?"

Alex was broadsided. Her eyebrows disappeared into her bangs. Her mouth opened and closed but she didn't speak. Lauren was sure she had read Alex correctly, up to and including the trip to Denver. She felt Alex wanted to see how and where she lived prior to crossing the nexus. Now she was uncertain.

"Don't you want to?"

"I would very much like to, Dearheart. I am simply shocked at how accurately you felt all that along our bond. I was not broadcasting, but I truly do want to go to Denver." Alex grabbed Lauren up and flipped them both onto the bed. "As for the other thing, let us focus on that now."

Lauren giggled. Their souls melded, and they were one, soaring outward, filling the universe with the essence of their love, as their bond expanded exponentially.

Chapter Seven

"But, Susan," Lauren pleaded.

"Don't 'But Susan' me, young lady. You traveling to Denver's a risk too great to even imagine, let alone act upon. No way am I letting the two of you leave here alone." Susan shook her head and her frown deepened. "I can't allow it."

"But, Susan, we'll fly back to Denver with Michelle in the jet. No one knows us, or me. Come on, the flight crew hasn't a clue who I am. And I'll wear a wig or something, a baseball cap maybe. We'll go into my building late at night. We shouldn't come across anyone on our way up to the loft. I want to show Alex Denver or at least the small part I lived in when I was there." The more she argued with Susan, the more she realized what Susan was concerned about. They would be taking a huge chance. Anyone could see them and if someone recognized Lauren, they would be well and truly outed. Lauren rolled her eyes at herself as she recognized her own double entendre.

Susan leaned a hip against the granite countertop and rubbed her temple. "I know you do, but it's such a gamble. We're so close to tying up all the legal stuff and to risk all that is more than I can comprehend. Have you asked Patricia what she thinks?"

Lauren knew she was caught. "No, I haven't, and I wasn't going to. I was going to run it by Michelle before she leaves tomorrow night. I know she's going to town for thirty-six hours to attend that court hearing she couldn't reschedule. I thought Alex and I could tag along. She could take us to the loft from Centennial Airport and pick us up after her hearing." Lauren knew she was starting to whine, and she hated that in others but most of all she hated it in herself.

Granddaddy's voice rang clear in her head. '*Stop acting like a spoiled brat, Lauren. You're better than that. Define the problem and then determine a solution which meets everyone's concerns. Most times when someone disagrees with you, they are concerned for you. Presenting your reasoning and discussing it allows them an opportunity to state their concerns. More importantly, you need to determine if this is a want or a need for you. Those two things are different. But no matter what, do not whine.'*

"I'm sorry, Susan. I've let my wants get in the way of everyone else's concerns. We'll figure out something else, some other way for the two of us to get away. I need a break." She absently rubbed her chest. Even with all the time since the Cador treason was ferreted out and the guilty punished, Lauren hadn't slowed down. Once the Council agreed to a course of action, she'd thrown herself back into her research. She and Newkirk had worked nonstop to get their science ready for this trip to Earth's reality. "I feel like I've gone two-forty since the blizzard, and I can't seem to catch up or slow down enough to rest."

Susan enveloped her in a huge hug. Lauren winced as pain shot through her chest, but she snuggled close to absorb the love and protection Susan offered. She still couldn't have her ribs compressed without discomfort. At least the pain generated by the random discharges from the Terran shield had stopped as soon as their group crossed the nexus into Earth's reality. The Terran shield technicians still couldn't stop them for some reason.

Susan pulled back and scrutinized Lauren clinically. "Are you okay?"

"I'm fine." She turned her head.

"Don't lie to me, Lauren. You winced when I hugged you. I know I forget how strong I am sometimes, but I didn't squeeze you that hard." Lauren again met Susan's eyes and saw Susan had her doctor glare going. "Are you sure?"

"I'm sure." She tried to smirk, but it was half-hearted at best. "I'm fine, sore from sparring yesterday."

Susan rolled her eyes. "I'm blown away by a culture so technologically advanced they can cure disease using nanites and travel through the universe at faster-than-light speeds, but they still fight with swords."

Lauren used to think the same thing. Even though she had experienced modern Terran weaponry firsthand, she hadn't understood their use of swords either. That was until Lady MacDonald explained. She shared Siobhán's explanation with Susan. "I get that. But what you don't understand is fighting with a sword brings you into the closest possible contact with your enemy. Literally face-to-face. You see, and in most instances, feel what's happening which forces you to be an active participant in the conflict. The Terrans can blast away with high-energy weapons from space, but that's a faceless action. In space, you're detached from the horrors you're causing." Lauren saw confusion on Susan's face, and she paused to organize her thoughts. "If you can't see your enemy, you can't be sympathetic to the pain you're inflicting. In some ways, not being sympathetic leads to more and more conflict. It builds walls between you and your enemies. Leaves you unfeeling and uncaring about what you're doing. Keeps you from determining a mutual understanding."

Susan moved around the granite island and plopped down on one of the barstools. "I guess I can see that. It's kinda like all the drones we're using in raids throughout the Middle East. The pilots are far away from the actual casualties and damages."

"That's a great analogy, but swords are even more integral to Terran culture than that. Our monarchy is magical. All the pageantry and rituals from times lost are important for one reason. They honor the dignity of our clans' past. Monarchy, and all its components, represent who we were, who we are, and what we aspire to be."

Susan whistled. "Wow. I never thought about it like that before." She tilted her head, and Lauren felt the intensity of her stare increase, almost physically slicing through her. She shivered. "And you said 'we' and 'our'. You've bought into all this, haven't you?"

Lauren felt her anger rise, but she tamped it down. She needed Susan to understand this. "It's not about buying in. It's about my family. I'm as much a part of them as they are of me. Doesn't matter that I'm adopted into the Fraser Clan, I love Merilyn more than I love my biological mother. Sharon understands this because she's part of a clan. Even though she was born here, in America, she still carries on the traditions of her family. She honors them and their heritage. She decorates her home with her clan's colors, their tartan. She identifies with her clan by wearing those colors on special occasions as a remembrance of who she is and who others in her history were." Lauren saw some understanding begin as a small grin danced at the corners of Susan's mouth. "Even without my soul-bond with Alex, I would have done what I did when I first crossed the nexus. Especially, as a physician. But after my adoption into Clan Fraser . . ." Tears rose in her eyes. Her vision blurred. "For the first time, I knew deep in my heart I was finally a part of something that mattered. Something greater than myself. Something I will protect and honor and cherish, today, tomorrow, and forever." Lauren knew she was lecturing Susan, but then Susan surprised her, as a beautiful smile bloomed across her face and it caused Lauren's tears to break loose and flow down her cheeks.

Susan leapt from her seat and grabbed Lauren up in another crushing hug. "Oh, my God, you've finally realized who you are, and how important you are to others. You've found your place in the world. I don't care it's on Terra. You've found it!" Lauren pulled back and her face must have shown her confusion. "When we first met you and as we got to know you, Sharon and I were always a little bit sad, because we knew you never allowed yourself to feel. To be a part of something greater than yourself. It wasn't you were self-centered or self-absorbed. You were so focused on your work. We knew you had the memories of your grandparents as your touchstone and that kept you centered, but you never allowed yourself to be you, to give your heart fully." Susan's voice trailed off.

Lauren felt the magnitude of Susan's insight hit home for her. She was stunned, but when she absorbed Susan's words, she had to agree. Her smile grew to match Susan's.

"I love you." Three simple words. Lauren hugged Susan back as hard. "And you're right, I have found my home."

A few minutes later, they were torn out of their hug as Snow crashed into the kitchen through the garage door. *"Come quickly, Lauren. Something is wrong. She will not get up, and she is in a great deal of pain."*

"What? What'd you say, Snow?"

The wolf danced in place, her anxiety evident. *"Ffrwyn! She is down and will not get up. Come quickly."* Snow raced back out the door she had entered. Lauren opened her bond fully and was immediately hit by an avalanche of pain. She staggered under its magnitude.

Susan reached out to steady her. "What, what's wrong?"

"It's Ffrwyn. Snow says she's down. She's in intense pain. Something's wrong."

"Don't panic. We'll take care of her. Go upstairs and get Sharon. Tell her to call my office. Have them bring the mobile-operating horse van out now. We may need to do surgery. They'll know what to do."

Lauren was frozen in place as Ffrwyn's fear and pain pounded through her psyche.

"Lauren, go now!" Susan turned her toward the inner door and gave her a shove. "Have Sharon call my office."

Lauren physically shook herself, her physician's training taking over. "Right. Sharon, office, surgery. Got it." As she ran from the kitchen, she called out to Alex. *"Ffrwyn's in trouble. Meet us in the barn, now."*

"I am already there. I felt her go down. The boys are trying to get Gríobhtha under control. We need you to talk to him. He will not listen to me. He is in a panic, and he will tear the barn apart trying to get to Ffrwyn."

Lauren extended her bond and felt for Gríobhtha. *There. "Gríobhtha you've gotta calm down. Doctor Susan and I are coming. But we need you to relax. Focus on Ffrwyn. Share your strength with her. You need to calm her down. You being this upset is hurting her."*

She didn't get an answer from him. *"Listen to me, now!"* She heard a far-off whiffle and then, something, but she couldn't understand what. *"Calm down, Gríobhtha and listen to me. We're on the way. Now, try again. What did you say?"*

"Pain. Lauren, help. Afraid. Hurts. My baby. Too soon." Lauren heard Ffrwyn's fragmented cries.

"It's going to be okay, Ffrwyn. Relax. Doctor Susan and I are coming. Everything's going to be all right." Lauren raced up the stairs and found Sharon in her office. She grabbed the door jamb to keep from falling, spinning into the room. "Call the office. Tell them to bring the horse van. Susan may need to do surgery. Ffrwyn's in trouble. And hurry." She turned and raced back to the stairs.

"Lauren, Gríobhtha is trying to reach her. We cannot keep him out of her stall."

"Then let him in. If he's near her, maybe he'll be able to calm her down. I can't reach him through our bond, Alex. He's so panicked, all I get are whiffles."

Lauren burst through the kitchen door, darted out through the garage, racing toward the far-off barn. As she ran, she reached out to Gríobhtha again. *"Listen, Gríobhtha, please settle down. Ffrwyn needs you, and you're going to need to be her strength. Do you hear me? We're all going to need you to be calm and steady. You must be brave for your mate and your foal."*

Finally, she heard him respond coherently. *"I am a pillar of strength and will give it all to My Heart."*

"Not all of it, Big Guy. Just enough for her to get through this. We will add ours, and you must pass it on."

"I understand, Lauren. I will channel your gifts to her. Ice and Snow are here, as are Alex and her companions. I must get to her. They will not let me in."

Running faster, Lauren mentally called Alex. *"You gotta let him in that stall. He's going to channel our shared strength into Ffrwyn."*

Dashing into the barn at a dead-run, Lauren took in the scene before her in a single glance. The half-door to Ffrwyn's stall hung off its hinges. MacD and Newkirk stood to the side, peering anxiously into the stall. The two looked up, faces grave with worry. She skidded to a halt outside Ffrwyn's stall, and placed a hand on each of their arms. "It's going to be okay, guys. We have to let Susan do her job. She's truly the best there is. Let's focus on that and send our strength to Ffrwyn through Gríobhtha."

Ducking into the stall, she gasped. Ffrwyn was down on her side, chest heaving, sweat glistening on her flanks. Gríobhtha was backed as far into a corner as he could get, but still touching Ffrwyn. He was lying sphinxlike, his massive head flat to the ground, nose touching the top of his mate's head, whiffling softly. McLaran lay half across Gríobhtha's broad back, arms around his great neck. He had his eyes closed in concentration, but Lauren could feel the strength he was sending to Ffrwyn through Gríobhtha. Ice and Snow huddled along Ffrwyn's back, their snowy fur contrasting sharply with her sweat-darkened coat.

Alex stood frozen in the other corner, hands clasped so tightly her knuckles were white. Lauren moved to stand beside her. She enfolded her in a hug. "Easy, Dearest. Susan's staff is on the way. We'll get her comfortable as soon as possible."

"But, she is in pain. It is awful." Lauren, feeling Alex's panic, knew she was shaken to her core.

"You've gotta be as strong for her as Gríobhtha is." When Alex didn't respond, Lauren shook her. "Alex, listen to me. Susan's the best vet in the western United States, if not the whole country. She's been watching and treating Ffrwyn since we arrived. You've gotta focus here. Your panic is upsetting Ffrwyn more." Lauren could see sweat starting to run down Alex's face in sympathy to Ffrwyn's struggles. She shouted along their bond, *"Focus, Alex. You can't lose yourself in her pain or efforts. Parcel the pain out. Send it away, and then send your strength back through our bond to Gríobhtha. You can't take on all her pain. You aren't prepared."*

Alex turned her head slowly and pleaded with Lauren. *"Help her."*

"We're going to, but we gotta help each other, too."

Alex nodded slowly.

Susan came around the corner of the stall, a large red case in each hand. "Whoa, okay, everyone out. We've got to have room to work here." Susan turned to Lauren. "I'm going to need your help before my staff arrives. Get the boys to rake out this stall and get some clean straw in here. I guess we'll have to work around the Big Guy. Him moving would upset Ffrwyn too much. Can you let Ffrwyn know what we're going to need to do?"

"I can." Lauren got the boys moving and Alex out of the stall. But Alex hovered in the open doorway, her anxiety ratcheting up with every groan from Ffrwyn.

Once the stall was cleaned, Susan turned to the group. "All right, here's how this is going to go. Newkirk, I need you to go to the tack room and get the big block and tackle that has the red rope on it." He darted away. She knelt beside Ffrwyn and scratched between her ears, her next comments directed at the horse. "Sweet one, your baby wants to meet her momma and papa, but she's a little overanxious." Ffrwyn whiffled softly. "I need you to relax as much as possible." Susan stroked her forehead. "Remember how relaxed you were when we did our massages?" Ffrwyn nodded. "I want you to focus on that and try and get that relaxed again."

Susan stroked her hands down the horse's side. Lauren saw the horse's belly visibly ripple with another contraction.

"Lauren, I need you to tell Ffrwyn the foal is turned properly and we shouldn't need to do anything more than help her along. But it's a big foal, even this early. Then I need you to go in the house. We can't have my staff see you. Once they arrive, I'll have them prepare everything we'll need, in case we need to do surgery." Susan stood and walked over to a large wooden bench along the near wall. She lifted the seat and took out a stack of blankets. "Time is of the essence here. I want to be prepared if I can't help the foal along the birth canal." She turned and dropped the blankets beside Gríobhtha and went back to stroke Ffrwyn as Lauren relayed the message.

"Once I start, I'll only have about twenty minutes to assist her with a natural birth. If I can't get it in that time window, we'll anesthetize her to alleviate the pain and relax the contractions. I'll try again, but I'll need to push the foal back to manipulate its position, all the while she's trying to push. Given the strength of a horse's contraction, it's a real battle. I may have to lift her hind quarters up." Susan pointed at the large ring embedded in one of the cross beams running over the stall. Newkirk dashed into the stall. "Newkirk, hang the block and tackle there."

Again, Lauren relayed the information. Ffrwyn nodded again, but even that small movement caused her pain and she snorted.

"If I need to do a cesarean section, we'll deepen the anesthesia and be as quick as we can."

"How can I help?" Alex had moved up to stand at Susan's side.

"Alex, I may need you to help me pull the foal out." Lauren watched as Susan wisely assigned a task to Alex. She knew keeping Alex focused on a physical activity would help her partition Ffrwyn's projected pain, and stop it from being transmitted along their bond. Alex nodded as Susan went on to explain how she was going to manipulate, and then pull the foal.

"All right, let's get this done." Susan bent and laid her forehead on Ffrwyn's heaving side and whispered. "All will be well, little one. We're looking forward to meeting you," Without lifting her head, Susan placed both hands flat on the horse's heaving side, rubbing in gentle circles. "And you will be fine too, Momma."

Susan stood and smiled at everyone. "Okay folks, you know what we need to do, we've got a new baby to meet."

Lauren felt the vet's confidence roll over her in waves. *Wow. That's so cool. How does she do that? Wish I could.*

"You do. Every time you are in healing ward, this is how you are." Ice reassured her.

It could have been minutes or it could have been hours, Lauren didn't know. She had the same odd sense of time displacement here as she felt when in the OR. She had watched the group's work through her bond with Alex. Susan's staff left after the successful birth and Lauren was now back in the stall.

After much effort on Susan and Alex's part, and more on Ffrwyn's part, they had a beautiful ebony filly. Her feet were feathered, like Ffrwyn's, but instead of white, they were caramel, as was her tail. The little horse was clean and bundled in blankets, curled beside her sleeping mother. They did have to anesthetize Ffrwyn, once that was done all the pain being transmitted along their bond stopped. At which point, all the companions turned their focus solely on Ffrwyn, sending love and strength. Breathing with her and keeping her from slipping away into the miasma of drugs Susan had administered.

Susan lay beside the tiny bundle, a warm bottle in hand, waiting patiently for the filly to wake up. "She'll need to eat as soon as possible. Once Ffrwyn's awake and we can safely get her to her feet, this little one will immediately seek a meal. In the interim, I'll start the process."

Ice and Snow lay on either side of the filly, watching with rapt attention. *"She is beautiful, Lauren."* Snow whispered along their bond. *"Gríobhtha and Ffrwyn should be very proud."*

"That she is, Snow, and I'm proud of them, too. After I get done kicking their butts for not telling us about her in the first place, I'll be even more proud."

"The animal techs on Terra could not have done better than Doctor Susan did. She is amazing. And I do not think Ffrwyn would have done as well there, without you and Alex near her. It would have taxed her even more having our bond stretched so thinly." Ice replied.

"She is correct, Lauren. Separation would have been hard on her," Gríobhtha said.

Lauren could feel his wonder as he stood watching the little filly. He whiffled over her head, her stubby mane moving with each of his exhalations.

Lauren knelt beside Ice and hugged her close. *"Always the voice of reason, Ice."*

"You are very lucky to have me." That comment brought a loud snort from each of the other companions.

"Watch it, furball. Your head is swelling again. We may need to have Doctor Susan examine you to check the size of your ego," Alex warned.

Lauren didn't share in their laughter. She was focused on Susan, who sat with the filly's head in her lap, holding the bottle as the now awake little horse drank the formula. It was the tilt of Susan's head, how her eyes were unfocused, and how she didn't seem to be breathing, which worried Lauren.

"Susan?"

Susan slowly turned her head away from the filly. "Her name is Làireach. She told me. She told me her name."

Alex bent down to lean over Susan, one hand on the vet's shoulder and the other on the filly. "Be easy, Susan, and let me listen." Lauren watched as Alex closed her eyes. She felt their bond sing as Alex drew her into the vortex of her mental quest. *"Can you hear me Làireach?"* Alex spoke with her mind-voice and also asked her question aloud for Susan to hear.

The little filly blinked her mahogany eyes rapidly, trying to focus. Alex opened her eyes and smiled. *"It is all right. You are safe. What may we do for you?"*

A tiny soprano voice tinkled brightly along the edge of their bond. Lauren watched the little filly smile. *"I am fine. I am happy to be here. I was afraid. But Siùsaidh told me to be easy. To let her do the work. She is my friend."* She punctuated her words with a whiffle that ruffled Susan's hair. Tears flowed down Susan's cheeks, as she sat awed by the small bundle in her arms.

Lauren's face was wet with tears. "So, this is how a bond is made."

"Yes, Dearheart, this is how Ffrwyn and I bonded at her birth. Susan must truly be special if this little one has chosen to bond with her."

"I did not choose. It was just there. And I like it. It feels good."

"So, it does, Làireach. You are amazing to recognize this and so brave to seek it out." Alex stroked the soft nose beneath her hand and cooed in reassurance.

"Oh, God, Lauren. Is this what you feel? I can't begin to explain how I feel." Susan's tears ran freely down her cheeks as she placed her cheek against the crown of Làireach's head.

"Sit back and enjoy it, Susan. It's an amazing thing. Can you hear Gríobhtha or Ice or Snow?"

Susan eyes unfocused, as she concentrated. Lauren felt her reach out along the small, tenuous bond which stretched between her and the tiny filly. "No, I don't think so."

Alex nodded. "Do not try to reach too far, Susan. Let the bond be. It will strengthen over the next few days. You may have one with Ffrwyn when she awakes. Do not be alarmed."

"I'm not alarmed. I'm . . . I'm totally blown away. I can't believe how rich the connection is." Susan hugged the filly and kissed her between her floppy ears.

"I am hungry, Siùsaidh." Làireach opened her mouth for the bottle Susan held out. She latched on and drank heartily.

"She's going to have an appetite almost as large as Ice's." Lauren heard the wolf growl in agreement.

"Now what're we going to do?" Lauren asked as they settled in for the night, warm and content in each other arms.

Alex rolled them on their sides, facing each other. "Do? Do about what?"

"About Susan and Làireach. What happens when we go back across the nexus to Terra? How'll they handle the separation?" Tears welled in her eyes and spilled down her cheeks. She couldn't imagine being separated any distance from Alex again. The pain of their first separation was still sharp and clear in her heart and soul. A shiver ran down Lauren's spine, as she remembered the cold of that early morning when

Gwenhwyfach expelled her from the Keep. But what had crushed her soul was the tearing-pain in her heart as she heard Alex tell her to go away.

Alex cupped her cheek in a large hand. "Easy, Dearheart. That time is over."

Lauren turned her head and placed a gentle kiss in the palm. Alex giggled. Lauren pulled away, "This isn't funny, Alex. We've gotta figure out how we're going to handle this."

"I was not laughing at you or the situation, Lauren. Your kiss tickled, and I giggled. That's all."

"Gawd, Alex, what're we gonna do?" Lauren flopped on her back and stared up at the ceiling.

Alex rolled on her back and laced her hands behind her head, crossing her legs at the ankles. Lauren knew Alex was either deep in thought on the problem at hand. Or, she already had the problem figured out and was preparing to give Lauren a lecture in bond development, the fostering of a newly formed bond, or something like that.

"Out with it. I can see you know something."

"What do you think I know?"

Was this another one of their experiments? Lauren and Alex spent the last several weeks testing the actual strength of their bond. They had determined that regardless of the distance they'd tried, and they had tried up to about seventy-five kilometers of separation, nothing prevented them from speaking easily to each other. Sleep didn't interrupt their link either. The one who was awake could slip easily into her partner's mind. Once there, they could influence the direction of the sleeper's dreams. They tried distraction, too, when one of them was engaged in a conversation or focused on a task. For example, when Lauren was working on the patent applications with Newkirk and Michelle, Alex found she could 'see' what was happening around Lauren as if she was in the meeting with them.

It was Gríobhtha who showed them the true nature of a strong bond. Several days after Làireach was born, the proud father informed Lauren he had informed Lord McLaran of the birth, and celebrations were planned when they arrived back in Terra. He also said Merilyn was preparing a special gift for the little filly when they all returned. Pressing for more details about this communication, the horse said he didn't actually 'tell' McLaran, he 'showed' him. When questioned further, he couldn't explain it any other way. He knew McLaran understood his feelings and was proud of him. Lauren deducted Gríobhtha was using some sort of emotion-thought, as she called them, to send McLaran a picture painted with feelings about the happenings on Earth.

Lauren sat up and mirrored Alex's position on the bed. "Let's see, what do you know?"

She opened her bond to its maximum. A cascade of images, feelings, emotions, and thoughts poured over her. Seeming to come from all directions, this torrent was generated from all the companions. She felt the filly sleeping and the happy parents watching over their baby. Snow and Ice snuggled together with Boscoe in the den and unsurprisingly, Ice was dreaming about food. Susan and Sharon slept soundly, both exhausted from the happenings since the filly's birth. Lauren's bond with those two had strengthened as Susan's bond with Làireach grew. These were all background noise, because Alex's mind was in the fore. A shining beacon which eclipsed all the others with its intensity.

"I think you know what we should do." Lauren tried to translate Alex's emotion-thoughts into words. "We should plan on taking them with us when we return to Terra."

Lauren hadn't consciously processed Alex's thoughts until she heard herself say the words of her translation out loud, and when she did, shock ripped through her.

"Alex, how's that going to work? Susan and Sharon are integral to our plans for the corporation and the foundation. How would they explain their absence? Plus, Susan has her vet practice, and Sharon has her foundation."

Alex chuckled and held up both hands. "Easy, Dearheart. Slow down a minute, and let your brain catch up with my thoughts. You are babbling."

"Sorry." Lauren rubbed her face, trying to clear her thoughts. "I do that when I'm worried or anxious."

"I know, and it is okay. I have realized it is one of the ways you process and work through a problem. But in this case, I have been thinking about this since Làireach was born and we realized the bond had established itself." Alex smiled at her.

"Well, Oh Great One, if you've got it all worked out, share." Lauren snuggled into Alex's side.

Alex dropped an arm around Lauren. "I did not say I had it all worked out. You raise some valid questions in your babbling which need to be addressed." Lauren pinched Alex in her side for the smart-aleck remark, making Alex squirm. "But the key point is Susan and Làireach cannot be separated in these early stages of the bond's formation. Therefore, Susan must travel back to Terra with us, because Làireach is too young to be separated from her mother and Ffrwyn will go with us. Since Susan would not leave Sharon, Sharon must go along."

"All right." Lauren drew the word out into several long syllables, as she thought about Alex's analysis. "Maybe we can set up a way to communicate with Jamie across the nexus, so he has access to their input into the tech work here. Or we can create a travel schedule. They spend time on Terra and then back here. Or when Làireach is grown, they live here, and we visit them." Lauren felt Alex draw her closer and she relaxed, the enormity of their problem shrinking to a manageable size in her mind.

"It will all work out. I do not think we have the right to answer all these questions without input from the others involved."

Lauren yawned. "You're right, Alex. We can work it out, but it's going to require another group meeting."

"Indeed." Alex's whisper trailed off as she dropped off to sleep.

Lauren agreed softly. "We can solve anything—together. Always together." Then she slid into slumber, joining Alex in their shared dream world of a green meadow, painted by a summer's sun. A tiny filly running toward the Keep.

Chapter Eight

The next several weeks passed in a whirlwind of activity. The attorneys completed their work. The two corporate entities were created and all the documentation was filed with the Colorado Secretary of State. They were able to establish some initial policies and outline a selection process for new employees. And thus, Nexus Limited was born.

Jamie was concerned about being the sole board member and only officer present to get the company rolling. So, Michelle agreed to take a leave from her position in Patricia's firm to help him full-time. Lauren and Newkirk had already parsed the Terran nano-tech into small, functional pieces, divided between medical and environmental applications. Michelle would have her hands full getting all the patent applications completed. She would stay at the ranch to complete the first applications and get them filed. There, she would be close to Lauren and Newkirk if any problems arose before they left for Terra. The group also decided they would base Nexus Limited in Steamboat Springs, not in Denver as originally planned.

Susan continued to strengthen her fledgling bond with Làireach. The bond began to include Ffrwyn. Susan spent every day and even some nights with Làireach. She and Sharon slept in the stall with the young filly. Alex wondered if the bond would grow strong enough to include Sharon at some point. She asked Newkirk about this. Angus knew his father would be ecstatic to study the pair when they returned to Terra as Lord Newkirk was the Terran expert on bonds and psi-activity.

It seemed Lauren's concerns about Susan and Sharon going to Terra weren't concerns at all. Sharon recognized the amazing offer for what it was and accepted it as she did everything else, with an open heart. She was most interested in continuing the exploration of her Scottish heritage with Newkirk, and with the Lady MacDonald once they returned to Terran reality. Newkirk and she had combed the internet for any indication Terrans had traveled to early Earth, especially to the Scottish Highlands. There were too many similarities for it to be a coincidence or a matter of parallel evolution. They would expand their historical review in the Terran archives as well.

The only remaining issue was Alex and Lauren going to Denver. Although Lauren acknowledged all the concerns and risks, she believed they could make the trip safely. Alex didn't try and sway the group one way or the other, except to say she would like to see Denver. See how large cities were managed in this reality, as a comparator to the cities on Terra Prime. But she bowed out of the debate and let her Consort do the arguing. At the end of the discussion, it was decided only the boys and Jamie would go back to Denver after they found a new home for Nexus Limited in Steamboat. When they left, Lauren and Alex would have the entire third floor of Susan and Sharon's home to themselves. This would have to do to get some privacy for the soulmates.

Lauren prepared a list of personal items she wanted from her loft to take back to Terra. Jamie would gather those things and return with them to Steamboat in a week. Lauren had purchased a new eReader, an MP3 player, and a tablet. She hoped she could surprise Alex with these gifts and maybe get hers back. She loaded all the devices with as much reading material, music, games, and research information as Alex wanted from the internet. She had already updated her own laptop and was downloading as much reference material as she could. She dumped entire databases on the new theories of loop quantum gravity, medical advancements, and general scientific achievements recorded since the blizzard onto portable hard drives. For Lady MacDonald, she prepared a new laptop and downloaded all the reference materials she could find on standing stone circles, Celtic history and lore, as well as the history of the Scottish Clans on Earth. Things were falling into place.

"I don't know, Jamie, is this a big enough building?" Lauren leaned over the blueprints of a large office and workshop complex owned by a construction firm leaving the Yampa Valley.

Jamie tilted his head. "I think it is, and if we can get the vacant thirty-five acres to the west and north along the Elk River, we'll have acreage to expand."

"The construction is sound, Lauren. We can convert the maintenance areas to laboratory space easily," Newkirk said, leaning over to point out the large open garage spaces on the plans to Lauren.

"I'll admit the price is right." Lauren stood straight and stretched out her back. "Is there something wrong we aren't seeing? I can't believe they're willing to let it go for only one and a half million. Doesn't make sense in today's real estate market."

Jamie nodded. "That may be true in Denver's hot market, but here the market is still quite soft. I think the company that owns the building is in financial trouble. We'll get Patricia to put together an intent-to-purchase contract and place some earnest money down, but the deal will be contingent on the results of a structural inspection. If an inspection finds something wrong, we'll cancel the purchase."

"I can go with that. And the vacant land?" Suddenly, Lauren laughed. She said to Newkirk and Jamie. "What am I doing here?" Neither Newkirk nor Jamie answered. "This is your company, Jamie, why am I meddling in the decisions which should be yours? I'm sorry, buddy."

"'S okay, Lauren. As far as I'm concerned, I'm the caretaker of this venture. It's your money and your technical discoveries." Newkirk cleared his throat and Jamie turned to him. "Sorry, Angus. I know you had a lot to do with all the discoveries. Isn't that why we're naming the nanites, NewKirks?"

That statement caused Newkirk's face to go slack with shock. "But they are not. I may have participated in Lauren's efforts, but they are her discoveries. Her stroke of genius was to use her DNA as a comparator. Her medical expertise led to the cure for the children. I cannot accept this." He vigorously shook his head. "It is Her Majesty's honor to have." He bowed deeply to Lauren.

Lauren acknowledged his gesture with a gentle nod, but she couldn't keep the smile off her face. "Oh, yeah, right. I was neither the one who suggested all the applications for environmental remediation, nor was I the one to reengineer the nanite size when the initial ones caused clotting problems. Sorry, Angus, but you gotta accept this honor and wear it proudly. Didn't we also agree we'd leave off on all the bowing, Her Majesties and M'lords in this reality? If anyone heard you call me that, they'd think I was an egotistical bitch or an absolute looney-tune."

"Oh, Your Majesty! I mean, Lauren, I would never call you a bird." Newkirk blushed.

"I'm not referring to a bird, Angus." Lauren clarified and his eyebrows rose in question.

Jamie dropped a long arm around the taller Newkirk's shoulder. "No worries. I'll show you what a looney-tune is when we get to Denver. In the meantime, I'll translate. What Lauren meant was, if people heard you call her Her Majesty, they would think she was crazy."

"But she is not crazy. She is the most intelligent and sane person I know." Newkirk's voice rumbled deep in his chest.

Lauren nodded her acknowledgement of his praise. "I appreciate you coming to my defense, Angus, but the United States isn't a monarchy. It's a democracy. We don't have any royalty, clan chiefs, lords, or ladies around here. It would be strange for someone to overhear you and wonder why you were calling me that. So, it's jeans, t-shirts and hoodies. No kilts or plaids. And no titles."

"Right, no titles." Newkirk seemed lost in thought as he tried to take in all of Lauren's warnings. "But, what is a democracy?"

"Nope, not going there, either," Jamie replied. "I'll get you a book when we get to my loft."

The royal couple relaxed in the hot tub on the back deck. The jets slowly circulated the warm water and small droplets of water effervesced to tickle Lauren's nose. Stars painted the night sky, and a full moon provided nearly enough illumination to read. The silver light sparkled and danced off Alex's wet ebony hair.

"This is amazing, but the stars do not seem as bright here as they are in Terra." Alex observed, as she laid her head back on the edge of the hot tub, gazing upward.

"I know what you mean. I used to think nowhere else had stars like here." She felt more than saw Alex frown. "I mean here in Steamboat. I've traveled around the globe, but always thought the stars were best here, especially in the cold, clear air of winter. But I was wrong. Nothing beats the night skies in Terra." Lauren rolled over in the hot water and stroked over next to Alex. “And the stars are in slightly different positions here due to the time displacement.”

“I would have to agree. You can see the sharp edge of the galaxy on Terra and here it is only a muted smear across the southern sky.” Alex pointed out the Milky Way.

“It’s the pollution in the atmosphere that’s responsible for muting the view.

No longer overly interested in the night sky, Lauren reached out and drew Alex close. “I’m so glad we came. Thank you so much for putting up with me and for allowing me to come back. It’s been a great trip and an even more wonderful gift.”

Happiness flooded their bond. “You are welcome. It was the right thing to do. I am sorry we were unable to do it sooner.”

“Don’t be sorry, Alex. There was too much going on in Terra to indulge my insecurities with a trip through the nexus. Newkirk was right. We wouldn’t have enjoyed this trip without having dealt with all that first. And I wouldn’t have come without you.” A kaleidoscope of images rolled through Lauren’s mind. Each difficult situation they overcame in sequence, but all with a positive outcome for Alex and for Terra. And for her, she realized. She wouldn’t have been happy taking Alex away from Terra if things hadn’t been resolved.

Alex leaned down and touched noses with Lauren. “I am glad we made the trip. Your friends are amazing, and I know they will be excellent stewards for your discoveries. This reality will benefit from them as Terra has.”

Lauren pulled Alex down lower in the water and placed a soft kiss on her forehead. She turned her around. “Right now, I’m glad we’re alone. These last few days have been wonderful beyond words.” She kissed Alex again, but on the lips this time. As the kiss deepened, Lauren felt her soul reach out and meld with Alex’s—into one entity.

“My turn, Dearest.” And then they didn’t need words anymore.

Lauren began the dance, slowly. An elegant waltz at first, each step choreographed based on the feedback she was receiving along their bond. Her hands slid down Alex’s strong back causing muscles to ripple in response. Then they came around, cupping each small breast, she gently squeezed, and lifted. Weighing each small orb in a hand. Circling inward, her fingers enclosed a taut nipple. A gentle tug pulled a soft moan from her partner. She splayed her fingers back out to massage again.

On her second moan, Lauren increased the tempo of their dance. She pulled Alex close and lifted her up onto the edge of the tub as she stood. Using the stimulus of their full-body contact, Lauren slid upward until her breasts were above Alex's, their nipples stimulated with each other's movements. With her center pressed tightly into Alex's lower stomach, another downward glide ratcheted their arousal skyward. She set up an even tempo of slide and glide. When Alex reached around and clasped her lower back and pulled her closer, Lauren leaned away, lost in sapphire eyes made silver in the waning moonlight. *"Who's in charge here, Dearest? I thought it was my turn to lead."*

Alex relaxed her hold on Lauren's back. She could feel Alex's need as easily as she felt her own and with it came an overwhelming desire to finish. She didn't want this moment to end in a crash. She wanted it to end in a crescendo. To do that, she had to control the rhythm.

All right, if Alex wants an end, I'll give her an end. Ravel's orchestral piece, *Boléro*, played in her head. She always favored this piece. Its mathematical synchrony amazed her even as a young child when she first heard it played at age six. Few realized it was originally composed as a ballet. Lauren wasn't interested in the flow and elegance of a ballet. She wanted the drive and insistent demand of a tango.

She wrapped one arm around her partner's waist as a strong and steady anchor. The other pulled Alex's head down into a deep, searching, seeking, demanding kiss. Pulling away, Lauren slid her hand around Alex's neck and down to trail a path between her breasts. As her hand finally arrived in Alex's curls, she delved deep. Finding her goal, she entered her, setting up a steady percussive rhythm. This in counterpoint to the building pressure she began with another gentle kiss, holding Alex in suspension. They were lost, driven by the cadence of emotion raging along their bond.

Lauren added another diatonic element as she stroked her thumb across Alex's distended clitoris. Lauren felt it peek from its hood and she focused her touch there. A variable stroke set up a contrasting melody, almost vocal, as Alex's breaths were synchronized with each increase of her thumb's pressure.

Lauren released her control and let their bodies set the tempo, driving her fingers deeper. Each stroke deeper than the last, as Alex relaxed and opened to her. Lauren's thumb became insistent. Her earlier melodic stroking of Alex's clitoris changed to a demanding, pounding beat which drove them higher, faster, farther along the path to perfection.

Syncopation was lost as Lauren's strokes became staccato. She couldn't maintain their rhythm as Alex's need to climax rushed through Lauren, overwhelming her. She fought for control and then with one last measure, succumbed to their mutual desire and together they reached crescendo.

A shout of ecstasy exploded outward. Their bond sang with the joy of their release. When they returned, each to their own bodies, they realized another piece of their soul was missing, yet there wasn't a void. For the missing piece wasn't missing so much as exchanged for a piece from their other half. Now, each more whole than before.

Jamie and the boys returned the following week, and final preparations were made for the Terrans, with the addition of Làireach, Susan, and Sharon, to return to Terra. Although each reality was unique and time was relativistic, Newkirk and Lauren were able to set up a travel schedule. It was based on how much time Làireach would need with Ffrwyn before the filly could return to Earth. With this schedule, Jamie would know when to be at the nexus to pick up the girls when they returned to the Zirkel Wilderness eighteen months from the date of their departure. Future trips would then be set based on the needs of Nexus Limited.

Everyone woke early on their last morning. Spring spread across the Yampa Valley and the air smelled sweet with the scent of hay and wildflowers carried on a gentle breeze. Susan loaded the three horses into her van. The Terrans had their packs ready, and they waited to load themselves into the cab of the large vehicle for the trip north to the Zirkel cave.

Lauren had bittersweet feelings about leaving Jamie again, but she knew she'd done all she could for this reality. It was now up to Jamie and their company to make the nano-tech available. Changes would come with their introduction, and Lauren hoped they would be positive. If nothing else, the impact in medicine would be profound, and she wouldn't have to worry about being helpless to prevent infant deaths in the future.

Alex dropped a long arm around her shoulders and smiled down at her. "You and Jamie have created a wonderful venue for helping this planet. I am very proud of you."

Leaning her head over, Lauren placed a soft kiss on the hand resting on her shoulder, "Thanks. This was a team effort, like all our discoveries and accomplishments. The success of Nexus Limited will also be a team effort. A lot of people will benefit, but it'll take the genius, ingenuity, and hard work of many to make it happen."

"Jamie is the proper person to get it done for you. You should be proud."

"I am, and you're right. Jamie's the person to get it all done."

"Come on, you two. Time to go if you want to be outta here before noon." Susan called from the cab of the horse van.

Ice loped over and nudged Lauren forward. *"Yes, it is time to go."*

The ride up to Clark and into the wilderness area was made mostly in silence, each person lost in memories of the last months. Once at trailhead, Susan unloaded the horses, and everyone shouldered large packs. Jamie had the nexus cave marked on a topographic map and didn't need to make the journey across the basin. He would drive the van back to Susan and Sharon's house once everyone was on the trail.

Jamie stood beside the van, tears streaming down his face, as the nexus travelers prepared to leave. Lauren gathered him close. "It'll be all right, Jamie. I know you'll do a terrific job."

Jamie wiped his eyes and nodded.

"Take care of yourself. I'm so proud of your ability to not only survive but excel in your new world." He hugged her tightly. "Now get going. Your court awaits." His comment turned the moment into something less sad.

"Is that anyway to treat royalty? I think not," Lauren said in mock irritation.

"You're the only royalty I know, so forgive me if I offend." He sobered. "Lauren, I'm going to miss you, but Nexus Limited will be up and running by the time you get back."

She wiped her eyes. "Take care, my friend. I love you."

"Love you, too. Now get outta here. I've got a lot of work to do and my boss is a real tyrant." They both laughed. And once their chuckles quieted, Lauren turned back to the Terrans, back to her family.

Sun glinted off the alpine lakes dotting the basin floor as the group crested the southern ridge and began their trek across the open basin to the cave. The towering granite peaks were still capped with snow, and Lauren smiled, realizing soon the snow would be acid-free and no longer pose a danger to this pristine wilderness area. Remediating the power-generation plants in the valley was one of the first projects on Nexus Limited's list.

The group arrived at Lauren's cave by mid-morning and began preparing to cross the nexus to Terran reality. Alex turned to the others. "All right. Since Lauren and I are the only ones who can open and cross the nexus unaided, we will pair off. I will open the nexus, and Lauren will cross over. Once in Terran reality, she will hold the nexus open using her soul-bond to me, and her bonds with our companions will guide each of you through. I will follow at the end and close the nexus once I am through. Does anyone have any questions?" A round of shaking heads answered.

"I know Lauren explained about the nexus, but could you go over it again?" Susan's unease was evident in the slight tremble in her normally steady voice.

Lauren stepped up to Susan and Sharon. "Of course. I think the best way to explain parallel realities was shared by Merilyn when we first discussed nexi after I arrived at the Keep. Imagine yourself standing between two mirrors which face each other. In them, you can see your reflection, reflected back and forth infinite times." Lauren watched closely to see if Susan and Sharon were following her explanation. Both of her friends nodded, as did Làireach. "Okay, each of those reflections is one universe or reality. The sum of all the reflections defines the multiverse. If you connected one universe with another along a tunnel, you would be able to traverse the tunnel and travel from one reality to another. The Terrans call these connecting tunnels quantum tubuli. If the tunnel connects two points in the same reality or on the same reflection it's called a geographic tubula, allowing you to move to another physical location but staying in the same reality. If the tubula connects two different realities or reflections, it's a quantum tubula connecting two different realities." She paused again, and again the friends nodded, following her explanation.

"Merilyn went on to tell me the orientation of the tubula defines 'when' you are as you pass from one reality to another. Since time is relativistic, if the tubula is straight, then time is similar in each reality. If the tubula is tilted then you would travel either forward or back in time relative to the two realities." Susan smiled in understanding, but Sharon frowned.

Lauren smiled crookedly at her friend. Talking about relativity always gave her a headache and she was a scientist. Sharon was obviously totally confused. "To finish my explanation, each end of the tunnel is protected by a nexus membrane. This prevents matter, energy, and time from leaking across from one reality to another." Lauren waved her hand at the cave in front of the group. This nexus has a tilted tubula, so once we cross over to Terran reality, we will be about thirteen thousand years in the future relative to Earth reality's time."

Susan draped an arm across Sharon's narrow shoulders. "It'll be okay, love. We're together and we have Làireach. No matter where we are." Susan chuckled. "Or when we are, we're okay."

Sharon smiled up at her partner. "You're right. Together."

"You may feel a slight disorientation as you pass through the quantum tubula, but that will pass quickly once you acclimate to the new reality. Keep a tight hold on your companion, they will follow our bond."

Lauren rubbed her hands together, excited to be returning to Terra. "Let's do this. I want to go home. Ice, you and Sharon are with me. Then Newkirk and MacD with Snow. Susan, Boscoe, Ffrwyn, and Làireach will follow. McLaran and Gríobhtha after them. Alex comes last." Lauren nodded at each small group as they got themselves organized. She moved down the line checking packs.

"Susan, can you handle Boscoe and Làireach?"

"He's good. Ffrwyn agreed to carry him on her back as we pass through. I've rigged a harness to his halter which will keep him in place," Susan said as Lauren passed the trio. Boscoe sat tall and proud on Ffrwyn's broad back, yipping in excitement.

"At least this time we can fly back to Terra Keep. No more treks through the wilderness," Lauren said. The Terrans had left the *Y Ddraig Goch* in the center of the basin on the Terran side when they travelled to the nexus. The return trip would be crowded with the additional passengers, but MacD was positive everyone plus their gear would fit. Alex's *Red Dragon* would fly easily.

Lauren stopped next to Gríobhtha, reaching up to adjust all the straps holding the various bags and boxes on his back. *"Are you okay?"* She asked quietly.

"I am fine, Your Majesty. I will be glad to be home. Please watch over Ffrwyn and the Little One," he said with a horsey snort, pawing the ground in anticipation of getting their trek started.

"No worries there, I'll watch over everyone." She patted his shoulder and moved forward.

"I will miss our hot springs at the Teton Cache." Alex sent a whisper along their bond and Lauren smiled.

"Me, too. But I won't miss anything else from that trip, especially your injuries." She said with a burst of love and excitement.

Lauren turned toward the small cave entrance and watched as Alex slowly inserted her blade into the invisible nexus membrane. She swung the blade in a wide arc and blue-green sparks flew. The membrane opened with a snap, and Lauren swallowed as her ears popped. She stepped forward. A full-body shiver travelled down her spine as she stepped into the curved entrance. Tingles of static electricity skittered across her skin but she knew what lay on the other side and didn't hesitate. Her bond vibrated, and she felt Ice step forward and follow her closely. Sharon had a death-grip in Ice's ruff. As Lauren crossed the nexus, she stepped aside allowing room for the other two to enter behind her into the small cave.

Snow walked out of thin air a few seconds later and moved toward them, Newkirk and MacD in tow. "Maybe we should step outside. It's going to get overcrowded in here as the others crossover." Lauren led the small group out of the cave into the sunlight of a Terran noon. She heard Sharon gasp as she got her first look at the Zirkel basin in this reality.

"Oh my. It's the same, but not. Everything's so bright and sharp." Sharon turned in a full circle, her gaze upward to trace the outline of the towering granite peaks above the cave they had exited.

"This world is exactly the same, except I've realized the differences which do exist are those created by humankind in Earth's reality. Here, there's no pollution or ozone depletion in the atmosphere or jet contrails or background noise. The air is clear and clean. The light of the sun is unfiltered by what man has dumped into the Earth's atmosphere." Lauren watched Sharon absorb her new surroundings, their group now immersed only by the sound of unadulterated nature. "Things appear brighter and more defined here. Almost closer. Like you can reach out and touch the mountain top." She gathered Sharon up in a fierce hug. "Welcome to Terra."

Drawing her thin blade, Lauren turned back to the cave entrance. Slowly, she inserted her blade into the nexus membrane on this side. A ribbon of green-white sparks flowed from the blade's tip as she drew her sword across the entrance. With her blade in the membrane, Lauren's connection with each of the companions strengthened. She held her blade steady as one by one each remaining group crossed the nexus. Lauren felt Alex along their bond, directing from the other side. Reaching out across the parallel realities to touch Lauren. It was almost a physical contact, and Lauren sent a burst of strength over the nexus back to Alex. She heard an almost instantaneous reply.

"We are done here. Is everyone safe?"

"Yes, we're all good. Just waiting for you, Dearest."

Her bond swelled, and Lauren's heart skipped a beat as the enormity of Alex's love was transmitted back at her. She saw the others had received Alex's burst, and heat rose up her cheeks.

"Do not be embarrassed, Lauren. Your bond and love are beautiful things which each of us is honored and privileged to be a part of. We thank you for allowing us to share in it." McLaran said softly for only her to hear. She turned toward him. He stepped beside her and wrapped an arm around her shoulders while she held her blade within the nexus membrane, surrounding her with added strength. She knew without a doubt the boys were now her companions as much as they were Alex's. They didn't stand by her out of duty to Alex but out of love and honor for her, and she was humbled.

Lauren was so caught up in her feelings for the companions, she didn't realize Alex hadn't joined them until Newkirk asked, "Where is she? She knows we want to head back before dusk."

Spinning out of McLaran's hug, Lauren closed her eyes and called, *"Alex, come on Dearest. We're waiting on you."*

"On my way, I wanted to ensure the membrane was fully sealed before crossing over."

Part Three

Luna Keep, Terra

We have to remember that what we observe is not nature herself, but nature exposed to our method of questioning.

~Werner Heisenberg

Luna Keep, Terra

"This is Sensor Platform Tau Alpha. Get me Chief McLeod, immediately please." The disembodied voice shattered the silence in the Central Information Control room of Luna Keep.

The three satellite technicians in the CIC looked at each other in question. The chief technician ordered, "Get me a plot on that platform. We never hear from them. I do not even know where they are in their orbital rotation."

Answering the hail from the platform, the chief keyed his ear microphone. "CIC, here. Chief McLeod is unavailable."

"This is Marcus McDowell, CIC. We have an unusual power reading at two-hundred-twenty-five kilometers out from the lunar ecliptic."

The chief turned to one of the technicians, "Put that up on the board and plot a trajectory, Shamus." He ran his fingers through his hair, and asked another one of the CIC techs, "What is out there? Do we have a cloaked probe coming in? Hail Chief McLeod's pilot. See if you can raise her and pass a message along."

"McDowell, what kind of reading are you picking up? Can you determine if it is a ship or is it a signal? We need to differentiate between an incoming probe or vessel and a remote signal from the outer system." The chief's voice rose as his fear increased about this unusual sensor reading.

"We do not think it is a probe or a vessel. It seems to be stationary."

"Sir, we cannot refine the plot. We have a main core analyzer test running," Shamus said and the chief watched the single red icon blinking menacingly on the master plot.

Another voice cut into the electronic conversation between CIC and the sensor platform. "CIC, Sarah Cameron, pilot for Chief McLeod here. I am in the flitter bay onboard the *Ruadh làn-damh* and I have a sensor reading, indicating a gravitational wave system is coming online. Do you have a test running that was unannounced?"

"Pilot Cameron, we have a lunar base central core system test running. Please confirm the coordinates of the energy source from your sensors. We cannot pin down the reading." Nothing but static filled the CIC.

"Pilot Cameron, this is CIC. Repeat your last transmission."

"Sir, I have a gravitational wave system powering up at two-hundred-fifty klicks off the lunar ecliptic."

"Continue to monitor and inform Construction Site Alpha we have a priority one request to speak with Chief McLeod immediately."

"Aye, sir. Calling Chief McLeod now."

The energy source built, and the red icon's glow intensified on the master plot. "CIC, Tau Alpha here. We are getting an increase in energy signature and are now picking up another energy wave. We do not have a source code identification on the new wave," McDowell's voice rose half an octave as he reported the new information.

"CIC, this is McLeod. What is going on down there?" The chief lunar technician's voice cut into CIC's conversation with the sensor platform.

The CIC chief exhaled in relief, as the voice of their chief roared through the control room. "M'lord, we have two unknown energy waves, rising in intensity off your ecliptic. The source should be approximately two five zero kilometers from your current location."

"I got that much from my pilot, chief. What is the nature of the wave and why can we not refine our analysis? Sarah's sensors indicate a gravitation wave system is powering up. Why can you not confirm?"

The chief gulped. "We have a central system test running and the core analyzers are in standby until the test is complete."

"Shut it down!" Chief McLeod's voice rang through CIC with a whip-crack of command.

"But, M'lord?"

"Now. I do not care about what we will need to repair due to an aborted test. Bring all the system backups online, and shut down that test. I want a pinpoint analysis, immediately. Our sensors are refining a gravitational wave system, and if that is the case, I need to know its source. We are powering up the Stag's systems too. But with a cold start, her sensors will need more than thirty minutes to get any detail. Leave this line open. I want to hear everything going on down there in real time."

The CIC chief nodded at the other two techs. "You heard him. Shut down that test. Call analyzer control, and tell them we are taking over operational control in . . ." He looked at the main chronograph. "In six minutes. Shamus, bring the backups online. Prepare to dump control from the central analyzers to them when they are hot."

Onboard McLeod's flitter, Chief McLeod turned to his pilot. "Sarah, recall all my techs who are EVA. I want everyone onboard the Stag in five minutes. Burn out their thrusters, if necessary, to get them inside as quickly as possible. Send a priority one message to McLaran at the Keep, dump all the details we are certain of in the message. Have him inform the Seneschal of this. Prepare to launch to the coordinates of that energy source. I want to be out there as soon as possible."

"Aye, sir. Flitter systems are at standby. We will have full power to launch in less than one minute."

"Very good." Chief McLeod turned to settle into his crash couch. "CIC, are you still with us?"

"CIC here, M'lord."

"I want a patch to the sensor platform that picked up the first signal."

"Patching you through to Sensor Platform Tau Alpha. You have an open comm."

"Sensor Platform Tau Alpha, this is Chief McLeod."

"Lord McLeod, this is Marcus Cameron, Sensor Platform Tau Alpha." The tech's voice quivered, anxiety evident in its thin, reedy quality.

Chief McLeod shook his head at Sarah as she grimaced at the fear-filled voice. "Easy, my boy. I need you to tell me what you saw. We will take this one step at a time. First, dump your raw sensor readings to the analyzer onboard my flitter. Then tell me what happened."

"Chief Newkirk, Shield Control." A comm message flashed on the main psi-Lab analyzer screen. The psi-Lab was located beneath the Keep, in the sixth subterranean level. The surrounding rock effectively isolated the lab and its psi-engineers from any external psi-energy generated by the Keep's occupants. The huge room was excavated from the solid rock foundation of the Keep. Fist-sized crystals of plagioclase and quartz glittered in the gray stone walls reflecting the low light given off by the numerous analyzers organized in a semi-circle before a huge wall monitor. This monitor was divided into twelve smaller displays, one for each section of the large psi-shield that protected the Keep above them.

"M'lord, I have a message for you from the Shield Control Room."

"Thank you. Please relay to my screen," Newkirk said absently. His desk sat above the row of analyzers and afforded Lord Newkirk a view of the entire room. Currently, he was lost in a simulation running on his desk analyzer. He was trying to determine the cause of the random energy bursts, which were impacting the shield's integrity. This was his three hundred and forty-seventh simulation and he still didn't have a clue where they were coming from. With the Consort due back any day, he wanted them identified and flushed from the shield before she returned. He vowed to himself he wouldn't cause her any more pain.

A coded message flashed as green alpha numeric characters began to stream across the header of Newkirk's analyzer. He punched in a keyed code to decrypt the message and frowned. *Why we have to use encryption to send a simple message from one office to another is beyond me.*

"Gil, remind me to send an order to the shield techs telling them to quit using an encryption when sending simple messages. All they probably want is permission to have lunch." He tapped his fingers on the desk surface as he waited for the message to change from gibberish to real words. But once the message resolved, he jerked bolt upright, sending his chair flying into the granite wall behind his desk.

"Gil, get me Lord McLaran and the Seneschal now! Andrew, call Luna Keep. Ask them what the blazes they think they are doing. Our shields are overloading from the energy pulse they are sending down. Our shield integrity is dissolving." He spun to his right. "Catherine, reroute power from the main geothermal generators and boost power to the shield. And call in all the psi-engineers who are off duty. I need everyone back here."

He turned to his analyzer and entered a long string of code, followed by an alpha-numeric key sequence he never thought he would need. Once he completed this action, he could feel the floor begin to vibrate.

He had activated a series of particle shield generators installed in the lowest levels of Terra Keep, ten floors beneath his lab. These generators had been dormant since they were removed from Clan Doouglas' *Iolar Mara* and installed beneath the Keep.

"Catherine, I need that power," he called to his harried technician.

"It is coming, M'lord. I need another five minutes to reroute power from the main lines and dump it into the sinks before I burn them out, and then I need to shut down the primary turbines."

"Overload them! I need that power!"

"We will bring down the power grid to the entire Keep if we do that, M'lord."

"I do not care, Catherine. Do it now. I need to route power immediately into the particle shield generators." His fingers flew over his board, moving packets of energy from one point to another. Rerouting lines from backup to primary. Creating a shortest-distance pathway to the particle generators. All the while, the vibrations in the floor increased. "Gil, get the energy grid plotted on the main analyzer."

"M'lord, I have Chief McLeod for you," Andrew shouted into the swirling chaos the psi-lab had become.

"Put it through." Static crackled over the comm. "McLeod, what the devil are you playing at?" Newkirk demanded as his fingers flew across his analyzer gel pads, routing power from one point to another, trying desperately to not overload any junctions. He had to keep as much power flowing to the generators as possible, while maintaining even power levels to the Keep.

"M'lord, reports from the Shield Control room indicate we have damage and injuries to two technicians." The tech's report interrupted the conversation.

"Playing at? Look here, Newkirk. I have an emergency situation up here and I cannot be bothered by a little imbalance in the Keep's shield at this time," Chief McLeod growled.

Newkirk could hear shouts coming from the background of the chief's comm line. "You? I have an imminent shield collapse. Psi-energy is being bled off and I have two psi-technicians down from the backlash. The particle shield generators are coming online but we are having trouble getting full power to their energy packs. I need you to shut down that energy pulse you are sending."

"Energy pulse. What the stars are you talking about? I have two unknown energy signatures up here, in stationary orbit. Hold on." Newkirk heard Chief McLeod mumble something to someone outside the pickup distance of his comm. "Newkirk, I have to go. We are isolating the signatures. I am en route to the coordinates now."

Newkirk blinked at his comm as the signal was abruptly cut.

Catherine broke in. "M'lord. You have full power available. We need to pull the psi-shield down before we initiate the particle shield. The two are incompatible, and we risk a shield detonation."

"I understand. Please monitor the particle shield generators. When they are fully spun up, prepare to activate the particle shield on my command." Newkirk's finger hovered over the large psi-shield abort key. "Andrew, what's the status from Shield Control?"

"We have four technicians down, one confirmed dead."

Newkirk startled. *Dead?*

"M'lord, Shield Control is not responding. I have lost communication." Andrew spun back to his board. "Remote damage reports coming in now. Fire control is activated. Energy was automatically cut to the control room once fire was detected by the analyzers." Andrew spun his chair back toward him. "It is a total loss."

Total loss? How is that possible? But he pulled himself together. *Not now, old boy. Focus!* "Andrew, route all shield control to this lab. Gil, where are those psi-techs? Message all of them and tell them to come here, not Shield Control. Catherine, hold the transfer."

As Newkirk was ready to transfer the shields, alarms sounded from all over the lab. The main analyzer board lit up like a firestorm had hit it, red lights flashing across the energy grid system. Junctions exploded across the Keep.

A warning klaxon blared over the communication system of the entire Keep. "Main shield collapse is imminent. Move indoors immediately. Stay away from all windows and doors. Do not use any powered devices. This is not a drill. Repeat. Main shield collapse is imminent—"

"Shut that off! Where are McLaran and the Seneschal?" Newkirk snapped, breaking everyone out of their temporary paralysis.

"We are unable to get any communications out of the lab, M'lord," Andrew replied.

Klaxons blared again. "Incoming psi-energy pulse detected. Twenty seconds to impact," a robotic voice warned.

Newkirk's finger stabbed the shield abort. "Now, Catherine. Put that shield up now!"

The foundation of the Keep rolled beneath the lab as the particle generators released their massed energy. A wrenching sound tore through the Keep as the particle shield began to form. The particle shield generators were originally designed to protect starships in flight, by broadcasting a shield around a ship as it flies through the near-emptiness of space. The particle shield was designed to deflect any stray bits of matter or radiation or energy away from the flightpath of the ship. However, they were not designed to generate a shield around a stationary object within the gravity well of a planet.

A massive energy burst exploded outward from the Keep, generated by the shield, as it tried to bleed off the excess energy into the ground. The excess energy traveled downward. As the downward burst crossed the different stratal boundaries of rock layers beneath the Keep, some of its energy was reflected off each boundary and directed back to the surface. Due to the differences in density from one rock layer to the next, a harmonic wave was established as the energy reflected back and forth between the layers. The bedrock beneath the Keep's foundations rang like a bell.

"M'lord, we are one hundred klicks from the point source." Sarah informed her chief. "You better have a look at this."

Chief McLeod unhooked his crash harness and floated carefully forward toward the pilot's chair. "What do you have?"

"It is the *Dubh Mogairle*, M'lord." Sarah pointed out the front view screen toward a point in space that was beginning to blaze. It was visible to the naked eye, even from a distance. He stared at Sarah's heads-up-display and counted the eleven flashing icons, each representing one of the clan ships where she floated in her docking cradle.

"She is coming online." Sarah flicked a toggle on her joystick and a circle icon began to flash around the bright point in space. A stream of numbers flowed down the left side of the HUD: power readings, generator status, gravitational wave systems status, and weapons status.

"Bring us around now. Get me the Keep. Quickly, Sarah, we must get out of her range."

Sarah swung the flitter in a gut-wrenching slew turn about the little ship's vertical axis. The inertial dampeners couldn't overcome the G-forces. McLeod was thrown into the row of seats behind the pilot. He heard Sarah grunt as the G-forces built with each maneuver. His vision tunneled as blood rushed out of his head. He was going to pass out.

As she completed her turn, Sarah slammed the throttles full to their stops, and the craft leapt forward. "Luna Keep, M'lord," she called through gritted teeth. *Would he be able to respond to the hail?*

"McLeod Flitter, Luna Keep Flight Control here. Please respond."

It took all his efforts to whisper, "McLeod here. Emergency override all systems. Prepare for a hostile incursion. Authorization 1-12-5-Alpha - 24. I repeat 1-12-5-Alpha - 24. Bring all clan ships to full power. Prepare crews for immediate launch. Charge the main lunar blaster batteries." He panted. He clawed his way forward over the seat back to the co-pilot position.

"McLeod Flitter, I need the second authentication code. Repeat, this action requires a second authentication."

"Second authentication code is 12-1-21 Lima 5." The Chief of Luna Keep grunted out the code a second time, fighting to remain conscious.

"Roger. We have authentication for full weapons activation. Blasters are priming. We will have firepower in two minutes. Flight crews are on alert. The clans are powering up."

As the G-forces diminished, McLeod finally made his way forward where he collapsed into the co-pilot's seat. He turned to his pilot. Neither of them had worn their helmets, and their white-suits weren't sealed. Perspiration ran in rivulets down Sarah's pale cheeks, and her jaws were clenched.

"Sorry about that, M'lord," she whispered.

"No need, Sarah. Comm to Construction Site Alpha and have them accelerate flight preparation as they power up the Stag. She's going to have to run before her shakedown cruise. And keep a lock on the *Dubh Mogairle*, I want to know if she so much as twitches."

"Aye, sir."

McLeod thumbed a toggle on the central console and a HUD popped up on his side of the cockpit. This one showed a view behind the little flitter. Centered in the display was a magnified view of the *Dubh Mogairle*. "Can you patch the data from the analyzers in her docking cradle into this display?" His display wavered for a moment, and then it stabilized with a crystal-clear image of the *Dubh Mogairle*. Her running lights were lit, and she had dropped mooring lines and umbilicals. The ship was beginning to back out of her cradle.

McLeod keyed his mic and shouted, "She has dropped her lines. She will be underway in less than one minute. Prepare to fire."

As he spoke, CIC called over his comm, "She has full power. Main fusion vessels are at maximum temperature for injection. Her systems are online. We have attempted to abort her power up remotely. However, our efforts are being blocked from the shipboard central analyzer system."

When McLeod didn't respond, Sarah keyed her mic. "Roger that, Central."

A tremor ran down McLeod's spine. "Patch me through to the *Dubh Mogairle*, Sarah."

"You have an open comm, M'lord."

"*Dubh Mogairle*, this is Lord Admiral McLeod. You will power down your systems, and prepare to be boarded. This is your only warning. If we do not see power falling and mooring lines reattached within one minute, we will open fire." He waited for a reply but knew one wouldn't be coming. "I repeat. Power down your systems or we will fire. You have forty-five seconds remaining to comply." He cut the open comm and switched to a secure channel.

"CIC, this is McLeod. Weapons status?"

"All weapons are hot and locked—" He didn't hear the remainder of CIC's status update because Sarah's shout deafened him.

"She's firing. Prepare for impact." Sarah threw the tiny craft into another gut-wrenching spiral turn, corkscrewing this time upward on her vertical axis, trying to yaw away from the energy beam which lanced toward them.

The inertial dampeners screamed as she held the turn. She pushed her joystick full forward, throwing the flitter into a dive. Their shock couches could not adjust fast enough to offset her violent maneuvers, and McLeod knew they were again close to losing consciousness again. The energy beam streaked past, missing a direct hit. But the flitter was close enough to absorb some of the beam's energy discharge, causing sparks to erupt from various control consoles.

Warning lights flashed on and alarms sounded as Sarah fought to control the craft. McLeod reached out and silenced the alarms. He grabbed thruster controls and sent a burst of energy out the starboard side of the craft. This slewed them sideways, farther away from the beam. Together the two got the flitter under control, but they had lost main power and were on an unpowered ballistic course away from Luna.

"Luna Control, this is McLeod Flitter. We're declaring an emergency. I repeat this is an emergency. We need assistance immediately."

"Roger that, McLeod Flitter. We have you on sensors."

While they waited, McLeod tapped the thruster controls again, and a small burst from the nose unit turned their craft toward the *Dubh Mogairle*. The great black ship was now free of her white docking cradle, pivoting about her vertical axis, turning away from Luna.

"Luna Weapons Control, you are free to fire. I repeat, you are free to fire. Do not let that ship exit the system."

McLeod's flitter had a ringside seat for the firestorm that erupted. Blue-white lasers shot up from the lunar surface toward the *Dubh Mogairle*. Several caught her amidships, but her particle shields deflected the beams easily.

"Damn," Sarah hissed under her breath as another series of beams lashed the great ship's hull. There wasn't any visible damage. The ship continued its turn away from Luna.

"Get a lock on her. Can you attach us with tractors?"

Sarah's fingers stabbed at the console between their seats. "I do not have full power to the generators."

"Rerouting power from main engine sinks. Get us locked on," McLeod commanded as his fingers danced over the forward console.

The tiny craft vibrated in place, but then began to slowly turn toward the *Dubh Mogairle*. "If we can get to her hull before she translates to gravitational wave drive, we can cling on magnetically."

"Right. Cling on. And then?"

McLeod knew his pilot did not understand his plan. But he knew if they could attach themselves to the great ship, they might be able to board her and stop her escape. All they had to do was catch her first.

"Lord Newkirk, we are detecting a psi-energy pulse coming from Luna."

"What the devil is going on up there?" Newkirk asked into the silence cloaking his psi-lab. Dust filtered down from the ceiling, but they had gotten the particle shield stabilized without too much damage to the Keep. Now all they had to worry about was induced terra-tremors. Hopefully, none of the reflected energy waves had activated hidden fault planes in the underlying strata of the Keep. They would know for sure over the next weeks.

"M'lord, the pulse does not appear to be aimed at the Keep." Catherine turned back to her analyzer. "It's focused approximately five hundred kilometers north of here."

Gil broke in. "It is not coming from Luna."

"What? From where?"

"It seems to be coming from a point in space approximately two-hundred and fifty kilometers off the ecliptic of Luna." Gil tapped some commands into his analyzer. "I am picking up energy weapons' fire. On the main board."

All heads turned toward the main projection Gil had patched through from Luna sensors. The room sat in stunned silence as they watched the exchange of weapons fire—blue-white energy beams sliced downward from a point-source in space and return-fire lanced upward from the lunar surface. "What is going on up there?" It was a purely rhetorical question, because no one in the psi lab had an answer for Lord Newkirk.

"Get me Luna Control, now!" Lord Newkirk demanded.

A woman's voice crackled over the comm in the CIC. "Luna Control, this is the *Dubh Mogairle*. We have the traitor. She is being held on charges of treason against Terra and all her clans, and for the theft of secure data from an ally. She will be taken to the scene of her crime and tried to the fullest extent of the law. *Dubh Mogairle* out."

The great ship completed its turn and streaked out of lunar orbit.

"Get a heading!" a shouted command rang through Luna Control. The red icon winked out of existence on the main plot as the ship exited the sensor boundary of the Terran solar system.

A small voice called from a corner console, "I have a bearing and heading, sir."

The Master Controller went over and peered at the plot. He dropped a hand on the young man's shoulder. "Good work son, very good, indeed."

"But, sir?"

The Master Controller shook his head at the young controller.

Turning to another station, he said, "Comm Terra Keep and inform the Seneschal and Head Guardian McLaran of the message. Send all relevant data to each of the clans. Prepare them for immediate departure."

Blue lightening shot from the nexus membrane and burned the ground at their feet. Debris rained down from the sheer granite cliffs above their heads. The mountain groaned as waves of energy tore through its rocky core. Lauren's blade was forcibly ejected from the membrane and lay, steaming in the grass at her feet. Her heart skipped several beats in arrhythmia, searching for its partner's stabilizing rhythm. Lauren collapsed to her knees, head lolling to her chest. The wolves howled in anguish. The horses neighed and whinnied, tossing their heads in agitation. The boys staggered. McLaran dropped to the ground and cried out.

"What's happening?" Susan yelled and ran to Lauren, reaching out to protect her from the falling rocks.

Làireach answered her bondmate's question. *"Alex is gone. Lost in the quantum tubula."*

"No. Not again. No—" Lauren's cry tore through the basin. Her pain engulfed the companions. Her soul was torn asunder as half was forcibly ripped away. A flood of memories crashed over Lauren. She was back in the Keep, kneeling in a snow-covered courtyard. The silence was deafening and she screamed through their bond, trying desperately to reach Alex. She was evicted again, like that winter's morning. Sent away. Banished. Alone. Her heart and soul bled.

Newkirk staggered to his feet and grabbed Lauren off her knees, lifting her into the air. He shook her hard by the shoulders, her feet dangling above the ground.

"Lauren."

She slowly raised her head.

"You must not succumb to the void of your bond. Fight it. Fight it hard. Alex needs you."

Lauren felt herself nod, but she was disembodied, standing outside the moment, watching the action from a different perspective.

"Good. Now reach out. Find Alex. Pull her back."

Lauren nodded again.

"You can do this. Your bond is strong enough."

As Newkirk placed her back on the ground, Lauren slowly gathered her strength.

"Do it now, Consort," Newkirk screamed. "Find your soulmate!"

Hands outstretched and eyes closed, Lauren ripped strength from each of the others. Sharon and Susan collapsed. Làireach squealed and dropped to her knees as the filly's bondmate lost consciousness. But Lauren did not stop.

More, I need more.

And then Lauren felt her, but Alex was far away and moving at tremendous speed. *"Alex, there you are. I have you."*

Nothing.

"Alex! Our bond can overcome this distance, but you must help me complete the connection."

Nothing again. Lauren screamed, raising her head to the bright afternoon sky. She spun on her heel, aligning her body in the direction her soul's other half was traveling. *"Alex, I need you! Now and forever! I am yours and you are mine. Hear me!"*

"I hear you," a pain-laced whisper answered Lauren's plea.

"Where are you?"

A pause, then another whisper, *"I do not know, but I feel her. She is near."* Lauren felt Alex gather her strength and then their bond snapped fully into place and hummed with strength. A command followed, and each of the companions bowed their heads as their Queen spoke. *"You will follow your Co-Ruler. She will lead Terra. You will honor and obey her. For Terra, for always."*

The companions answered her in their own way, with voice, growl, and neigh. "For Terra, for always."

Then a whispered blast meant for Lauren tickled her bond. *"You are my love and strength, Dearheart. Protect Terra and all she stands for. You are Consort, but now you are Ruler. I love you."*

No more words followed, regardless how loudly Lauren called. She knew Alex was alive. She may not be well, but she was alive. Their bond stretched taut, drawn out into a nano-thin filament of pure psi-energy, but the bond held firm. Emotion-thoughts raced back and forth, even as Alex streaked away from Terra at faster-than-light pulse speeds.

"I swear to you, I will find you! I will bring you home! Home to Terra. Home to Me!"

incerto tempore . . . incertisque loci

an uncertain time . . . an uncertain place

~Lucretius, *On the Nature of Things*, 70 BCE

End of Book Two

About The Author

CA Farlow grew up amidst the verdant fields of midwestern farm country. From the age of four, she spent summers on an island in northwestern Ontario, Canada, and winters among frozen fields. Her grandfather imparted his love for the natural world to her. CA earned degrees in geology and tectonics. She worked for an international petroleum company for many years and traveled the globe. Now she lives in the Rocky Mountains. Science is the focus of her writing and her ongoing research is in earthquake mechanics. She lives with her cat, Peet. CA tries to balance her passion for long-distance cycling with writing.

A Quantum Singularity

Nexus Series Book Three

In the previous book of the Nexus Series, Lauren and Alex's return from Earth reality was interrupted by the exiled traitor Gwenhwyfach, Chief of Clan Cador, when the traitor grabbed Alex out of the quantum tubula connecting realities and spirited her away on her clan's interstellar ship, the *Black Orchid*.

Now, in book three, Lauren is left to mount a rescue. But first she must prove her ability to lead Terra as Ruler. Challenges to her right to rule comes from all sides, allies and enemies alike. Will she find the strength to overcome these challenges, in time? Her only strength comes from her soul-bond with Alex which is stretched nano-filament thin.

With her companions at her side, Lauren knows they must beat the *Black Orchid* to their final destination. To do so, they must find a new, shorter route and travel faster than the Terrans have traveled before. Will Lauren be able to vanquish her foes and still have time to discover new technologies to catch up with the traitors? Alex's life and the bond between them depends upon it!

List of Major Characters - The Nexus Series

Lauren Beckwith: Ph.D./M.D., pediatric oncologist and environmental scientist in Earth Reality. Nexus traveler and healing technician; adopted daughter of Clan Fraser; soulmate of Alexandra, Regain Rìoghachd Fuar Ćala, Queen of the Planet Terra; Cáraid Rioghail, Royal Consort to Alex, Co-Ruler Fuar Ćala. Considered by the people of Terra as the Savior of Terra, Terran Reality.

Alex: Alexandra Aoeron Aonwyn nighean mic Fionnaghal, Regain Rioghachd Fuar Ćala, daughter of Fionna, 14th Doouglas Ruler of Terra, Royal Ruler of Cold Harbour, soulmate of Lauren, Terran Reality.

Jamie Gilchrist: Co-worker of Lauren's at GeoDynamics, Earth Reality.

Ffrwyn: Animal companion to Alex and Lauren, Horse, partner of Gríobhtha.

Snow (Sneachda): White Wolf, Animal companion to Alex and Lauren, partner of Deigh (Ice).

Ice (Deigh): White Wolf, Animal companion to Alex and Lauren, partner of Sneachda (Snow).

Merilyn: Merilyn Arrin Can Fionna Fraser Doouglas, The Seneschal of Fuar Ćala. Mentor and Guardian to Alex. Adoptive Mother to Lauren, Terran Reality.

Robert McLaran, the Elder: Chief Guardian, Leader of Alex's Black Guard; Chief of Clan McLaran; father of Robert McLaran the Younger; Terran Reality.

Gríobhtha: Horse companion to Chief Guardian McLaran, partner of Ffrwyn.

Angus Newkirk: Companion to Alex and Lauren, Alex's Wisdom and Skeptic, Master Technician, Terran Reality.

Robert McLaran, the Younger: Companion to Alex and Lauren, Alex's Compass and Conscious. Son of Robert McLaran, the Elder, Terran Reality.

Tavish MacDonald: Companion to Alex and Lauren, Alex's Strength and Right Arm. Son of Lady Síobhan MacDonald, Mastersmith and jeweler, Lauren's Guardian, Pilot, and Protector, Terran Reality.

Lady Síobhan MacDonald: Our Lady of the Ancients-Chief Historian of the Terrans, Chief of Clan MacDonald, Lauren's teacher, mother of Tavish MacDonald, Terran Reality.

Newkirk, the Elder: Chief, Clan Newkirk, Chief Shield Technician and Master Psi-technician of Terra Keep, father of Angus Newkirk, Terran Reality.

Iain McLeod: Chief, Luna Keep; Chief, Clan McLeod; Admiral of the Terran Intragalactic Fleet; Spacing and Engineering Technician; Terran Reality.

Hamish McLeod: Interim Chief, Clan McLeod on Terra; Inventor, Master Weaver; Terran Reality.

Stewart McGuiness: SwordMaster, Champion of Terra and the People; Member, Clan Campbell.

Gwenhwyfach: Chief, Clan Cador, Traitor to Terra; in exile, Terran Reality.

Susan Stanley: DVM-Veterinarian, Friend of Lauren, Partner of Susan Frasier, Earth Reality.

Sharon Frasier: Head of Steamboat Heritage Foundation, eco-environmentalist, Friend of Lauren, Partner of Susan, Earth Reality.

Boscoe: Pembrook Welsh Corgi, dog of Susan and Sharon, Earth Reality.

Altair Doouglas: Chief of Clan Doouglas in the time of The Fraser and The Doouglas (First Foremothers of Terra Prime).

The Doouglas: First Foremother, Terra Prime, Chief of Clan Doouglas, Pilot/Spacing technician, Inventor of faster-than-light pulse flight technology, Partner of The Fraser, Terran Reality.

The Fraser: First Foremother, Terra Prime, Chief of Clan Fraser, Healing technician, Partner of The Doouglas, Inventor of immersion therapy used in the Ruler's Rite, Terran Reality.

Pronunciation Guide and Translations

Some of the terms, names and titles are taken loosely from Scottish Gaelic. A translation guide is included below for some of the more intricate terms. These pronunciations could then be used as a guide for pronunciation of other words in the books.

Scottish Gaelic uses just eighteen letters, each of which is named after a tree or shrub. The consonants all have more than one pronunciation depending on their position in a word and which vowels precede or follow them.

The orthography of Scottish Gaelic was regularized in the late 1970s. For details see: http://www.smo.uhi.ac.uk/gaidhlig/goc/

Thanks to a reviewer for suggesting this be included.

a' Mhaighdeann - A mai den. Translated as "a lady"

Bhean chéile aquas Comh-rialóir - Van Hail a Coo Re-al. Translated as "a Royal Lady"

Cáraid Rioghail - Kar id REE-na. Translated as "Royal Consort"

céile - cee lə. Translated as "partner"

Deigh - dāy

éideadn an - edh ən A. Translated as "Investiture"

Ffrwyn - frē num

Fuar Ćala - For Kăla. Translated as "Cold Harbour"

Gríobhtha - Grĭf fin a

Gwenhwyfach - Guine Vak

nighean mhic Fionnaghal - Nee-an ic FYOON uh gaul. Translated as "daughter of Fiona"

Rigain Rioghachd - Rīoga REE-nah. Translated as "Royal Ruler"

Sneachda - snau

subhachas - su exes. Translated as "a celebration"

Y Ddraig Goch - ə ðraig gox. Translated as "the Red Dragon"

Reading List - Book Two

A Quantum Uncertainty

Guerrier, Simon, editor. *Short Trips: The History of Christmas (Doctor Who Series Anthology)*. Berkshire, UK, Big Finish Productions, 2005.

Lindley, David. *Uncertainty: Einstein, Heisenberg, Bohr and the Struggle for the Soul of Science.* New York, Doubleday, 2007.

Rovelli, Carlo. *Reality is Not What It Seems: The Journey to Quantum Gravity.* New York, Riverhead Books/Penguin Random House, 2017.

Rovelli, Carlo. *Seven Brief Lessons on Physics.* New York, Riverhead Books/Penguin Random House, 2016.

Rovelli, Carlo. *The First Scientist: Anaximander and His Legacy.* Pennsylvania, Westholme Publishing, 2011.

Sobel, Dava. *The Glass Universe-How the Ladies of Harvard Observatory Took the Measure of the Stars.* New York, Viking Press/Penguin Random House, 2016.

Stewart, Ian. *Calculating the Cosmos-How Mathematics Unveils the Universe.* New York, Basic Books/Hachette, 2016.

Tegmark, Max. *Our Mathematical Universe: My Quest for the Ultimate Nature of Reality.* New York, Alfred P. Knopf, 2015.

Reading List – Book One

A Quantum Convergence

Crease, Robert P. and Alfred Scharff Goldhaber. *The Quantum Moment: How Planck, Bohr, Einstein, and Heisenberg Taught Us to Love Uncertainty*. New York, W.W. Norton, 2015.

Greene, Brian. *The Fabric of the Cosmos: Space, Time, and the Texture of Reality*. New York, Alfred P. Knopf, 2003.

Greene, Brian. *The Elegant Universe: Superstrings, Hidden Dimensions, and the Quest for the Ultimate Theory*. New York, W.W. Norton, 1999.

Greene, Brian. *The Hidden Reality: Parallel Universes and the Deep Laws of the Cosmos*. New York, Alfred P. Knopf, 2011.

Gribbin, John. *In Search of Schrödinger's Cat: Quantum Physics and Reality*. New York, Bantam Books, 1984.

Gribbin, John. *Schrödinger's Kittens and the Search for Reality: Solving the Quantum Mysteries*. Boston, Little Brown & Co, 1995.

Gribbin, John. *In Search of the Multiverse*. Hoboken, Wiley, 2009

Kaku, Michio. *Parallel Worlds: A Journey Through Creation, Higher Dimensions, and the Future of the Cosmos*. New York, Doubleday, 2004.

Randall, Lisa. *Warped Passages: Unraveling the Mysteries of the Universe's Hidden Dimensions*. New York City, HarperCollins, 2005.

Smolin, Lee. *Time Reborn: From the Crisis in Physics to the Future of the Universe*. Boston, Houghton Mifflin Harcourt, 2013.

CPSIA information can be obtained
at www.ICGtesting.com
Printed in the USA
LVHW011047300821
696400LV00014B/325